Treat Me
Thrill Me

One Night with Sole Regret Anthology
Volume 4

Olivia Cunning

CONTENTS

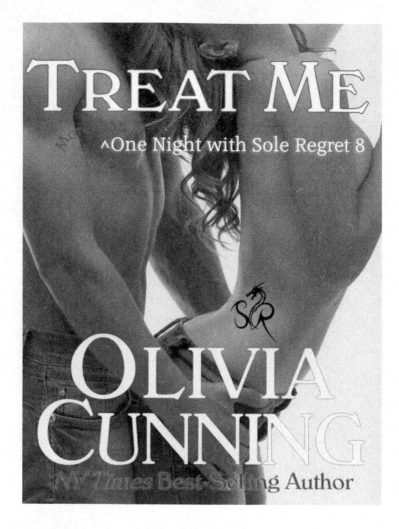

TREAT ME

^One Night with Sole Regret 8

OLIVIA CUNNING

NY Times Best-Selling Author

Treat Me
One Night with Sole Regret #8

CHAPTER ONE

SHADE CHECKED over his shoulder to make sure no one was on the tour bus—they'd only reached the venue in New Orleans an hour ago, but the overcrowded vehicle had cleared out almost immediately. Finding the place deserted, he pulled Adam's notebook out from under its bunk-mattress hiding place and flipped through the pages. Shade knew he shouldn't be going through Adam's private stuff again, but just as he suspected, the lead guitarist and head composer for the band still wasn't writing jack shit. Comparing the pages to the snooping he'd done that morning—when Adam had caught him with the same notebook— Shade discovered a new, lifelike and detailed sketch of a spider on the corner of one page, but not a single verse. Fuck, there was only a single *word* written: *the*. What would happen to the band if Adam couldn't compose new music? Shade had tried his own hand at a few verses, but as much as he hated to admit his own failings, he sucked at writing lyrics. He could sing life into them, but write them? No way in hell. He'd always had some sort of mental block when it came to written language.

Maybe Adam needed a bit of encouragement—perhaps in the form of a boot to the ass. Shade had talked to him earlier that day about his progress, and Adam had assured him that he was locking himself in the tour bus bedroom to work on new songs, but the pages were still as devoid of ideas as they had been when Shade had examined them earlier. He wasn't sure if badgering Adam was the best way to spark the man's creativity, but as leader of the band, he felt he had to do something. No one but him seemed to care enough about the band's future to be a nuisance. And if Adam didn't get his shit together soon, Shade would be forced to do something drastic.

He shoved Adam's void-of-creative-genius notebook back into its hiding place and went in search of the man in question. He started by asking the road crew if they'd seen him.

"I think he went off on his own," said Kris, head of their stage crew. He contemplated Shade with a pair of dark eyes nearly lost in the shadow of the wide skull-and-crossbones bandana he had fashioned over his forehead to keep sweat from dripping. Shade didn't envy the road crew having to unload the trucks in the sultry heat. "I'm pretty sure he had the limo driver take him somewhere right after we arrived," Kris added.

"Thanks," Shade said. After giving Kris a friendly whack on the back, he went in search of the limo driver. He found the long black car parked behind the tour bus and its driver sitting nearby in the shade of a huge cypress draped with swags of Spanish moss. When Shade asked about Adam's whereabouts, the young man stopped fanning himself with a pamphlet long enough to answer.

"He had me drop him off at a Harley dealership," said Parker—assuming his engraved nametag could be trusted. "Told me he was renting a motorcycle, so I didn't have to wait around for him."

So much for offering to brainstorm with Adam so they could come up with some new songs. "All right," Shade said. "Thanks."

Maybe Shade could try writing lyrics with the other guys and see what they came up with. How hard could it be? Gabe was a smart guy. Even though he was their drummer, surely he could throw a few meaningful words together for a song. Or maybe he should talk to Kellen. His female guest was a classical music composer. Unfortunately, that meant she never had to create lyrics. Inspiring, complex music scores, yes. But words? Nope.

A feeling of hopelessness began to seep into Shade's pores, but he shook it off. He wasn't the kind of guy who took anything lying down. Except women. He also took them standing up, kneeling, against the wall, suspended from his ceiling and— Shade shook his head to clear his thoughts. Maybe he shouldn't have asked Amanda to wait for him at home. If she were here, he could have filled his spare time, and her, instead of sticking his nose in

Adam's business. But since he had nothing or no one better to do . . .

Shade had had every intention of talking his bandmates into attempting a new song without Adam's assistance when he entered the dressing room backstage, but somehow he got distracted by socializing. He'd never been the type to isolate himself the way Adam did. Shade craved human contact. He didn't like to be stuck in his own head for long. Maybe that was why he was so bad at writing lyrics.

While listening to some local lackey in charge of making beer runs drone on about the Saints' draft picks, Shade noticed that poor Owen looked like he needed rescuing. The pregnant chick, Lindsey, who they'd somehow managed to pick up in Houston, was leaning so heavily into the guy that he looked like he might fall over.

"Hey, Owen," Shade called to him, interrupting Saints-fan in the middle of his spiel on the importance of getting the right bench warmers from the third round of draft picks. "You want to go somewhere with me?"

Owen didn't even ask where—which was good because Shade had no real plan. Owen pried Lindsey's claws from his arm and excused himself.

"Can I come?" she asked, waddling after him. Shade noticed that she waddled more when she was trying to get Owen's attention. He wondered if she did it consciously.

"Not this time," Shade said. "We have important band business to see to. Very important *secret* band business." Shade scanned the large dressing room for a savior—even he wasn't cruel enough to subject the poor woman to Saints-fan—and spotted the youngest member of their road crew, Jordan, stocking a small refrigerator with various beverages. "Hey, Jordan, keep an eye on Lindsey, will you? Get her anything she needs while Owen and I conduct our business."

Jordan glanced over his shoulder at the pregnant woman and flushed, his smile strangely grateful. "Will do, boss."

"And have this guy go out for more beer," he said, jabbing a thumb in beer-run-lackey's direction.

Owen followed Shade out of the dressing room and into a wide corridor. Roadies and stage crew were bustling about getting the stage ready for their first of two shows in New Orleans, but the band members weren't needed for a while, so they could get out of the building for a few hours. Owen walked beside Shade as they headed toward the exit where the tour bus was parked.

"So what's this important band business you need me for?" Owen asked.

"No idea," Shade said with a shrug, wondering if he should broach the subject of writing songs behind Adam's back. He decided Owen was the least likely of his band to do such a thing. Owen would want to include Adam; he was just too nice not to. "I thought you looked like you needed to get away from Lindsey for a few minutes."

"She won't leave me alone for five seconds," Owen said. "It's like she's afraid I'll disappear if she lets me out of her sight."

"I'm sure you want to disappear right about now."

Owen raked a hand through his dirty-blond hair and groaned. "Is it that obvious?"

"Can't blame you. I'm just glad she didn't adhere to me." Of course, Shade wasn't as sympathetic as Owen, so if Lindsey *had* taken an interest in him, Shade would have found a way to get her off tour at the very least and shipped off to a convent as a last resort. She was a distraction that none of them needed. "What are you going to do with her, Owen? She can't follow us around for the rest of the tour."

"I'll take her back to Austin tomorrow and leave her there. I'm sure my mom will look after her for a few months until she gets settled and the baby is born and we figure out what needs to be done."

"Don't you have the feeling there's more to her story than she's letting on?"

Lindsey had explained that she had nowhere else to go, but Shade wasn't as gullible as Owen—at least when it came to women—so he didn't automatically trust her word. Shade wanted some goddamned evidence before he started forking over child support payments and paying her living expenses and medical bills. Though Shade wouldn't mind having a few more kids, he'd rather have them with someone he cared about. Like Amanda. Amanda would make beautiful babies. He figured they'd look a lot like the light of his life, his Julie. The two did share a lot of genetic material.

Shade shook his head, troubled by the direction of his thoughts. While Amanda would make a wonderful mother and he could only imagine how sexy she'd be with his baby growing inside her, he didn't think knocking her up would be a wise decision. At least not until they had Tina's blessing. Like that would ever happen. His ex-wife would kill them both if she knew they were seeing each other. He didn't imagine she'd approve of her ex-husband dating her older sister.

"Probably," Owen said. "There's probably a lot Lindsey hasn't told me." He waved a hand between himself and Shade. "Told *us*. But does it matter? When someone asks for help and you have the means to help them, it's what you do, right?"

It was what Owen did apparently. There was a sucker born every minute.

Recalling that he'd invited Owen along on his undefined adventure to get away from Lindsey, not talk about her, Shade changed the subject. "Do you think they have any good Cajun restaurants around here? I'm craving something spicy."

"In New Orleans?" Owen scrunched up his face. "Actually, someone told me about this amazing food truck out in the sticks. Even though it's in the middle of nowhere, they always sell out of their daily catch of crawdads."

Shade's stomach rumbled, and he licked his lips eagerly. "Crawdads?"

"The best around. But how are we going to get there? I'm not sure it's wise to show up in a limo. Unless you want to cause a stir."

Shade usually liked the attention, but sometimes he preferred to be anonymous. "I'm not in the mood to be recognized. We'll find another way to get there."

He talked an event coordinator into lending him a company pickup truck. It hadn't been much of a challenge. Once the guy had realized who he was talking to, he'd handed over his keys with a stream of worshipful stammering.

"How do you do that?" Owen asked as he slid into the truck beside Shade.

"Do what?" Shade started the truck and cranked the air conditioning to max. As a Central Texan, he was used to the heat. It was the oppressive fucking humidity that was liable to do him in.

"Get anything you want."

Shade grinned. "It just takes confidence and persistence."

"And being someone more important than the band's

bassist." Owen chuckled.

"I'm sure he'd have given you the keys if you'd asked . . . And explained that you knew me." Shade grinned at Owen's scowl. "Where to?"

Owen sent a text to someone he knew locally, and within a few minutes they had directions and were on their way to Shay's Shrimp Shack, someplace miles outside the city.

"Shrimp? I thought you said they had crawdads," Shade grumbled.

"They do, but they must have shrimp too."

As the buildings became farther apart and twisted mangrove trees crowded each other, reaching gnarled, moss-strewn branches toward the narrow road, Shade's thoughts returned to his biggest concern.

"Do you have any idea why Adam isn't writing on this tour?" Shade asked.

Owen smirked. "Since he hooked up with Madison, he seems to be thinking with his dick most of the time. Maybe the little head lacks his usual creative spark."

Adam had recently been spending a lot of time with his rehab counselor turned lover. Could that really be the problem? He did seem distracted when she was around, and downright irritable when she wasn't.

"We need to reinstate our no-women-on-tour rule," Shade said. "They always lead to trouble."

"Speaking of trouble, is Amanda coming to the show tonight?"

Shade shook his head. "While I loved seeing her the other night, I asked her not to surprise me again."

"And how pissed off was she when you told her that?"

Shade shrugged. "Not at all. She's a reasonable person."

"She didn't assume you didn't want her to show up unannounced because she might catch you doing something she wouldn't approve of?"

"Such as?"

"Banging some other chick."

Shade scratched his head over his left ear. "She didn't say anything about it." But he did have such a reputation. He had cheated on her sister while they'd been married, but at least he hadn't cheated *with* her sister. He hadn't slept with Amanda until well after his divorce from Tina had been finalized. "Amanda trusts me, I guess." She was the complete opposite of her sister, who had never trusted him. Maybe that was why he liked her so much.

"Are you going to see her this weekend?"

"Yep, all weekend. And Julie too."

"Well, that should put a damper on your fun," Owen said with a laugh.

"How so?"

"You'll have to keep your interactions with Amanda rated G in front of Julie."

That might pose a bit of a challenge since he couldn't keep his hands off the woman. "Do you think I'm incapable of controlling my urges?"

Owen snorted. "Yep, pretty much. Does Tina know you're banging her sister?"

"Nope."

"She's going to find out eventually," Owen said. "She'll probably take it better if you're up front with her about it."

Shade laughed. "I can't imagine her ever taking it well. Do you remember how crazy she went when she found out about that groupie I fucked in Vegas?"

"That was before you were divorced," Owen said. "You were legally and morally obligated to keep it in your pants and you didn't."

Shade rubbed his suddenly queasy belly. It always got tied in knots when the subject of his infidelity was broached. He still felt guilty about it. Tina had started accusing him of cheating long before he'd sought comfort in the arms of other women, but Owen was right. He should have divorced Tina *before* he'd succumbed to his weakness for a good piece of compliant ass. Tina had never been compliant—not even in the bedroom—and while her fire had been hot as Hell in the beginning, eventually it had burned him to ashes.

"Sorry," Owen said after a long moment of silence. "Shouldn't have brought that up."

Shade shrugged, though his stomach was still clenching. Maybe he was just hungry. "Can't change any of it." And he couldn't change the way he felt about Amanda either. Maybe they should just come out and tell Tina that they were getting serious.

Were they getting serious? He was leaning that way. However, he wasn't so sure about Amanda's feelings. He knew she liked him. They always had a good time together—and how could she resist his prowess in bed—but did she have deeper feelings for him? Was she willing to confront her sister and claim him as her lover or did she think he wasn't worth the trouble their relationship would cause?

Owen pointed out the window. "I didn't know they had cows in this part of the country. Stop the truck."

"What?"

"They look bored."

"Cows are supposed to be bored."

"Just stop the truck."

With a resigned sigh, Shade pulled the truck to a halt in a short gravel drive before a metal gate. Owen opened his door and hopped out.

"What the hell are you doing?" Shade asked as Owen opened the gate and entered the pasture with a small herd of bovines that watched him warily with large brown eyes as they chewed their cud.

"Bringing entertainment to the lives of these poor creatures."

Shade pulled out his phone and readied his camera, certain that Owen was about to do something that required photographic evidence. While he was fiddling with the phone, he noticed that he had an alert that Adam was nearby. Shade no longer kept tabs on the guy—well, not as extensively as he had when Adam had been hooked on heroin—but it did make him smile to see his friend so close. He'd almost given up on pestering him about writing songs today, but maybe he could convince Adam to hang out with him and Owen.

Shade sent Adam several quick text messages—*hey* and *you busy* and *yo Adam*—before switching to camera mode and focusing on Owen. He wasn't sure what had Owen up to his typical antics, but it probably had something to do with Shade's undeniably foul mood. Owen couldn't stand it when his companions weren't happy.

"Here, Bessie," Owen said, pulling a tuft of grass out by the roots and approaching the animals who had all stopped midchew to stare.

"Owen, don't harass the cows. You're liable to get shot by an angry farmer."

Owen paid Shade no mind as he crept closer to the cows, shaking his clump of grass at them. "Come get the grass. Yummy grass."

"Watch out for that—"

Owen gingerly stepped sideways to avoid a fresh cow pie. If Owen got shit on his shoes, he'd be riding in the bed of the truck.

"Don't you ladies want some yummy grass?"

When Owen got a bit too close for the cows' comfort, they began to take uneasy steps backward, tossing their heads and rolling their eyes. A few produced loud, disgruntled moos.

"Fine," Owen said. "Be that way." He tossed the grass aside and reached for the button of his jeans.

"What the fuck?" Shade asked. As confused as he was as to why Owen felt it necessary to drop his pants and moon the cows, it didn't stop him from laughing and taking pictures of Owen's exposed ass.

"Still think you're too good for my grass?" Owen called to the cows. "How do you feel about viewing my ass?"

Shade took his eyes off his phone screen to scrutinize Owen more closely. He could rhyme lines of equal length; was he capable of writing profound lyrics? Ones not about mooning cows?

When the herd began to bellow in distress—and who could blame them—an enormous, pissed-off bull popped up over the hill. When he recognized that his herd had been insulted, his massive body tensed and he swished his tufted tail threateningly before releasing a deep bellow.

"Owen, I think you'd better make a run for it," Shade said.

Owen glanced over his shoulder. With an "Oh, shit!" he raced toward the gate, struggling to keep his pants up. "Open the gate!" he yelled. "Open the fucking gate!"

Shade had been laughing so hard, it hadn't occurred to him that Owen could be in mortal danger. And he'd been too busy snapping pictures to think about helping.

The bull was rapidly closing in on Owen; there was no way he would beat the animal to the gate. The massive beast's hoofbeats thundered across the ground and churned up puffs of dust as the bull attempted to trample the human who dared insult his cows. Owen dodged left and scaled the plank fence beside the gate like an expert rodeo clown.

Shade waved one hand at the bull, trying to gain its attention. "Hey, Ribeye. Over here!"

Distracted by Shade, the bull hesitated long enough for Owen to flip over the top of the fence and land on his back in the long grass between the road and the pasture. He lay there for a long moment, catching his breath, while on the other side of the fence the bull pawed the ground, snorted, and flicked its tail in annoyance.

"Are you okay?" Shade asked, chuckling at Owen.

"I'm alive!"

"I'm not sure that fence will hold back a pissed-off bull. We'd better get out of here."

Owen dragged himself off the ground and stumbled back to the truck. He'd mooned the cows, but he gave the bull the finger.

"You're fucking crazy," Shade said as he slid into the truck beside Owen.

"Made you laugh." Owen grinned at Shade. "Did you get any pictures?"

Shade handed him his cellphone and Owen flipped through the shots, laughing so hard at what must have been a terrifying situation that Shade wondered if the guy needed a psychiatrist.

"Are you sure you're okay?" Shade asked.

Owen hesitated, the smile dropping from his friendly face. "Um, yeah. Why wouldn't I be?"

"You seem a little crazier than usual."

Owen shrugged. "Just a little stressed."

"About?"

"Caitlyn."

Shade scowled. "I thought her name was Lindsey."

"Lindsey's the reason I'm stressed about Caitlyn. I was hoping to make her a more permanent part of my life."

"You're seeing someone seriously?"

"I'm trying to. I met Caitlyn at a sex club several nights ago. She's everything I've ever wanted in a woman. Smart, sexy, rich . . ." He grinned his best boy-toy grin.

"A cougar?"

"Oh, yeah. You know I like my meat well-seasoned."

Shade laughed. "Typical. So she knows about Lindsey?"

"She was there when Lindsey showed up. I don't know what to do. I'm supposed to see Caitlyn this weekend and make it up to her, but how am I going to pull that off while I'm taking Lindsey to Austin?"

"And where's this other chick from?"

"Houston."

"So drop Lindsey off tonight and head directly for Houston. Don't look back."

"I'm sure that'll go over well with my mom. Hey, Mom, I might have gotten this woman pregnant. Can you keep an eye on her for a few months while I go fool around with this other woman? The one I actually *want* to be with. I know how much you like me to date older women." His words dripped with sarcasm.

"You could tell Lindsey to figure out her own problems," Shade said, squinting at the map on his phone that seemed to be leading them nowhere.

"But if it is my baby, I'd feel like shit if I disregarded his mother."

Shade rubbed his nose with the side of his finger. He'd never understood where Owen was coming from, and this situation was no different. "If Lindsey had been your girlfriend or something, your concern would make sense to me, but she slept with every person on the bus that night, including her best friend. If you act like a whore—"

Shade's words were cut off by Owen's hard punch to his arm. Shade rubbed the aching spot and scowled.

"Don't talk about her like that," Owen said. "We all make mistakes."

Why was he defending her? Shade didn't get it at all. But, whatever. If Owen wanted the woman to be his problem, Shade wasn't going to beg him to hand over the responsibility.

Shade's phone produced a familiar tone. It was an alert that told him that Adam was within a certain radius again. They must be driving down parallel roads or something. Shade had put the app on Adam's phone over a year ago, when he was still struggling with addiction. He wasn't sure why he kept it now that Adam was clean. Shade supposed he still didn't trust him not to do something completely idiotic.

"I wonder if Adam is busy," Shade said. "The limo driver said he rented a bike, so maybe he's driving around. Maybe he'd like to eat crawdads with us."

He had no idea why Adam would be riding a motorcycle out

in the middle of nowhere—because he and Owen were definitely in the middle of nowhere—but this was the perfect opportunity to boot him in the ass. Shade hoped Adam was riding to clear his head so he could write lyrics. But more than likely he was fucking his girlfriend in the bayou, which would likely only muddle his thoughts further.

Owen shrugged. "We can ask."

"Text him," Shade said.

Owen reached into his pocket, but Shade handed him his phone. "Use mine."

"I'll have to send him a picture of my cow prank. See what he says."

Shade snorted. "He'll think you've lost your mind."

"But I'm sure it'll make him laugh." Owen sent the picture and waited. "He's not responding."

"If he's on a bike, he'll have to pull over to answer," Shade said.

"True." He sent several more messages. Eventually Adam started to respond.

"Where the hell are you guys?" Owen read from the screen.

"Here, give it back to me," Shade said.

"You shouldn't text and drive," Owen said, but he handed him the phone.

Shade rarely texted more than a couple of words at a time; he used his voice-to-text app almost exclusively. After explaining to Adam where they were, he asked him to meet them for lunch. He was surprised when Adam agreed. He seemed to be in a much better mood than he had been that morning. Shade decided he wouldn't bust Adam's balls about not writing lyrics until they were back at the venue. Well, unless Adam broached the subject.

"So he's going to meet us there?"

"If he can find it," Shade said. "Where in the hell is this place?" Besides the narrow highway and some fencing, Shade hadn't seen any manmade structures for miles. "Are you sure it exists?"

Owen consulted Shade's map app. "We'll be turning in a few miles."

"Well, don't let me miss it or we'll end up in Mississippi."

"Or Florida."

When his phone's navigation program finally told him to turn right, they bounced down a short gravel drive before coming upon a small open picnic area in front of a trailer that had been converted into a mobile kitchen. Shade wondered if they'd set up business here to avoid city health inspections. The place made gas station restrooms look sanitary.

"Are you sure this place is legit?" Shade asked. He wouldn't want to get food poisoning and spend his evening on the toilet instead of onstage.

"It must be—it's packed." Owen handed him his phone, opened the truck door, and slipped outside.

Shade watched a nearby patron crack open crawdad after crawdad and stuff them into his mouth. When the guy didn't collapse from intense stomach pain or start projectile vomiting, Shade climbed out of the truck and followed Owen to the order counter.

"What will you have?" the aged, dark-skinned woman asked in a thick Cajun accent.

The menu board was limited in variety; Cajun-seasoned crawdads and shrimp, gumbo, and a few traditional side dishes were all they offered. But as far Shade was concerned, they only needed one item on their menu.

"A double order of crawdads," Shade said.

"Good idea," Owen said. "We can share them."

Maybe if they were disgusting. But Shade figured Owen would be going hungry.

Shade was halfway through his mess of tongue-tantalizing bliss when the rumble of a huge Harley announced Adam's arrival. He had his woman with him—the sweet little drug counselor from Dallas—but Shade was too busy stuffing his face and fending off Owen's attempts to sample one of his crawdads to offer either of them a proper greeting.

Dear lord, Shade had never tasted more delicious crawdads in his life. He was glad Owen had thought of this place.

He was starting to feel full, but the bit of spice stinging his tongue and lips made him crave more. He did love spicy food— not so hot that you couldn't taste other flavors, but hot enough to cause a tingle. This place got the flavor and the sensation exactly right. He was so intent on devouring his meal that he scarcely noticed the rest of the group had abandoned him to order at the counter. Until he noted his pile of crustaceans was quickly dwindling.

He was contemplating getting a second mess as he watched the others return with their smaller orders. *Smaller?* He wasn't sure how anyone could show restraint when it came to crawdads. Especially these crawdads.

He caught the tail end of their conversation.

"I'm a perpetual party, baby," Owen said as he sat next to Shade on the bench.

"Your perpetual party is in your pants," Shade said, checking out the line at the counter. It would be quicker and easier for him if his friends would share. The line of four customers seemed long. He tried staring down Madison—of the three, he figured the woman was most likely to succumb to his charm—but she pulled her basket closer and snapped open one of her crawdads, obviously not willing to share a single morsel, the scrooge.

"Better be careful with that kind of party." Madison laughed at Owen's expense. "Or you'll end up knocking up some groupie."

Shade shuddered as he was reminded that they currently had a knocked-up groupie in tow. Way to ruin his appetite.

"Yeah," Owen said, his voice barely above a whisper. "We wouldn't want *that* to happen."

Too late. Shade shoved his few remaining crawdads to the center of the table. Few things could diminish his enthusiasm for his favorite dish. Talking about Lindsey was right there at the top.

After a long moment of uncomfortable silence, Madison said, "What's wrong?"

She didn't know? It had been a coincidence that she'd brought up the subject? Shade glanced at Adam. Did he lie to her as much as he lied to everyone else? "You haven't told her?"

"Told me what?" Madison asked, her eyes on Adam as she slurped her soda.

"Nothing." Adam nodded toward her cup. "Do you want another drink?"

Nice try, Shade thought. "You'd better tell her. It might be yours." Shade shook his head. "No sense in making this worse than it already is."

"What might be yours?" Madison asked, frowning at Adam, then at Shade, and then at Adam again.

"It's probably mine," Owen said. "Damn party in my pants was bound to get me into trouble sooner or later."

Once Madison understood the situation—carefree band orgy turned lifelong responsibility—she completely lost her cool, going so far as to threaten Adam with a plastic fork. "How could you do this to me, Adam?"

Amanda hadn't taken the news quite so hard, but then Madison and Adam had been seeing each other off and on for over a year. Shade was surprised Madison wasn't angry about him cheating with another woman. Her only concern seemed to be that he hadn't used protection and might have contracted an STI. Huh. Where did Shade find a woman like her?

"I did wear protection," Adam insisted.

"Then how could you potentially be the father of this baby, Adam?" She jabbed him with her fork. "How?"

"We all wore protection," Shade said. They had. He wasn't just saying that to put Madison at ease.

Madison looked unconvinced. "Then *how* is she pregnant?"

"Wish I had the answer to that," Owen said.

Shade didn't remember all the details of their wild night with Lindsey and her friend Vanessa, but he'd fucked them both, he couldn't deny that. But he was certain he'd used a fresh condom each time he'd penetrated. He sure as hell didn't need two baby mamas in his life. A loving wife and several kids at home? Sure, he could go for that. But it was hard enough dealing with one court order for visitation—how the hell would he handle two? If Lindsey's baby did turn out to be his, he'd deal with it. He'd never turn his back on his own child. But he prayed this situation didn't further complicate his home situation. He was already struggling to stay an important part in his daughter's life. Was he capable of adding another kid to his mix of responsibilities?

"If you all wore protection, what's to say she got pregnant by any of you?" Madison's question jerked Shade out of his troubled thoughts. "Maybe she's a goddamned liar."

Maybe. If she was capable of fucking six guys and her best friend in a single night, who knew how many potential fathers she'd spread her legs for. She could have fucked the entire state of Idaho and all of its potatoes for all he knew.

". . . make her get a paternity test," Madison was saying. "Prove it isn't any of yours. Get rid of her once and for all."

Lindsey had a few more months before she gave birth, so worrying about what could be was going to make for a long summer. "We'll have one done as soon as the baby is born," Shade said. "Until then, we're just playing a waiting game."

"Fuck that," Madison said. Shade had never heard her cuss before. She must be really upset. Not that he blamed her. "They can do the test during pregnancy now. You don't have to wait until she delivers."

Well, hallelujah! He'd be sure Lindsey had the test as soon as possible. Then the poor sap who had drawn the knock-up-a-groupie card from the *Game of Rock Star* could figure out how he was going to handle the situation before the kid took its first breath. The rest of them could get on with their lives and thank their slow-swimming sperm.

When Madison and Adam started arguing about Adam's decision to get a vasectomy, Shade shifted uncomfortably on the bench and decided it was a good time to leave. Conversations about permanent nut alterations should never be discussed over a fine meal. He went back to the food truck and ordered all the remaining crawdads for the crew. Soon they were headed back toward the venue with Adam and Madison trailing them on their noisy rented Harley.

"He still isn't writing any music," Shade said to Owen as conversationally as possible. He didn't need to say who he was referring to. They both knew Adam was the catalyst for the band's creative output.

"I guess he has writer's block."

"Any suggestions as to what we should do about it?"

Owen thought for a moment and then shrugged. "I don't think we can do anything but wait it out."

"We could try writing something without him."

Owen turned his head and scrunched his brows at Shade. "Why would we do that? Just be patient. It'll come to him. You busting his ass about it all the time isn't going to help."

Shade had never been a patient man, but Owen was probably right. He was going to confront Adam about his lies—he was sick of the guy getting away with shit—and maybe put a little pressure on him, but perhaps if Shade tried to be supportive instead of adversarial that would help Adam break through this block of his.

"I'll give him some breathing room," Shade promised. But only an inch or two.

And now for the band's other major issue . . .

"So are you going to tell Lindsey she's getting that paternity test as soon as fucking possible, or do you want me to do it?"

Owen released a long sigh and returned his attention to the scenery outside. The gnarled trees had already given way to city sprawl. The drive back to civilization seemed a lot shorter than the one that had taken them to the food truck. Of course, they hadn't stopped to harass cows on this leg of their journey.

"I'll tell her," Owen said.

"I'm not sure why you voluntarily interact with her. Do you get off on her attention or what?" Shade would probably never understand the dynamic between that particular groupie and his bass player.

"I don't know." Owen shrugged. "It's kind of nice to be one who's sought after for a change."

Shade released a bark of laughter and slapped Owen on the shoulder. "Trust me, dude, you do not want her kind of attention."

Back at the venue, Owen took the large foil trays of crawdads to the crew while Shade followed Adam and Madison onto the bus. Madison disappeared into the bathroom to change out of her riding leathers—which she looked fantastic in, Shade couldn't help but notice. Shade took the opportunity to ask Adam how his supposed songwriting session had gone that afternoon.

"Fine." Adam said, his body stiffening defensively.

Fucking liar.

"So you wrote something?" Shade asked.

Adam refused to meet his eyes. "Yeah."

Liar, liar, uninspired.

"Is it good?" Shade asked.

"Of course it's good."

"I'd like to hear it."

Just admit you're fucking lying. Admit it, Adam.

"I'd rather surprise you," Adam said.

Shade's jaw tightened. Why couldn't Adam just say that he hadn't written anything? Shade fought the urge to grab him and shake sense into him. Shade supposed he'd have to play the asshole—*again*—and force Adam to tell him the truth.

"Is it in your notebook under your mattress? Let's see it." *I know it's still fucking blank, because you didn't write shit.* Shade headed toward Adam's bunk, and Adam raced after him.

Adam darted between Shade and his bunk, bodily preventing

Shade from going after the notebook. "You'll see it when I'm ready for you to see it."

Which will be never, because you haven't written anything! Shade wanted to yell, but he managed to keep his shit together. At least a little.

"Just be straight with me, Adam," Shade said calmly. "You're not as good a liar as you think you are." Shade had no problem telling when Adam was lying because junkie-Adam had lied to him innumerable times in the past. It was hard to believe someone who always let you down.

Adam glared at him for a long moment and when Shade refused to give him an out, he lowered his gaze and for once, his guard. "I didn't write much," he said and took a deep breath. "Or anything," he whispered.

At least he was owning up to it. That was a start. Shade figured a guy with a year of rehab under his belt would realize the first step in solving a problem was admitting there was one.

"I kind of figured that," Shade said. "So what's the problem?"

"I don't know." Adam shook his head, a scowl crumpling his dark brows. "I think . . ."

Shade waited not so patiently for him to confess what was on his mind.

"I think maybe I'm too happy."

That had not been what Shade had expected him to say at all. "Huh?"

"The music always came from the darkest part of me," Adam said.

And that was what made it awesome.

"It was a balm to my miserable soul," he continued, his eyes haunted. Worried? Was Adam actually worried about this? "And now that I'm not miserable . . ." He held Shade's gaze, shrugged, and shook his head.

If he needed assistance, why didn't he just ask? "Do you want me to make you miserable?" Shade joked. "I'm probably up for the task."

"I don't know. If it would help."

Shade didn't want to make him miserable. He wanted to help him through this. He offered a couple of suggestions—asking Kellen's composer girlfriend for opinions or letting the rest of the band try their hand at writing music—but Adam refused to take

Shade's advice. Shade could tell he was struggling. Adam probably felt like a failure, so Shade backed down. Still, he wasn't going to let the issue rest for long. They needed new material, but he'd give Adam a little more time to sort himself out.

"I'll work on some stuff this weekend," Adam promised.

Shade opened his mouth to remind him that Madison would be making him happy all weekend, so he probably wouldn't write a single word, but he thought better of it. He was *glad* that Adam was happy. There had to be a way to keep him that way and off drugs *and* writing music. There just had to be. Shade would give it more thought and in the meantime try to be supportive. "I can't wait to see what you come up with."

Madison came out of the bathroom having changed into her typical country girl attire. Adam looked ready to jump her bones, which was Shade's cue to leave, though he couldn't resist offering Adam one more little push on his way out the door.

"I still think you should talk to what's her face." Kellen's woman.

"Dawn?" Adam said.

"Yeah, her." Shade left on that note, hoping the suggestion would stick in Adam's craw and irritate him into seeking Dawn's advice. She might be invaluable to him or not, but Adam wouldn't know unless he asked.

As Shade walked away from the bus, he checked his phone for the time. Occasionally, he could catch Julie between appointments in the late afternoon. He wasn't sure why her mother thought it was necessary to schedule every hour of their four-year-old's life with activity. Whatever happened to just being a kid? Discovering that it was almost five, he decided to risk a phone call. He dialed Tina's number and leaned against a wall for moral support. He hated calling her. She was always busting his balls.

"What do you want?" Tina asked in greeting.

"Just called to talk to Julie. Is she there?" Hearing his daughter's sweet voice was exactly what he needed at the moment.

"She's busy."

Too busy to talk to her father on the phone for a couple of minutes? "Doing what?"

"She's on a very important play date with Riley Callahan."

Shade rubbed at one eye under his sunglasses. There was no use arguing with Tina. He was sure she actually thought Julie's playdate with Riley Callahan was important. "What time do you want me to pick her up in the morning?"

"I'll just have her dropped off."

"I don't mind pick—"

"I *said* I'd have her dropped off. Why is everything an argument with you, Jacob?"

He hadn't been arguing. He was just trying to be helpful.

"We're going to the zoo tomorrow," he told her, "so make sure she wears something comfortable."

"I know how to dress our child, Jacob," she snapped.

His ire was starting to rise. This woman knew exactly how to push his buttons and she so enjoyed poking at them all.

"I didn't say you didn't know how to dress her. Jesus Christ, Tina, I can't say more than two words to you without you jumping down my throat."

The line went dead. He pulled his phone away from his face and stared down at it in disbelief. She'd fucking hung up on him. That figured.

"What a bitch," he grumbled under his breath, before taking a deep, steadying breath and shoving his phone back into his pocket. Thank god that personality trait wasn't genetic. Julie was a perfect angel. No one would ever convince him otherwise. And Amanda was fun and cheerful and level-headed. Hard to believe the two were sisters. Maybe Amanda was adopted, he thought as he headed toward the building.

Shade stalked through the backstage door into the venue. Here he was in his element. But as he ventured further down the corridor, he recognized someone who shouldn't be in his element at all. He'd already told the woman that he wasn't interested in seeing her again when they'd parted ways in Tulsa. What in the hell was Nikki doing backstage? And with Gabe?

"Why is she here?" Shade asked Gabe, not sure why he cared so much.

Gabe immediately bristled, standing to his full impressive height, his bright red mohawk making him look even larger and more intimidating. But Shade wasn't the least bit frightened.

"If Amanda can come to our shows, then so can Melanie."

Shade shook his head. "Not Melanie. If you have a thing for her, of course she's welcome." He reached behind Melanie and pulled Nikki out from hiding. "Her! What is *she* doing here?"

Nikki tightened her hands into fists and glared at Shade. "What, did you forget my name already, asshole?"

Why did women always call him that? Because he refused to let them walk all over him? Because he knew what he wanted or didn't want and made no apologies for either? Did that make him an asshole? Shade shook his head. "No, darling Nikki, I didn't forget your name, but you can't be here. I don't want you here." And why did it bother him so much that Nikki was there? Was it because she was the last woman he'd slept with before losing himself to Amanda? Her presence made him uneasy. He didn't think he'd fall to her seductive charms again, but he didn't want to compromise his growing relationship with Amanda. If Nikki wasn't around to test his resolve, he'd have nothing to worry about. He knew the chick was still interested in him. Why wouldn't she be?

Nikki's lower lip quivered, all the fight going out of her in an instant. She totally wanted him—and he'd probably hurt her feelings—but he had a long history of interacting with women he wasn't interested in and he knew from experience that if he showed them kindness and respect, they thought it meant he liked them and then he couldn't shake them. Maybe that was why he'd been labeled an asshole. Better an asshole than a dude with dozens of crazy stalkers.

"I invited her," Gabe said. "I invited both of them, okay? It's none of your concern."

Shade's eyebrows shot up. Gabe had *invited* Nikki? Really? There was only one reason he could think of to invite a girl like Nikki along on a romantic weekend with your new girlfriend.

"So they'll double up on your dick, but not mine?" Shade was teasing because Gabe was being entirely too serious about the situation. Unfortunately, Gabe's girlfriend took his jest at face value.

"You are the biggest pig I've ever met in my life!" Melanie screamed at him.

Hmm . . . pig is a step up from asshole. Maybe she hates me less than I thought.

Melanie continued her tirade while Nikki smirked at him. "I don't know why anyone would do anything with you other than kick you in the nuts."

Or not . . .

Nikki stepped forward, apparently thinking Melanie had compromised his armor. "Can I talk to you?" she asked, looking up at him with those bedroom eyes of hers.

"No," he said flatly. "I have nothing to say to you. If I had, I would have called you."

Melanie actually growled at him. "You have no problem fucking her in a public hallway . . ."

He had to admit that he'd had a good time with Nikki. She was a fun party girl, but not someone he wanted to get close to. Not someone he wanted in his life. Not someone like Amanda.

"Or a sauna," Nikki supplied.

Shade's balls tightened at the memory of what wonderful things Nikki had done to them in that sauna. Yeah, Nikki needed to get lost as soon as possible. Not that he couldn't control his libido, but he'd rather not have to worry about it.

"Or a sauna," Melanie spat. "But you don't have the common decency to carry on a polite conversation with her?"

Did Melanie have any idea what kind of woman her friend was? Nikki wasn't interested in polite conversation. She wanted to fuck, and that was all she wanted to do. Which was fun for a weekend, but it didn't amount to anything. The fact that she was here set off all sorts of warning bells in Shade's head. His big head. The little one would consider a second go at her. She was exceptionally bendy.

"That about sums it up," he said and turned on his heel to stalk away. He didn't want to hurt Nikki's feelings by pointing out her loose transgressions to her best friend—who seemed to think she was Nikki's guard dog—but at the same time he didn't want Nikki to think she had a chance to be with him. So his best course of action was to walk away. He managed not to grin at the sound of rage Melanie bellowed at his back. That chick really hated him. What the fuck did Gabe see in her?

Shade entered the band's dressing room and was immediately wrapped in the arms of their tour manager. He couldn't help but be aware of Sally's large, soft breasts pressing into his chest, but she was like an older sister to him, and he knew how much she and her husband—a member of the crew—loved each other. Shade would never make a move on Sally, and he was pretty sure she'd refuse him if he tried. But he did enjoy her hugs and not only because she had a great rack.

"I've been looking all over for you," Sally said. She pulled away and looked up at him, her bright blue eyes set off by thick black eyeliner. She dressed like a groupie, but was entirely professional when it came to running Sole Regret's tour.

"Am I in trouble again?" he asked with a teasing grin.

"I'm sure you are, but that's not why I need to talk to you. There's an opportunity for Sole Regret to play at Rock on the Range on the *main* stage. One of the scheduled bands had to cancel and the event coordinator called me—desperate and begging."

Shade shook his head. "I already told you we aren't performing at Rock on the Range this year. It's during Julie's weekend—"

"Jacob," Sally interrupted. She only called him Jacob when she was flustered. "I know you want to see your daughter. I understand that. Bring her with you—"

"No," he said. "She doesn't like the loud place"—which was what the four-year-old called concerts—"and I don't want her exposed to that environment. She's very impressionable." He dropped his eyes, unable to stop himself from staring at Sally's boobs. He swore that some women had eyeball magnets on their chests. Their tour manager was one of them.

"I think the band should vote on whether or not to perform—"

"They're going to have a hard time performing without a vocalist. I'm not—"

His words were cut off when Sally suddenly stumbled forward. She bumped into his chest before he could catch her. "You okay?" he asked, steadying her. But Sally didn't answer because she was being screamed at by one very upset Nikki.

"You fucking bitch, I saw him first." Nikki grabbed Shade by the arm and tugged.

What the fuck?

"I already told you I'm not interested," Shade said

"Yeah, because you've moved on to this *slut*," Nikki spat.

"I'm married," Sally said, shaking her head in disbelief.

"This *married* slut," Nikki said.

Sally shoved Nikki, who stumbled back and then with an angry growl launched forward and took a swing at a stunned Sally. Luckily Shade's reflexes kicked in. He managed to grab Nikki's wrist and prevent the blow from connecting.

"Not cool," Shade said to Nikki, lifting an arm to block the blow she directed toward him. Her half-assed slap turned out to be a diversionary tactic so she could grab a handful of Sally's thick black hair.

Sally shoved Nikki again. "Back off!"

Melanie was the one who pulled them apart. She didn't say a word, just took Nikki by the arm—Nikki went inexplicably docile beneath her friend's touch—and escorted her out of the dressing room and into the corridor.

"What the hell just happened?" Sally said, smoothing her hair with both hands.

"I fucked that chick last weekend. She seems to want a repeat performance."

Sally rolled her eyes at him. "Why don't you try keeping it in your pants for a change?"

Shade chuckled. "*It* doesn't get off on dry humping. *It* prefers hot, slick orifices."

Sally shook her head. "You probably get what you deserve, stud. But I'm not sure why *I* was assaulted."

"She obviously thought you were her competition."

"For you?" Sally snorted. "She can have you."

Shade's ego stung slightly. He knew Sally had eyes only for Kris, but she didn't have to be so harsh. "Guess I'll go tell her that you gave us your blessing."

He started to walk away, but Sally caught his arm. "You do *not* have my blessing. I suggest you stay the fuck away from her," she said.

He planned to do exactly that.

"And I think you owe me for putting up with your crazy sex partners."

"Fine," he said. "I owe you one."

Sally grinned deviously. "So I guess you'll be performing at Rock on the Range after all."

Shade scowled at her. "Nice try. I already said no. Julie comes first. You can run me into the ground on any day except my weekends with Julie. I'm not bending on this issue, so you might as well quit pushing."

She sighed with resignation. "Fine. I get it."

"You aren't going to mention this to the rest of the guys, are you? The last thing I need is everyone ganging up on me." Not that it would change his mind.

Sally shook her head. "No, I'll keep it to myself. That daughter of yours is a lucky little girl, you know."

"I do my best to be a good father." Yet he always felt as if he wasn't measuring up and that he didn't get to see her nearly enough. That was why he was determined to make the most of the time he did get to see her and why he guarded those precious moments ferociously. Performing at Rock on the Range on the main stage was a big deal, but nothing was more important than his daughter.

Sally left him while she went to make sure the setup was running smoothly. She was excellent at her job, and usually Shade had a hard time telling her no, but she knew better than to try to schedule performances or events during his visitation weekends.

Shade ventured out into the backstage area to chat with other musicians, the roadies, and the fans who had lucked into backstage passes. Next to performing onstage, this was his favorite part of the rock star gig. He met so many interesting people, and there was always someone to talk to, always someone to share a beer with and pass the time. The cellphone in his pocket vibrated, and he pulled it out to see who wanted to interrupt his good time.

His heart stumbled over a beat when he saw that the message was from Amanda. God, he couldn't wait to see her later that night. And if he was lucky, all weekend long.

I know you're probably busy, her text said, *but I can't stop thinking about you.*

Understandable, he texted her back in jest.

Egomaniac, her return text accused.

Any man lucky enough to have you thinking of him would have a swollen head.

In his mind's eye, he could see her smile. See her eyes light up and the green flecks in their hazel depths brighten with mischief. Very soon he wouldn't have to imagine what she looked like as she thought of him. He would see for himself.

Her reply came quickly. *I hope you have TWO swollen heads when you think of me.*

He laughed out loud. *No doubt. I'll see you soon.*

Not soon enough.

She sure made it difficult to keep his head on his work. A pretty brunette stopped in front of him and smiled. "Can I get a picture with you?" she asked shyly.

"Sure." He stood and wrapped an arm around her slight shoulders, smiling for the camera phone. He did have the best job on the planet. Now if he could only create the perfect home life to match it.

CHAPTER TWO

AMANDA WAVED at the pretty black-haired woman who walked through the front door of Jack's Bar and Grill. Leah was stretching every inch of her five-foot frame to try to spot Amanda through the crowd. Their favorite table had been occupied when Amanda had arrived, so she'd been forced to sit at a counter-high table in the corner.

"Leah!" Amanda shouted, waving more vigorously.

Leah smiled when her gaze landed on Amanda, and she pressed her way through the boisterous crowd. She hugged Amanda before climbing up on the tall stool across from her.

"The nachos should be out in a few minutes," Amanda said.

Amanda waved a hand at the cute Latino waiter who'd already brought her margarita and would know what Leah wanted to drink without asking. The chicken nachos, the margaritas—hers lime with salt on the rim, Leah's strawberry with sugar—the flirting with their regular server, and the dissuasion of inebriated cowboys were all part of their Friday night routine. They'd been coming to this bar since they'd turned twenty-one. Before that they'd hung out at a coffee shop every Saturday morning and studied together each night in the library. Before that, they spent almost every afternoon at the mall. And before *that*, they'd been together every waking moment playing with frogs in the Carmichael's backyard koi pond. Leah was no longer Amanda's next door neighbor, but they still saw each other regularly. They even worked in the same school district.

"I thought you might bail on me tonight," Leah said with a wry grin. "Isn't that new man of yours coming home for the weekend?"

"I'd never miss our girls' night." Amanda took a sip from her straw; the cold lime kick bathed her tongue and traced a frigid path down her throat as she swallowed. "Besides, he won't be home until after midnight."

Leah grinned knowingly. "Ah, so you'll need to leave here by eleven thirty."

Amanda wanted to leave early and meet Jacob at his house, but she wasn't sure that was a wise approach. She'd seen what had happened to the last woman who'd stripped off her clothes and surprised him—wet, naked, and gorgeous—in his hot tub. As the lead singer of a popular metal band, Jacob was used to women chasing him. Perhaps he'd like to do the chasing for a change. But Amanda wasn't sure she could keep herself from pursuing him; she'd had a crush on him for ages. Their one night together had turned into two when she'd surprised him backstage at his show in San Antonio. If she hadn't taken the initiative to hunt him down, he'd have likely forgotten about her by now. The man's attention span was more miniscule than most of her sophomore biology students' fascination with cellular mitosis. So she could hold the man's interest for five minutes. Tops.

"Maybe," Amanda said with a shrug. "I haven't decided yet."

Leah snorted. "Coward."

"I'm not a coward," Amanda insisted. She folded her arms on the table and leaned over to press her forehead into her forearm. "Just a little yellow."

"I don't get what the problem is. You've been lusting after the guy since he started dating your sister."

"Reprehensible behavior," Amanda muttered.

"You've always gotten along well with him—even when Tina was trying to destroy him in the divorce. Then he finally notices you as a woman, you have the best sex of your life with the guy, and *now* you're backing off? What your deal, Amanda?"

"I don't know." Amanda lifted her head from her folded arms and stared into Leah's dark brown eyes. "Do you think I'm a horrible person for having an affair with my sister's ex-husband?"

Leah lifted both eyebrows. "You know how I feel about your sister. How many times did she steal your boyfriends? Ones you actually wanted? Do you think she felt a twinge of remorse for causing you so much heartache over the years? And Tina hates Jacob now. *Loathes* him. You're not a horrible person, Amanda. You're incapable of being a horrible person."

"*You're* incapable of being a horrible person. I'm capable of lusting after my brother-in-law for seven years."

"*Ex* brother-in-law."

"And then at the first opportunity, I screwed him until I

couldn't move."

A bright red drink was set before Leah and an enormous plate of nachos topped with fragrant, steaming chicken placed in the center of the table.

"Who did you screw?" their regular server, Tomás, asked.

"None of your business," Amanda said.

"Her sister's ex-husband," Leah said at the same time.

The woman's infallible openness could be a liability at times.

"Ooh," Tomás said. "Sounds scandalous. Does your sister know you're screwing her ex?"

Amanda shook her head with marked exaggeration. "Noooo. She'd flip."

"Only because she's a mean, selfish whore," Leah said.

Tomás jerked back and blinked at Leah. The sweet, shy Asian woman—with her narrow frame, pink sweater set, and smart black-rimmed glasses—didn't seem the type to call others names.

"Who could make my life miserable," Amanda added.

Leah leaned closer and laid a hand on her shoulder. "If he's not worth it, then you should back out now."

Tomás nodded his agreement, as if he had suddenly earned a degree in relationship counseling.

"But he *is* worth it. He's so worth it." Amanda dropped her head back down into her crossed arms. "Argh! I'm so conflicted," she said to the floor.

Her cellphone, which was sitting on the table, dinged as a text message arrived.

"Not for long," Leah said and giggled.

Amanda lifted her head to find Leah eying her cellphone screen and part of the message that was openly displayed for a few seconds before the screen went dark.

"Snoop," Amanda accused before lifting her phone and typing in her password so that she could read the message Leah had already seen.

"Is it from the guy?" Tomás asked, standing on tiptoe to try to read over her shoulder.

"Don't you have work to do?" Amanda asked, tilting her phone so he wouldn't be able to see the screen, and elbowing him in the chest to get him to back off.

"Probably," Tomás said, "but it will wait."

As Amanda read her message from Jacob, a smile spread

across her face and her heart fluttered in her chest.

I hope I find you waiting in my bed when I get home. Nothing would make me happier than holding the most beautiful woman in the world while I sleep.

She couldn't resist teasing him in her reply. *Are you sure your bed is big enough for you, me, AND Pamela Anderson?*

It was a running joke between them. When she'd surprised him backstage in San Antonio, he'd pretended to think it was Pamela Anderson who'd come up behind him and put her hands over his eyes.

Probably. He texted back. *But I want you. Only you.*

Leah was right—as usual. Amanda was no longer conflicted in the slightest. If Tina couldn't handle the thought of her big sister making the moves on her ex-husband, well, tough titty,kitty. And what Tina didn't know couldn't hurt her.

"So you're going, right?" Leah said.

"Could you say no to him?" The man was even more gorgeous than he was a master of smooth talking.

Leah chuckled. "It wouldn't even cross my mind."

"Living dangerously," Tomás said before he left them to eat their nachos in peace.

Are you sure you want to see me tonight? I figured you'd be tired. She sent that text to give him an out if he wanted one.

An instant later her phone buzzed. *Can't you take a hint?*

She chuckled. Another running joke between them. *Hint taken. I'll see you when you get home. Though sleeping is not my favorite thing to do in your bed. ;-)*

He replied, *Hint taken.*

She set her phone aside and glanced at Leah, who was slurping her strawberry margarita through a straw.

"How's summer school going?" Amanda asked as she scooped cheese and chicken onto a chip.

Leah searched their plate of shared nachos for a chip with minimal cheese. "You know those kids that you privately celebrate when they're absent?"

All teachers had them. Whether the student in question was a troublemaker, a mouthy brat, or the teacher just had a plain old personality clash with a kid, every teacher had a few students on her roster that drove her absolutely nuts. One mark of a good teacher was never letting the student know you'd like to strangle them.

"Yep," Amanda said.

"That's my entire class this summer."

"You always find a diamond in the rough and make a personal connection. Change a life forever," Amanda said. She knew that was what excited Leah about teaching.

"At this point, it isn't looking promising. Maybe it's time I took summers off. It's only two weeks into summer term and I'm already drained."

"I highly recommend summers off," Amanda said, lifting her nearly empty margarita glass in toast.

"And maybe I'll start taking Christmas breaks too."

Which reminded Amanda of something she'd meant to ask Leah but kept forgetting. "Are you doing your GED prep class this December?"

Leah sighed. "Yeah. I already signed up to do it. But next year . . . Next year I'm going to take some time off for me before I completely burn out."

"Is the class already full?" Amanda asked, setting her drink down and reaching for another nacho.

"Isn't it always full?"

"That's because you work miracles." Yep, Amanda was buttering her up and for a very good reason. A reason she'd be seeing in a few hours.

Leah flushed with pleasure at Amanda's compliment and took a sip from her bright red cocktail.

"Any chance you could squeeze one more into the class?" Amanda asked, biting into her chip and using her free hand to tip escaping crumbs into her mouth.

"I'm already stretched to my limit."

"Please? It was nearly impossible to get him to agree to it in the first place."

Leah scowled. "Who are you talking about?"

"Jacob."

Leah jerked her hand back from the plate of nachos, hit her drink with her elbow, and barely rescued the tottering glass before it dropped from the table.

"What?" Leah sputtered, mopping up a few escaped drops with a napkin. "He didn't graduate from high school?"

Amanda shook her head. "We were talking about regrets, and

he said his only regret was not finishing high school. So I mentioned getting his GED and taking your prep class. He was against it at first, but I told him how great you are and he eventually came around to the idea. But I don't think he'll go through with it if you can't work him into your roster this winter."

"So basically you're saying that if I don't let him into my class, I'm crushing his dreams and will be responsible for turning him into a shell of a man. Is that what you're implying?"

"Pretty much."

Leah shook her head at Amanda. "Why don't *you* teach him?"

Amanda chuckled, imagining that the only studying he'd get done around her was the study of her anatomy. And she was more than okay with that.

"You're the miracle worker. I just teach biology."

"You're a great teacher," Leah insisted.

"I'm a good teacher," Amanda admitted. "*You're* a great teacher." A little extra butter never hurt.

"Fine," Leah said, using both hands to flip her long straight hair behind her ears. "I wouldn't do this for just anyone, you know?"

Leah was lying. She was always burdening herself to help others, but Amanda appreciated her friend's giving nature far more than she would ever realize.

"You're the best!" Amanda leaned from her stool to give Leah a hug.

"You can make it up to me," Leah said.

Amanda released her and scooted back onto her stool. "Anything. Name it." She reached for her margarita and sucked down the melting dregs of her growing-tastier-by-the-minute drink.

"Does the hot cowboy at three o'clock look a little lonely to you?"

"My three o'clock or your three o'clock?" Amanda asked, turning her head slowly to try to locate the man in question.

"My three o'clock. White Stetson. Blue shirt. Great ass."

There were several white Stetsons in the general area Leah had indicated, but Amanda knew the woman's tastes, so she didn't have to ask which cowboy had caught her eye. "I'm on it," Amanda said, and she hopped off her stool.

She grabbed her empty glass and headed toward the bar.

Tomás would have refilled it for her, but she needed a reason to bump into Leah's dreamboat. And the whole "going to the bathroom to powder her nose" thing felt trite.

When she reached the back of the guy Leah was interested in, she paused and turned to glance at her friend, lifting her eyebrows to seek her approval. Leah grinned and nodded. Yep, predictable. Leah liked her cowboys tall, blond, and with a little meat on their bones—pretty much the woman's physical opposite. If the man had blue eyes and a bit of beard scruff on a strong jaw, Leah would be in insta-lust.

Amanda took a step back so she could gain momentum and then rushed forward and bumped into the cowboy's broad back. "Oh, excuse me," she said, rubbing the guy's shoulder to undo any damage. "I was in such a hurry to refill my drink, I wasn't paying attention to where I was going."

The guy turned, and Amanda immediately began her Leah-checklist as she assessed whether to introduce him to her friend or not. Leah was painfully shy, so approaching men was difficult for her. Amanda held no such reservations.

The man's eyes were shadowed by the brim of his hat, but were light in color—either gray or blue—so were sure to melt Leah into a puddle. Check. He had a friendly face, a bit too round to be handsome, but he was definitely cute. Hesitant check. His smile was pleasant and he didn't leer at her or stare down her shirt. Enthusiastic check. So far, he was getting good marks. He wasn't completely approved yet as he hadn't spoken, but she had a good feeling about this one.

"Did you hurt yourself?" he asked.

Showing concern for her well-being but not using it as an excuse to paw her. Check.

"Oh, I'm fine. I was more worried about you. I just plowed right into you like an idiot."

"A pretty little thing like you is going to have to hit me a lot harder than that to do any damage."

His come-on was a bit oafish, but not the worst introductory flirting she'd encountered. Not by a long shot.

"Can I refill that for you?" he asked, nodding toward her glass. "What are you having?"

A little fast, but he probably thought she was hinting for him to buy her a drink.

"No thanks. I don't think my boyfriend would appreciate me accepting a drink from a gorgeous stranger." She waited for his response, hoping he didn't disappoint her by suggesting she ditch her boyfriend and go back to his place. No way would she introduce a jerk like that to Leah. And more than one guy had said exactly that in this same situation.

He frowned slightly, but tipped his hat at her. "Lucky guy," he said. "You take care now, darlin'." He turned back toward the bar, cradling his drink between both hands and yep, looking a little lonely.

Amanda set her empty glass on the bar and caught the bartender's eye for a refill.

"Are you here alone?" Amanda asked the cowboy as she waited.

"I thought you had a boyfriend," he said, glancing at her out of the corner of his eye and blushing slightly.

"I do. I'm going to level with you. What's your name?"

"Colton and yes, I'm flying solo tonight."

"Nice to meet you, Colton. I'm Amanda. I'm not trying to pick you up. My friend thinks you're cute, but she's too shy to come hit on you herself."

The guy chuckled and turned in his stool, glancing around, presumably for the smitten friend she'd mentioned.

"Don't be obvious," Amanda said, clutching his arm. "She'd kill me if she knew I was doing this." Not really. Leah *expected* Amanda to do this. "She's over there in the corner. Black hair. Pink sweater." Amanda tilted her head in Leah's direction and then noticed she was cornered by two guys who were obviously drunk and checking none of her boxes. Cringing away from the one trying to wrap his arm around her, Leah looked ready to bolt. Crap.

"Just a minute," Amanda said to Colton. "I'll be back."

Amanda rushed to the table. "Is there a problem here, gentlemen?" she said loudly.

"Yeah, there's a problem," said a guy who looked barely old enough to shave. "She won't dance with me." His words were slurred, his eyes unfocused.

"Maybe she doesn't want to dance with you," Amanda said, checking with Leah for validation. Staring at the hands she held twisted in her lap, Leah shook her head vigorously. "She's probably afraid that you're so drunk you'll fall on top of her and crush her."

"You look a lot sturdier than she does," the guy said, leaning heavily into his silent friend looking ready to fall flat on his face. "You dance with me."

Sturdier? Oh yes, Casanova, how could I resist that wonderful compliment?

"Get lost," a deep voice said from behind Amanda. "You're bothering the ladies."

The drunk whirled to confront the intruder, but seemed to recognize that Colton was much sturdier than himself—*and* Amanda—and he was also steady on his feet.

Leah's harasser stumbled away with his friend's assistance. "Whatever," he grumbled. "She was ugly anyway."

Amanda's foot automatically shot out in front of him, and he had to grab some random dude in the crowd to keep from face-planting on the dusty wooden floor. "Asshole," Amanda muttered under her breath.

"Are you okay?" Colton asked Leah.

She flushed prettily and nodded. "Thanks for chasing them away," she said.

"My pleasure, miss." He lifted his hat, momentarily exposing hat-flattened blond hair, and Amanda smiled at the flush that rose up Leah's face.

Yep, Leah was definitely interested.

"Would you mind sitting with us for a while?" Amanda asked. "Just to keep drunk jerks from hitting on us."

"I reckon so," Colton said, smiling at Leah, who was currently stealing glances at him but who had yet to make steady eye contact.

It must suck to be shy, Amanda thought.

As the trio munched on nachos and nursed their drinks, Amanda ushered her tight-lipped companions through small talk. She had no problem getting both of them to talk to her, even if they weren't talking to each other. Or even meeting each other's eyes. Perhaps Leah would be better off if she didn't have Amanda there as a crutch.

Amanda allowed the conversation to lapse, watching her friend for cues. Maybe Leah didn't like this guy after all. Did they need to have a BFF conference in the ladies room? Amanda opened her mouth to announce her need to use the restroom, but Colton turned to Leah and said, "Say, Leah?"

Leah glanced up into his eyes and flushed before focusing on the second button of his Western-cut blue shirt. "Yes?"

"I'm not much of a dancer," he said.

"Oh," Leah said before lifting her gaze and offering him a sweet smile. "That's okay."

She was totally into him, and apparently Colton had been too polite to tell Amanda to shut the fuck up and get lost so he could make his move.

"If you're not against a few crushed toes . . ."

"I'm not," Leah said a bit too eagerly.

"Would you care to dance? Or rather, endure my clumsy attempts at dancing?"

"I'd love to."

Amanda smiled to herself as Colton stood, offered Leah his hand to help her from her barstool, and put a protective arm at her back as he led her off to the dance floor. Ah, nice guys with manners. Perhaps a perfect match for Leah, but Amanda's tastes ran a bit on the darker side.

Finding herself alone, Amanda fiddled with her phone, wishing Jacob was offstage so they could text each other while she waited to see him again. She couldn't remember the last time she'd been so giddy over a guy. Her last couple of boyfriends had been more like Colton—settled, considerate, *not* forbidden—and those men sure hadn't made her heart thud, belly quiver, or her pussy ache the way it did for Jacob. She wasn't sure if those feelings would last, but holy hell, she was definitely enjoying the ride. Even if it was making her a little crazy.

Amanda kept half of her attention on Leah in case Colton turned out to be one to bolt on and she needed to intervene. But heck, the guy hadn't even pulled Leah up against him yet. Yawn. The other half of her attention was fixed on her cellphone as she waited for Jacob to get in touch with her again. He would be offstage soon. Would he call her? Should she call him? Should she chill the fuck out and try to have a good time tonight? Yeah, she should definitely do that.

She lowered her head to the table and took several deep breaths as her brain tried straightening out her heart.

This is just a fling. He's really not that into you. Get off your bar stool and go flirt with someone. Anyone. Maybe Mr. Right was at this very bar at this very moment.

But even if he was, it didn't matter. Mr. Wrong—aka Jacob

"Shade" Silverton—had her complete devotion. Might as well not fight what she was feeling—it was no use anyway. She had more than the hots for her former brother-in-law—she liked him. Liked him in the way that an addict *liked* methamphetamine.

Someone took the seat across from her and she could tell by the very large set of feet attached to the person that it wasn't her petite friend returning from the dance floor. "Hey, beautiful, why are you sitting here all alone?"

"How do you know I'm beautiful?" she asked, her forehead still pressed to the table. "Maybe I'm sitting alone because I'm ugly enough to melt the paint off a furnace."

"With legs like those?"

Amanda rolled her eyes and lifted her head. "You're wasting your time," she told the handsome young man, who she normally would have found attractive. He had dark hair and startling green eyes and was filling out his plain white T-shirt in exactly the right way. If he'd hit on her just a week ago, she would have probably already given him her phone number. "I'm completely infatuated with Mr. Wrong at the moment."

"Maybe I can help you get over your infatuation."

She snorted and shook her head. "I'm not looking to get over him just yet," she said. "But maybe after he breaks my heart, you could try again."

"Do you come here often?" Green-eyes asked.

He lost points for unoriginal pick-up lines, but the green eyes made up for his lack of creativity. "Every Friday night."

"Maybe I'll see you again then."

She shrugged. "Maybe."

Still not rising from his seat, he traced the bottom of Leah's margarita glass with one finger. "How will I know when you're ready to move on?" He blinked, and when his eyes reopened, his gaze had shifted from staring at his finger to boring into hers.

Jeez. Why did guys like this only hit on her when she was happily taken?

And she was happily taken. So she figured she'd best scare the guy away since he seemed the type to like a challenge.

"Depends." She shrugged. "If you're interested in a broken shell of a desperate woman—that will be obvious by the endless sobbing—I'll be super easy to seduce, if that's all you're after."

"It's not," he said evenly, never breaking eye contact.

Yeah, right, she thought. *What a little player.*

"Good, because in that state I'll be absolutely no fun and the sex will be awkward and icky."

"Not the way I do it."

She snorted. "If you wait until just after I stop breaking into spontaneous bouts of tears, you'll get my man-hating angry-bitch phase. Unless you like to be treated like shit—and some guys do— you'll want to avoid me entirely during that stage. Very scary."

"That has possibilities." She noticed his hand was starting to move across the table toward hers. She lifted her eyebrows and it returned to tracing the bottom of Leah's glass.

"If you're interested in normal Amanda, you'll have a long wait. This guy is likely to do a number on me and it'll take me a while to recover my normal personality."

"If you're expecting it to end badly, why bother dating the guy in the first place?"

"Never in all the history of Mr. Wrongs has there ever been one more perfectly right." And secretly she was hoping things would work out between them, even though she knew there was no way they could. Tina would find out about their relationship eventually, and nothing good would come of that. "So you're probably best off hitting on someone else."

"I can take a hint," the guy said. That made one of them. "I'm Anthony."

"You should probably take your hint elsewhere, Anthony," she said.

"Am I really that offensive?" he asked.

Amanda shook her head. "No, but there is zero chance of you taking me home tonight." She made a goose egg shape with her thumb and forefinger.

"Why don't you relax and tell me about yourself?" he asked.

She tilted her head, wishing she had someone to exchange incredulous looks with. She didn't mind Anthony's company since she'd been left sitting by herself by Leah, who was now several inches closer to Colton as they continued to sway on the dance floor. But she wasn't the kind of woman who led men on for sport, and Anthony just wasn't getting it. Leah's eyes met hers, and she apparently took Amanda's stare as a plea for help. Leah said something to Colton before surging through the crowd to their table.

"I thought you were going to save my seat," Leah said.

Anthony stood. "Sorry, I didn't realize I was intruding. It was nice to meet you, Amanda." He slipped into the crowd before Amanda could say *likewise*.

"You *did* want me to chase him off, didn't you?" Leah asked.

Amanda shrugged. "I'd already told him I wasn't interested. I'm not sure he believed me." Amanda glanced around to make sure Colton was out of hearing range. He was at the bar trying to catch the bartender's attention. "So what do you think of Colton?"

Leah flushed. "He's very . . . ." She bit her lip. ". . . *polite.*"

"Too polite?"

Leah shrugged. "I'm not sure. He doesn't act like he wants to touch me."

There could be a lot of reasons why he didn't want to touch her. It might be good manners, or it might be something deeper. He had looked a bit lonely and lost at the bar when he'd first caught Leah's eye.

The man in question set three drinks on the table. Leah might be too timid to pump the guy for information, but Amanda held no such qualms.

"So, Colton, why haven't we seen you around here before?" Amanda asked, reaching for her margarita and thinking this had to be her last one or she wouldn't be able to drive.

"It's my first time in this bar," he said. "I haven't been in Austin long."

"Where are you from?" Leah asked.

He smiled at her. "Miami."

Leah's eyebrows shot up. "Florida?"

He didn't sound like he was from Florida. He had a hint of Texas twang.

"Naw. Up in the Texas panhandle. Not far from Amarillo."

"Oh," Leah leaned in closer to him. "So what brings you to Austin?"

"There's not much of a music scene in Miami, Texas. Though I wasn't expecting Austin to be so focused on rock. Maybe I should have tried Nashville."

"So you're into country, I take it?" Amanda asked.

He nodded.

"There are plenty of country musicians in Austin, Colton," Leah said. "It just takes a while to find the right crowd."

"Are you two in with the right crowd?" He looked so hopeful that Amanda almost didn't have the heart to tell him he was singing to the wrong choir.

"Well, Amanda's dating a rock star," Leah said. "Maybe Shade can help."

"He sings in a metal band," Amanda reminded her.

"But he probably knows someone who knows someone. Or something."

Amanda shrugged. She wasn't going to volunteer Jacob to get this guy noticed. She didn't even know if Colton was any good. Heck, she didn't even know if he sang or played an instrument. He could play a washboard or a jug and sing like a strangled goose for all she knew.

"Don't put her on the spot," Colton said. "I'll get it figured out."

"So do you sing?" Leah asked.

Amanda wasn't sure if their friendship could survive them *both* dating vocalists. In her experience, front men were high maintenance.

"I do my best to sing," Colton said. "And I'm not bad on a guitar."

On second thought, Colton wasn't anything like Jacob, who had an ego that spread across the entire state of Texas and the self-confidence to back it up. Colton was self-deprecating. But perhaps with notoriety came swagger. Jacob had plenty of both.

"I'd love to hear you play," Leah said. "Do you write your own songs?"

"That I do."

They now knew what Colton was doing in Austin and maybe why he'd looked lost earlier, but that information still didn't explain why he hadn't held Leah tight on the dance floor. Her friend was definitely giving off the right signals. Perhaps the guy was blind. Or gay.

"So was your trip to Austin a recent decision or a lifelong dream?" Amanda asked.

Colton flushed and lowered his head to shield his face with the shadow of his cowboy hat. He reached for his beer and drew it toward himself before lifting it and taking a long swallow.

"Don't mind her," Leah said. "She's naturally nosy."

Nosy? Amanda preferred the term *curious*.

"It's all right," Colton said to the froth in his mug. "I was content to stay in Miami, get married, raise a family, and work for a living, but my girl . . ."

Leah and Amanda cringed at each other across the table.

". . . she broke it off with me. Said I was meant for bigger things."

Leah slumped in her chair, and Amanda couldn't blame her. It was obvious that Colton was pining for the woman who'd sent him packing.

"Why didn't she come with you?" Amanda said, her curiosity—okay, fine, her *nosiness*—getting the better of her.

"Said she wanted a settled life." Colton took another draw off his beer. "Not with me, I guess." He shrugged, his expression hidden in the shadows of his hat brim.

Leah touched his shoulder. Was she willing to be his rebound girl? Amanda had to advise her against that. Maybe Leah could mend Colton's heart—she was definitely nice enough to do it— but eventually she'd have to stop falling for these sob stories and find a man who could make her happy. Still, Amanda wasn't sure that she was the best person to offer relationship advice these days. She *was* sleeping with her sister's ex-husband, after all.

"Someday I'm sure she'll regret sending you away," Leah said.

Or maybe telling Colton he was meant for "bigger things" had been the woman's way of getting rid of his ass, Amanda thought. She'd dated too many toads to assume any man was a prince. Leah had dated her fair share of toads as well, but she always expected them to be hiding a prince beneath the slime and warts. Leah never shied away from cleaning them up and patching them back together. She actually seemed to like doing it, no matter how many times it resulted in her heart being broken.

"You're awfully sweet to me, Leah," Colton said.

"And you'd better be sweet to her, or you'll have me to deal with," Amanda said.

Leah scowled at her.

Recognizing her limit, Amanda slid her glass to the center of the table. When she started to get combative, she knew it was time to lay off the liquor.

"You two have been friends for a long time, haven't you?" Colton asked.

"Since we were toddlers," Leah said. "Our moms made us

play together even though I didn't understand English. Amanda used to take all the toys."

Colton laughed. "I can see that happening."

"What's that supposed to mean?" Amanda asked, giving him the evil eye.

"I was happy to share. Amanda always sticks up for me," Leah said. "It wasn't easy being the only Asian in our class, you know."

Leah had been targeted by bullies early. She'd always been meek, and it was easy for kids to taunt someone who'd been adopted from another country. Amanda had punched more than one boy in the nose for making Leah cry.

"Which part of Asia are you from?" Colton asked.

"China. I was one of the first girls adopted by American parents. Before that time, foreign adoptions weren't allowed. Many girls older than myself were abandoned to grow up in orphanages." She closed her eyes briefly and swallowed. "Or worse."

Amanda reached under the table and gave Leah's hand a comforting squeeze. Sometimes Leah still dwelled on what could have been. Amanda didn't even want to think about what her friend's fate might have been if the Carmichaels hadn't brought her home.

"Oh," Colton said, and then after a reflective pause, added, "I bet you were a cute kid."

"She's *still* cute," Amanda said tersely, her combative attitude showing no signs of easing.

"I'd say she's beautiful," Colton said.

Leah flushed prettily and lowered her gaze.

Well, okay then. Amanda wouldn't sock him in the nose. *This* time.

Amanda's phone dinged. She grabbed for it, expecting to see a message from Jacob but finding one from her sister.

Are you busy in the morning?

She hoped to be very busy in the morning. With Jacob. In his bed.

Probably, she texted back. *Why?*

Can you drop Julie off at her dad's house? I have an appointment on the other side of town.

I'm sure Jacob would come pick her up. Just call him and ask.

I don't even want to look at him. I sure don't want to talk to him. Will you PLEASE just take her for me?

No problem. What time?

Eight.

I'll be there.

Thanks.

Amanda placed her phone back on the table within easy reach. Colton and Leah were talking and laughing about adventures from their school days. Amanda decided to text Jacob rather than try to catch the thread of her companions' conversation.

Is your show over yet? Tina just texted me. She wants me to pick up Julie in the morning and drop her off at your house. Do you think I'll be able to crawl out of bed before eight?

She set her phone down when he didn't reply immediately. He was likely still onstage, or maybe he'd found a nice groupie to entertain him before he caught his plane home. She scowled at the thought.

"Bad news?" Leah asked.

Amanda lifted her gaze to meet her friend's. "Huh?"

"You look mad."

Amanda shook her head. "I'm just a little drunk. You know how I get when I've been drinking."

"She's a mean drunk," Leah informed Colton.

"I figured she was a li'l spitfire," Colton said.

Well, tarnation! Amanda thought, but somehow she kept the taunt locked inside.

"Tina wants me to drop Julie off at her dad's house in the morning," Amanda said.

"That's convenient," Leah said with a laugh.

"I know it's selfish, but I wish it wasn't his weekend to have her," Amanda said.

"What?" Leah lightly slapped the back of Amanda's hand. "You love Julie to pieces!"

"I do. But I'm sure it's going to make jumping her dad's bones a *bit* awkward."

Jacob's response to her text dinged on her phone.

You'd better bring a pair of crutches. I don't think you'll be able to walk unaided after I fuck you all night.

At reading his words, a distracting throb pulsed between her thighs.

Are you almost home?

Getting on the plane now. Have to shut off phone soon.

Ugh. She wasn't sure she could wait several more hours to see him.

He sent another text. *What are you doing? I'm imagining you lying in my bed touching yourself while you wait for me.*

Well, *there* was a plan she could get behind. It would sure beat sitting here at the bar with her friend and the guy she was getting to know. Amanda was glad the two had finally started talking to each other, but she felt like an unnecessary and unwanted accessory to their good time.

That's quite the imagination you've got there, she messaged Jacob. *Let's see if I can make those fantasies a reality.*

If you do, you'd better record it so I can watch later.

I'd rather you watch in person.

I'm not going to argue with that. Got to go. Plane is taking off.

See you.

Amanda sighed as she dropped her phone on the table again. "Are you ready to head for home?" she asked Leah.

"You don't have to stay," Leah said.

They had a rule about abandoning each other at bars. Especially when one of them was in the company of a man neither of them knew well. "I'm not leaving you here by yourself."

"She's not by herself," Colton said. "She's with me."

Leah smiled at this, but Amanda scowled. "You know our rule, Leah. I won't leave here without you."

Leah's shoulders sagged. "I'm not ready to go yet."

"Okay," Amanda said. "Let me know when you are." She ordered a glass of water—no more alcohol for her tonight—and munched on the now soggy nachos, waiting for Leah to get bored with Colton so she could go to Jacob's house and wait for him. It seemed she would have a long, long time to wait for Leah to be ready to leave. Especially now that Colton had found the balls to rest his hand on her lower back.

Maybe she should call Anthony back over for a chat. He wasn't very good at pretending he wasn't watching her. Or maybe he wasn't even trying. Best to ignore him, she decided. Jacob probably wouldn't appreciate her flirting with another man. Or maybe he wouldn't care. She wasn't sure where their relationship was headed. Did Jacob want more than a hot and dirty fling? And if he did, what in the hell was she going to do about it? If they became an item, Tina would gut them both and tie their entrails together.

Oddly, that gruesome thought didn't stop her from counting the minutes until she could see him again.

CHAPTER THREE

SHADE COULDN'T remember the last time he'd been this excited for two days off. Unless it was his weekend to have Julie, he usually stayed in a hotel near the next scheduled venue and partied the nights away, slept most of the day, and pretended he wasn't miserably lonely the entire time. He surrounded himself with people, but didn't feel that any of them knew the real him. Amanda was different. And this tour was different. He'd exercised his clout so that he had every other weekend free—he would not be missing any of his scheduled time with Julie if he could help it. In the past, their tour dates had centered around weekends because many concert goers preferred shows on Friday and Saturday nights. He'd given up so much time with his little angel to make the fans happy, and his ex-wife seemed to think the court's visitation order was gospel—weekend meant weekend, not a random Thursday—but he was through putting his daughter last. He could maintain a rigorous concert schedule and see Julie as much as the courts and Tina allowed. And if half of his eagerness to get away from the grueling life on the road for a weekend was due to a certain lovely lady he had no business sleeping with, so what? Amanda made him laugh, chased away the loneliness he could never seem to shake, made him feel good about himself, fucked him just right, and she wasn't bad to look at either.

Inside the small private plane, Shade reclined his seat, crossed his arms over his chest, and tried to catch a nap on the trip from New Orleans to Austin. As usual, he'd given his all to his performance that night, and he wanted to restore some energy for his night with Amanda. Plus, it was easier to ignore the band's white elephant—was it crass to think of a pregnant woman that way—when he had his eyes closed.

When he pulled into his driveway hours later, the house was dark. He supposed it was well after midnight. He smiled in relief when he noticed a familiar sedan parked on the street across from his house. Amanda had probably crawled into his bed and fallen asleep—hopefully naked with her hand between her legs. He parked in the garage, plugged the Tesla into the recharging bay, collected his overnight bag from the trunk, and let himself into the house, turning off several zones on his home security system so he could make his way through the house and to the back yard without alerting the local police. His dick was already half hard with wanting her. God, what the woman did to him. He peeked into the great room to see if she'd fallen asleep on the sofa, but there was no sign of life. The kitchen was equally empty. No dishes in the sink or snacks on the counter. He hoped she realized she should make herself at home in his house and not just in his bed. He had already formed a plan to wake her with passionate kisses when he entered his bedroom. His heart sank when he found the bed empty and meticulously made. Amanda wasn't there waiting for him. She wasn't there at all.

He had been sure it was her car parked across the street when he'd pulled up, but it was dark outside, so maybe he'd been mistaken. Was she still at that bar? Had she picked up some other guy, deciding he was more trouble than he was worth?

Not likely. She was probably out in his hot tub. Naked. Touching herself as she thought of all the things he'd do to her when he found her there wet and rosy skinned waiting for him. He opened the French doors that led from his bedroom to the pool area, but with the exception of the soothing trickle of the waterfall that fed the pool from the spa, nothing moved. The hot tub across the yard that was fenced for privacy was also empty. What was the point of having two hot tubs—one for relaxing in and the other privacy screened for discreet fucking—if Amanda wasn't in either of them?

He pulled out his phone and called her. Before the second ring, his house lit up as every light switched on and a loud siren blared from the massive structure. He raced inside and found Amanda in the foyer, poking buttons on his alarm system.

"Shit! Shit," she said as she squinted at the keypad. "Six seven two four, dammit! No, it's seven six four two. Wait."

The landline started ringing. Jacob lifted the receiver and was greeted by the security system operator. "We have evidence of an unauthorized front door entry."

"Everything is fine," Jacob said. "My girlfriend accidentally set off the alarm." And she was adorable when flustered. He was strangely glad he hadn't shut off the entire system when he'd entered through the garage. Amanda spun around and splayed her hands, shaking her head when she recognized she wasn't alone in the room.

"These things happen. We'll cancel the call to the police and reset the system on our end. What's your pass phrase?"

"One day the light will fade, the end will come, his debt repaid." It was a line from one of Sole Regret's songs—"Darker." He sang it almost every night, so it was easy to remember.

The alarm stopped blaring. Jacob's heart rate didn't slow, however. Not with Amanda in the room.

"Thank you, sir," the operator said pleasantly. "Have a good night."

"Oh, I will," Jacob said, his gaze drifting down the slender curves of Amanda's bare legs.

Jacob hung up the phone. The lights dimmed to darkness.

"Well, that's one way to announce my late arrival," Amanda said.

Jacob chuckled and approached her in the dimly lit foyer. The lights on the exterior of the house filtered in through the glass of the front doors, but otherwise it was dark.

"I had hoped to beat you here, but I'm glad I didn't set that thing off while I was by myself. You'd have had to bail me out of jail."

"I was expecting to find you naked in my bed when I arrived," he said. "I must admit I was a little disappointed."

A little? Fuck, he'd been devastated.

"I couldn't get Leah to leave the bar. She met some guy and they really hit it off."

"So why didn't you just leave her with him to get acquainted?"

"I have trust issues," she said.

He was close enough to touch her now and to feel the heat of her body through his clothes. But he kept his hands at his sides, knowing that as soon as their skin made contact, he'd be unable to control himself. Unfortunately, his condoms were all in his bedroom, so fucking her against the foyer wall was out of the question.

"You have trust issues? Since when?"

"I don't trust anyone to treat Leah the way she deserves to be treated."

Jacob smiled and forced himself not to drag her against him. He doubted he'd be able to keep his desire in check much longer. "You mean you're overprotective of your friend."

"I guess so. Especially after I've had a few drinks."

"You didn't drink and drive, did you?" He thought she had more sense than that.

"No, I stopped drinking early. Been sober for hours. Those two would not shut up."

Jacob took a step closer. Her breasts brushed against his chest, and he tilted his face toward hers, inhaling her familiar yet unsettling scent—a hint of spice, a touch of sweet, and something exotic that tugged at his balls.

"Well?" she whispered, her breath tickling his throat.

"Well what?"

"Are you going to kiss me or do I have to take the initiative here?"

"You messed up my plan," he said.

"Mmm." That little sound did things to his tenacious grip on control. "Maybe we can make an adjustment to that plan," she said.

"Or maybe you can strip off your clothes, climb into my bed, and pretend to have been waiting for me all along."

"Mmm," she murmured again. "But if I'd done that, I wouldn't have been able to think of anything but how much I wanted you to join me, how it feels to have your strong, hot body against mine, your cock filling me. You probably would have discovered me with my fingers in my pussy, imagining they were yours."

That was exactly how he'd hoped to find her.

"Amanda." He lifted his hands, holding them a hair's breadth from the skin of her arms. He fought the urge to grab her, throw her over his shoulder, and claim her as his. She shivered.

"I am a little tired," she said with a—hopefully—feigned yawn. "Maybe I should just go on to bed without you."

"Amanda." He couldn't seem to come up with anything more profound to say.

"I guess I won't need this," she said. Her shirt brushed his face as she lifted her arms and stripped it off. "Would you mind holding it for me?" She handed him her shirt, and he bunched it into a ball against his chest.

He wished there was more light so he could see her standing

there in her bra, but the limited illumination was at her back, and he could only make out her silhouette.

"Won't need these either."

She unfastened her waistband, wiggled her hips, and then bent to collect her discarded shorts. He soon had them bundled up with her shirt against his chest.

"Or this."

She released her bra and draped it over his shoulder. He should have turned on the light, he thought thickly.

"It's chilly in here," she said. "My nipples are hard." She leaned close and whispered in his ear. "Or maybe it's because I crave your mouth on them."

Her bare breast brushed his arm, and he groaned. Damn, he wanted her. And he could take her; he knew she'd let him. But he was so enjoying her tease. He could only imagine what she'd do next, and he didn't want to interrupt her little game.

"Do you think I should take my panties off as well?" she asked.

"Yes."

"Are you sure you don't want me to leave them on? Sometimes when I think of you, I slide my hand inside them and touch myself. I did it this afternoon on my back patio."

"What?" It was more an aroused sigh than a word.

"Remember when I texted you that I couldn't stop thinking about you?"

He nodded and licked his lips.

"I wasn't just making conversation, Jacob. After you signed off, I took matters into my own hand right there in my longue chair."

He sucked in an excited breath.

"I was soaking in the warm rays of the sun, thinking about how you fucked me against that window in your hotel in San Antonio. I could almost feel the cool glass against my back, and I kept thinking about that excited-nervous feeling pulsing through me as you took me. I was so worried about us being seen."

Unable to resist, he nibbled on her jaw. "But you liked it, didn't you? The thrill of wondering if you'd be caught?"

Her huffed breath brushed over his cheek. "Yes. I think that's why I slid my hand down my shorts right then and there. I don't think anyone can see me in my backyard, but I don't know that for sure. I barely had to rub my clit at all. I was already so turned on thinking about you that I came almost immediately."

"Wish I would have been there to catch you touching yourself."

"I could show you what you missed, slide my hand into my panties. I'd know what I was doing, and you could imagine what I was doing, but you wouldn't be able to see my fingertips rubbing over my clit, dipping into my slick pussy."

Dear lord, the woman was driving him insane with words. Had she really masturbated in her backyard while thinking about him? He'd always been very visual when it came to sex, so why was her dirty talk making him so fucking hard for her?

"So do you think I should leave my panties on while you watch me touch myself?" she asked in his ear. "Sometimes imagination is sexier than reality."

"Amanda."

She slipped around him and walked slowly through the foyer toward the hall that led to his bedroom. He could make out her shape, but no details of her body as he trailed after her in the darkness, a slave to her whimsy.

When they reached his bedroom, he reached for the light switch, but she covered his hand to stop him from turning it on.

"Leave it off."

"How will I see?"

She covered his lip with one finger. "I'll let you see in a little while. Right now I want you to listen."

"Amanda," he said against her fingertip.

"No bright lights, no cameras, no video monitors this time, Jacob." She kissed him briefly and stepped away. "Intimacy. That's what I want from you tonight."

Intimacy? Whenever he had sex in his bedroom, it was basically a stage performance. He couldn't imagine why she wouldn't want the whole setup. She'd enjoyed the live camera feed well enough the first time she'd experienced his routine.

"Amanda?"

"Shh, I'll do the talking. You listen. And later, I'll let you feel."

He liked the sound of that *feel* part. She took her clothes from his arms and dropped them on the floor. He didn't resist when she pulled his shirt off or when she unfastened his jeans. As she lowered them to the floor, her warm breath against his belly made his body jerk. What was she going to do while leaning over him like that? But she didn't touch him, didn't drop to her knees and suck his cock into her throat as he anticipated. Didn't lick its head or cradle his nuts in her palm. Hell, besides the teasing sensation of her breath on his skin, he couldn't feel her at all.

"It's a good thing it's dark in here," she said. "I know I wouldn't be able to keep my hands off your hard chest or my mouth off your gorgeous cock if I could see you clearly."

"Then we'd better turn on the light."

"Mmm. Maybe just a taste," she whispered before her hot mouth closed over the head of his cock.

Her lingering sucking kiss on his sensitive flesh made his belly tighten. His balls ached with heaviness. He moaned and reached for her, but she drew away.

"Sorry," she said, her voice low and throaty. "I couldn't help myself. I'll behave."

"I don't want you to behave."

Her shadowed form crossed the room—an inky black shape on a dark gray background. He trailed after her, his eager cock pointing the way.

"Stay back," she warned as she crawled up onto the bed and disappeared from sight when her figure blended into the bedding.

"How can I touch you if I stay back?"

"Tell me where your hands would be if you were touching me, Jacob."

"First, I'd want your breasts in my hands."

The mattress creaked slightly as she shifted on his bed. And why wasn't he on it with her?

"They're cool to the touch," she said. "Would you massage them to warm them up?"

"Are you touching them now?"

"Just holding them."

"Squeeze them."

"Yes."

Damn, he wished he could see that, but he could imagine what she'd look like: her golden-brown hair tousled in waves against her suntanned shoulders and the red satin pillowcase; her lids heavy, partially closed over her green-flecked hazel eyes as she gazed at him; her back arched, breasts thrust forward, soft hands cupping them, red-tipped fingers digging into the soft globes.

Wow. Apparently he was a visual lover even when he couldn't see a damned thing.

"I'd rub your nipples gently with my thumbs until they were so hard you'd beg me to suck them."

There was a slight rustle of the bedding, and she produced a sensual purr that grabbed him by the balls and demanded he take everything he wanted from her.

"I can imagine your tongue flicking over a tip," she said, "before you suck it into your hot, wet mouth."

He could imagine that too. And he was wondering why he was standing at the end of the bed with a hard-on while they discussed such delights rather than actually acting on his desires.

"I'd slide one hand down your smooth belly," he said. "Slow. Gentle. Drawing goose bumps to the surface."

"Yes," she whispered. "God, you have the sexiest voice. Do you have any idea what it does to me?"

He grinned, silently thanking the universe for the gift he'd been given. "Are you quivering, Amanda?"

"A little. I'd be quivering more if it were your hand instead of my own teasing my skin. Touching me. Stroking. Mmm. Feels good."

It occurred to him that she was testing his resolve. He wasn't sure if she wanted him to be stretched so far beyond his limit that he'd devour her, but she was quickly working him up to such a state.

"Slowly I'd move my hand closer to that sweet pussy between your thighs."

"Mmm."

"Closer."

"Yes, Jacob."

He loved when she called his name. His real name. Most of his lovers called him Shade.

"But I wouldn't touch it," he said. "Not yet."

"Please."

"I'd brush the backs of my fingers against the curve of your hip. Light touches. Slow and easy to make you squirm. Then I'd jerk your thighs apart and—"

He heard a sound much too wet to be her stroking her hip. He smirked at her apparent haste. "Amanda, are you cheating?"

"Why don't you turn on the light and find out?"

He almost tripped over the jeans circling his ankles in his haste to find the light switch. He kicked them aside impatiently and turned on the light. When his eyes adjusted to the glare, he found her in a position that far surpassed what he'd been imagining.

She had one breast gripped in her hand, her painted fingertips twisting desperately at her pebbled nipple. Her other hand was between her splayed legs. Her panties had vanished, so no imagination was required on his part. He could see exactly what she was doing to herself. Her ring finger and middle finger worked her slick pussy, delving deep and stretching herself in wide arcs. Her little finger popped in and out of her ass. Her thumb massaged her clit in desperate, rapid strokes. She rocked her hips into her hand and lifted her head from the bed as her body shuddered with pleasure.

Jacob stood at the end of the bed—mouth dry, balls tight, feet rooted to the floor—and watched her stunning performance.

"This is what I wanted to record for you while I waited in your bed," she said, gasping as her pinkie finger slid deeper. "I was going to send you a dirty video on your phone to keep you company on your plane ride."

He didn't look at her face, couldn't draw his gaze from the sight of her manicured fingers disappearing and reappearing as she plunged them in and out of her pussy. What was it that was so sexy about a woman's fingers pleasing a pussy? Her own or another woman's, he was absolutely riveted by the sight.

"I prefer live performances," he mumbled, surprised he could form a coherent sentence.

Amanda's thighs began to shake. Was she going to come? He glanced up to her face for cues and found her staring at him.

"How long do I have to keep this up before you take over?" she asked.

He grinned. "You seem to be doing fine on your own."

"I think you can do better."

He glanced down between her thighs again and found that she'd moved her hand. Her fingers were no longer buried inside her, they were spreading her lips, holding them open so he could see the emptiness at their center. Her gorgeous pussy begged to be filled with him. He crawled up the bed slowly, forcing his gaze to lock with hers rather than fixating on the parts of her that demanded his attention. He moved over her until he was suspended above her body on hands and knees, then he lowered his hips and brushed the head of his cock against her mound. She squirmed and when he didn't move—merely stared down into her eyes—she took his cock in her hand and rubbed its sensitive head against her. Pleasure teased his nerve endings as she used his tip to stimulate her clit.

"Do you have a condom?" she asked breathlessly.

He wished he didn't have to deal with them, but he hurriedly applied one for her. Now he was in command of her pleasure. Free to take her. Or not.

He stared into her eyes as he rubbed her clit with two fingers, working the hardened nub until her mouth dropped open, her eyes rolled back, and she shuddered with orgasm. He shifted his hips and slowly slid inside her, his breath catching with the pleasure her clenching pussy provided his entire length. He rubbed her clit faster and faster, making her sputter and quake as he filled her with slow deep thrusts.

Jacob's arm began to shake with fatigue. It was holding his full weight so he could free a hand to work her clit, but at this rate he'd have to give up his plan to stimulate her clit while he fucked her. Hell, if he'd had another free hand he could have used it to finger her ass at the same time. He could probably manage what he envisioned if he fucked her on her knees, but then he wouldn't be able to stare into her eyes. He wondered how she'd feel about using his sex swing tonight. She'd said she didn't want the theatrics, that she'd wanted intimacy, but he wanted to please her without doing permanent damage to his body.

"I know you said you wanted intimacy tonight," he said, totally lost in her eyes.

She reached up and stroked his face. "This is perfect," she said, a gaspy moan escaping her as his touch on her clit slowed and he rubbed in deep circles. "Exactly what I want."

"Is the sex swing intimate?" he asked, hoping she'd see that it was. Or maybe she needed another demonstration. He could show her how intimate weightlessness could be.

Amanda's eyes popped open wide and her breath caught. "How could I have forgotten about the sex swing? Yes, please. Let's use that."

He chuckled at her unexpected enthusiasm. The woman was amazing.

Jacob lowered the device from its hidden panel in the ceiling. Amanda shivered as the padded harness descended toward her.

He took his time with her, getting to know her body as he slipped a black strap beneath her back and eased each of her limbs through loops. He trailed kisses between her breasts as he adjusted the length of each strap so that when he tightened the tension, she'd rise from the bed in the exact position he had in mind.

He wasn't sure how intimate trussing her up in a sex swing could be, but he was doing his best to give her the experience she wanted. He knew if he pleased her, he'd receive more than his share of pleasure in return. He remembered a time when he'd thought that taking what he wanted from a woman was the best way to get his rocks off, but he'd come to realize that the more pleasure he gave, the more he received. Funny how that worked. So while his body demanded he get to fucking, his head reminded him to take it slow, put her needs first, make her want him with the same desperation that he wanted her.

He tugged a strap that popped the overhead tension rod into place, and Amanda was lifted from the bed. She gasped in surprise at the sudden change in position but smiled at him with trust in her amazing hazel eyes as she swayed gently in the swing. She was basically sitting in midair, her legs held wide open by the contraption's straps. He hoisted her body another foot higher and then knelt between her legs, leaning forward to thrust into her pussy with his eager-to-please tongue.

While teasing her clit with rapids licks, he explored her body with both hands. The swing allowed him to simultaneously massage her breast and grab her ass. When her sighs of pleasure intensified to moans begging for release, Jacob yanked a strap that tilted her into a more upright position and then grabbed her hips to pull her down onto his lap. He sank into her molten pussy, his biceps straining as he stretched the spring suspension at the ceiling to its maximum tension. He shifted his hips forward, finding the perfect tilt to increase the depth of his penetration. God, she felt good.

"Jacob," she groaned as he ground into her, pushing deeper still.

"I want to be so deep inside you that you forget how to breathe."

Her eyelids fluttered as she forced them open to look at him.

"You're there."

He loosened his hold and the swing recoiled, yanking her body away from his until only his tip remained inside of her.

"Oh!" she cried out and looked down between her thighs as if unable to comprehend what had happened.

He used his arms to pull her toward him again, burying himself deeper, deeper, and when her bottom rested firmly against his balls, he released the swing again. This time when she shot away from him, his cock fell free of her body, so he shifted forward on his knees slightly and adjusted the swing, lowering it an inch.

"What are up to?" she asked, a crooked grin on her face.

"Do you like how quick withdraw feels?"

She nodded eagerly.

"Then give me a second to get our positions exactly right so I don't break my dick."

She chuckled. "I definitely wouldn't want that to happen."

He did another trial run—pulling her down onto him, claiming her so deeply that her breath caught in her throat, and then releasing the tension in the swing to pull out quickly. Tightening his arms, he stopped her recoil a scant inch before his cock fell free of her body.

"You sure you can handle this?" he asked with a teasing grin.

Her soft laugh made his heart thud. "Do your worst, Silverton."

"My best," he corrected.

He could fuck a woman fast or he could fuck her deep, but with the swing he could do both simultaneously. He claimed her with a perfect cadence of pull and thrust, release and withdrawal. As he perfected the motion, he increased his tempo. Her breasts bounced with each hard, deep, fast penetration. His mouth watered—he wanted those rosy tips between his lips, against his tongue. But if he shifted to suck her hardened nipples, he'd lose their momentum.

Amanda's moans had become frantic cries. Her back arched, forcing him to compensate for her shift in position. He squeezed his eyes shut, fighting his sudden need to come.

Oh God, her pussy was clenching over him so hard, adding a squeezing sensation to the already blissful hot, rapid strokes. If he didn't pull out soon he was going to lose control, but he didn't want to deny her the orgasm that was ripping through her body with the force of a hurricane.

"Jacob, Jacob!" she screamed.

Her cum dripped off his balls as her entire body went rigid. He wanted to follow her over the edge, but he wanted more than guaranteed bliss; he wanted their time together to last. He pulled out with a groan of torment and shifted to sit on his heels. He grabbed the harness at her back and pulled her pussy to his mouth. He drew in a deep breath and rammed his tongue inside her as far as he could before tightening the suction around her still-clenching hole and sucking her slick flesh.

Slick, hell. She was fucking gushing.

Amanda cried out, her body shuddering violently at the change in sensation.

Jacob's balls tightened, and he fought to keep his load from spurting, but he couldn't stop the pleasure from pulsing through his length. He grabbed his cock, pressing his fingers hard against the thickened ridge along its underside, holding his cum back, refusing to let this be over.

Suddenly unable to find enough air, Jacob released Amanda's pussy and rested his forehead against her mound, his breath coming in rapid, jagged gasps.

"Oh my God, Jacob," Amanda said, her body falling limp in the swing. "I've never come like that before."

He grinned, his breathing still harsh and irregular, the cock in his hand still as hard as granite and soon to be ready for round two.

"Was it as intimate as you'd hoped?" he asked.

"Intimate? I came so hard I think I blacked out."

He kissed the softness between her thighs before lifting his head and looking up into her eyes. "I'll do better next time."

"Next time?" She released a weary chuckle. "If you came even half as hard as I did, you won't be able to get it up for a week."

"I didn't come at all."

She lifted her head to stare at him incredulously. "You didn't?"

He shook his head.

"Mmm."

His cock twitched. What was it about that throaty sound that always drew a response from his nether regions?

"Stand up and turn me around," she said.

"How?"

"I want to suck your cock."

He didn't mind taking orders when they benefited him. He stood on the bed and rotated her so that her head was toward him. Her long hair trailed down behind her and brushed his legs as she swayed gently on her back within the swing. Smiling at him, she stripped the condom from his length and tossed it aside. At first, her touches, kisses, and delicate licks were reserved, but apparently something about his soft groans of encouragement made her bolder. He gasped when she drew him into her mouth and took as much of his length as she could into her throat. Her throat constricted as she sucked at him, her glorious hair tickling his thighs rhythmically as she used the sway of the swing to pull him in and out of her mouth. He stroked her breasts and plucked at her nipples as she sucked. The feel of her mouth tugging at his bare skin soon had him again teetering on the edge of release.

She must have tasted his impending orgasm because she suddenly pulled away. "Don't come yet," she said. "I want to try something."

The green flecks in her hazel eyes caught the light. He couldn't resist leaning forward to kiss her in her upside-down position.

"What did you have in mind?" he asked.

"Can I use the swing in reverse cowgirl?"

"You can use it any way you want."

He soon found out how imaginative his new lover could be. Smart girls rocked his world. And this one in particular had stolen his heart.

CHAPTER FOUR

…plastic, it's fantastic!

AMANDA CAUGHT the tail end of that very specific ringtone when she was woken by her blaring cellphone. She accidentally smacked herself in the face when she tried to open her eyes. Her lids refused to budge. Why the hell was Tina calling at this ungodly hour? And why did it feel like a log was resting on her belly?

The log shifted and slid up her torso to grasp her breast. She smiled when she realized the log belonged to Jacob. Her phone stopped ringing, and she relaxed back into her pillow. She had no desire to speak to her sister this morning. Not when she had a hot and hunky man at her disposal. Amanda rolled onto her side and trailed a hand over Jacob's hard-muscled back. He buried his face in her neck and inhaled. Amanda shivered and dragged her fingertips along his hip, the curve of his ass.

Aqua's "Barbie Girl" blared from her phone again.

Amanda groaned. Ugh! Too early for that annoying, perky shit.

"Are you going to ignore that?" Jacob said, his warm breath teasing the skin along her throat.

"That was my plan," she said.

Jacob tugged her closer, seeming to agree that ignoring Tina was a great idea. "What time is it?"

"I dunno," Amanda said, caught by an unexpected yawn. "Five a.m.? Six?"

Jacob lifted his head to peer at the clock next to his bed and stiffened. "It's almost nine."

"Nine? Nine! Oh shit, I was supposed to pick up Julie at eight!"

Amanda scrambled from the bed and reached for her phone. It fell silent in her hand. "Tina's going to be so pissed."

"We can pick up Julie together," Jacob said.

Amanda slowly turned in his direction, her eyes burning from being stretched wide. "Are you fucking insane?"

"Why? It's my weekend to have her. Tina can't keep her from me."

"If Tina sees us together, she'll flip. Have you ever seen her lose her shit? Scary. Very scary."

Jacob shook his head. Of course he'd seen Tina lose her shit. He'd been married to her once. "You can tell her you picked me up on the way to get Julie."

"Then she'll know we talk to each other."

Jacob grinned crookedly. "We do a lot more than talk to each other."

"Jacob, Tina cannot find out about us."

Jacob's jaw hardened. Avoiding her gaze, he rolled out of bed and reached for the switch that raised the swing into the hidden panel above the bed. God, she loved that swing.

"After last night, I thought maybe you were willing to declare me as yours."

"I wish I could," she said. "You know she'll use our involvement against you. You know she will."

"Well, maybe I'm sick of letting her dictate my life. We aren't married anymore. She has no claim over me."

"She has a claim over your daughter. Do you want to risk losing visitation rights?"

"The courts can't take Julie away from me just because I'm in love with someone my ex-wife wouldn't approve of."

Amanda's phone rang in her hand, and she dropped it. Jacob didn't mean he was in love with her. He'd just been stating a broad example, hadn't he?

Oh God, hadn't he?

Amanda scooped her phone off the floor and answered it, because dealing with her sister was far easier than dealing with the idea that Jacob Silverton had done the stupidest thing imaginable and fallen in love with her. Shit!

"Hello?" Amanda said, hoping her voice sounded normal.

"Where are you? I thought you were going to pick up Julie and take her to Jacob's for me."

The sound quality was grainy, and Amanda could hear Julie singing "Itsy Bitsy Spider" in the background. Tina must be calling from her vehicle.

"Sorry," Amanda said. "I was out late with Leah last night and I overslept. I'll get dressed and be right over."

"Don't bother. I'm already on my way to her dad's. If I miss my spa appointment because of this—"

"You're on your way?" Amanda blurted, searching wildly for her discarded clothes.

"I probably should have called Jacob to let him know, but I'd love to catch him with some bimbo in his bed, and then Julie will see what kind of asshole she has for a father."

Well, the poor child must definitely see what kind of bitch she had for a mother. Amanda couldn't believe Tina would say something like that within hearing range of her four-year-old daughter. On second thought, Tina making such an inappropriate statement didn't surprise Amanda in the least.

"You can't do that kind of stuff to her, Tina. She's just a little girl."

"I'm a big girl, Aunt Mander!" Julie called, presumably from the back seat of the car.

"Yes you are, sweetheart," Amanda said, crushing the phone between her ear and shoulder as she hopped into her panties. "Are you going to see your daddy today?"

"Yes! And we're going to the zoo. I want to see a lephalant."

Amanda grinned at how adorable her niece was. "You mean an elephant?"

"That's what I said—a lephalant. He has ears as tall as me."

Amanda found her shorts and wriggled into them. "Wow, those are big ears! He must be able to hear really well."

"I will sing a song for him with my daddy."

Amanda grinned and glanced at Jacob, who'd already found all of his clothes and was watching her with a scowl on his handsome face. "They're on their way," Amanda mouthed to him. "Where's my bra?"

While Julie told Amanda everything she knew about lephalants, Jacob retrieved her remaining clothes and shoved them at her chest. He left the room without saying a word.

What the hell was his problem?

"I hope you have fun at the zoo," Amanda said. "I'm going to let you go now."

"Bye, Aunt Mander!"

"Have a nice day at the spa, Tina." She hung up before her sister could get in the dig she knew was coming.

Finally dressed, Amanda headed for the front door. She

hesitated with her hand on the door handle when she remembered her alarm-greeted welcome from the night before. "Jacob," she called. "Can you let me out? I don't want to set off the alarm again."

After what seemed like an eon, Jacob came out of the kitchen and disarmed the alarm system. When he started to walk away without so much as glancing at her, she grabbed his arm.

"What's wrong?" she asked.

"I say I love you and you don't even acknowledge it?"

So that hadn't been a slip, he'd actually meant it? Shit!

"I haven't even had time to process it yet, Jacob. I'm sort of in a hurry to get out of here before Tina catches us together."

"Whatever. Just go," he said, turning his back to her and raising a hand in farewell.

"I'll be back in less than an hour." She needed to grab a quick shower and fresh clothes. "Or have you changed your mind about wanting me to come with you and Julie to the zoo?"

"See you in an hour," he said before disappearing into the kitchen.

She would have stood there for a while and tried to puzzle him out, but she knew Tina would arrive any minute and she had to leave immediately.

As Amanda sat at a stop sign waiting for traffic to clear so she could turn onto a cross street, she glanced in her rearview mirror and sighted Tina's enormous cream-colored SUV turning onto Jacob's road behind her. Amanda scrunched down in her seat automatically, even though if Tina was paying attention, she would recognize Amanda's car. She drove a common beige Toyota Camry, not a rare, attention-grabbing vehicle, but she didn't want to get caught. Panicked, Amanda jetted into the flow of traffic, surely cutting off some unsuspecting driver and prayed that Tina hadn't noticed her.

CHAPTER FIVE

HE COULDN'T believe Amanda had walked out on him. Well, that wasn't exactly what she'd done, but it sure felt like it.

Jacob was jolted from his turbulent thoughts by the ring of his doorbell. Thinking about seeing Julie brought a smile to his face. His sweet angel was probably the only thing on the planet that could have dredged up any feeling of joy in him.

What the hell was Amanda's problem? He knew he shouldn't have blurted his feelings to her so soon into their relationship, but how could she blow him off so easily? He thought they had something special and had a difficult time believing she didn't at least like him enough to explain her own feelings. Maybe it was because she'd been too busy getting dressed and fleeing the house to talk to him about it. Frankly, he didn't give a shit if Tina knew all about his affair with her sister. He almost wanted to rub it into her conniving face. But the one who'd be most hurt by such actions would be Julie, and his protective instincts kicked into high gear where his little girl was concerned. So he'd try to keep Amanda a secret for Julie's sake, but not for Tina's and not even for his own.

He opened the door to Tina's scowl. At times he wondered how he'd ever thought she was beautiful. Of course, when they'd been in love, she hadn't perpetually shot eye daggers at him.

"Took you long enough," Tina grumbled. "I'm in a rush here. Didn't you hear me honking in the driveway?"

"No."

"Probably going deaf from all that loud music," she said as she shoved an overnight bag into his chest.

"Daddy!" Julie called as she squeezed between her mother's leg and the doorframe to peer into the house.

Jacob's mood instantly brightened. He dropped her bag with a disconcerting crunch and bent to scoop her into his arms. She was light as a feather, but he pretended she weighed a ton and that he couldn't lift her from the floor. "You've been growing again," he accused, grunting with exertion. "Didn't I tell you to stop doing that?"

"I eat all my vegetables. Did they make me too fat?" Julie rubbed her hands over her belly and scowled down at her petite figure.

Why would a four-year-old even think to ask such a thing? Jacob turned an accusing glare on her mother. Tina avoided his gaze. "Give me a hug, Jules," she said. "I'm already late for my appointment."

Julie hugged and kissed her mom. "Love you!"

"Love you too, baby. I'll see you on Sunday."

"Okay, Mommy. Have a nice time at the sprawl."

Jacob pursed his lips to stifle a grin as he imagined his ex-wife sprawled on the ground. Good place for her as far as he was concerned. He knew it was wrong of him to think of her in duress and enjoy it, but he couldn't help being amused at her expense.

"I'm sure I will." Tina stood and met Jacob's eyes for the first time since she'd arrived on his doorstep. His heart produced an uneasy thud as she held his gaze. "Take good care of her," Tina said.

"Of course."

She leaned a bit closer, her lips pursed as if she was considering kissing him goodbye, and he took an automatic step backward.

"Uh, Tina?" Surely he was mistaken about her intentions.

She blinked up at him and covered her lower lip with two fingertips, her bright eyes beguiling in her beautiful face. He remembered when that look used to bring him to his knees. Now it produced a knot of displeasure in his gut. Tina backed away and turned, rushing toward the huge SUV idling in the driveway. She honked and waved goodbye to Julie, who waved back enthusiastically. When the vehicle turned out of the driveway, Jacob crouched down to four-year-old level.

"What do you want to do first?"

"Eat. I'm practly starved to death over here."

He grinned at the morose expression on Julie's face and reached out to tickle her ribs. She giggled, twisting away from his digging fingertips.

"Pancakes?"

"Do you know how to fix anything else?"

"Eggs."

Julie crinkled up her nose. "I don't like eggs."

"I think I have some fruit." He hoped Tammy had remembered to restock his kitchen. He and Amanda had cleared out his fruit supply almost a week before.

"Nanas and pancakes."

They might have to go to the store to get bananas, but Jacob didn't mind. As long as his little princess had what she wanted.

Jacob picked up her overnight bag and followed her into the house, smiling at her attempts to skip and sing "Old McDonald" at the same time. Perhaps he was a tad partial, but the kid had inherited a talented set of pipes. She came to an abrupt halt in the doorway of the kitchen and held out both hands to encourage him to stop.

"Wait! I almost forgot. I brought you something," she said.

"A present?"

"Well . . ." She cocked her head at him, a tiny fist on each hip. Sometimes she did remind ~~her~~ him of her mother. "You can just borrow it. Okay?"

She dashed to his side and pulled open the zipper of her overnight bag and yanked out two pairs of sparkly fairy wings made of some gauzy material. They had elastic loops where child-sized arms could go through. He knew she would talk him into wearing them before she'd even slipped the pair of pink ones onto her narrow back.

"I brung you the blue ones 'cause you're a boy."

He chuckled. "Are you sure these are for boys?"

Wide-eyed and irresistibly adorable, she nodded up at him. "I'm sure, 'cause they're blue. And I'm the fairy princess, so you must be the fairy king. Little girls are princesses and their daddies are kings."

"Do fairies have kings?" he asked, slipping one arm through the elastic band and stretching it to its limit over his man-sized shoulder.

"Yes. I saw it on the TV."

"It must be true then," he said, struggling to get his arm through the second loop. "I don't think these will fit me, sweetheart."

"Come down here. I'll help you."

He squatted, deciding kids were hard on the knees, and Julie pulled and wrestled with the wings until she finally managed to get them onto his back.

"Well?" he asked, glancing over his shoulder at the lopsided and crumpled set of glitter-covered wings between his shoulder blades. He wondered what his bandmates and the fans would think if they could see him like this. Not that he cared, because Julie broke into a fit of giggles. She had the cutest laugh. He couldn't help but smile at her.

"You look silly, Daddy!"

"Are you sure?" He wiggled his shoulders to try to make the wings move. He only managed to set them further askew.

She nodded and covered her mouth with one tiny hand. "I don't think you can fly with those puny things."

"I can if I'm magic."

Her blue eyes widened with wonder. "Are you magic, Daddy?"

He chuckled and tapped her nose with a fingertip. "I just like to pretend. Maybe I should take them off so I can cook your breakfast." He'd probably need to cut the strings or dislocate his shoulders to remove them.

"No! You're the fairy king. Fairy kings cook the best breakfast in the land." She spread her arms wide.

Well, Jacob was sure he looked like a fairy. Wasn't so sure about the king part.

"You just need to get some big wings for growed-up people," she said as she assessed his attire with her head cocked to one side.

"I'll keep that in mind the next time I go shopping at the growed-up fairy store."

Her belly growled loudly, and she covered it with both hands. "Excuse me."

"I think we'd better get you fed first."

In the kitchen, she sat on a stool at the breakfast bar and ate bites of bananas he'd cut into circles for her while he prepared pancakes. He attempted to delight her by making her pancakes shaped like butterflies, but getting them to look like anything but blobs was a losing battle.

"It's supposed to be a butterfly," he told her as he set a plate of his best attempt in front of her. The first few were even less impressive than this one.

"Cool, Daddy! She needs eyes." She used a few of her

remaining banana slices to make eyes for the hopeless creature and drew a smiling mouth with the syrup. "Now she's perfect."

Jacob was glad his child had a vivid imagination and a kind heart.

"Are we going to the zoo after we eat?" she asked.

"We have to wait for your surprise to get here first," he said. Assuming Amanda wasn't hiding from him after what he'd said earlier. She'd sure been in a hurry to leave.

"Ooh, what is it?"

Jacob used a butter knife to cut his butterfly masterpiece into bite-sized pieces for her.

"I'm not telling. If I did, it wouldn't be a surprise. Eat your pancake."

"I think my surprise is a lephalant," Julie said and then stuffed a bite into her mouth. "Yummy!"

Jacob touched her hair and smiled, his heart light. There was only one other person on the planet who gave him a similar feeling of joy and she'd soon be there to share the day with them. He couldn't remember the last time he'd felt so damned happy.

CHAPTER SIX

IT DIDN'T take Amanda long to reach her house. The small bungalow was only a couple of miles from Jacob's place, in an older subdivision populated by working stiffs like herself.

After her shower, she stared into her small closet wondering what to wear. She wanted to look sexy for Jacob—because, holy shit, the guy actually had feelings for her that she still wasn't ready to face—but not too sexy since young and impressionable Julie would be with them all weekend. She decided on a pair of black shorts that accentuated her long legs while still managing to cover her ass, and a cute white top made of eyelet material with cup sleeves and tiny buttons down the front. The shirt hugged her figure and gave a hint of cleavage, but didn't make her look like she was trying too hard. She hoped.

Amanda examined herself in the mirror while she blow-dried her hair and simultaneously swished mouthwash through her teeth. Was she pretty enough to have someone like Jacob "Shade" Silverton fall in love with her? She'd probably rank herself above average in looks, but she wasn't a stunner like Tina. Amanda shrugged at herself before spitting into the sink. Whatever. She was comfortable in her skin, and she wouldn't be changing how she looked to appease a man. Not even Jacob. After applying mascara and lip gloss—the only makeup she ever wore—she found a comfortable pair of canvas shoes suitable for walking around the zoo. She was heading out of her bedroom when her gym bag caught her attention.

Was she brazen enough to pack an overnight bag? It probably was a bad idea for her to spend the night with Jacob when Julie was there, but she wanted to stay with him. They didn't even have to have wild and crazy sex all night long. Just knowing he was within reach was enough. At least for a couple of nights. Truth be told, she wouldn't mind staying with Jacob whenever he was home from Sole Regret's tour, but she still wasn't ready to flaunt their relationship. Just thinking about Tina's response and all the horrid things she could do to make Jacob's life miserable made Amanda queasy.

She decided to pack her bag but leave it in the trunk unless she needed it. On her way out, she gave Tinkerbell a scratch behind the ears while the cat devoured a bowl of her favorite tuna dinner.

Scrunching low in the driver seat of her car, she approached Jacob's drive cautiously, just in case Tina was still there. Amanda was fully prepared to speed on by without stopping, even though it was unlikely that Tina had hung around for any length of time. Amanda wouldn't have been surprised if Tina had deposited Julie in the driveway and tossed her bag at her feet before speeding off to her spa appointment.

Finding Jacob's drive empty of gigantic German-engineered SUVs, Amanda pulled in and parked under a shade tree. What excuse would she use if Tina just happened to drive by and saw her car parked in Jacob's driveway? She supposed she could claim that Jacob needed help caring for Julie, but that was a lie and Tina would use such a claim as ammunition against him.

Leaving her presumptuous overnight bag in the trunk, Amanda scurried toward the front door and rang the doorbell.

"Is that my surprise?" she heard Julie squeal inside the house.

"It's not a great surprise," Jacob said on the opposite side of the closed door.

Gee, thanks, Jacob. Amanda chuckled to herself.

"What is it?" Julie asked.

"It's not a what, it's a who." Jacob opened the door, and Amanda didn't know which of the pair made her heart swell with more emotion: the gorgeous dark-haired, blue-eyed, muscled hunk who was currently wearing sparkly blue fairy wings on his back or the adorable blond four-year-old who had no doubt convinced him to wear them.

"Aunt Mander!"

"Surprise!" Amanda said. She held out her arms for an exuberant hug, lifting Julie off the ground and into her arms, getting several kisses on the cheek for her effort.

"This *is* a great surprise, Daddy," Julie said. "I love my Aunt Mander." She bestowed more kisses on Amanda.

"And I love my Julie Bean," Amanda said, giving her a squeeze. "Can I come to the zoo with you and your daddy today?"

"Yes! I was waiting so long for my surprise so we can leave."

Amanda supposed an hour felt like an eternity to a young child.

"Did you have breakfast?" Jacob asked Amanda.

"Daddy made me pancakes and they look like butterflies."

Amanda grinned at Jacob, who appeared rather flushed. "He did?" When Julie nodded, Amanda asked, "Did they *taste* like butterflies?"

Julie crinkled up her nose. "No, silly. They taste like pancakes. You can have some. He cooked about a hundred of them."

"You said you were hungry," Jacob said.

Amanda set Julie on her feet, and the girl skipped into the house toward the kitchen.

Jacob leaned close and whispered in her ear, "You look beautiful."

She turned her head to offer her thanks and found their lips a hair's breadth apart. She leaned into him, her hand on his waist, wishing his T-shirt would disappear so she could touch his bare skin. A deep longing curled in her belly.

"Daddy! Where's the butter?"

Jacob jerked away and spun on his heel. "Don't go near the stove," he warned as he hurried toward the kitchen, his bouncing fairy wings slightly askew.

Grinning to herself, Amanda trailed after him, feeling lewd for admiring a fairy's ass. But who could blame her? She found the pair in the kitchen. Julie was kneeling on a stool at the breakfast bar and arranging butterfly-shaped pancakes—well, they were pretty much blob-shaped, but she was certain Julie was too sweet to criticize her father's creations—on a plate. Jacob stood beside her, a steadying hand at her back.

"How many do you want?" Julie asked.

"Just two," Amanda said. These two specifically, even though she knew she could never have the Silverton pair to herself. Even if a relationship worked out with Jacob, Julie was Tina's daughter and she always would be, no matter how much Amanda adored her.

"Could you keep an eye on her for a bit?" Jacob asked. "I want to grab a quick shower."

"No problem."

When Amanda scooted onto the stool next to Julie's, Jacob leaned in with puckered lips to kiss Amanda's temple. Wide-eyed, she jerked away. What was he thinking? Julie was drizzling syrup all over Amanda's pancakes and not paying much attention, but she'd have heard the sound and probably wondered why her father was kissing her aunt.

Jacob's jaw hardened as he glared at her. "Seriously?"

Amanda shook her head at him. What did he expect her to do? Shove her tongue down his throat and her hand down his pants?

"Aunt Mander, I made you a smiley face on your butterfly!" Julie said.

"Looks delicious," Amanda said. "That's enough syrup for me." Her pancakes were liable to float away on the lake of liquid sugar flooding her plate.

"We need to talk," Jacob grumbled into her ear before stroking Julie's soft blond curls with one hand and then turning to leave them alone in the kitchen.

Apparently so. She'd thought they were in agreement about keeping this fling of theirs a secret, but he didn't seem to think secrecy was important. Surely he couldn't want Julie to know they were involved. Julie liked to talk about everything she witnessed. *Every*thing. If she caught her father and her aunt being overly affectionate, Tina wouldn't be the only person to hear the tale.

"Mommy is mad at you, Aunt Mander," Julie said as she watched Amanda dig into her pancakes.

"I know. I'm sorry I didn't come get you this morning. I stayed up past my bedtime and didn't wake up early enough."

"What's a sprawl anyway?" Julie asked.

"Huh?" Amanda lifted an eyebrow at her niece.

"Mommy said she was late for her sprawl appointment."

"Spa."

"Spraw," Julie mimicked, her dainty face screwed up with concentration.

"Spa."

"That's what I said."

"A spa is a place grownups go to get pampered."

Julie's eyes widened and she gasped. "Mommy wears a diaper there?"

Amanda didn't follow her train of thought. "A diaper?"

"My friend Rachel's baby sister wears Pampers all the time. She's not a big girl like me and Rachel yet. She still poops in her pants." Julie whispered the last part as if it were an embarrassing secret.

Amanda chuckled at the thought of Tina getting Pampered at her sprawl appointment. "No, sweetie. Mommy goes to the spa to get a massage and a mud bath and, well, I don't know what all goes on there. I've never been to one." Her sister regularly went to the spa with her friends and left Amanda with babysitting duty. Not that she minded. She'd rather spend time having tea parties with stuffed bears than sit in a tub of mud and gossip about other women.

"Sounds like a silly place. I'd rather go to the zoo."

"Me too. Are we going to the big zoo in San Antonio or the little one in Austin? Did your dad tell you which one?"

"The one that has lephalants."

"It's a long drive to the zoo that has elephants."

"That's okay," she said. "Daddy's car goes really fast. We'll get there in no time."

His two-seater Tesla was known for its quiet speed, but it didn't have room for three people.

"We'll have to take my car," Amanda said. She already had a booster seat in the back since she often had Julie in tow, especially in the summer when she had so much time off.

"Is it time to leave now?" Julie asked, drawing Amanda's attention to the gorgeous hunk of a man who'd entered the room while Amanda had been stuffing her face with pancakes.

"Is everyone done eating?" Jacob asked.

As soon as she'd noticed him, Amanda had paused with her fork halfway to her mouth as she ogled the man. He'd removed his fairy wings in favor of a black tank and black-and-white-plaid board shorts. She could see the hint of the lion tattoo on his chest above the low neckline of his shirt, and the gold cross necklace he always wore swayed slightly with his motion as he approached the breakfast bar. Wide shoulders, firm chest, ripped arms, narrow hips, and long legs—from his damp black hair to his tan, sandaled feet, the man was gorgeous.

Julie poked Amanda to gain her attention and stared at her hopefully. Amanda stuffed a final bite into her mouth and shoved her plate away. "I'm about to bust!"

"We'll clean up later," Jacob said as he tossed plates into the sink. "We're off to a late start."

"We could just go to the Austin Zoo," Amanda suggested. "It's much closer."

"Is that the one with the lephalants?" Julie asked. The child was completely fixated on the creatures.

"No elephants. There are some bear cubs. And a bunch of monkeys. And a train ride." Amanda often volunteered at the little rescue zoo, so she was a tad partial. It wasn't the biggest zoo and the exhibits were small, but she was proud of the fact that they took in animals other zoos didn't want.

Julie studied Amanda for a moment. It was obvious that she wanted to please her aunt, but she also wanted to see her favorite animal. She turned to Jacob and leveled him with her most adorable pleading expression. "Can we go to two zoos today, Daddy?"

"I don't know if we'll have time, princess."

"Please!" She knotted her hands together and gave him the puppy dog eyes.

The poor man didn't stand a chance.

"Um . . ." He turned to Amanda for assistance.

"How about we go to the Austin Zoo first, since it's really close, and if you still want to go to San Antonio afterwards to see the elephants, we'll go there second?" Amanda hoped Julie would be too tuckered out to want to go on two zoo adventures in a single day.

"Okay! I will get to see *all* the animals today. Catch me, Daddy!" she said, spreading her arms and taking a leap from the bar stool. Amanda's heart skipped a beat, but Jacob caught her and cradled her against his chest as they made their way outside.

Amanda started her car and cranked up the AC while Jacob helped Julie out of her fairy wings and then fastened her into the back seat.

"Can you give me a hand packing up the trunk?" he asked Amanda. "I'm not sure if I've remembered everything."

"Sure." She slid from the driver's seat and shut the door before circling to the back of the car. She gasped in surprise when he pulled her up against him, both hands on her ass. He tilted his head to whisper in her ear.

"I'm assuming you're keeping your distance because you don't want Julie to see us together."

"Yeah," she said.

"So since she can't see us now, you won't brush me off when I do this."

Amanda shivered in delight as he sucked thought-shattering kisses along her neck. Goose bumps rose to the surface of her skin, and she tilted her head to give him access to her tingling flesh. His hand slid up her hip and waist, his knuckles skimmed the side of her breast, and then his hand pressed into her back to draw her closer.

His lips traced a gentle trail along her jaw before capturing her mouth in a deep kiss. She moaned into his mouth and, unable to keep her hands to herself any longer, she grabbed his ass in both hands.

He drew away slightly, and her eyelids fluttered open.

"So you do still want me," he said in that low, smooth voice of his. Parts of her craving his mouth on them began to throb distractingly.

"Of course I still want you." She breathed in his clean scent, marveling at how it made her heart race and her belly clench.

"Daddy, are we going now?" Julie's muffled voice drifted out from inside the car.

"Be patient, princess," he called to her before lowering his head and capturing Amanda's tender lips in another kiss.

By the time they finished packing the trunk, Jacob had somehow managed to ignite every inch of Amanda's skin with little touches and stolen kisses. She was on fire—burning for him—and that inferno had absolutely nothing to do with the sizzling Texas heat.

"What taked you so long?" Julie asked when the adults finally entered the cool interior of the car.

"Couldn't find the sunscreen," Jacob lied as he fastened his seat belt on the passenger side of the car.

"We need to hurry up if we're going to two zoos today," Julie said, holding up two fingers and waving them at her distracted caregivers.

Resigned to a long day, Amanda shifted the car into drive. She was overly conscious of the man beside her as they headed to the hills just outside the suburbs. Though he wasn't touching her, she could feel his gaze, and if his thoughts were even half as sensual her own, she had a reason to squirm in her seat beneath his avid attention.

CHAPTER SEVEN

JACOB SLID his fingertip up the outside of Amanda's smooth thigh. He grinned to himself when the car decelerated suddenly as her foot slipped off the gas pedal. She caught his hand just before his questing finger reached the hem of her shorts and turned her head to glare at him.

"Are we there yet?" he asked in a low tone—the one he knew aroused her—and leaned close to inhale her spicy perfume.

"Soon," she said, pushing his hand off her leg.

This could be fun, he decided. She'd made him promise that he wouldn't touch her when Julie was a witness, but there would be plenty of opportunity to tease her when his daughter's attention was elsewhere.

"Can we sing a song, Daddy?" Julie asked.

His daughter's sweet voice was like a bucket of cold water in his lap. He shifted away from Amanda, his bare shoulder pressing against the warm glass of the passenger-side door. "What should we sing?"

"You pick it."

"I know a song your Aunt Amanda likes to sing when she thinks no one is watching."

Amanda took her eyes off the road just long enough to glance at him, one eyebrow raised comically.

"How does it go again? *I'm walking on sunshine,*" he sang. He'd caught her singing when she'd been washing dishes, completely unaware of his presence. What she lacked in vocal talent, she made up for in enthusiasm. He wasn't sure if that was the moment he'd fallen for her or if her carefree singing had only added to already blossoming feelings.

Amanda flushed, which made him want to kiss her pink-stained cheeks. But despite her embarrassment, she sang along in her ever-off-key, wholehearted style. "*Whoa oh!*"

They sang alternating lines—Julie in the back seat clapping along in perfect time—and when they reached the end of the chorus, Julie sang, *"And don' I feels good?"*

Surprised, Jacob chuckled and turned in his seat to look at his wriggling daughter. He was surprised her booster seat held out under her vigorous dancing.

"You know this song?" he asked.

"Aunt Mander always sings it when we do dishes."

"And does she always sing it off-key?" he teased, glancing at the gorgeous woman in the driver's seat.

Amanda swatted at him, and he jerked up against the door to avoid her blow.

"I try to help her sing it right," Julie said.

"She does," Amanda said. "But it's a lost cause, I'm afraid."

"It's okay, Aunt Mander," Julie said. "We still love you."

Amanda stole a glance at Jacob, her hands gripping the steering wheel as if she feared she was about to spin out of control. She still hadn't acknowledged his words from earlier that morning. Would she accept them coming from Julie's innocent lips? Was he moving too fast? Did he care? He wanted Amanda in his life. She was just going to have to come to terms with that, because he refused to back down. He might be convinced to slow down, however. Maybe.

Oblivious to the tension between the adults in the front seats, Julie asked, "Can we sing more "Sunshine," please?"

They sang the chorus, each of them taking their own line, and repeated it over and over until they arrived at their destination. Jacob was pretty sure there was more to the song than three lines, but he was having too much fun to worry about getting the lyrics right or about the odd stares their vehicular performance received from passing motorists.

Jacob had never been to the Austin Zoo. He was stunned by how small the graveled parking lot was and surprised that it wasn't teeming with humans looking to examine the caged wildlife.

"Are you sure this is a real zoo?" Jacob asked Amanda as she shifted the car into park.

"It's not your ordinary zoo, but I'm sure it's a zoo."

Jacob shrugged and got out of the car, opening the back door to release Julie from her booster seat. "Should we bring the stroller?" he asked Amanda, who was opening the trunk.

"I'm a big girl!" Julie insisted. "I don't want a stroller."

Yeah, she said that now, but in ten minutes her feet would be hurting and she'd want to be carried for the next three or four hours.

"The paths aren't good for strollers," Amanda said. "And it only takes an hour or so to see everything."

Which would give them plenty of time to make the hour and a half drive to San Antonio for a second zoo visit.

Jacob sighed in resignation and set Julie on her feet in the gravel. Within two steps, he had a rock in his sandal. He was already wishing he'd opted for tennis shoes as he fished the sharp stone out with his finger. "I think you two are going to have to carry me if I keep getting rocks in my shoe."

Julie giggled. "You're too big to carry, silly."

"Come get your sunscreen on," Amanda said, tugging a large bottle of SPF 80 out of Julie's bag.

Amanda filled her palm with the coconut-scented stuff and handed the bottle to Jacob, who followed her cue. They each worked on one side until Julie was sufficiently coated with enough sunscreen to stop a solar flare.

"Here's your hat," Amanda said, handing Julie her white straw hat. His baby was incredibly fair skinned, and her pale-blond hair didn't provide much protection to her scalp from the harsh Texas sunshine.

"You need sunscreen too," Julie said. "I don't want you getting wrinkles."

Jacob chuckled. She'd probably heard that from her mother, but he found it humorous that a four-year-old would have such concerns.

"Allow me," Jacob said, taking the bottle from Amanda and squeezing a healthy dose into his palm. He rubbed his hands together to distribute the lotion between them and then worked the sunscreen into Amanda's sun-kissed shoulders, her graceful throat, the back of her neck, and—after peeking at Julie to make sure her attention was elsewhere—the tops of her lush breasts. Amanda released a breathy sigh as his fingertips rubbed her warm, pliant flesh. She leaned closer, and he lowered his head, craving her kiss and the feel of her body pressed against his.

"Daddy, did you bringed me a drink? I'm thirsty!"

Amanda jerked away and after discreetly rubbing her arm over the erect tips of her breasts, began to rummage through Julie's bag again. Jacob admired the curve of Amanda's ass as she bent over the trunk. That and the long graceful lines of her legs. The woman had amazing legs. They looked especially fantastic wrapped around his waist as he drove his cock into her hot, slick pussy.

Holy hell. Jacob rubbed a hand over his face, trying to clear the erotic images suddenly bombarding his thoughts.

"Apple juice?" Amanda asked, holding up a juice box for Julie to see.

"Yes, please. I want to do the straw."

This behaving himself stuff was going to be far more of a challenge than he'd anticipated.

"Daddy, hurry up and put on your sunscreen," Julie advised while she held the juice box against her belly and jabbed the little foil circle with a pointed straw. She was soon slurping juice and watching a family with six small children unload from a minivan.

"Allow me," Amanda said with a devilish grin as she filled her hands with the thin white cream.

Dear lord, did she have to stare up at him with her gaze full of longing and promise? He couldn't take it.

Amanda's hands were cool and slick against his heated fleshed as she took care to make sure every inch of his exposed skin was fondled—er, covered with fragrant lotion. Amanda squatted at his feet and ran both hands up his right leg from ankle to knee and then up the leg of his shorts. The father corralling his flock of kids toward the only visible building walked into the bumper of a car as he gawked at them. Julie waved at each of the passing kids, oblivious to the spectacle her aunt was making of her father.

"I think I have enough sunscreen," Jacob said, his voice raspy with arousal. He crouched and captured Amanda's shoulders in his hands, drawing her to her feet. It took every shred of his willpower not to crush her body against his and devour her mouth as she stared up at him beguilingly.

"What about your other leg?" she asked, blinking at him with faux innocence.

"It will just have to burn," he said.

By the time they'd collected everything, Julie had finished her juice and wanted to hold onto Amanda's left hand and Jacob's right so she could swing between them. Jacob couldn't help but grin at the cute giggles his daughter produced each time her feet flew out from under her as she placed complete trust in her companions.

They entered through the gift shop, a smallish wooden structure that reminded Jacob of an old general store. Julie was immediately drawn to the stuffed animals and bestowed on him the look of longing she knew he couldn't resist. "You can pick one on the way out," Jacob promised. "You don't want to have to carry it the entire time."

"I didn't know you were volunteering today," the friendly woman behind the counter said to Amanda.

"I'm not," Amanda said. "I brought my niece and her father for a visit. Thought I might get them the backstage experience if it's okay with Margie."

"The backstage experience?" Jacob had thought he was the only one with such privileges.

Amanda grinned at him. "You'll see." She opened her purse to grab her wallet, which sent Jacob scrambling for his cash supply.

"I got this," he said. "My treat."

"You don't have to pay," the cashier said. "God knows you do enough for this place."

"We insist," Amanda said. "And we'll also buy three bags of sheep pellets."

Sheep pellets? Jacob paid their admission and purchased three little brown bags that were stapled shut.

"What is this?" Julie said as one of the bags was passed to her.

"Don't you want to feed the goats and sheep?" Amanda asked.

Julie worried her lips together. "Do they bite?"

The cashier leaned close to her. "They don't bite, but watch out for the big brown goat. He's a greedy one who will try to steal your entire bag."

Julie nodded in understanding and cradled her sack of feed against her chest.

"I'll let Margie know you're around," the cashier said to Amanda.

"Thanks, Frances."

Jacob followed his two ladies across the hollow-sounding wooden floor, out onto a porch, and down a set of dusty steps to an uneven path. He glanced around, looking for signs directing them to the exhibits, or at least to a wide cement path that would be easy on sandaled feet.

"Chickens!" Julie cried, approaching the free-roaming birds that didn't look like any chicken Jacob had ever seen.

The dark-gray-and-white-speckled birds fluttered away from her, releasing a chorus of raucous chirping that made Jacob wince. The noisy creatures were definitely *not* chickens.

Amanda chuckled and squatted next to Julie, rubbing the center of her back soothingly. "Those are guinea fowl," she said. "You'll have to stand still and watch them quietly, or they'll run away."

"Can I pet one?" Julie looked up at her aunt, and Jacob was struck by the resemblance between the two.

Julie's eyes and nose resembled her mother's, and he hadn't ever noticed that Amanda had the same nose. Amanda's eyes were a different color—hazel rather than blue—but the shape of them was definitely a Lange family trait. His attraction to her was inevitable, it seemed. While Tina had the personality of a cactus, outwardly she was one of the most beautiful women he'd ever laid eyes on. He'd always liked Amanda for her personality, but he couldn't deny that she had the physical looks he admired most. So why had he fallen for Tina first? It was an unfortunate fact that he'd probably never understand. But if he hadn't married Tina, he wouldn't have Julie, and he'd face any hardship to have his little girl in his life. Even put up with her mother.

"Guinea fowl don't like to be touched," Amanda said, "but watch what they're doing while they walk. They eat all sorts of bugs. Even ticks and wasps."

The small flock of birds marched across the grass side by side, devouring any living creature stirred up by their scaly feet.

"And butterflies?" Julie asked.

"Sometimes. If you keep these birds in your orchard or vegetable garden, they'll keep all the pest insects away."

"Better than bug spray," Jacob said, knowing this kind of nature stuff inspired Amanda.

She smiled up at him, the sunshine catching golden highlights in her hair. "Exactly."

"What's an orch herd?" Julie asked.

"Where they grow lots of trees," Jacob said. "Like apples and oranges and stuff."

Julie looked to Amanda, who nodded her agreement.

Did Julie think he was an idiot or something? Her mother

certainly made that opinion of him well known. Jacob scowled, pulled a pair of sunglasses from the low collar of his tank top, and shoved them onto his face.

"Want to see a lemur?" Amanda asked.

"Like on *Madagascar*?" Julie asked.

"Exactly."

Jacob was underwhelmed by the first exhibit. A lemur sat on a platform just above eye level, his long striped tail dangling several feet behind him. He watched them with enormous yellow eyes as he used human-like hands to grab fruit from a bowl and bring it to his mouth. His cage was clean, but barely the size of a small closet. One side was draped with a blue tarp, presumably for shade.

"Up, Daddy!" Julie said, lifting her arms to him. "I can't see his face."

Jacob lifted her onto his shoulders, and she reached out to grab the wire cage as she peered inside.

"He has fingers," Julie said.

"All primates do," Amanda said. "And where most animals have sharp claws, primates have flat fingernails."

Julie shifted against Jacob's neck as she looked down at Amanda. "Can I put some nail polish on them?"

Amanda chuckled. "I don't think he'd hold still long enough."

This was why Jacob had wanted to bring Amanda along today. One of the reasons. She was so smart. She knew things about animals and stuff. Julie could learn new things from her, where Jacob mostly felt like an escort on such excursions. And he'd never tell Amanda, but he liked learning science-type things from her as much as Julie did. He'd been terrible at school, not because he hadn't wanted to learn, but because he got absolutely nothing from books. As far as he was concerned, books were only good as paperweights. And even when he'd paid attention in class and understood everything the teacher explained, when it came to tests, he hadn't bothered trying. He couldn't make heads or tails out of them. So he'd focused on the only thing he was good at: singing. He was so glad that Julie was smart like her aunt and hadn't inherited the brick her father had for a brain.

"Why is his cage so small?" Jacob asked.

"Most of the exhibits are small here," Amanda said. "This is a rescue zoo. So you'll find animals that other zoos didn't want or couldn't keep, injured animals that need to be isolated, exotic animals that someone had thought would make a good pet but couldn't keep, and retired service animals."

Jacob scowled. "Like dogs?"

"Monkeys," Amanda said. "Every animal here has a story." She pointed to a little sign on the cage that explained the lemur's origins and how he'd come to the zoo. Beneath it was a collection box. Amanda read the sign to Julie—and Jacob, not that he was willing to admit that.

"Just because he didn't get along with other lemurs doesn't mean he should be kept in such a small cage," Jacob said, staring intently into the creature's intelligent eyes as it nibbled on an orange wedge.

"They do the best they can here," Amanda said. "All the funding comes from paid admissions and donations. They don't get any financial assistance from the government. That's why I volunteer."

Jacob reached into his back pocket and pulled out his wallet. He took out a twenty-dollar bill and stuffed it into the slot of the lemur's collection box.

"What are you doing, Daddy?" Julie asked.

"Giving this lemur some money."

"Can I give him some money too?" she asked.

Jacob pulled Julie from her perch on his shoulders and handed her another bill. She stuffed it into the collection box and smiled up at him with pride. Jacob stroked her silky hair and kissed her on the forehead. "It's nice to give when you can."

Which reminded him of something Owen had said the day before. He fleetingly wondered if Owen's plans to dump Lindsey on his mom had worked out.

They continued around the zoo. Amanda shared interesting facts about all the animals. Julie insisted on shoving a twenty into every collection box. Feeling a bit light in the wallet but full in the heart, Jacob wandered the small zoo, having to stop every so often to dig sharp stones out of his sandals.

The tortoise exhibit had low walls, and Amanda said it was okay for Julie to touch the hard shell of a roaming creature when it got close.

"Why is there so many turtles here?" Julie asked.

"These are tortoises," Amanda said. "Turtles live in water."

"Why *do* they have so many tortoises?" Jacob asked. There

were over a dozen of them crawling about in their dusty pens, and he was pretty sure others were hiding out in the central shelter and thus weren't visible.

"Tortoises live a long time—some of these are over fifty years old. So when they're bred in captivity, it doesn't take long to have a surplus population, and when other zoos run out of room, they send them here."

"This turtle is as old as Grandma?" Julie said, looking up at Amanda with wide eyes. "I mean, is this *tortoise* as old as Grandma?"

Amanda laughed and touched her hair. "This tortoise is even older than Grandma."

While Julie reached over the wall, trying to get a hand on the mossy green back of the land tortoise, Jacob took the opportunity to move in close to Amanda. He was enjoying her company so much. It didn't seem fair that he couldn't openly display his affection.

When she turned to look at him, he couldn't resist stealing a kiss. Her hand moved to his shoulder and instead of pushing him away as he'd anticipated, she drew him closer.

"Daddy, I can't reach him," Julie said with a grunt of exertion.

Amanda pulled away, but not before Julie spied their unusually close proximity.

"What are you doing?" Julie asked, her slim blond eyebrows drawn together.

"Amanda . . . uh . . ." Jacob racked his brain for a plausible explanation. *Amanda is utterly delicious* didn't seem like a good enough reason.

"I had something in my eye," Amanda said, rubbing at one lid with the back of her hand.

Jacob was glad the woman was brilliant. "And I was helping her get it out."

Julie pursed her lips and shifted them to one side. Jacob didn't know if she'd actually seen them kissing or had just seen them standing inappropriately close.

"Can I pet the tortoise again?" she asked.

Jacob scooped her up airplane style and made zooming noises as he shifted her over the wall. She giggled, both arms extended, and managed to skim a hand along the tortoise's back.

"Is it okay to do this?" Jacob asked Amanda as an

afterthought.

Amanda nodded. "Just don't drop her in there. Tortoises like to nibble on little girl toes."

Making gobbling noises, Amanda grabbed the tips of Julie's tennis shoes. Julie squealed, "He's getting me, Daddy!"

Jacob scooped her up against his chest and squeezed. "I've got you. I won't ever let anything hurt you."

They watched a mischievous trio of bear cubs climb and tumble around their large enclosure, and Julie completely emptied Jacob's wallet into the collection box for an aged black panther with a lame leg.

"She's very compassionate," Amanda said as they sat on a bench and watched Julie talk to the pacing cat, telling him everything was going to be all right.

"I think she gets that from you," Jacob said, sneaking an arm around her back and stroking the bare skin of her shoulder with his fingertips.

"From me? How would she get that from me?" She inched closer to him on the bench until their knees touched.

"What do they call it, nature or nurture?"

Amanda lifted a questioning eyebrow at him.

"She's around you a lot," Jacob continued. "It's only natural that she's picked up some of your characteristics. She's shaped by more than her genes."

Amanda smiled. "You don't think she gets her compassion from her mother?"

They shared a hearty laugh over that idea.

"What's funny?" Julie asked, wriggling her slight form into the nonexistent space between them.

"Nothing important," Amanda said. "Are you getting tired?"

Julie shook her head. "Can we ride the train now?"

"Don't you want to feed the goats first?" From the diaper bag Amanda had been hauling around for over an hour, she pulled the three sacks of animal food they'd purchased at the main entrance.

"Yes!"

Julie was very careful to make sure each goat in the fenced corral got exactly one pellet. She giggled as their lips wiggled over her palm to collect her offering. Jacob watched closely, wondering if goats carried rabies. They sure didn't smell very clean.

A big brown goat butted his way between his fellows and

stole another goat's pellet from Julie's outstretched hand.

"No!" Julie shouted, waving a chastising finger at the crazed-looking animal. "That's not yours."

Brown-goat didn't look the least bit ashamed, and Jacob had to admit the animal's oblong pupils weirded him out. Did they all have bizarre eyes like that? Or just the crazy, rabid ones?

"What is it with their eyes?" Jacob asked Amanda.

She opened her mouth to answer but was cut off by Julie's piercing scream.

Jacob's heart slammed against his breast bone, and expecting to find his little girl with fewer fingers, he couldn't help but laugh at what had her so upset.

Brown-goat, having identified Julie's stash, had gone straight for the bag in her hand, biting into the brown paper and tearing off a chunk. The animal seemed satisfied with his meal until he swallowed and went back for a second bite.

"No!" Julie screamed. "You're a stupid, stupid idiot!"

"Julie!" Amanda admonished. "That's a terrible thing to say. You should never call anyone stupid or an idiot."

Amanda went still and her head jerked, turning her stunned face in Jacob's direction. She grimaced, her brows crumpled with sympathy. What the fuck? Why was she looking at him all apologetic-like?

"My mom does it," Julie snapped, throwing the remnants of her bag into the pen.

She crossed her arms over her narrow chest, stuck out her lower lip, and stomped off toward a mesquite tree in the center of the clearing surrounded by the petting barn's fences and the reptile shed. Brown-goat snatched up the bag and scattered the remaining tan pellets in all directions.

"Sorry," Amanda called to Jacob's back as he went after Julie.

Why was she sorry? Because she'd shouted? Because she'd upset Julie? Or was it because she thought *stupid* was his trigger word? Yes, Tina called him stupid on a regular basis, but Amanda didn't have the same opinion of him, did she?

Jacob squatted beside Julie and watched her kick at a tree root.

"Are you mad?" he asked.

"Yes," she grumbled.

"What about?"

"That stu—" She glanced at her Aunt Mander and adjusted her word choice. "That greedy goat taked all the food." Her eyes welled with tears. "Now the nice goats don't get any."

And wasn't that the way of the world? But that wasn't something he wanted her to simply accept. "Do you want to feed the nice goats my bag of food?" he asked, holding his full bag of pellets out to her.

"But the stupid—I mean, that *brown* goat—will just take it all again."

Jacob couldn't resist stroking her soft hair. "I have a plan to outsmart that brown goat."

Julie perked up, and it warmed his heart that she didn't even question his ability to outsmart a goat. "What is it?" she whispered, obviously not wanting Brown-goat to overhear his plan.

"We'll dump the pellets into our hands, and Aunt Mander can take the empty bag over there." He pointed to the far end of the corral. "And make Brown-goat think she has all the food."

Julie scrunched up her face and giggled into her tiny hands. "That's a good trick, Daddy."

Surprisingly, his trick worked. Brown-goat was so accustomed to being fed out of a paper bag that he was distracted by the bait long enough for Julie to make sure all the nice goats had several pellets each.

"Thank you, Daddy!" Julie said, hugging him as tightly as she could. "You saved the day."

Smiling, he squeezed her back. He wished she would stay this size forever. She'd eventually become a teenager and his ability to outsmart goats wouldn't seem quite as heroic to her.

A loud train whistle sounded, its playful tone carrying across the clearing. "Can we ride the train now?" Julie asked.

"Do you want to look at the snakes first?" he asked, pointing at the small building across the way that was labeled as the reptile house.

Julie's eyes widened, and she shook her head. "No, thank you," she said in a squeaky voice.

He didn't care much for snakes either. "Let's go find that train."

He beckoned Amanda with a wave and found her staring at them while Brown-goat nibbled on the empty bag she was still clutching in one hand. She relinquished the bag to the goat and hurried to catch up.

"Ready for a train ride?" he asked, and Amanda nodded, tripping over her feet as she slowed to walk beside him. He took her hand—an automatic reflex on his part—and was surprised when she didn't yank it away.

At the ticket booth, Jacob peered into his empty wallet. Well, shit, Julie had completely cleaned out his cash supply with her donations.

"Do you take credit cards?" he asked the clerk in the tiny booth.

"I've got this," Amanda said, shifting in front of him and handing bills to the cashier. "It's my treat."

"Amanda . . ." he tried to protest.

"How many hundreds of dollars did you donate to this place today?"

"Julie donated it," he reminded her.

"*You* donated it." She peeked at Julie around Jacob's shoulder. Julie was engrossed in talking to the green parrot in a nearby cage—*pretty bird, pretty bird* they echoed each other. Her eyes shifting to Jacob's, Amanda slid a hand up his neck and rose up on tiptoes to kiss him. "Julie didn't get her compassion from me. She got it from you," she whispered against his lips before turning to the cashier to get her change.

From him? From Jacob "Shade" Silverton? He was a badass metal singer with only sex, partying, and rock 'n' roll on his mind. Didn't she get that? The rest of the world understood him perfectly.

Honestly, the train ride was entirely underwhelming.

Wooden cutouts of dinosaurs and forest elves stood scattered in the mesquite forest that the train wound through. Or maybe the colorful mystical creatures were gnomes. They definitely weren't the wild animals he'd expected. Julie got overly excited when she spotted a small shaggy pony housed behind a chain-link fence. What excited Jacob was the ability to casually place an arm on the back of the bench and run the silky strands of Amanda's hair between his fingertips. And with Julie squashed between them, with one of her hands on Amanda's knee and the other on Jacob's thigh, they felt—the three of them—like a family. He had to admit it was exactly what his heart desired—a good woman to love him and his daughter. Someone special to him who could also serve as

Julie's role model as well as her mother.

It was a wonderful dream, but just that: a dream.

A dream he wanted to keep close to him. He pulled out his cell phone and held it at arms-length in front of them. When he had all three of their faces lined up in the shot, he said, "Say cheese!"

"Pickles!" Julie said and laughed at her naughtiness.

As he smiled down at the perfect picture he'd captured he decided they looked good together. And happy. He tucked his phone back into his pocket and gave Amanda's shoulder a squeeze. She peeked at him over Julie's head and offered him a flirty wink.

After the short train ride, they checked out a famous goose and some ordinary deer before winding their way to the interior of the zoo where a bunch of small monkeys were housed.

"There you are," said a middle-aged woman in khaki shorts and an Austin Zoo polo shirt. Her dark hair was streaked with gray, her lean body sinewy and tanned, likely from spending her days working outside. She had a friendly face and gentle brown eyes. Jacob was pretty sure he'd never seen her before, but a lot of people he didn't know recognized him.

"Excuse me?" Jacob asked.

"Hello, Margie," Amanda said, offering the woman a brief hug. "This is my niece, Julie, and my . . ." She glanced Jacob. "Uh . . . Julie's father, Jacob."

"Nice to meet you both," Margie said, nodding at them in turn.

"Margie's one of the head zookeepers here," Amanda said.

"Do you get to play with the animals?" Julie asked.

"Sometimes," Margie said. "Most of the time I take care of them."

"And clean up their poop?"

It was an honest question, but it gave the adults a chuckle.

"Unless Amanda's here. Then I make her do it," Margie said with an ornery grin.

Julie gave Amanda a look of pity.

"Do you think Jojo would like a young guest today?" Amanda asked.

"I'm sure she'd love one," Margie said with a smile at Julie.

They followed the zookeeper through a tall gate marked Employees Only and down a narrow path and then stopped behind one of the monkey cages. Margie took out a set of keys and fit one into a lock. The small dark brown monkey in the cage scurried up a faux tree to a platform and sat watching them with her thumb in her mouth.

Jacob's heart thudded when he realized they were about to stick his daughter in a cage with a wild animal.

"Amanda," Jacob said, taking Julie's hand and keeping her at his side. "Are you sure this is safe?"

Amanda smiled at him. "Would I ever put Julie in danger?"

He didn't think she would, but then he'd heard stories of apes going crazy and ripping off people's faces, so while Amanda wouldn't intentionally harm Julie, he wasn't so sure the monkey had gotten the memo.

"Jojo has been with us for about a year. I assure you she's very gentle," Margie said. "Especially with children."

"I'm sure you feel that way about all wild animals," Jacob said.

"Jojo's not really wild," Amanda said. "She was a service monkey for a disabled woman and when her owner passed away, they brought her here to live out the rest of her life. She loves people. Her owner had several grandchildren she adored. She gets lonely without a lot of human contact. But if you're afraid—"

"I'm not scared, Daddy," Julie said, her eyes locked with the monkey's. "Can I please hug Jojo?"

She turned her gaze to Jacob's, and his resolve crumbled. He didn't know why he had such a hard time telling his daughter no.

"You're sure it's safe?" he asked Amanda.

She nodded. "I'll go in with her. Jojo knows me."

"Jojo loves visitors," Margie said. "She's a little more leery of men. If you weren't here, she'd already be reaching through the cage for Amanda."

"Should I leave?" Jacob said, not wanting to upset the creature. Especially since these animal-lover types seemed determined to lock his daughter in a cage with it.

"You can stay out here and observe," Margie said. "It's not that Jojo is upset by men. She's just a little shy around them."

Jacob squatted down and captured Julie's shoulders between his palms. "You mind your aunt and do whatever she tells you to do."

Julie backed away and lifted a hand to Amanda, eager to start her adventure.

"Promise you'll mind her, Julie," Jacob said firmly, "or you won't be allowed to see the monkey."

"I promise I'll do whatever Aunt Mander says," Julie said, her gaze locked on Jacob's. "Even clean the poop."

Jacob chuckled and gave Julie's slight form a hearty squeeze. Even though he trusted Amanda to keep her safe, he still found it difficult to let Julie go.

Margie opened the cage, and Amanda stepped inside, ducking her head through the small door. "Wait there for a minute, Julie," Amanda said to the eager child.

Julie wrapped her fingers around the cage door, but did as she was told and didn't enter the enclosure.

"Come, Jojo," Amanda said to the monkey.

"What kind of a monkey is that?" Jacob asked Margie as the small dark brown animal climbed down from her perch and settled at Amanda's feet. Jojo curled her long tail around her body. She looked up at Amanda and then glanced at Julie before finding the tip of her tail uncommonly interesting. The monkey began to pick at her fur with tiny black fingers.

"She's a capuchin. They're very intelligent." Margie patted his back. "And friendly."

Amanda sat on a cement step inside the cage and Jojo climbed into her lap, immediately settling into Amanda's arms and snuggling into her chest for a hug. Amanda stroked her thick fur and murmured to her in soothing tones. "Do you want to meet Julie?" Amanda asked the monkey.

As if the animal could understand her, she lifted her head and peered at the child waiting just outside her cage. She reached toward Julie with a paw that looked remarkably human and vocalized softly. Julie smiled and mimicked the sound. "*Ooo*."

"You can come in now, Julie," Amanda said.

Margie helped Julie through the cage door and shut her inside.

CHAPTER EIGHT

AMANDA KEPT a soothing hand on the back of Jojo's shoulder as Julie took timid steps in her direction. She didn't fear that the monkey would bite or scratch, but she might get excited enough to jump in Julie's arms and accidentally knock her over.

"Come sit beside me," Amanda instructed as she patted the patch of bare cement next to her hip. She glanced at Jacob, who'd stepped forward to stand just outside the cage, watching his daughter walk closer to where Amanda sat with Jojo on her lap. She could sense his anxiety even though she couldn't see his eyes through his sunglasses, but it meant a lot to her that he trusted her with Julie. She knew how much Julie meant to him and how important it was that she was safe and happy. If not for his desire to make Julie happy, Amanda wasn't sure Jacob would have allowed her into a cage with a baby bunny.

Julie sat on the cement step, her blue eyes wide and fixed on Jojo, who had shifted away from Amanda so she could examine the newest intruder in her dwelling. Julie lifted a trembling hand toward Jojo, and the monkey scurried onto her lap. Julie's eyes widened when Jojo wrapped both arms around her narrow chest and hugged her. Jojo's fluffy cream-colored eyebrows rose expressively, as if to ask Amanda, "Am I doing this right?"

"You can hug her back," Amanda said. "She likes you."

After a lengthy embrace from Julie, Jojo scurried up her tree and grabbed something from her platform. In an instant she was back on the ground and dropping a slice of apple on Julie's lap.

"She's giving you a gift," Amanda explained.

"Don't eat it," Jacob warned as Julie picked up the slice of apple and eyed the browning piece of fruit with disgust.

"Jojo, get your ball," Amanda said.

Jojo had been trained to retrieve lots of objects while caring for her human in her former role. She ignored all the other objects in her enclosure and picked up a small red ball, racing back toward Amanda on her hind legs as she carried it between her front paws.

"Give it to Julie," Amanda said. Jojo paused and glanced at the child who was watching intently. "Yes, that's Julie."

The monkey vocalized a soft *ooo ooo*, and deposited the ball in Julie's lap.

"Good girl!" Julie said.

Jojo moved to stand behind Julie and began grooming her pale-blond hair. Julie giggled and scrunched up her neck. "What is she doing?"

"She thinks you have bugs in your hair," Jacob said from outside the cage.

The sound of his voice danced along Amanda's nerve-endings. God, the man had an amazing voice. She couldn't wait to get him alone later.

"She's picking them out."

"I don't have bugs in my hair, silly." Julie lifted her face to Amanda's, the corners of her mouth drawn down. "I don't, do I?"

Amanda tugged one of her silky curls. "I don't think so. Jojo's just checking to make sure."

Julie giggled, melting her Aunt Mander into a pile of sappy goo. "Monkeys are silly."

Julie certainly enjoyed Jojo's silly antics as she retrieved the items Amanda and Julie requested. The capuchin watched them put objects inside different compartments of a small box. Amanda closed all the doors of the box, and Jojo had no problem opening the correct door to reveal whichever item she requested.

"She's so smart," Julie said. "I want to take her home." She turned to her father. "Please, Daddy!"

Before Jacob could deny his daughter her request, Margie spoke up. "She has to stay here with us, sweetheart. But you can come with your aunt and visit her again. How does that sound?"

Julie's lower lip quivered, but she pressed it against her upper lip and nodded. "We have to come here to be with Jojo *all* the time, Aunt Mander. She wants me as her best friend." Julie reached her little hands out to the monkey, and Jojo dashed into her arms to give her another hug, picking imaginary nits out of Julie's hair over her shoulder.

"We'll come visit when we can. School will be starting soon."

"I love school," Julie said.

Amanda glanced over her shoulder at Jacob. She had yet to bring up Leah's class to him. She wasn't sure if he'd be grateful or annoyed that she'd weaseled him onto the roster. He looked kind of lonely outside the enclosure without them. Or maybe he was just interested in what they were doing. How could she tell with his eyes hidden behind his shades? Those things needed to go.

"Jojo," Amanda said, "go get glasses."

Jojo knew this command well since her previous owner had often requested her glasses. Jojo hopped off Julie's lap and looked around for the requested object. Amanda pointed at Jacob, who was standing against the fence, clinging to the wires with both hands. He was so close that the tip of his nose was actually inside the cage. Jojo dashed toward him, climbed the cage, and before he could stop her, reached through the fence and pulled the sunglasses off his face.

"Hey," Jacob protested.

Jojo offered a sheepish grin and raced off holding his sunglasses over her head. She promptly dropped them in Amanda's lap.

"Good girl, Jojo!" Amanda said, stroking her head. "He looks much better without them."

Julie laughed. "She took Daddy's glasses."

"Little thief," Jacob accused, but he was smiling.

It took them a long while to coax Julie out of the cage. She didn't want to say goodbye to her new friend. "I will miss her so much," Julie said.

Jacob swung her into his arms and tugged her against his broad chest, one strong, masculine hand gently cradling the back of her head. Amanda tripped over her feet as she watched them. What was it about daddies protecting their little girls that Amanda found so irresistibly sexy? When Julie had been an infant, Amanda's ovaries had practically exploded every time she'd seen the man with his baby in his arms.

Suddenly, music declaring life in plastic as fantastic blared from Amanda's cellphone and she scowled at the sound of her sister's ringtone. It was as if Tina knew Amanda was coveting her family and needed to put a stop to such thoughts at once.

"What's up?" Amanda answered.

"Brenda can't make it to lunch, so I thought maybe you'd like to join me. Get out of the house for a while."

Tina was under the impression that Amanda left her house only to jump at Tina's whims or, during the school year, to go to work.

"I can't make it. I'm busy today."

"Is that Mommy?" Julie asked. She must have recognized the "Barbie World" ringtone. Crap!

Amanda grimaced and cupped her hand around the bottom of her phone to muffle sound.

"I want to tell her about Jojo!" Julie squealed excitedly.

And when Julie did tell told her about Jojo, she'd undoubtedly mention she'd been with Amanda. And that Jacob was with them both.

"Is that *Julie?*" Tina asked.

Amanda's grimace deepened. She wondered if it would be better to come clean now or to convince Julie to keep a secret. Amanda was sure the child would try, but Julie was much too excited about the monkey to keep her trip to the zoo from her mother for long.

"Yeah. I was volunteering at the zoo today." Amanda decided on the fly that a partial lie would be best. "And Jacob just happened to bring Julie by. I think she wants to talk to you about the monkey she saw. I'll put her on."

She handed the phone to Julie, who told her mother all about her adventure with Jojo, but didn't—thank God—mention that Jacob and Amanda had arrived at the zoo together. Or that her aunt had a strange way of getting dirt in her eye whenever her daddy was near.

"You know," Jacob said quietly to Amanda. "I don't give a shit if Tina knows we're together. She's going to have to come to terms with it eventually."

"I know," Amanda said, deciding *eventually* would be best a few years into the future. "I think we should break the idea to her very gradually. It's enough that she knows I saw you today."

"At random," Jacob said flatly.

"Exactly."

"Okay, Mommy. I love you!" Julie shoved her phone into Amanda's hand and skipped ahead to peer at another capuchin monkey through the wires.

"What have you done?" Tina said accusingly.

Amanda's stomach dropped. "Um, we just— I thought— He invited—"

"Now she wants a goddamned monkey," Tina interrupted

Amanda's disjointed stammering. "A *monkey*. You'd better get that idea out of her head before you send her home. Jacob will go out and buy her one. You know how stupid he is. I had to put her fucking birthday present in a lockbox at the bank."

Amanda's spine straightened, and her jaw hardened. "He's not . . ." She glanced around to make sure he wouldn't overhear. He had lifted Julie into his arms so she could see into an exhibit and wasn't paying Amanda any mind. ". . . *stupid*," she whispered harshly into her phone.

Tina snorted. "He has a brick for a brain, that one. He's lucky he's attractive."

Jacob had so much more going for him than his looks. Even more than the vocal talent that had made him successful and rich. Yes, even more than his exceptional skills in the bedroom. As far as Amanda was concerned, Jacob's best trait was his big ol' heart, and Tina was the stupid one for discarding it.

"I've got to go," Amanda said. She didn't think she'd be able to stay civil with Tina for another second. She didn't care if Tina was her sister.

"Rain check?"

"Yeah, fine," she said, although at that moment she doubted she'd ever want to go to lunch with her again. "Bye."

She hung up immediately, so she didn't know if Tina had anything else to say. And frankly she didn't care. How dare she turn Julie's joy into an excuse to belittle Jacob?

"Look, Aunt Mander," Julie said, pointing to the cage. "This monkey looks like Jojo, but he has blond hair like me."

Amanda took a deep breath and plastered a smile on her face. "He does look like you."

"Wanna know how I know he's a boy?" Julie asked slyly.

The monkey was naked and letting everything hang out, so it was obvious that he was a male. "Uh . . ." Amanda bit her lip and glanced at Jacob, who was laughing silently, his lips pursed, face reddening by the second.

"'Cause he has big eyebrows," Julie said. The monkey did have wild, bushy eyebrows going on. "Girls have to pluck theirs."

"Oh," Amanda said, deciding it was best to leave the boy-versus-girl anatomy discussion for a later time and a more private location.

"And he has a penis," Julie added knowledgably.

Jacob snorted and then burst out laughing. Julie leaned back in his arms and gaped at him.

"Is a penis funny?" she asked.

"Nope," Jacob said, blinking back tears and touching the back of his hand to each eye in turn. "I was just laughing at these crazy monkeys."

Those crazy monkeys were currently sitting quite docilely in their enclosures.

"You're a boy," Julie said. "So you have a penis. But me and Aunt Mander are girls, so we don't have one."

"You are correct," Jacob said, "but we don't talk about private parts while we're out in public."

"Penis is a secret?" Julie asked, glancing around for eavesdroppers.

"Not a secret," Jacob said, obviously struggling to find the right explanation.

"It's a bad word?"

"No, we just don't talk about certain things in public," Jacob said. "If you want to talk about private parts, you can ask me or Aunt Mander about them when there aren't any strangers around. They might get offended."

"What's offended mean?"

Jacob paused for a moment as he thought up a child-friendly definition. Amanda didn't interfere. She didn't want to come to his rescue.

"It means—sort of—that they don't like what you're saying, so they don't want to hear it."

"But penis is just a fact of life," Julie said.

Amanda pressed her lips together so she wouldn't laugh. Jacob was holding it together quite well now.

"You're right," Jacob said with a shrug. "I just didn't want you to get into trouble for talking about something that many people think is inappropriate."

Julie squished his face between her palms. "I don't want to get into trouble. I hate time out. I'll just talk about penis to you later."

"Good." Jacob's smile was a bit false—he probably didn't want to talk about penis to his four-year-old daughter *ever*—but he gave her a tight squeeze and set her on her feet.

"Are you ready for lunch?" Amanda asked. "Your dad made

all sorts of good things to eat and packed them in your bag."

Jacob rubbed the back of his neck. "Well, actually Tammy knew I had Julie this weekend, so she stocked the fridge with sandwiches and stuff. I just tossed them in the bag."

"You did good," Amanda said and patted his arm. Her pat turned into a light touch and then a caress. And then she was leaning in closer, longing for him to wrap her in his arms and kiss her.

"I want to see more animals," Julie said.

Amanda took a step back from Jacob so she didn't try to jump his bones in front of his impressionable daughter.

"You've already seen them all," Amanda said. "This place isn't very big."

"So we can go to that other zoo now? The one with the lephalants."

Amanda glanced at Jacob, who shrugged and nodded. "It's only about an hour and a half drive. We'll eat lunch on the way."

They made a pit stop at the bathroom. Amanda froze when Jacob leaned in to brush a kiss across her cheek. "Take good care of my girl," he said.

If Julie had noticed his affectionate peck, she didn't mention it.

After they used the toilet—Julie insisted she didn't need help because she was a big girl—Amanda made sure she washed her hands.

"Get all the monkey stink off," Amanda said. Julie sniffed her wet hands, made a face, and washed them again with double the soap.

Jacob was waiting for them outside the bathroom when they came out. He placed a hand on the small of Amanda's back as they walked down the ramp, with Julie skipping ahead. All the sudden touchy-feely he had going on worried Amanda. It wasn't that she didn't like it—she wished they could show their growing affection for each other openly. But she didn't want anyone to get hurt. She didn't much care how Tina would feel anymore, but she did care if Jacob and Julie suffered.

They had to exit through the gift shop, so their trip to San Antonio was further delayed. Jacob picked up a new set of sunglasses; a small capuchin monkey now had possession of his old pair. And Julie thought she needed an entire collection of stuffed animals.

"You can pick one," Jacob said.

"But I need them all," Julie insisted.

"Only one." He wrapped one of her curls around his finger. "Choose wisely."

She examined each display as if making a life-altering decision. Amanda wandered over to the far corner to look at posters. She liked hanging them in her classroom. She didn't get to spend much time teaching about mammals in her biology class, but they were her favorite part of her subject. Well, other than the dark reactions of photosynthesis and chemiosmosis. Fascinating stuff. But most students looked like they wanted to cry when she discussed anything biochemical. Even the students who struggled with biology liked to look at posters of animals, however.

"What did Tina want?" Jacob asked her.

Amanda slid the poster of a wolf back into its slot—she already had that one—and pulled out one of a red fox.

"She just asked if I wanted to go to lunch with her." Amanda didn't look at him when she said it, afraid this was about to turn into a confrontation. She didn't want the day to turn sour.

"And you told her you couldn't go?"

"Right."

"Because you were with me?"

Amanda slid the fox poster back in place and pulled out one of a brown bear. "Tina heard Julie's voice in the background, and I figured she would tell her mom about being allowed in Jojo's exhibit, so I was sure Tina would find out that we'd seen each other."

"Randomly?"

"Don't you think that's best?"

"What I think's best?"

She nodded, lifting her gaze to meet his.

"I think it's best not to hide." He moved to stand directly behind her, the heat of his body burning through her clothes, stirring her awareness, her desire. "So if I want to touch you." His palms slid down her bare arms and her breath quickened, eyelids fluttered shut. "Or kiss you." He brushed the lightest of kisses against the sensitive spot where her shoulder met the back of her neck. She shuddered and swallowed a groan of delight. "I can do so without hesitation."

"But Julie—"

"I don't think Julie would have a problem with us being together," he said. His hand slid under the hem of her top, and his fingers traced the waistband of her shorts, making her squirm and brush her ass against him.

His soft growl of torment against her ear made her pussy ache from its emptiness.

"It's not that," she said.

He turned her to face him, pressing her into the wall with the length of his body.

"Then what?" he murmured. "I know you're into me."

She was very into him. She took a deep breath just so she could delight in the feel of his hard chest against her taut nipples.

"If Julie catches on to what's going on between us, she'll tell her mother."

"So what?" Jacob said, his blue-eyed gaze hard with anger or frustration, she wasn't sure which.

"Tina will use her leverage to keep Julie away from you."

"I'd like to see her try," he said.

"Would you?" Amanda asked. "Would you really? What if she succeeds? Then what?"

"Daddy," Julie said from across the rectangular room. "What are you doing to Aunt Mander?"

"I've got something in my eye, sweetheart," Amanda said.

"Again? Aunt Mander you need to wear safety glasses. The lawn-mowing guy says he wears them to keep stuff out of his eyes."

Jacob pushed off the wall, leaving Amanda feeling hopelessly exposed. He ripped the tag off the sunglasses he intended to buy and perched the eyewear on his face to hide the turmoil in his expression. Speaking of safety glasses . . .

Julie eventually decided on a stuffed monkey—which she promptly named Jojo—and they piled back into the car. Even though it was Amanda's car, Jacob insisted on driving. She didn't mind. If he drove, it would be much easier for her to stare worshipfully at his masculine beauty.

And with him driving, she could cool down a bit. She was still overwarm from his little show of posturing in the gift shop. Why had it turned her on when he'd cornered her like that?

Maybe because he made her feel desirable.

Once the interior of the car had cooled enough, Julie was

fastened into her booster seat and given her lunch. She was soon sharing her peanut butter and jelly sandwich and carrot sticks with her new toy. "Eat your lunch, Jojo."

Amanda dropped her bag into the trunk and riffled through it for more sandwiches for her and Jacob. Seemed she'd be having ham and cheese on wheat. An apple tumbled out of the bag and rolled to the far reaches of the trunk. She reached for the wayward fruit, pulling it from the corner. It dropped from her hand when Jacob stepped up behind her and pressed the ridge in his shorts against the aching heat between her thighs.

"Do you have any idea what seeing you bent over the back of this car does to me?" he said in her ear.

Probably the same thing the low rumble of his voice did to her.

"I could hazard a guess," she said with a grin.

"I want to peel those shorts down your thighs and fuck the sassiness out of you."

"That would take a whole lot of fucking, Silverton."

"I'm up for it."

She wriggled her hips, rubbing his hardening cock against her. "I can feel that you are."

His arms wrapped around her waist, and he crossed them in front of her so he could grasp her breasts. He pinched her nipples, sending a jolt of pure lust through the center of her body. Dear lord, what was this man trying to do to her?

"Have you forgotten where you are?" she asked, grabbing his hands and glancing around the currently vacant parking lot.

"Trust me," he said. "If I'd forgotten where we are, my cock would already be buried inside you."

"Daddy!" Julie's muffled voice called from inside the car. "Jojo is thirsty."

Jacob huffed a half laugh into Amanda's ear and pulled away. "My four-year-old-daughter's voice," he said with a resigned sigh. "So much more effective than any cold shower."

Turning to face him, Amanda chuckled and handed him a lukewarm juice box from Julie's bag. "We don't have time for a public quickie against the trunk of my car anyway."

"You'd better prepare yourself for tonight," he said, and though his expressive blue eyes were hidden behind sunglasses, she could feel the heat of his gaze as he examined her body. "I have a whole lot of sexual frustration to work through. Once Julie goes to sleep, you're mine."

"Oh?" she teased. "Are you sure about that?"

He leaned in and stole a quick kiss that had her swaying with dizziness. Must be this heat, she thought as she gripped the trunk behind her so that she didn't sink to her knees at his feet.

"I'm sure," he said. Wearing a crooked grin, he circled the car to give Julie her juice box.

Amanda collected their lunches in a spare plastic sack, shut the trunk, and climbed into the passenger seat. Jacob waited for her to fasten her seat belt before leaving Austin Zoo behind. While he drove, she handed him food, glad that he was too busy concentrating on driving and lunch to touch her. Okay, that was a lie. No matter how unsettling she found his physical attention, she would never be glad he wasn't touching her.

"Julie's already asleep," Jacob said, his gaze on the rearview mirror.

Amanda turned in her seat and smiled at the peacefully sleeping angel in the back seat who held her stuffed monkey wrapped in a tight embrace, her own neck bent at an uncomfortable angle. Amanda unfastened her seat belt and grabbed the neck pillow off the floorboard. She carefully used it to straighten Julie's neck before flopping back into her seat and buckling up.

"She looks much more comfortable," Jacob said, reaching for her hand and giving it a squeeze. "Thanks."

"She'll be fully rested and raring to go when we get to San Antonio." Which was far preferable to dealing with a tired, cranky child who'd missed her nap.

"I'm glad you came with us today," Jacob said. "You make her walk on sunshine."

Amanda flushed. "Thanks."

"And me too."

"You both make me happy as well," Amanda admitted around the knot in her throat.

This conversation was rapidly turning serious. And she wasn't sure she was ready to have this talk just yet. She shifted in her seat and said, "Did you feel left out while we were in Jojo's enclosure?"

"Not at all. Are you changing the subject?"

"Totally," she said.

"Still not ready to admit you're in love with me?"

Amanda's lips went numb. "Um . . . Well . . . I-I'm not sure."

"You'll come around," he said with a confident grin. He shifted his free hand to rest on her thigh.

If he was that sure, he knew more about her feelings than she did. If she was in love with him, the feeling hadn't first sparked recently. It had been growing for a long time. But she didn't want to believe that she'd fallen for him while he'd still been married to Tina. That was a betrayal to her sister that she didn't want to face. And she definitely needed to change the subject. Again.

"So last night I was talking to my friend Leah," she said. Which reminded Amanda she needed to text her and see if Colton had contacted her for a second date.

"Your cute Asian friend?" Jacob asked, glancing over his shoulder as he changed lanes to pass a lagging semi-truck.

"What's with the cute qualifier?" Amanda asked, narrowing her eyes at him.

"What? I said she was cute, not that I want to screw her."

Amanda shoved her feelings of unwarranted jealousy into the pit of her stomach. She knew that Tina's jealousy had been the primary catalyst for her breakup with Jacob, and Amanda refused to follow the same path.

"Yes, my cute Asian friend Leah. She's the one who does the GED prep course around Christmas break. Remember when we talked about that?"

Jacob moved his hand from her leg to rest on the automatic transmission gear shift. "I remember," he said after a moment.

"Her class is totally full already."

"So I guess that idea is shot." He didn't seem too upset about it.

"I thought you wanted to get your GED."

"I do," he said.

"Are you sure?" she pressed.

"Yeah, I'm sure."

"Then you'll be glad to know that Leah agreed to let you into the class as a favor to me."

He didn't see her bright smile of encouragement, because he didn't look at her. He didn't respond either. "Jacob?"

"The band will be working on our next album then," he said.

"It's only a few nights a week. I'm sure you can make it work if you want to."

"I don't want to embarrass myself in front of your smart friend," he said quietly.

"You won't," Amanda said. "Leah works with struggling students all the time."

"What's that supposed to mean?" Jacob took his eyes off the road long enough to glare at her.

"I don't know why this is escalating into an argument," Amanda said. "You told me you wanted to get your GED but didn't think you were prepared. Leah is the best teacher around for your exact situation. She's willing to put her neck out for you at my request, and you act like I've done something wrong. I don't understand what your problem is."

"My problem? You're the one so fixated on this GED thing."

"Me?" she shouted, and then she lowered her voice when Julie mumbled incoherently in her sleep. "I don't care if you ever get your GED. You said you regretted never graduating from high school."

"I do," he said.

"Jacob, I don't want you to regret anything. Not your unfinished education. Not your relationship with Tina." Not being with me, she added silently.

"I don't regret marrying your sister," he said. "Without Tina, there'd be no Julie. I don't want to even think about what life would be like without her. I also don't regret divorcing your sister. She's a huge pain in the ass. We don't belong together."

Amanda couldn't help but draw parallels between herself and Tina. Maybe Jacob thought she was being a huge pain in the ass for meddling in his life.

"I appreciate that you're trying to help," he said.

She lifted a skeptical eyebrow at him. "Do you?"

"Yeah. I just—" He shook his head and reached for an open bottle of water, tipping his head back as he chugged half its contents. He returned it to the cup holder and gripped the steering wheel in both hands.

Amanda traced the edge of the skull tattoo on his right shoulder. "Do you want to talk to Leah? Maybe she can convince you that you'll do just fine."

"No, I don't want to talk to Leah. What do you do in her class? Sit and read books?"

"I think she does a practice test on the first day."

"A test on the first day?" Jacob blurted.

"Practice test," Amanda said. "It's to see where your weaknesses are. She uses it to customize her instruction for each student. She forms study groups to work on topics and determines if there are issues that the entire class needs to be instructed on. And she does a lot of one-on-one instruction for students who are really struggling."

Jacob massaged the back of his neck.

"You don't have anything to be nervous about. If you're not ready to take the real test at the end of the class, you can sign up to take the class again. You can take it as many times as you want. It's not for a grade or anything, it's just to help you do your best on the test. I know you're smart enough to do this, Jacob."

He snorted. "Oh yeah," he said. "I'm a real genius."

He was too hard on himself. She leaned over and kissed him on the arm. "You're smart enough," she repeated. "I know you are. You can trust my judgement. I'm a professional educator, remember?"

"You aren't the first professional educator I've duped with sex," he said.

Amanda's jaw dropped. "What?"

He shrugged. "Let's just say Mrs. Cranston wasn't helping me improve my essays when she kept me after school." He laughed and rubbed at the center of his forehead.

"That's terrible," Amanda said. "Please tell me you reported her and got her fired. Hell, got her arrested."

"For what?"

"For molesting you."

"I honestly didn't mind," he said. "I was a lot better at making her moan than making heads or tails out of those boring-ass books she made us read."

"She was your *teacher*, Jacob. Jesus, how old were you?" Not that it mattered. Even if he'd been a consenting adult of eighteen, a teacher was in a position of authority, one that should never be abused. Exchanging sexual favors for passing grades? It was positively disgusting.

"Uh, fourteen, I think."

"*Fourteen?*" Amanda clutched her stomach to stave off the nausea. "I don't even know what to say."

His jaw hardened. "I'm sorry if what I did disgusts you. Failure was not an option."

"You don't disgust me, baby. *She* fucking disgusts me!"

"Are we there yet?" Julie asked groggily from the back seat.

"Not much longer," Jacob told her, smiling at her in the rearview mirror. "About twenty more minutes."

"Okay," she mumbled before drifting back to sleep with her stuffed monkey snuggled tightly in her arms.

"Did you report that teacher?" Amanda said, still feeling sick over what he'd told her.

"It isn't that big a deal, Amanda. Just drop it."

"It is a big deal," she insisted. "Would you think it was a big deal if some teacher coerced a fourteen-year-old Julie into offering sexual favors in exchange for better grades?"

Jacob's face went ashen. "I'd kill the fucking son of a bitch."

"So now do you get why I'm so upset about this?"

"It's different," he said. "Julie's a girl."

"But it isn't different," Amanda said, shaking her head. "And I'm so sorry it happened to you."

"I've always had a thing for teachers," he said, reaching for her hand, capturing it in his and drawing it to his lips.

Amanda frowned and turned to him. "Please don't tell me that your attraction to me has anything to do with what that sick bitch did to you as a kid."

"But I wasn't a kid," he said with a chuckle. "I landed on the other side of puberty like a champ."

"Perhaps you were physically mature, but psychologically, you were a kid, Jacob."

"Did you know me then?" he asked and dropped her hand.

"My students are all between the ages of fourteen and sixteen. Trust me, they're kids. They don't think they are, but their decision-making processes are far from mature. Would you still sleep with a teacher for a better grade?"

"Depends on how hot she is," he said with a soft chuckle.

Amanda's nostrils flared.

"That was a joke," he said, patting her knee. "I don't understand why you're so pissed. It happened over a decade ago. No one got hurt. No one got caught. I was okay with it then and I'm still okay with it. Mrs. Cranston was definitely okay with it."

"She gives teachers a bad name." Amanda crossed her arms

over her chest and tried to glare a hole into the dashboard.

"Oh," Jacob said, the hand on her knee beginning to explore her bare skin in a most distracting fashion. "So this is really about you."

"Of course it isn't about me."

Well, maybe it was about her. Nothing grated on her nerves more than a person of authority using their power to do wrong. Teachers, cops, CEOs—in her mind, they had the moral obligation to do the right thing. And requiring a student to exchange sexual favors for a better grade was outlandishly wrong. "Was she the only one?" Amanda asked, wishing she could see his eyes behind his sunglasses.

"You don't want me to answer that," he said.

Amanda slumped against the door and rubbed her face with her palm. "How many?"

"A few," he said. "My education was a joke, okay? Can we just drop it?"

Amanda watched a muscle twitch in his jaw. She hadn't meant to upset him. Maybe it was best to leave such things in the past.

"Is it any surprise that I turned out to be such an idiot?" he said under his breath.

Amanda's heart shattered. "You aren't an idiot, Jacob."

He snorted. "I know what I am, better than anyone. Better than my teachers, better than you, better than—than *Tina*." He pounded a fist against the steering wheel and held it there, clenched so tight that his knuckles turned white.

As far as Amanda knew, Tina was the only one who actually called him stupid, and she did it because she knew how much it hurt him. Amanda had never gotten along with Tina, but at that moment she actually hated her own sister. Despised her.

"You're not an idiot," Amanda said.

He turned his face from her as far as he could while still keeping his eyes on the interstate stretching before them.

Amanda needed him to believe her, but how could she erase years' worth of negativity?

She unfastened her seat belt, which drew his attention back to her.

"What are you doing?" he asked.

She shifted to kneel in her seat and leaned across the car until her lips were an inch from his ear. She held onto the back of his seat with one hand. The other hand slid across his chest to rest against his pounding heart.

"I know you're not an idiot," she whispered to him. "I know it, because I could never care so deeply about an idiot."

His heart thudded harder and faster against her palm.

"And I do," she whispered. "I care about you, Jacob. I don't ever want to hear you refer to yourself as stupid again or believe what my bitch of a sister says about you. You're brilliant and talented and warm and generous." She brushed a kiss against his jaw, and his free hand moved to press her palm more firmly into his chest.

"Aunt Mander, put on your seat belt!" Julie yelled from the back seat. "That's dangerous."

"Listen to your niece," Jacob said, his voice tight with emotion.

"Do you believe everything I said to you?"

He squeezed her hand, and his mouth twisted into a crooked smile. "I'm pretty thick headed. I think you'll have to tell me more than once."

"Aunt Mander, *please!*" The terror in Julie's voice was not fabricated.

Amanda shifted to sit back in her seat and fastened her seat belt. "I'm safe now," she said to Julie.

"If you need to hug my daddy, do it later," she said. "If we got in a wreck, you would die."

"You heard the child," Jacob said with a soft chuckle and a toe-curling smile. "Hug me later."

Amanda planned to do a lot more than hug him.

CHAPTER NINE

SOMEWHERE ALONG THE PATH between the warthogs and the elephants, Jacob purposely stepped on the back of Amanda's shoe. She stumbled forward, hands flying out to catch her balance. He grabbed her around the waist and pulled her up against him—belly to belly—relishing the feel of her soft body pressed to his.

"I've got you," he said, his lips a scant inch from hers. He wanted to kiss her so badly he almost said to hell with hiding anything from Julie. "You're awfully clumsy today," he teased.

"That might have something to do with the fact that you keep tripping me."

"Who me?" He offered his most angelic smile as he slid a hand down her ass and tugged her closer.

"What if you don't catch me?"

"I'll always catch you," he promised. "I'd never let you fall."

"I've already fallen." Her happy smile seemed to brighten the green flecks in her remarkable hazel eyes as she gazed up at him.

Could life possibly get any better? The only thing he needed to feel complete was for her to actually say she loved him while he was tangled in her bare arms and legs, his cock buried deep in the slick, molten heat between her thighs. If Julie hadn't interrupted, worried about Amanda without her seat belt, he was positive Amanda would have said those three little words he longed to hear.

Julie had wandered ahead several paces. "Lephalants!" She dashed farther ahead, and Jacob released his hold on Amanda to chase after her.

"Wait for us," he called.

When he reached the observation area, Julie was already trying to climb up the short wall for a better look.

"She's huge!" she said.

"Do you want up on my shoulders?" he asked, knowing that Julie had been dying to see elephants more than any other animal. He wanted to make sure she had the best vantage and plenty of time to enjoy them.

"Yes, please." She lifted her arms and leaned toward him.

He swooped her up and deposited her on his shoulders, holding onto her ankles so she didn't topple from her perch.

"Look, Daddy! She's eating hay."

"She certainly is." His body jerked involuntarily when Amanda stepped up behind him and slid her hand up his back. He was uncomfortably aware of her and had been all day. While Julie provided commentary about everything the elephant was doing, Amanda slipped a hand under his shirt to touch his bare skin. He squirmed and dropped his gaze to give her a look of warning. He did not want to become visibly aroused, and being around Amanda made it difficult to keep his shorts from tenting. She offered him a devilish grin and leaned closer to playfully nip the back of his arm.

"Are you almost ready to go home?" he asked Julie hoarsely. Please, he added silently. As wonderful a time as he was having being out and about in public with his two favorite ladies, he was very much looking forward to putting Julie to bed for a full night sleep so he could take her aunt to *his* bed and get no sleep at all.

"I want to see a kangaroo," Julie said, "but I like this lephalant. Where is her friends and family?"

"Beats me," Jacob said. "Maybe they're inside the elephant house."

Amanda read the story of Lucky the elephant from a nearby sign.

"So she's all alone?" Julie asked tremulously.

"She likes to be alone," Amanda said.

"I will be her friend," Julie said. "Hi, Lucky!" she called to the elephant, which took a step backward and swayed her massive trunk.

"She hears me," Julie insisted.

A woman with a pair of boys near Julie's age entered the observation area. Both boys climbed to stand on a ledge so they could get a better look into the exhibit.

"Put me down," Julie said. "I want to stand by myself."

Jacob lifted her over his head and set her on the ledge by the two boys. She smoothed her blond curls with both hands and said to the bigger of the two, "My name's Julie, what's yours?"

The boys stared at her as if she were an angel that had fallen from the sky. Jacob cringed as his brain automatically fast-forwarded ten years. There was no doubt she'd grow to be a stunner like her mother. Should he lock her in a tower guarded by a fire-breathing dragon *now* or wait until she hit puberty?

"She's already a little flirt," Amanda said with a chuckle.

Jacob shook his head in denial. "She's just saying hello." Though it wasn't lost on him that both boys were following her and mimicking her motions as if driven by instinct.

"She's adorable," the mother of the boys said. "How old?"

"Just turned four," Jacob said.

"She looks so much like you," she said to Amanda. "I'm still holding out for a daughter to spoil."

"Oh," Amanda said, "she's not mine. I'm just her crazy aunt." She smiled and patted her chest.

The woman glanced at Jacob. "You're so good with her, I thought for sure you were her father."

"Guilty as charged," Jacob said.

The woman glanced from Jacob to Amanda and back again. Based on her expression, he guessed she'd seen Amanda copping a feel earlier.

"Julie's mother and I are divorced," Jacob said, not that it was any of her business, but he didn't like the judgmental way she was looking at Amanda.

"I'm sorry to hear that. Jeffrey, Mitchell, let's go see the rhinoceros," she called to her sons who were listening in rapt attention to Julie's story about playing with the real Jojo. She used the stuffed version to demonstrate her interactions with the monkey.

"I want to see a monkey, Mama," the smaller boy said. "Julie got to hold one."

"That was at a different zoo," Amanda said helpfully. "In Austin."

"We're not driving all the way to Austin," she said as she ushered her sons away.

"Bye, Julie!" They both waved until they were out of sight.

"Daddy," Julie said, a slight pout on her sweet face. She stared at the ground and toed a pebble with the tip of her tennis shoe.

"Yeah, princess?"

"I want a little brother."

"Oh." That was not what he'd been expecting her to request. "I'll get right on that." Jacob glanced at Amanda and grinned. Her eyes widened and her face went white. She shook her head even as he imagined her pregnant with his son growing inside her.

"Can I have two baby brothers?" Julie asked, holding up two fingers.

"Maybe someday," Jacob said.

He lifted her back onto his shoulders and continued down the path, looking for signs pointing to kangaroos.

"Why do you want brothers and not sisters?" Amanda asked.

"I don't want to share my princess castle."

Amanda laughed. "You share it with me."

"But you won't break it. My friend Courtney has a little sister. She breaks everything and she cries all the time."

"I think most babies break things and cry," Jacob said.

"Did I do that?" Julie asked, planting her hands on the top of his head and shifting forward to look down at him.

"You were a perfect baby," Jacob said, giving her ankles a reassuring squeeze.

Amanda snorted. "How soon he forgets. I don't think you slept once for the first six weeks of your life, Julie. All you did was cry and poop."

Julie sniggered. "Was it stinky?"

"The stinkiest baby poo ever," Amanda assured her.

Jacob had forgotten. He'd been on tour when Julie had been born and had missed out on most of her first weeks. He did remember Tina complaining about his absence and accusing him of sleeping with other women. He wondered how different things would have turned out if he'd called off the rest of the tour to be with his wife and newborn that summer. Would they still be married?

He reached over and wrapped an arm around Amanda's shoulders, and for once, she didn't push him away.

"Why don't you have any kids, Aunt Mander?" Julie asked.

"I haven't got a husband," Amanda said.

"Yet," Jacob said, tugging her closer to his side.

"Yet," Amanda echoed.

"I know who you can marry," Julie said.

Jacob's heart warmed as he anticipated Julie saying Amanda should marry him.

"Who's that?" Amanda asked, looking above Jacob's head at her niece.

Julie snorted on a laugh. "SpongeBob."

"SpongeBob?" Amanda shook her head. "He's nice and all, but he's a little too square for my tastes." She made a square shape with her thumbs and index fingers and peered at Julie through the opening.

"Who do you want to marry Aunt Mander? A prince? I want to marry a prince."

Amanda shrugged. "I don't know. I think princes are in short supply these days."

"How about a rock star?" Jacob asked.

"Ooh, rock stars are cool," Julie said. "I think Daddy knows some of those guys."

Jacob bit his lip so he wouldn't laugh. Just how much hinting did he need to do here to get his daughter onboard with his plan to make her aunt a permanent fixture in their lives?

"I've heard relationships with rock stars never last," Amanda said. She looked up at him, the golden sunshine dancing through her hair and a question in her hazel eyes.

"Depends on the rock star," he said, leaning closer to Amanda. He wanted to kiss her so badly, he could already taste her sweet lips.

"Giraffe!" Julie yelled, startling him into backing away.

He'd just have to save all of Amanda's kisses for later.

He hoped her lips were well rested.

CHAPTER TEN

THEY STOPPED for dinner on the way home, so by the time they reached Jacob's house, the sun was already setting, casting an orange glow on the world. Amanda couldn't remember a day she'd enjoyed so much. She always loved spending time with her sweet niece, and the kid's father wasn't half bad either. As she retrieved Julie's bag, and—after only a second of consideration—her own, she watched the two walk hand in hand to the front door.

"Daddy, can we have a tea party now?" Julie asked.

"I'm tired, baby," he said as he released Julie's hand and fit his key into the lock. "Can I take a rain check?"

Julie glanced up at the sky. "Okay, I'm checking, and I don't see no rain clouds."

Amanda chuckled at Julie's literal rain check.

"Can we do a tea party tomorrow?" Jacob rubbed at one eye beneath his sunglasses.

Julie had her new stuffed monkey under one arm and her new stuffed elephant under the other. "Jojo and Lucky need to meet their new friends before bed. So we need to have a tea party tonight. Would you like it if you had to sleep with strangers?"

Jacob laughed, and Amanda wondered just how many strangers the man had slept with. "I guess I can't argue with that logic."

He opened the door and turned off the alarm. "You go set it up and come get me when you're ready."

Julie hopped through the foyer and down the hall singing, "I'm a little roo. I'm a little roo."

Jacob turned to Amanda, who'd entered the house behind them with a bag slung over each shoulder.

"I could have helped you with that," he said, reaching for one of the bags.

"I'm fine," she assured him. "They're not heavy." Not after they'd devoured every smidge of food that had been packed in Julie's bag. "Should I put my bag in your bedroom?"

"You're staying the night?" he asked, cocking his head to one side.

She couldn't tell if he was teasing, because he was still wearing his damned sunglasses.

"If you'd rather I go—"

His arms were around her and his mouth against hers before she could complete the thought. She dropped both bags to the ground with successive thuds before lifting her arms to draw him closer. His strength, his heat, and his heady scent engulfed her, pulling her under. She was drowning in him and didn't want to be rescued.

"God, I want you," he growled, his fervent kisses moving to her jaw and throat. His fingers tangled in her hair, tugging her head back as he nibbled his way to her collarbone. "Do you have any idea how hard it is to behave myself when I'm around you all day?"

"Yes," she whispered, tilting her head to give him better access to the flesh he was already igniting with lips and tongue and teeth.

Small footsteps echoed off the tiles in the hallway. Jacob tensed. "Fuck," he murmured against her throat before slowly pulling away.

"Do you have something in your eye again, Aunt Mander?" Julie asked.

Yeah, tears of frustration.

"All better now," Amanda said tersely. "Thanks to your daddy."

"The tea party is ready," Julie said.

"I'll be right there," Jacob said, still facing Amanda. "I need to go to the bathroom first."

Amanda offered him a puzzled look, but he was too busy taking deep breaths to sate her curiosity.

"Are you coming to the tea party, Aunt Mander?"

Amanda realized Jacob's predicament was located in his shorts, and while she was still as hot for him as he obviously was for her, at least her excitement wasn't so blatantly obvious.

"Wouldn't miss it," Amanda said, stepping around Jacob and taking Julie's hand to lead her back to her room while Jacob regained control. They were going to have to keep a more appropriate distance from each other until they could be alone.

Julie showed Amanda where to sit on the floor next to a child-sized wooden table. The small chairs were overflowing with various stuffed animals and dolls. In the seat of honor—Julie's small white rocking chair—sat her two newest friends, Jojo and Lucky.

"They're already best friends," Julie explained.

"I can see that. What kind of tea are we having?" Amanda reached for a tiny porcelain cup decorated with pink rose buds.

"The good kind," Julie said.

"Ah," Amanda said. "My favorite."

"What's taking Daddy so long?" When Julie headed for the door, Amanda caught her arm and drew her into her lap for a vigorous tickle.

"I think he needs some privacy," Amanda said.

"Oh. I don't want to start without him."

"Did you have fun today?" Amanda asked, hoping to distract her from going in search of her father.

"Oh yes! When I grow up, can I work at the zoo and be a singer too?"

Lost in Julie's wide blue eyes, Amanda stroked her silky hair and smiled at her. "You can be whatever you want to be."

"And I want to be a princess," Julie said.

"You're already my princess," Jacob said from the doorway.

Julie lit up like a Griswold Christmas light display and squirmed off Amanda's lap. She soon had her father seated on the floor next to Amanda and introduced everyone at the table—real and imaginary—to the newest additions to her eclectic menagerie.

"I do think she needs a little brother," Jacob whispered to Amanda.

Amanda's head swiveled in his direction, and she choked on her imaginary tea. "Let's not get ahead of ourselves."

"There's only one way that's going to happen," he said.

She lifted inquisitive eyebrows at him.

"Stop being so terrific. You're putting strange thoughts in my head."

"Apparently," she said.

Telling her he loved her that morning had progressed to hints of marriage and blatant requests for more children. He was obviously delirious. Hopefully once he got laid, he'd come back to his senses. Amanda wasn't prepared to let her sister know she saw him even casually. If she started birthing Jacob's babies, Amanda was pretty sure Tina would put two and two together.

But he did make beautiful babies and he was a spectacular father. He was also a rock star. She tended to forget about that part of his life when they were outside the arena. There was no way that her boring self would keep his attention for long. Still, she wasn't going to let that knowledge stop her from enjoying her time with him while she had him.

Julie yawned sleepily and started to sway. Amanda snuck a peek at her cellphone, delighted to see it was the tyke's bedtime.

"Which pajamas do you want to wear?" Jacob asked, groaning as he staggered to his feet from the hard floor.

Amanda felt a bit intrusive as she watched him prepare Julie for bed. He helped her into her nightgown—Julie didn't even protest that she was a big girl and could do it herself—and combed her hair while she brushed her teeth. Once she was tucked into bed with her all of her tea party guests, Amanda leaned over her to kiss her goodnight.

"Are you going home now?" Julie asked with another sleepy yawn.

"I'm going to stay the night so I can go swimming with you tomorrow. I hope that's okay."

Julie scrunched up her brow as she considered that bit of news. "I think my bed is too small for you."

Amanda chuckled. "That's okay. I'll sleep on the sofa."

"My daddy has a big bed," she said. "You can sleep with him."

Gladly, Amanda thought. "Don't worry, I'll find a good place to sleep. Good night, Julie Bean."

"Can you read me a story, Daddy?" Julie asked.

Jacob eyed the bookshelf near the bed as if it were swarming with cockroaches. "Um . . ." he murmured. "How about I sing to you instead?"

Julie smiled sleepily. "Sing the angel song."

Amanda stepped outside the room but leaned against the wall just outside the door and closed her eyes, listening to Jacob's smooth, soothing voice as he sang his little girl to sleep. The sound made her heart swell with love. What would her life be like if he became a permanent fixture in it?

Heaven. It would be heaven.

Yet she couldn't let herself think that way. If she got too attached, she would be destroyed when they ultimately parted ways.

But maybe it was okay to imagine a future with Jacob in it. A little dreaming couldn't hurt.

Jacob's voice softened on the next chorus and softened yet again on the next. Amanda peeked into the room to find him sitting on the edge of Julie's bed, stroking her hair gently as he sang to her. Julie's eyes were closed and her face had gone slack. The tender smile on Jacob's face and the love in his expression melted Amanda's heart.

Amanda's own father had always been a minor player in her life. He'd doted on Tina, as all men did. Amanda had a much closer relationship with her mother. Seeing Jacob with Julie made her ache for the kind of blind devotion a father had for his little girl. Julie would probably never realize how lucky she was to have this man's heart in the palm of her tiny hand. Amanda hoped Julie didn't mind sharing a bit of it.

Jacob finished the song on a whisper, and his hand went still. He waited for a moment, watching Julie for signs of wakefulness. He carefully stood, disturbing her mattress as little as possible as he moved away. He shut off her lamp, which looked a lot like the castle at Disneyland, and tiptoed out of her room.

Amanda smiled at him and said, "I think—" But Jacob's finger against her lips silenced her.

He took her arm and led her to his room, not releasing her until the latch clicked shut behind them and he'd locked the door.

"Whatever you do, don't wake her up," Jacob said.

"Sorry," she whispered.

"I'm in desperate need of some adult time."

Amanda released a breathless laugh. "I'm with you on that."

He tugged off her clothes while she pulled his off. They were mostly naked when his patience reached its end and he lifted her off the floor to carry her to the bed. They collapsed on the mattress, a tangle of arms and legs. He shattered her with deep passionate kisses while he used hurried motions to cover his length with latex. Amanda cried out in bliss when he filled her. He took her hard and fast, his breaths excited and ragged against her ear. She dug her nails into his shoulders and hung on as he brought her closer and closer to the brink of release. Unexpectedly, he called out, clinging to her hips with strong fingers as he buried himself so deeply, it stole her breath. And then he shuddered against her as he let go.

She couldn't believe he'd finished so fast. He usually outlasted her several times over.

"Sorry," he murmured against her jaw, his sweat-slick belly bumping against hers with each of his labored breaths. "I probably should have rubbed that one out in the shower."

She hugged him close and snuggled into his neck. "I'm glad you rubbed it out in me."

He chuckled and went slack in her arms, pressing her into the mattress. "Just let me catch my breath and I'll make it up to you."

She had absolutely no doubt that he would, but lying beneath him, with his breath in her ear and his heart thudding so hard in his chest she could feel it in her breast, meant more to her than she could express. She was pretty sure what she felt for Jacob was love, but she was in no way prepared to tell him she felt so strongly. He was already much too close to her, and he didn't realize that loving her could destroy an important part of his life.

But she had no time to fret. His touch soon chased every troubled thought from her head until nothing mattered but the two of them, their bodies connecting in a way she wished was someday possible for every facet of their lives.

CHAPTER ELEVEN

JACOB SMEARED extra waterproof sunscreen on the bridge of Julie's nose. He couldn't help but smile when she scowled at him and wiped at the goop dripping from the tip.

"Don't want you to get burned," he said, splattering another glob on her nose.

"Can I get in the water now?" Julie asked, peering out through the sliding patio door at the inviting blue pool in the backyard.

"Wait for your aunt. She's putting on her swimsuit." Thank you, God.

"I can swim," she said, rubbing the excess sunscreen off her nose again. "I take lessons and everything."

"I know you can. Amanda should be out any minute."

Jacob heard a throat clearing and turned his head to smile at Amanda. The smile dropped along with his jaw as his gaze traveled up her legs. The well-muscled curves seemed to go on for miles, accentuated by the high cut of her tiny orange bikini bottoms. He sucked drool back into his mouth as his stare moved up her flat belly to the beguiling cleavage spilling from the cups of her bikini top. His heart was thudding so hard by the time his eyes met hers that he feared it might burst.

He patted Julie on the back. "Go sit by the pool," he said, rising from his crouched position to his full height. "I need to ask your aunt something."

"Can I jump in?"

"Not until we're out there with you. Go sit and don't move."

"But I'm a big girl."

"Julie," he said sharply.

"Fine," she grumbled, and her bare feet slapped against the decking as she headed out the door and toward the water.

Jacob watched to make sure Julie sat outside the pool and then took the two steps that separated him from Amanda and pulled her against him. His mouth claimed hers as he filled his hands with her scrumptious ass and lifted her slightly so he could press his suddenly attentive cock into the beckoning crevice between her thighs. How long had it been since he'd been buried inside her? An hour? Two? Jesus, this woman had him out of his head.

Would he ever get enough of her? He hoped not.

"After Julie goes home," Amanda whispered in his ear, "I want to go swimming with you alone and mysteriously lose my swimsuit bottoms."

"And I mysteriously want my—"

A loud splash made his heart skip a beat. He pulled away from Amanda and rushed around the corner to the tiled decking around the pool. Julie was not where he'd left her. Ripples marred the surface of the water at the deep end of the pool.

"Julie!" he yelled before diving into the water and swimming to the bottom. Chlorine stung his eyes as he searched the pool. He located Julie sitting calmly on the bottom of the pool, bubbles blossoming from her nose and an impish smile on her face. He didn't know whether to be terrified or angry. Admittedly, he was both. He grabbed Julie by the upper arms and kicked off the bottom of the pool, launching them upward until their heads surfaced.

"Oh, thank God," Amanda said from beside the pool.

"I can hold my breath for a really long time," Julie said, beaming with pride.

"Don't you ever, *ever* jump into the pool when I'm not with you!" Jacob shouted, his heart thundering so hard in his chest that his ears were ringing.

"It's okay, Daddy. I'm a big girl."

"It's not okay, Julie," he said, his voice still booming. He didn't know the best way to get his point across. He'd never yelled at her before, and he refused to spank her. He knew how much she hated time out, but this lesson needed to stick. "You could have drowned." He hauled her to the side of the pool and sat her on the edge. "If you can't do what I say and stay out of the water until I tell you it's okay to get in, then you can't go swimming."

"But, Daddy . . ." Her tiny lips pursed, and her eyes filled with tears. His thudding heart twisted at the look of devastation on her face.

"Do you understand why I'm mad at you?"

Her tears began to fall, and he could see how much his words affected her by the way her face twisted. "You're mad at me?" she asked brokenly.

And boy was it hard to cling to that anger when all he wanted to do was hug her and tell her everything was all right. She looked like her entire world was crumbling at her tiny feet.

"I'm very mad at you, Julie. You scared me. I thought you were hurt."

"I'm sorry, Daddy." She held out her arms for a hug, but he wasn't going to let her off the hook that easily, no matter how much he wanted to.

"You're in time out."

Her face fell. "I don't want to be in time out," she yelled at him.

"Go sit on that chair," he said, pointing at a nearby lounge chair that sat low to the ground. She should be able to climb into it without his assistance. He really hoped he didn't have to bodily drag her to the chair and make her sit in it.

"But, Daddy, I won't do it no more. I promise." She touched his shoulder, the look on her face so sincere that he almost laughed.

"You won't do what anymore?" he asked.

"Go swimming by myself."

"I'm glad. Now go sit in time out so you don't forget."

She wailed a protest as she climbed to her feet and ran to the chair, flopping herself into it with dramatic flair. "I hate time out!" she screamed.

"Four minutes," Amanda said, handing Julie a kitchen timer.

"Four minutes?" Julie shouted. "I only have to do it for three minutes!"

"You had a birthday, remember?" Amanda said. "You're four—a big girl—so that means time out is now four minutes."

Julie frowned at her aunt, but didn't argue. The timer beeped as Julie started the countdown and sniffled miserably. Apparently, this was not a new punishment to her even if it was the first time Jacob had been forced to use it. And why did he feel so bad for yelling at her and putting her in time out? She needed to be punished so she learned an important lesson.

Amanda slid into the water beside Jacob and patted his shoulder. "You handled that well," she said quietly.

He flashed her a brief smile for the vote of confidence. "I

shouldn't have yelled."

"She needed to see how upset her actions made you. You don't get cross with her often, so when you do, it has a big impact on her."

"It breaks my heart when she cries."

She kissed his cheek and whispered in his ear, "Your tenderness with Julie is what I like most about you."

"Hmm," he said and shrugged. "I thought it was the tight leather pants."

Amanda chuckled and slid a hand down his back, gripping his ass beneath the surface of the water. "Maybe I should reevaluate my priorities," she murmured near his ear.

"Three minutes!" Julie announced. She was watching the countdown on her timer as though she was about to celebrate the arrival of a new millennium, which gave him the opportunity to reciprocate Amanda's exploration. Only *he* slipped his fingers beneath the seat of her bikini. His hand gripped the curve of her ass and then shifted until his fingertip breached her tight back entrance.

Amanda's mouth dropped open and she pulled away. "Naughty," she hissed at him.

"Are you going to put me in time out?" he asked quietly, not even trying to conceal his ornery smirk.

"Your punishment shall be slow and torturous," she promised. Her hand slid into the front of his trunks, but stopped short of touching him where he most wanted her slow, torturous touch. "But it will have to wait until after lunch."

She didn't need to say why. That was Julie's naptime. And Jacob planned to exhaust the poor child with swimming and then fill her up with plenty of food so she'd sleep soundly.

"Two minutes," Julie said, still staring down at the timer, but getting a bit squirmy in her seat.

"For as much as she protests, she doesn't seem too upset to be in time out," Jacob said, not feeling quite so bad about making her sit there.

"It's the timer," Amanda says. "If she has something to focus on, she doesn't scream bloody murder the entire time and she knows exactly how much time she has left."

By the time the gadget beeped, Julie had stopped sniffling and fidgeting. "Can I come swimming now?" she called from her chair.

"You'd better," Jacob said. "Your Aunt Mander is pretty boring. All she does is float on her back." And he was doing a piss poor job of not ogling the shiny wet globes of her cleavage peeking above the surface of the water. Her orange swimsuit could not be ignored.

Amanda sent a half-assed spray of water in his direction for his insult. "I'm relaxing," she said.

"Watch me jump, Daddy!"

He turned just in time to catch the splash from Julie's rather impressive cannonball directly in his face.

Amanda laughed as he wiped the water from his eyes, and then he held out his arm for Julie to hold onto as she surfaced and treaded water.

"You got him, Julie Bean!"

"That was a huge splash," he said to Julie's smiling face. "My turn."

Julie swam over to Amanda as Jacob climbed out of the pool. Julie was still mostly doggie paddling, but she added a few breaststrokes to expedite her journey through the water. She took to water the same way Jacob had as a child and somehow that little connection between them made him proud.

"Are you ready for a tidal wave?" he asked as he climbed the diving board's ladder at the deep end of the pool.

"Can I do the diving board, Daddy?" Julie asked.

"When you're older," he promised. He'd love to teach her to dive, but not until he got past the fear of her getting hurt. Which would likely be never.

When he was sure his two guests were out of harm's way at the far end of the pool, he took a brisk step toward the end of the board, feeling it dip beneath his weight. At just the right instant, he used the momentum of the upward swing of the spring board to push himself into the air. He did a front summersault in midair—yeah, he was totally showing off for the ladies—and extended his body to enter the water with a quiet slosh. He surfaced to cheers and a vigorous round of applause.

"That was an awesome flip," Julie said. "But you only made a tiny splash."

"Guess I need more practice," he said with a soft chuckle. He showed Julie how to dive from the side of the pool. She dove in head first, climbed the ladder, hurried around to the edge of the pool and dove again. He couldn't believe how quickly she caught on or that she wasn't exhausted yet.

"Maybe I should get her a diving coach," Jacob said to Amanda.

"I think you've got yourself a little Olympian there," Amanda said, still floating lazily on her back. He mostly used the pool for exercise, but was starting to think Amanda had the right idea. "Wish I had half her energy."

"Can I do a flip this time?" Julie asked, jumping up and down in the puddle she'd made on the decking.

"You need the diving board to do that."

She eyed the diving board without a shred of fear in her gaze.

"And if you try to climb that thing and jump off without permission, you'll be in time out for four *years*," he threatened.

"I wish I was big," she said glumly.

And he wished she would stay this size forever.

To divert her attention from the diving board, Jacob collected pool toys from the deck box. Amanda joined their games, though she really sucked at diving for batons. She kept grabbing Julie's ankle instead. Julie giggled every time. They had sword fights with pool noodles and contests to see who could hold their breath underwater the longest. By the time Julie said, "I'm hungry," a couple of hours later, Jacob was running low on fuel and energy. Who would have thought a tiny little girl could completely wear out two adults?

"I'll start the grill," he said and pulled himself out of the pool with shaky arms.

While he got lunch cooking, Amanda started a rousing new game of Who Can Float on Her Back the Longest without Sinking. He supposed it was her version of the Quiet Game. Julie didn't have flotation devices built into her chest yet—and thank God for that—so the game was a real challenge for her and kept her well occupied.

"Do you want a hamburger?" Jacob called from behind the grill. "Or I can cook some brats?"

"I'm not a brat," Julie assured him. "Don't cook me."

Jacob grinned and shook his head. "I'm talking about a brat*wurst*."

"What's worse than a brat?" Julie looked to Amanda for direction, but Amanda was caught in a fit of giggles.

"This," Jacob said, holding up a bratwurst for Julie to see.

"Oh, a fat hotdog," she said and crinkled up her nose. "I don't like those kind."

"One hamburger for Julie," he said. He flopped a raw patty onto the grill. It hissed satisfyingly. "Amanda?"

"Would you think I'm a pig if I asked for one of each?"

"You'll get fat, Aunt Mander."

"There are worse things," Amanda said, and Jacob flopped a couple more burgers and several brats onto the grill. With all the physical activity they'd been getting, he doubted a few extra calories would hurt either of them.

"Mommy says princesses can't be fat, so I can't eat junk food if I want to be a princess when I grow up."

Jacob supposed such a claim would be a good deterrent from unhealthy eating. Of course, it might instead lead to a lifelong harmful relationship with food.

"Are you sure you want to be a princess?" Amanda asked. "Sounds like a lot of rules to me."

"I'm not sure she's being exposed to the right kind of role models," Jacob commented as he closed the grill lid. "Why are all the female characters in Disney movies princesses? Gives a girl a skewed perception of romance and the real world, doesn't it?"

Jacob started when a wet hand touched the small of his back. Lost in his musings, he hadn't heard Amanda get out of the pool. "Gives a girl something to dream about."

"Is that what you dreamed about?" he asked. "Having some girly prince rescue you?"

"And live out my life in a castle, wearing beautiful gowns, and attending balls every night?"

"And singing!" Julie said. "All princesses sing."

Jacob turned to look at her. "Is that why you want to be a princess? So you can sing?"

She smiled, her eyes lighting up with excitement. "I love singing." She stopped beside him to stare up at him worshipfully, her pruned fingers supporting her chin.

Another way she was just like him. Well, except for the wanting to be a princess thing. He cupped the back of her head and hugged her against his hip. "I think you need to be exposed to other ways girls can be singers."

"Daddy, your singing place is too loud." She titled her head back and cringed, as if she'd insulted him.

"My singing place *is* loud," he said agreeably and glanced at Amanda for help.

"There's opera," Amanda said.

Jacob produced a breathless laugh. "Loudest singers on the planet. They don't even use sound equipment."

"What's opera?" Julie asked.

"Singing in Italian."

"I don't know Italian," Julie assured him. "Is there singing in Spanish? I like learning Spanish on *Dora*."

"There's singing in every language, baby." He stroked her hair, trying to think up ways to expose Julie to more than singing princesses. He wished he had more time to spend with her than every other weekend.

"We could take her to the theater," Amanda suggested. "A musical."

The thing he liked most about that suggestion was the "we" part.

"Is there a thing with singing and swimming and hugging animals and wearing crowns?" Julie asked, touching her hair where she'd wear a gilded crown. Her imagination was obviously running wild.

Jacob tapped her nose. "Not that I know of, but you can do anything you set your mind to."

"Tina will never forgive you if she joins a circus," Amanda said with a laugh.

"The Little Mermaid," Julie said, jumping up and down when the answer came to her. Yet her face fell almost right away. "But Ariel hugs fish. I don't think I'd like to hug fish. They're smelly."

And they were back to Disney princesses. "This kid needs to get out," he said to Amanda, who smiled in agreement.

Lunch started with the excited chatter of Julie's ideas for her swimming and singing animal show—a crown would be involved, of course—but as her belly filled, her enthusiasm began to wane and soon she was nodding off in her plate. Within a few minutes, she slumped back in her chair midchew.

"Julie," Jacob said quietly, "finish what's in your mouth." He didn't want her to choke while she slept.

Eyes shooting open, she jerked upright in the chair, chewing vigorously. An instant later she was asleep again—her tiny elbow on the table supporting her tiny chin on her tiny hand. Jacob stood and scooped her into his arms. She lazily opened her eyes.

"Are you finished eating?" he asked.

She swallowed the bite in her mouth and nodded. He snuggled her against his chest, and she pressed her face into his shoulder. Her swimsuit had dried while they ate, so he didn't bother changing her out of it. He entered the house and tucked her into her bed for a much deserved nap.

He returned to the outdoor dining table to find Amanda had deserted her lunch. He located her in the pool.

She was floating on her back in the water again, but this time she was topless.

CHAPTER TWELVE

AMANDA HID a self-satisfied grin when Jacob entered the pool with a loud splash. She figured removing her top would instantly put him in the mood, and for that, she was thankful. Watching that man wander around in nothing but swim trunks all morning had been hell on her self-control.

When he surfaced between her legs and latched on to her mound right through her bikini bottoms, Amanda's head went under and she sucked in a mouthful of water. She flapped her arms to push her head above the surface and forced the water out of her mouth before she took a deep breath.

"You're going to drown me," she said, reaching out until she touched the top of his head with one hand.

"I'd rather make you come," he said. He started towing her through the water toward the edge of the pool.

She'd rather he did that as well. Hard cement dug into her shoulders when she leaned back against the pool edge and Jacob grabbed her ass to lift her pussy to his mouth. She watched him with wide eyes as he blew hot breaths through her wet suit bottoms and then sucked water up through her seam before forcing it back down in a warm gush over her clit. She shuddered, surprised by how good a little water could make her feel.

Jacob's tongue pressed fabric into her aching center, driving her mad with need. She wanted his tongue inside her, licking her in deep, wide arcs. She reached for him, but felt herself slipping into the water, and had to cling to the pool edge instead, giving the man free rein over everything between her legs. His fingers slid beneath her suit, touching bare skin. He stroked her sensitive lips while drawing water through her bikini bottoms and into his mouth.

She gasped when the tip of his finger slipped inside her. "Take them off," she pleaded. "I want your tongue inside me."

He bit into the fabric and tugged. The action did little to relieve her of her bikini bottoms, but the excitement of it had her core clenching with need.

His lips and tongue and teeth worked against her swollen flesh through the thick fabric, and the sensation drove her insane. She grabbed the strings tied into neat bows at both hips and tugged them loose. This time when he grabbed the bikini bottoms with his teeth and yanked, the fabric tore free. The small scrap of orange material floated along the surface of the water beside her.

"In a hurry?" he asked with a soft chuckle.

He had no idea. Taking a deep breath, she pushed off the wall and sank to her knees before him, her head disappearing under the water. Chlorine stung her eyes as she searched for the object she was after. She'd never been good at collecting items from the bottom of the pool, but she had a sturdy guidepost to help her find her way this time. She tugged at the bright red trunks Jacob wore until they slipped down his slim hips. His cock sprang free, rigid and proud, but she'd already run out of air, so she had to surface.

Water sprayed from her lips as she took greedy gulps of air.

"Find what you were looking for?" he asked.

She smiled her naughtiest smile and nodded before taking another deep breath and going down for a second look. Afraid she'd accidentally draw water into her lungs if she tried to suck him off, she settled for stroking his length between both hands and licking the swollen tip. When she surfaced the second time, his eyes were glazed with passion.

"I'd try to suck—"

Her words ended in a gasp of surprise when without warning he spun her around, grabbed her by the hips, and lowered her onto his cock. She reached between her legs to help him find her opening, then gasped as he struggled to enter her. The water kept washing away her natural lubrication, so he could only claim her an inch at a time. She grabbed the edge of the pool and straightened her arms to give him an anchor to push against. When he was finally buried inside her, he moved his hands from her hips to her breasts and pressed his face into the center of her back.

"I love you," he whispered. "Amanda."

Tears sprang to her eyes. She loved him too. She knew she did. But instead of saying the words, she rocked her hips impatiently, working his cock in and out of her body as best she could.

"You're still not going to say it?" he asked, kissing her bare shoulder. "What are you afraid of?"

"Julie waking up from her nap and catching us like this."

"We'll just tell her you have something in your eye." He chuckled.

"And you're assisting me by standing behind me and grabbing my tits?"

"I'm talented that way," he said.

Her attempt to distract him worked. His hips began to pump, driving his cock deep inside her before withdrawing. She bent her knees, hooked her feet together behind him, and let him carry the rhythm. His gentle kisses along her spine intensified her pleasure, and the rhythmic squeezing of her nipples made her pussy tighten around his driving cock. She soon forgot where they were entirely. Only the building excitement of being joined with him—two bodies as one—mattered. Within moments she was spiraling out of control, her hand diving beneath the water to grab her pussy and squeeze her mound as the intensity of the waves of pleasure ripping through her demanded to be contained.

"As much as I want to come inside you . . ." Jacob murmured against her shoulder before he pulled out. She felt the warm bursts of his cum against her ass as he groaned into her hair.

Amanda's post-orgasm daze lifted quickly when she realized what had happened. "Shit, Jacob! You weren't wearing a condom?"

"You had to know that," he said. "You're the one who forced me inside you that way."

It wasn't a lie. She had jerked his trunks down, taken his bare cock in her hand, and pressed it inside her. She obviously hadn't been thinking clearly.

"I pulled out in time," he said, rubbing his still hard cock against her ass. "And being inside you felt amazing. Don't make me regret it."

"You'll regret it if I get pregnant," she said.

"I won't," he whispered, pressing tender kisses along her shoulder. He brushed her hair aside and continued up her throat, his mouth igniting a trail of pleasure toward her ear. "I'd be the happiest man on earth."

What? Her brain struggled mightily with his claim. First he said he loved her and now he was thinking that making babies with her was a good idea? Was he out of his fucking mind?

"Daddy!" Julie called from inside the house. "Where are you? I had an accident in my bed."

"I'll be right there, princess," he said. He adjusted his trunks to leave the pool. "Accidents happen."

Amanda turned and slumped against the pool wall, her bare breasts concealed beneath the sparkling blue water and watched him—dripping wet and more gorgeous with every breath—enter the house. When he loved someone, this man was all in. No reservations. No fear. But was Amanda ready to plan a future with Jacob when she couldn't imagine telling her sister that she even *talked* to him?

"Oh, Jacob," she whispered. "How will this ever work?"

CHAPTER THIRTEEN

JACOB HANDED Julie her stuffed monkey and set her bag on the floorboard of the SUV. He squatted down in front of her next to her mother's car and stroked her silky hair, her smooth cheek. "I'll call you this week when I can."

"Okay, Daddy. I know you'll be singing a lot." Their schedules never seemed to mesh. When he was bored on the bus or in his hotel room, Julie was busy with school and activities. When she had free time in the evenings and before bed, Jacob was preparing for shows, dealing with bullshit, and entertaining the fans.

Julie kissed him with sticky smacking lips and gave him a huge hug before climbing into the back seat of her mother's SUV.

"Did you have fun with Daddy?" Tina asked as she fastened Julie into her booster seat.

"Oh yes. We went to Aunt Mander's zoo and then the other zoo that has just one lephalant and we had a tea party and Daddy singed me a song and then I went swimming and—"

"That's nice," Tina said as she shut the car door.

"Did you want me to swing by your house to pick her up weekend after next?" Jacob asked. He missed the kid already, and she was only a few feet away.

"I'll just drop her off," Tina said with an annoyed huff. "Can't seem to rely on anyone but myself."

Jacob bit his tongue so he didn't remind her that he had offered to pick up Julie, but she had refused because she hadn't wanted to "deal with him."

"What time?" Jacob asked.

Tina shrugged. "Whenever I get around to it. You'll wait."

He would wait, but it grated on his last nerve that Tina would consciously use that fact just to annoy him. Why couldn't she be more reasonable, like her sister? How could two people with such similar genetic makeup, who'd been raised in the same household, be so very different?

Tina touched his arm and leaned closer. So close, he caught the familiar scent of her perfume. He fought the urge to step back. A year ago, he might have considered this an opening to get close to her, to win her back. But now? Now he didn't want to win her back. If not for Julie, he'd have gone out of his way to avoid his ex entirely.

"I guess I'll see you in a couple weeks," she said. "Maybe . . ." She blinked up at him with a set of beguiling blue eyes. "Maybe we can take Julie somewhere together or something."

"I don't think that's a good idea." He wondered how pissed Tina would be if he told her that Amanda was the only woman he wanted to go on outings with. He kept silent, though. Julie was sure to drop enough hints that Tina would figure their situation out very soon, and he was pretty sure Amanda would forgive a four-year-old for being unable to keep their secrets. He wasn't so sure she'd forgive him, however. He didn't have the excuse of being a child. He should know better than to intentionally stir up shit.

"Well, think about it," Tina said. Before he could say anything else, she reached up to touch his cheek with her fingertips. She stared into his eyes for a long moment before slowly backing away as if she didn't want to lose contact with his skin.

He was too stunned to do anything but gawk at her as she hurried around the SUV and climbed inside. Julie's enthusiastic wave caught his attention, and he bent his head so he could see her better and waved back. He kept waving even after the vehicle pulled away and turned out of his driveway onto the street.

What the hell had that been about? Tina had seemed almost rational. But she also acted like she wanted to forge some sort of relationship with him again. His life would be a lot more tolerable if they got along better, but he prayed she didn't think he was interested in her as something besides his baby's mommy. He didn't love her anymore, and he knew without a doubt that he'd never be able to love her again. Not after Amanda had showed him that his passion could burn just as brightly with someone who made him feel good about himself. Tina had been a beautiful trophy, and for a while it had been enough to be referred to as the guy with a hot wife, but she'd always made him feel bad about himself, as if he'd never be good enough to make her happy no matter how much he tried. Amanda was so different. She seemed to think he was just fine the way he was and that her happiness was her own responsibility and not someone else's. Even though she hadn't said she loved him yet, he believed that she did. He knew he loved her.

Jacob grinned when the woman he loved pulled into the driveway and stopped directly in front of him—missing his toes by less than a foot. Amanda climbed from the car and peeked at him over its beige top.

"Is it safe?" she whispered.

His grin turned wicked. "Depends on what you mean by safe."

Now that Julie was back with her mother, possibilities for sexual adventures with Amanda were limited only by their imaginations, vitality, and bendiness. She circled the car, and he lost all power to resist her.

He pulled her against him, whirled them both around, and pressed her against the side of the car, holding her there with his rapidly hardening cock against the beckoning warmth between her thighs. His fingers clutched at her hair as his mouth crushed hers in a devastating kiss. Her hands slid up the back of his T-shirt, nails digging into his flesh. He had a mind to fuck her right there against the car. He might even have gone that far if the sounds of a gunning engine and screeching tires stopping just short of ramming the back end of Amanda's car hadn't yanked him out of his lust-fueled daze.

"I knew you were seeing someone!" Tina shouted as she jumped out of her SUV. "I knew it. Did you fool around with your little whore in front of Julie?"

Jacob instinctively shifted Amanda behind his back to shield her from Tina's wrath. He could feel Amanda trembling as she clung to his shirt with both hands.

"Hi, Aunt Mander!" Julie called from inside the car.

Tina stopped in her tracks, her furious gaze shifting from Jacob's face to the car parked in the driveway. Her jaw dropped, and for a minute Jacob was certain her head would explode as her face turned from a shocking red to a violent purple.

"You're sleeping with my sister?" Tina blurted. "My *sister*?"

"It's none of your business," Jacob said calmly. His belly was churning itself into a massive knot of anxiety, and he was pretty sure Amanda was going to shake herself to pieces if she didn't stop trembling so hard behind him, but what he did with Amanda *wasn't* Tina's business. He refused to deny what was going on between the two of them just to make Tina happy.

Tina's arm shot out, her fingers bent into vicious claws. Jacob threw up an arm in defense, but Tina didn't grab him. She went after Amanda.

"How could you?" Tina screeched, yanking Amanda out from behind Jacob.

"Ow!" Amanda protested, throwing off Tina's hold before Jacob could intervene. "Calm down."

"I'm not going to calm down," Tina yelled. "I'm going to fucking *kill* you."

Amanda stepped back to avoid an incoming blow. Jacob didn't understand why Tina was attacking Amanda and not him. He tried to catch Tina's flailing arms to prevent her from hurting someone.

"Will you stop?" Jacob said, grabbing Tina's left wrist in an iron grip. He trapped her right arm against her side as he wrapped his arms around her from behind. She struggled against him, lifted one leg, pressed her foot against the door of Amanda's car and shoved. Jacob had to take a couple of steps to regain his balance, but he didn't release her. "Have you lost your mind?"

"How can you do this to me?" Tina railed at Amanda, who'd taken a defensive stance with her back against her car, her arms in front of her body and her hands clenched into loose fists. "You know I still love him!"

Jacob was so stunned, his grip went slack. Tina immediately launched herself toward Amanda.

"If you hit me, I *will* hit you back," Amanda warned as she slid sideways around the hood of the car. She obviously didn't want to fight, but Jacob was glad she didn't plan to take a beating lying down.

"And what do you mean you still love him?" Amanda yelled. "You hate his guts. You just don't want *me* to have him. You never want me to have anyone."

Tina shook her head, her silky blond hair dancing around her shoulders. "I only hate him because I still love him so much. I don't want to love him. But you, *you* can't have him! I'll kill you before I'll let you."

"Do I have a say in this?" Jacob asked, wondering if he still had water in his ears from swimming and was hearing everything entirely wrong. Tina loved him? She had a strange way of showing it.

"You know you're with her because you still want me," Tina said, taking another swing at Amanda, who proved to be quite good at dodging blows. Jacob wondered if the sisters had turned to physical violence in the past. "Why be with a poor substitute when you can have the real thing?"

"Actually, I have no desire to be with you at all, Tina," Jacob said. "I've been trying to get Amanda to tell you we were involved, but she was afraid you'd freak out, so we decided to keep it a secret."

"I told you she'd freak out. She hates to lose to me more than anything," Amanda said and then she narrowed her eyes at her sister. "But you lost, Tina. Jacob is mine now."

Amanda wasn't quite quick enough to avoid Tina when she launched herself over the hood of the car and tackled her to the ground.

"You, bitch," Tina snarled, battering any inch of Amanda she could connect with.

Jacob grabbed Tina around the waist and tried to pull her kicking, punching, screaming body off Amanda, but Tina grabbed handfuls of Amanda's hair and refused to let go. Gritting her teeth, Amanda slapped Tina across the face, sending her head flying back to connect hard with Jacob's shoulder. If anything, Amanda's slap pissed off Tina even more. She yanked Amanda's hair so hard, Jacob feared she'd rip it all out.

"Let me go!" Amanda kicked at her sister, but couldn't reach her without scalping herself.

"Stop this," Jacob demanded, squeezing Tina's wrists until she cried out and the strength went out of her grip. Free at last, Amanda scrambled to her feet.

The sisters glared at each other like a pair of wolverines. Jacob was sure they'd tear into each other again if he released Tina's wrists.

"You should go," he said to Amanda. There was no way he'd be able to calm Tina down as long as Amanda was there.

"What about Julie?" Amanda asked.

Now that the two women had stopped screaming, Jacob could hear Julie wailing inside the SUV. He turned and peered in at her through the windshield. Julie's face was streaked red, her eyes were overflowing with tears, and she wasn't simply crying, she was sobbing. This was not something a child should witness. Hell, this wasn't something *he* should witness. He'd known Tina would be upset, but the woman was practically insane with irrationality. She couldn't take care of a defenseless child in her current state of mind.

"Take her with you," Jacob said to Amanda, who nodded and rushed for the back door of the SUV.

"If you fucking touch her," Tina railed, "I'll have you arrested for kidnapping."

"And I'll have you arrested for assault," Amanda shot back before opening the car door.

"Why are you fighting?" Julie shrieked. "Why are you fighting with my mommy?"

"Shh, it's okay Julie Bean," Amanda said. "I'm going to take you to see Grandma."

"I want my daddy!" Her piercing scream was like an ice pick to Jacob's heart.

"I'll see you soon, princess," he said as Amanda lifted her out of the car. "Go with Aunt Mander. I need to talk to your mom."

"I'm not talking to you, you fucking imbecile," Tina said. "You'd better let me go."

"I'll let you go when you calm down."

"I'm not going to calm down, you piece of shit. I said let me go!" Tina wrenched her wrist from his grasp and immediately started swinging her free fist. He backed away, but not before catching a sharp blow to the temple. The enormous diamond on her finger scraped his flesh as she pulled back to hit him again. The open wound stung as blood welled to the surface and trickled down his face. Jacob struggled to keep his grip on Tina's other wrist while fending off her attack with his free hand. She was a lot stronger than she looked, he decided as he tried to contain her fury without knocking her out.

"Daddy!" Julie screamed as Amanda tried to get her struggling body into her car. "You're bleeding. Daddy!"

With his attention diverted, Tina landed another sharp blow to his collarbone before he finally caught her hand.

"Stop this," he said. "You're upsetting Julie. What do you think hitting me will accomplish?"

"I want to hurt you as much as you've hurt me," Tina growled, yanking on her arm.

"I've never hit you," Jacob said. "Never."

"God, you're stupid."

Jacob stiffened as if she'd punched him again. Actually, he'd rather she punch him than call him stupid. "Don't call me that."

"Why? You're a fucking idiot. You don't understand anything."

"Maybe if you tried explaining it to me in small words," he said tersely. But he wasn't interested in what she had to say. He wanted to comfort his daughter, who was still screaming for him in the back of Amanda's car, not listen to more of Tina's bullshit.

"You never fought for me, Jacob," she said. "For us. We had—*what?*—one big argument about your infidelity before you left me."

"You accused me of cheating on you all the time, Tina. Even when I hadn't cheated."

"But you did cheat, Jake. You admitted it."

"Yeah, I admitted I wronged you and I left. That's what you said you wanted."

Tina shook her head, her eyes filling with tears. Jacob didn't feel the least bit sorry for her. She'd driven him away. Made his life so miserable he had to force himself to go home. If Julie hadn't been there, he'd have avoided going home at all.

"Maybe I wanted you to fight for me."

"Who the hell was I supposed to fight for you? Were you cheating on me with some guy?" He kind of hoped she had been. Then he wouldn't have to feel so low about his own infidelity. God knew the woman needed to get laid.

Tina blinked at him and shook her head. "You're so dense, Jake. There wasn't anyone else. Ever. There still isn't anyone else."

"I'm taking Julie home," Amanda interrupted. "I'll call Mom to come watch her, and I'll leave."

"You're goddamned right you'll leave," Tina spat. "I never want to see your whore face again."

"She's not a whore," Jacob said.

"Did you fuck her?" Tina asked. When Jacob didn't dignify her question with an answer, Tina snorted. "Then she's a whore."

"Go to hell, Tina," Amanda said before climbing into her car, starting the engine, and driving away.

"Somebody call the police," Tina screamed. "She's taking my child!"

"Will you just stop?" Jacob said, releasing both of Tina's wrists now that Julie and Amanda were gone and safe from her wrath. "Julie didn't need to see you blow up like that. She's probably scared to death. You know Amanda would never take her from you or harm her. Why don't you try acting like an adult for once in your life?"

"Like you can talk," she said.

Jesus. Why had he ever thought this woman was attractive? She was nasty. Rotten to the core. He hoped her influence didn't rub off on Julie, but he'd witnessed Tina's effect on Julie's thought processes more than once.

"I'd like to talk, not fight," he said, raising both hands in truce. "Just talk. Do you think you can calm down enough to do that?"

Jacob scowled at the sound of approaching sirens. "I think someone called the cops on us," he said. He wiped his bleeding temple with the neckband of his T-shirt. He wasn't surprised the neighbors had called the police. He just wished they'd arrived when he'd been trying to break up the fight and gotten knocked around by his ex-wife.

"You're not going to see Amanda again," Tina said.

"I plan to see her this evening, as a matter of fact."

"Then you'll never see Julie again."

Jacob's eyes narrowed. "What are you talking about?"

"Promise you won't see Amanda again or I'll . . ." Her eyes narrowed maliciously. "I'll send the cops after her for kidnapping Julie. She'll go to jail, Jacob. Do you want that for her? How do you think that will affect her life? Her career? She's a teacher. They'll fire her over this for sure."

Tina's cold smile turned Jacob's blood icy in his veins.

"You wouldn't lie to the cops just to keep us apart," Jacob said. *Hoped.*

"It's not a lie. She took my daughter without my permission. That's kidnapping."

"Amanda had *my* permission to take Julie," Jacob reminded her. "She's my daughter too."

"Maybe. But which of us is the custodial parent? Whose decision will matter to the court?"

Jacob wished he'd fought for split custody, but at the time, having Tina as the custodial parent seemed best for Julie. Tina had been the one to convince him of that, so maybe she was right; he was incurably stupid.

He didn't want Amanda to get in trouble, but Tina's threat didn't hold water. "They won't keep Julie from me because her aunt took her home without your permission."

"But they will if her father is physically abusive and her mother has a restraining order against him."

"You don't have . . ." It occurred to him that she was threatening to tell the police that he'd done the attacking, not her. And who would they believe, the gorgeous blonde with bruises on her wrists, a torn shirt, and scraped-up legs and arms, or the hard-muscled metal singer with a small gash on his forehead, but was otherwise unharmed? Amanda would back up his story, but did he want to put his faith in the legal system and risk losing Julie?

With lights flashing and sirens wailing, two police cruisers pulled up his driveway and screeched to a halt. Jacob didn't even have a chance to explain what was going on before he was face down on the asphalt with his arms handcuffed behind his back. Someone hauled him up into a sitting position, and he glared up at Tina.

"Don't do this," he warned.

"Are you going to keep fucking her?" Tina asked.

"Who I fuck is *my* business, not yours," he growled.

"What happened here, folks?" one of the officers asked.

"He grabbed me," Tina accused, thrusting her reddened wrists in the officer's direction.

"Self-defense," Jacob said.

The officer lifted an eyebrow at him. "You needed to crush her wrists to defend yourself? You must outweigh her by a hundred pounds."

"Would you rather I had punched her in the face?" He was mad enough to do it now.

"Are you threatening her?" the officer asked.

Jacob took a deep, calming breath and released it slowly. His shoulders were starting to ache from the position the handcuffs held his arms in. And he sure didn't want to take a trip downtown to the police station. "No. She attacked her sister, and I was trying to break up the fight."

"Her sister?" The officer glanced around. "And where would

she be?"

"She took my daughter," Tina said, suddenly acting frantic. "Without my permission."

"Is that why you attacked your sister? To prevent her from taking your daughter?"

Tina blinked. "Uh . . ."

"Is the child in danger?" the other officer asked. Immediately he spoke into the communication device at his shoulder. "We need to issue an Amber Alert." To Tina he said, "Can you give me a description of the child, the kidnapper, the vehicle?"

"This is ridiculous," Jacob said. "Amanda took Julie home. To her own house. Just go there and you'll find our daughter safe and sound in her room. There's no reason to issue an Amber Alert. She wasn't kidnapped."

"We'll be the judge of that," the officer said. He took Tina aside and questioned her out of Jacob's hearing. He had no idea what Tina was telling the officers, but Jacob's only means of defense was to stick to the truth. He knew he wasn't in the wrong, but would the law see it that way?

He needed to call Amanda and warn her that her sister might do the unthinkable. He tried shifting his arms so that he could reach the phone in his front pocket. He wasn't sure how he thought he'd get a call to connect if he actually managed to reach the device, but he was desperate.

"Do you have something in your pocket?" one of the officers asked.

"No." Jacob realized a second too late that he shouldn't lie to cops who thought he assaulted women and was an accessory to kidnapping a child. In the blink of an eye, he was face down on the asphalt and being frisked.

"Nothing in your pocket, huh?" the officer said.

Jacob cringed when his phone thudded on the ground in front of him.

"Nothing *illegal* or dangerous in my pocket," he clarified.

"Who were you trying to call?"

"His whore, I'm sure," Tina said snidely.

"I told you not to call her that!" Jacob bellowed. It was hard to keep his cool in the humiliating position he currently found himself in.

"Is that why you attacked your wife?"

"*Ex*-wife," he said between gritted teeth. Currently he didn't even want to claim her at all.

"Did you attack Ms. Lange because she insulted your new girlfriend?"

"I already told you that I didn't attack her. Tina attacked Amanda, and I was trying to separate them." Perhaps he should call a lawyer before he blurted statements. No one had read him his rights, so he assumed he wasn't under arrest. At least not yet. But if he didn't keep his temper in check, he was bound to find himself behind bars. "Why don't you call Amanda and ask her what happened?" Jacob said, glad his voice sounded reasonable—not demanding, not pissed as hell. He recognized that the police responded better when he remained calm.

"She'll just say whatever he tells her to say," Tina said.

"Not if we question her before she speaks to him," the officer said as he scooped up Jacob's phone.

That shut Tina up. For the time being.

With Jacob's direction, the officer dialed Amanda's number. Jacob prayed she just told the truth and didn't try to protect anyone.

"She says the child is with your mother," the officer said to Tina. "Do we need to follow up on this claim?"

Tina sighed and shook her head. "No. I'm sure Julie's fine."

"She also says that you went crazy and attacked her when you found out she's in a relationship with your ex-husband."

"I didn't attack her," Tina said.

"Miss," the officer said into Jacob's phone, "would you mind returning to the scene? It would make this a lot easier."

Jacob's stomach dropped. He couldn't protect Amanda if he was handcuffed. Would Tina try to harm her sister again while the police were present? What about after the police were gone and then when Jacob was on tour? How would he protect Amanda then? Maybe he should ask her to follow him out on the road so he could keep an eye on her. He didn't think Tina was capable of killing her, but then he hadn't thought she'd attack her when she'd found out that he and Amanda were involved.

A few minutes later, Amanda's car pulled into his drive. Jacob was still in cuffs, but now seated on the bottom step of the walkway to his door. Looking disheveled and a little scared, Amanda stepped out of the car and her eyes met his. Her brow crinkled when she noticed why he had his hands behind his back. She turned a questioning gaze on the officers.

"Why is he in handcuffs?" Amanda asked. "Is he under arrest? I told you he didn't do anything."

"The stories we're hearing aren't correlating," the officer said. "Maybe we need to take you all downtown for questioning."

"Excuse me," interrupted Mrs. Barbury, who lived across the street from Jacob. She was a sweet elderly lady who always brought Jacob a big plate of homemade cookies around Christmas time, but otherwise, didn't interact with him much. "I was walking past with my dogs when it happened. I don't mean to intrude, but I saw the whole thing up until I ran to the house to call nine one one."

If that was true, then Jacob would be baking Mrs. Barbury cookies this Christmas.

"This one's car was here for two nights in a row," Mrs. Barbury said, jabbing a thumb in Amanda's direction. Then she pointed at Tina. "This one shows up every couple of weeks with Mr. Silverton's little girl." Mrs. Barbury smiled. "She's a real cutie pie."

An officer took pity on Jacob and helped him to his feet to ease the crick in his neck developing from staring up at everyone.

"About half an hour ago," Mrs. Barbury continued, "I was walking past with my dogs and saw these two going at it in the driveway." She pointed from Amanda to Jacob.

"What do you mean by *going at it*?" the officer asked.

"Kissing. Well, more like trying to swallow each other's faces." She fanned her flushed throat. "I thought he was going to strip her naked right there in the driveway and have his way with her. Land sakes alive! And that's when *she* showed up." She jabbed a thumb in Tina's direction.

"Her name is Tina," Jacob said.

Tina narrowed her eyes at the woman and crossed her arms.

"Tina started yelling and chasing this one around the car. And when she finally got a hold on . . ." She looked to Amanda and raised her eyebrows.

Amanda supplied her name.

"When she finally got a hold on Amanda, I thought Tina was like to kill her. Mr. Silverton was tryin' to break them up, and all the while that poor little girl was in the SUV screaming for her daddy."

Usually Jacob hated nosy neighbors, but at that moment, he felt blessed to have them.

"So Mr. Silverton finally got the two women separated and he told this one"—she pointed at Amanda—"to get away to safety and take his daughter with her so that poor child didn't have to watch her parents argue and such. That's when I ran home to call the police."

The officers nodded at each other as the story was repeated for the third time. Now the only one with a different tale was Tina, and as Mrs. Barbury was an impartial witness, Tina's false account was completely discredited.

"Would you like to press charges?" an officer asked Amanda. She blinked at him, her eyes wide with shock. "What?"

"Would you like to press assault charges against Tina Lange?"

Amanda glanced at Tina and licked her lips, her throat constricting as she swallowed.

"Are you actually considering having me arrested?" Tina asked, her eyes wide in disbelief.

Amanda turned her gaze to Jacob, and he shook his head. He didn't want Tina to wind up in jail. He just wanted her to behave like an adult and come to terms with the fact that he was in love with her sister.

"It was a family squabble," Amanda said. "You know what sisters are like." She laughed as if they got into knock-down drag-out fights all the time. "How about we just let her off with a warning?"

"It's your call."

While Jacob was released from his cuffs, Amanda spoke to the other officer. Tina stared at the asphalt between her shoes, her expression and body language completely unreadable. Jacob could only guess what was going on in her mind, yet he was positive it was nothing good. He walked toward her, rubbing the ache from his wrists as he approached.

"I know finding out about Amanda and me was a shock."

"How long have you been with her?" Tina asked. "Was this going on while we were married?"

"No," he said. "Of course not. We've only been involved for a week."

"So it won't be too big of a deal to break it off with her." Tina's gaze lifted to his, and he saw a brief flash of malicious hatred in her eyes before she smiled.

"I'm not breaking it off with her just because you don't like it."

Tina licked her lips as she stared into his eyes as if searching for answers. Or maybe she was looking for his soul so she could suck it out of him.

"Okay," she said. She turned away from him and toward the nearest cop. "Am I free to go?"

He told her she could leave, and Jacob watched her climb calmly into her SUV and drive away. He wasn't sure why she was behaving so rationally all of sudden, but her model behavior frightened him far more than her uncontrollable rage.

CHAPTER FOURTEEN

AMANDA LEANED into Jacob's side as the police pulled out of the driveway. Her knee and the palms of her hands were still throbbing, but her heart was surprisingly light. Their relationship had survived Tina. If it could overcome her disapproval, Amanda was sure they could get through anything.

She glanced up at Jacob and cringed at the ugly bruise on the side of his head. It was bleeding slightly. "How's your head?" she asked, reaching up to touch it but thinking better of the idea and resting her fingertips against his jaw instead.

"It'll be fine. It's always been like a brick. What about your hands?" he asked. He captured her wrists in his and turned her hands over to gaze down at their abraded palms. "Let's go get you cleaned up."

He took great care in applying antibacterial ointment to her hands and kissed her wrists tenderly. "Thank you for taking Julie away from that mess."

"She'll be worried about you," Amanda said. "You should call her."

He bit his lip and nodded slightly. "I should."

"Are you hesitating?" she asked, lifting a cotton ball saturated in peroxide to the jagged gash on his temple.

He released a heavy sigh. "Tina will probably answer," he said. "I don't think I can talk to her right now."

"But Julie—"

"Is what's important." He nodded and dialed Tina's landline number. Amanda held his hand for support while he listened to it ring.

"You have some nerve calling here!" Amanda could hear her mother's harsh greeting from several feet away.

"Hello, Mrs. Lange. Can I speak to Julie?"

"She's very upset," Mom retorted.

"I understand that. It's why I called. She needs to know everything is going to be okay. If you don't let me talk to her on the phone, I'll come over." There was no threat in his tone, but it was obvious he meant what he said.

"Julie," Mom called. "Do you want to speak to your father? If you don't, I'll—"

There was a brief pause and then Julie was on the phone. Amanda leaned closer so she could listen to what her niece said. Julie had been so upset when she'd taken her home.

"Daddy? Are you okay? You were bleeding."

"I'm fine, princess. Don't worry about me. Okay?"

"Why did mommy get mad at you?"

"She doesn't like me to spend time with your Aunt Mander." He gave Amanda's hand a squeeze, and she leaned her head against his shoulder.

"That's silly, Daddy," Julie's sweet voice came from Jacob's phone.

"I agree, but sometimes grown-ups get mad for silly reasons. So it might be a good idea not to talk about me and your aunt when your mom's around."

"I don't like mommy when she's mad. She hit you." Julie sniffed her nose, and Jacob turned his face into Amanda's hair. His arm went around her back to pull her close. He—Jacob "Shade" Silverton—was leaning on her for support. She hoped she could always be there when he needed her.

"Don't cry, honey. Mommy isn't mad at you. She would never hurt you."

"I know. But Mommy shouldn't be mean to you. You're my daddy. I love you so much."

"I love you so much too, Julie. What your mom does and says to me doesn't matter as long as you love me. You make me feel all better."

"I do?"

"Yep. Now that I talked to you, I'm smiling again."

Amanda wiped at a tear. How could Tina even consider keeping these two apart? Julie would be devastated, and Jacob would likely die from a broken heart.

Julie giggled. "I like you smiling. How many sleeps until I see you next time?"

Jacob sighed and his hold on Amanda went slack. "Twelve," he said flatly.

"How many fingers is that?"

"All of them," Jacob said. "Plus a couple of extra."

"I'll just hug Lucky really tight every day and pretend she's you, okay?"

Jacob chuckled. "That is one lucky elephant."

"That's her name. Lucky. Just a minute!" she yelled at someone else before talking to her dad again. "Grandma says I have to get off the phone now."

"Do you feel better?" Jacob asked. "Not scared? You can call me if you're afraid or sad or worried."

"I'm okay, Daddy. Bye."

"Bye," he said. And then, "I love you." But Julie had already hung up.

"Are you okay?" Amanda asked, rubbing the center of his back.

"Yeah. It's just she means everything to me, you know?"

"I know." And his infallible love for his daughter was what made him irresistible to Amanda. His looks and personality, his passion and generous nature—she could have fallen for any of those traits. But his devotion to his little girl? That was what had Amanda head over heels in love with the guy. "You mean as much to her." *And to me.*

Amanda licked her lips and took a deep breath. She should tell him how she felt. She wanted to tell him. She wasn't sure why she was still holding back. Maybe because everything had happened so fast. She was a practical woman. She wasn't the type who fell for a guy in a week. But she'd known Jacob much longer than that. Maybe she'd been falling for him for years.

"Jacob . . ." she whispered.

"Let me fix up your knees," he said.

She sucked in a pained breath as he poured hydrogen peroxide on her scrapes. *Way to kill a mood, Silverton.*

He wiped up the liquid dripping down her calf with a hand towel and then lowered his head to kiss the inside of her thigh just above her knee. Amanda's breath caught at the intensity of the passion that small tender move sent swirling through her body.

Way to put me in the mood, Silverton.

"I'm so sorry I got you involved in this mess," he said.

She winced as he picked a small stone out of her scraped skin.

"Jacob," she said, "I *am* this mess."

He chuckled and slid both hands down her calf as he tilted

his head to look up at her. "I guess you are."

She touched his face with her fingertips, her heart swelling.

"Am I worth it?" she asked.

"Tina's hatred?"

She nodded.

"Well, considering she already hates me . . ." He shrugged.

But she'd claimed to still love him. Amanda hadn't forgotten that shocking revelation. Had Tina just been saying it to cause a bigger stir or had she meant it? If she'd meant it, Amanda was sure things between herself and her sister were going to get a lot worse and would probably never get better.

"But does she really hate you?" Amanda lifted her gaze to meet his. "Or is she out of her head in love with you?"

"It doesn't matter. I'm in love with you."

He smiled at her expectantly, and she licked her lips. She knew what he wanted her to say, and she felt the words deep in her heart, but she was terrified of what Tina was capable of doing. Not to her, but to Julie and to Jacob. How could she protect them? "Jacob, maybe she'd calm down if we—"

He silenced her with a finger to her lips. "Can we not talk about Tina anymore?"

"I'm not sure you know . . ."

"What she's capable of?"

Amanda nodded.

"I'll figure out a way to handle her," he said. "But not right now. Right now I need you in my bed so I can feel what you're refusing to say."

"Jacob," she whispered against his fingertip, but he replaced it with his lips and kissed her until her resolve crumbled. Her arms circled his neck.

He scooped her from the toilet lid and carried her to his bed. He tasted every inch of her as he removed her clothes. She was delirious with need by the time he pushed himself inside her. His hands linked with hers on either side of her head, and he stared into her eyes as he filled her with slow, gentle strokes. In her head and her heart, she told him how she felt about him a thousand times. And when they tumbled over the brink together, he had to see the love in her eyes, but she still couldn't say it. What was holding her back? Fear, yes. But fear of what?

Jacob held her close as their heart rates slowed and their

breathing became even again. Everything seemed so calm after the storm they'd weathered together. She relaxed against him and told herself everything was going to work out between them. And maybe someday Tina would give them her blessing and Julie would come to live with Amanda and Jacob as *their* daughter. She already loved her niece as if she were her own. It was a foolish dream— she knew that. Tina would never let it happen, but wrapped in Jacob's strong arms, his heart beating strong and steady against her ear, she allowed herself to believe anything could happen.

Amanda's belly rumbled unexpectedly, tearing her from her moment of perfect contentment, and Jacob laughed when she covered her stomach with one hand.

"Do you want to go out for dinner or eat in?" he asked, drawing her closer to his bare chest.

"I'd much rather eat in." Because that would mean they could spend more time alone together.

"All right," he said. "What are you cooking?"

She chuckled. He *had* cooked for her several times over the weekend. "I have some chicken in my fridge that I need to cook before it spoils. Do you want to come over to my place and have dinner?"

"Will it require me putting on pants?" he asked.

She grinned, picturing him in her passenger seat buck naked. She wouldn't mind that arrangement in the least, but her neighbors might find his nudity offensive. Or at the very least mind-bogglingly distracting. "Don't bother with pants. I can bring it over here and cook it in your enormous kitchen. But I need to check on my cat anyway. She's probably shredded the drapes by now."

"I didn't know you had a cat," Jacob said.

"She hides from strangers. Not that you've ever been to my house."

"Next time I'm home, I'll stay with you at your house."

"I don't have much room. Or a pool." She waggled her eyebrows at him. They did have a good time in that pool.

"That doesn't matter. As long as you're there, I'm sure I'll have plenty to keep me entertained."

"And what will we do with Julie? I don't even have a spare bedroom." She doubted Julie would appreciate being holed up on an air mattress with all the unfiled papers Amanda stacked all over the floor in her home office.

"She's small," he said. "I'm sure she'll fit in a closet or something."

Amanda slapped his belly playfully and squirmed out of his arms. She wasn't sure if she could wait two weeks to see him again. At least they had tonight and a few hours the next morning to be together, even if it wouldn't be enough. She doubted she'd ever get enough of him. "Would it be okay if I came to see you after a show sometime this week?"

He watched her dress from the bed. "Women on tour are a distraction."

Her heart sank.

"But having a lonely, cranky lead singer is far more dangerous." He chuckled. "When should I expect you?"

She pulled her T-shirt over her head, unable to suppress her joyful grin. "I'll check the schedule and let you know."

He climbed from the bed—still gloriously naked—and pulled her into his arms for a deep, satisfying kiss. She eyed the bed, but her stomach rumbled again and he released her.

"I'll hurry back," she said a few minutes later as she opened the front door. Jacob had followed her—still gloriously naked—and drew her near for one last kiss.

"I'll be counting the seconds until I get to see you again."

Sometimes he said the most wonderful things.

"I'll only be gone twenty minutes," she reminded him. "Keep your pants on."

He glanced down at his current pants-less state. "A bit late for that."

She gave his bare ass an appreciative squeeze and then dashed across the driveway to her car before she wound up naked again. The man did have an uncanny skill for relieving her of her panties.

She was still smiling when she pulled into her drive a few minutes later. She'd been so wrapped up in her musings about Jacob that she didn't notice she'd been followed until a familiar SUV pulled up behind her car, blocking any hope for escape.

"Shit," she muttered under her breath. She sat in the car weighing her options. If Tina attacked her again, what would she do? A sharp knock on her window startled her out of her thoughts, and she looked up at her sister's smiling face. Funny how she found that friendly grin far more terrifying than Tina's face twisted in rage.

"We need to talk," Tina called through the glass.

"I don't want to fight with you, Tina."

"I don't want to fight with you either."

Sure she didn't. As soon as Amanda got out of the car, she was sure to get her eyes scratched out and her hair ripped from its roots.

"I just want to talk," Tina said.

Amanda glanced in her rearview mirror, but the SUV was too close to her rear bumper for her to see inside the hulking vehicle. "Is Julie with you?"

"No, she's with Mom. Can we talk?"

"I can hear you just fine," Amanda said loudly. "We can talk like this."

Tina laughed. "Are you seriously scared of me, big sis?"

Amanda narrowed her eyes and opened her car door. If Tina wanted a fight, she was going to get a fight. But Amanda wasn't going to start it. She closed the door and leaned against the overwarm metal, crossing her arms in front of her chest.

"Why did you come here?" Amanda asked.

"You have to break up with Jacob."

Amanda rolled her eyes. "I'm not breaking up with him, Tina. I don't care about your feelings on the matter."

"Do you care about *Julie's* feelings?"

Amanda scowled. "What do you mean?"

"Don't you think she'll feel bad if the reason her mommy is always crying is because her backstabbing whore of a sister is fucking her father?"

Amanda's jaw hardened. "You wouldn't do that to her."

"And won't you feel terrible when Jacob doesn't get to see Julie because—I don't know—she's too sick to get out of bed during his visitation weekends."

"You can't keep them apart, Tina."

"I can't? Are you sure about that?"

"It would destroy him." And Amanda obviously wasn't the only one who realized that.

Tina smiled coldly. "And won't Jacob feel horrendous when he realizes the reason he's not allowed any happiness is because he couldn't keep his dick in his pants *again*."

Could anyone really be that cruel? What did Tina want from him? "He doesn't love you, Tina. Just let him go."

"You're going to break up with him," Tina said. "You're going to do it tonight in person at Jack's Grill so I can make sure it's done. And you're not going to mention that I had anything to do with your decision."

"I'm not."

Tina shrugged. "I guess you don't care if you destroy our entire family. Making your niece hate you will be easy. It might take a little more effort to get Mom and Dad to disown you, but I don't doubt I can do it." Tina tapped her jaw with one finger as her gaze focused upward. "So, should I tell Mom about your fling first? She's always thought you were a good person. This slut move is sure to change her opinion of her darling daughter. Or maybe I should go crying to Daddy first and let him tell Mom. Daddy never really liked you anyway."

"Why would you do any of this? Why do you care so much that I'm with Jacob?"

Tina didn't answer her questions. Instead she said, "So are you going to do as I ask and break up with him?"

"No!" Amanda said. "I'm not breaking up with him just because you can't stand that he's with me. Jacob is worth any shit you can throw at me, Tina. Do your worst."

Amanda shoved Tina aside and headed for her front door. Her hands were shaking so bad she dropped her keys twice on her way up the brick path.

"Having him between your thighs is worth your parents hating you?"

Amanda figured they'd get over it pretty quickly. They were the type of parents who forgave their children, though Amanda didn't really think there was anything to forgive. She'd fallen in love with someone they didn't particularly care for—they still believed he was a horrible man who'd done their youngest daughter wrong—but if they saw how good she and Jacob were together, they'd eventually understand. Maybe.

"Is he worth your niece turning against you?" Tina called after her. "I'll find a new babysitter for her. You'll never see her."

Amanda stopped in her tracks. Tina wouldn't really manipulate her four-year-old daughter to get what she wanted, would she?

"I wonder if Jacob thinks *you're* worth losing his daughter's devotion over. Maybe he's willing to risk it. And by the time he realizes how much Julie despises him, it will be too late to fix their relationship."

Amanda pressed her lips together to stop their trembling. Her throat tightened, choking a sob from her. She tilted her head back and blinked up at the darkening sky to keep the tears in her eyes from streaming down her cheeks.

Jacob was worth any adversity to her life, but to Julie's? Amanda wasn't cruel enough to hurt her Julie Bean in any capacity, but she knew Tina was. Tina wasn't making veiled threats. She would keep Julie out of Amanda's life. She would find a way to keep Jacob from seeing his own daughter. Make his little girl hate him. Tina would do anything in her power to destroy Amanda's fledgling relationship with Jacob, even if she had to use Julie as a pawn.

The fucking bitch.

"If I break up with him tonight, you'll leave Julie out of this."

Amanda could picture her sister's smile of victory, even if she didn't have the stomach to turn around and look at her.

"Of course," Tina said brightly.

Rage boiled in Amanda's gut. She wondered how much time she'd have to serve for murdering the cunt on her front lawn. Surely it would be deemed a crime of passion; that had to carry a lighter sentence than cold-blooded, premeditated murder, didn't it?

Or maybe there was a way to prove Tina was an unfit mother and have her lose custody of Julie. Was using a child's happiness to manipulate your sister into breaking up with your ex-husband grounds for a custody battle? Amanda doubted it. She couldn't see a way out of this. The only door open to her was the one Tina was holding wide.

With Tina watching over her shoulder, Amanda fished her phone out of her purse and dialed Jacob.

CHAPTER FIFTEEN

JACOB WAS SEARCHING his fridge for items to round out a chicken dinner when his cellphone rang. He smiled indulgently when he saw who the caller was: Amanda. She missed him already? He knew the feeling.

"Hey," he answered. "Did you get lost?"

"Um, not exactly," she said. "Can you meet me at Jack's Grill? The meat in my fridge is beyond saving."

"I can probably find something here to cook." Would she mind having pancakes for dinner?

"You just don't want to be seen in public with me." Her teasing laugh sounded breathless, but maybe it was just the phone connection.

"Of course I do," he said. "I want the whole world to know you're mine."

"So you'll come?"

"I've already done that with you several times today, but I can probably go for another quickie."

"Jacob," she chastised.

He scowled, puzzling over her lack of reciprocal flirting. One of the traits that he loved most about her was that she always countered his teasing with a comeback.

"I'll meet you there in ten minutes," he said. "I still need to put on pants."

She hung up without saying goodbye.

The entire drive to Jack's Grill, Jacob couldn't shake the feeling that something was off. Not only was it odd that Amanda wanted to meet for dinner in a public place when she knew he was naked and waiting for her, but he'd sensed a tension in her that he'd never felt from her before.

He spotted her car in the parking lot, but it was empty, so instead of dragging her into the back seat for that quickie he'd mentioned, he entered the noisy establishment and scanned the crowd for signs of her. He smiled when he spotted her, but she was staring into a bright green cocktail with a tight expression on her lovely face. Had her cat died while she'd been at his place or something?

Jacob sat on the stool across from her and reached for her hand. She tugged it away and hid it between her knees.

"I can't see you anymore," she said.

His breath caught in his throat, threatening to choke him. "What?"

"I've given it a lot of thought," she said, her words hurried, almost practiced, as if she were reciting a speech. "The sex is great and all, Shade, but our little fling isn't worth destroying my family over." Her lips pressed together, and she looked down at her lap. "It's best if you just stay away."

"Where is this coming from, Amanda? We both know this is more than a fling. I love you."

She flinched away from him as if he'd slapped her.

"And I know you love me too."

She released a brittle laugh. "Yeah, well, I don't or I would have said so. I always thought you were hot and all, but now that I've had what I was after, I'm moving on. You need to move on too."

She slipped off the stool, but he grabbed her arm.

"What the hell?" he said. "An hour ago we were trying to figure out how to spend more time together and now you're cutting me off entirely? What happened between then and now?"

She tugged at her arm, refusing to meet his eyes. "Why are you being so stubborn? I said I don't want to be with you anymore."

"But what you're saying doesn't make sense. You can't just turn off your feelings like a switch."

She laughed. "You can if you never had feelings to begin with. Now let go of my arm."

"I'm not letting you go, Amanda. Tell me the truth. What's going on?"

"Don't you get it?" she yelled. "Or are you too fucking stupid to grasp the simplest concepts?"

The background noise went silent, or maybe his ears just stopped working. The confusion holding his hurt at bay shattered. Anguish clenched his gut, expanded within his chest, and clawed up his throat.

"Do you really think someone like me would fall for an idiot like you?" she spat at him. "I just wanted to get laid by a rock star. That's all this was."

The strength melted from his fingers, and her arm slipped from his grasp. She backed away several steps, but apparently felt the need to deliver another blow to the metal stake piercing his heart.

"Thanks for the nice time, Shade, but I have better things to do than you."

He was too stunned to fight for her. For them. Who was this person? It wasn't Amanda. Not the Amanda he knew. Not the Amanda he loved. But maybe she was just like her sister and kept her inner bitch at bay to get what she wanted and then unleashed all her darkness and cruelty when it served her purpose.

"I'm going to the ladies room," she said, "and when I get back, I want you to be gone. Don't try to contact me. You'll only make it harder for yourself. I'm through with you, Shade. Do you understand?"

The only thing he understood was how it felt to have his heart ripped from his chest and kicked around a dusty wooden floor, but he nodded anyway.

"Good," she said. "Leave. Now. No one wants you here. Least of all me."

She turned—golden brown hair dancing around her shoulders with the motion—and stalked away. That was when Jacob noticed everyone in the bar was staring at him. More than one person was recording his misery on a cellphone. He was sure that within the hour, the entire world would be able to watch him—Shade "Rock Star" Silverton—get his heart broken on YouTube.

Why had Amanda done it in public? Why had she done it at all?

Jacob pulled the sunglasses from the neckband of his T-shirt, flicked them open, and crammed them onto his face. Jaw set, Shade made his exit through the bar's front door, giving everyone watching a one-finger salute as he went back to the life he knew best.

Thank God he could still rely on his fucking band.

CHAPTER SIXTEEN

AMANDA STOPPED just outside the ladies room. The guy who'd hit on her on Friday was standing next to the door with his arms crossed over his chest and a knowing smirk on his handsome face. "I guess you skipped step one and went directly to full-out, man-hating bitch mode."

Her eyes narrowed. She hadn't skipped step one. She hadn't even gotten to step one yet. "Go fuck yourself," she spat at him before slamming both hands into the bathroom's swing door. She gave zero fucks what he thought of her. Wasn't sure why he'd taken the time to rub the breakup she'd predicted into her face. Asshole.

Before Amanda had even managed to cross the threshold, the tears she'd been holding in check started to fall. She somehow managed to stifle an anguished sob until the door swung shut behind her. Thank God Jacob hadn't followed her. She wouldn't have been able to force herself to say another cruel thing to him no matter how loudly her sister's threats rang in her ears.

"That was brilliant," Tina said as she burst into the ladies room a moment later. "He left all pride and swagger as usual, but for a minute there, I thought he was actually going to cry."

"If you value your life, you'll get the fuck away from me," Amanda said in an animalistic growl. Her hands balled into tight fists and her eyes narrowed into slits. She wanted to hit something—*hard*—and Tina's face would serve as the perfect target.

"You did the thing properly, at least," Tina said with a self-serving chuckle. "He'll never take you back after that public humiliation. Half the bar was recording it on their phones."

Amanda's stomach clenched, and she pressed her fingertips against her quivering lips. How could she have been so heartless? And to Jacob? He was always so good to her. Had she really called him stupid? An idiot? She knew how sensitive he was about his intelligence, and she'd fucking used his greatest weakness and insecurity against him? How could she have done that to him? In front of all those people?

But she had to go for the death blow, otherwise he wouldn't have left. She'd had to break him to save him.

Oh God, Jacob, I'm so sorry.

With a wave of crippling grief, her stomach lost its battle and she raced into a stall, barely making it to the toilet before she heaved up everything she'd eaten in her entire life. Tina left Amanda sobbing and puking her guts out, kneeling on a grimy bathroom floor over a less-than-sanitary toilet. Amanda was surprised her sister hadn't snapped a picture of her triumph before she abandoned her.

Tina had won. As usual. The bitch who always fought dirty had won.

So this is what rock bottom looks like, Amanda thought as she used cheap, scratchy toilet paper to wipe her mouth. *It's better than I deserve.*

Thinking of what she'd done to Jacob brought on a new set of tears. She wasn't sure how long she sat on the floor of the stall crying—several women entered the bathroom and a few even tried to help her—but she was completely inconsolable. She just wanted to cry until she was so dehydrated she couldn't make any more tears.

It was Leah's voice that finally reached her.

"Amanda, it's me, honey. Unlock the door."

"Leah?" Amanda croaked. Her throat felt as if she'd taken up sword swallowing as a new hobby.

"Tomás called and said you'd been crying in the restroom for over an hour and needed me to come get you. What happened?"

"I broke up with Shade." She sniffed. The entire time she'd been focused on Shade, not Jacob. Making herself believe she was tearing apart the *rock star*—who must have a heart like a polished diamond—had been the only way she'd been able to get through that ordeal. But that rock star had looked like Jacob and acted like Jacob, and the pain in his expressive blue eyes had definitely been Jacob's.

"Oh God," she sobbed and curled into her knees, covering her head with folded arms as the tears began to flow again. She felt as if someone had kicked her in the stomach a few hundred times. But what was worse was that she knew she deserved any pain she had to endure.

"Amanda," Leah called through the narrow crack in the door. "Open up and let me in."

Amanda shook her head. She didn't want Leah to make her feel better. She wanted to wallow in this misery.

"If you don't unlock the door, I'm calling the fire department," Leah warned. "You wouldn't want a bunch of sexy firemen to see you with crying-jag face, would you?"

Amanda didn't give a fuck, but she figured she'd already hurt one person she loved today. She wouldn't want to upset Leah too.

Amanda wiped her face on the hem of her shirt and pressed her hand against the wall to gain enough leverage to get her wobbly legs beneath her. Her stomach heaved, but she didn't have anything left in it to hurl. She swallowed against a parched throat and released the bolt with a trembling hand. The door swung out, and Leah peeked around the green metal. Her jaw dropped, and she scurried into the stall to join Amanda, bolting herself inside.

"Oh God, sweetie, you're a mess," Leah said, but she didn't try to clean Amanda up with cheap toilet paper. Instead, she immediately folded Amanda into a comforting embrace, setting off another flood of tears. "It's going to be okay," Leah repeated over and over again, but her words didn't mean a thing to Amanda. It decidedly was not going to be okay. Nothing would be okay ever again.

When Amanda's sobs turned to sniffles and her full-body quaking lessened to occasional shudders, Leah drew away and stroked Amanda's tear-drenched hair from her cheeks. "Tell me everything that happened. It'll make you feel better."

"Nothing will make me feel better, Leah." Well, maybe if a meteor shot out of the sky and struck her sister dead . . . No, even that would suck because Julie would have to go through the pain of losing her mother. And even with Tina out of the picture, Jacob would never love Amanda again. Not after the heartless things she'd said to him.

"I promise it will, sweetie." Leah glanced around their less-than-inspiring surroundings. "But maybe we should go home first. It smells like vomit in here."

"That would be my fault too," Amanda said dully, her energy completely sapped.

She allowed Leah to lead her out the back exit so there'd be fewer prying eyes burning into the back of her neck. Thankfully, the asshole—Anthony was his name, she recalled—was no longer leaning outside the bathroom door. She probably would have kicked him in the nuts if he'd still been there. Because Amanda was too shaky to find her keys, much less drive, they took Leah's car, leaving Amanda's in the parking lot.

The distance to Amanda's house wasn't far, but as soon as Leah turned out of the parking lot, she said, "Start talking."

"I don't know where to start," Amanda said, clutching her small purse to her chest. The phone inside had been silent for over an hour. Part of her had hoped that Jacob would call and fix the mess she'd made—that Tina had insisted upon—but part of her was glad he hadn't. A clean break would be easiest for all of them. If she kept telling herself that, maybe she'd start to believe it.

"Start at the beginning."

Amanda told Leah about setting off Jacob's alarm and spending Friday night and Saturday morning alone with him.

"That morning, he told me he loved me," Amanda said, the ache in her chest so sharp, her heart struggled to beat.

Leah pulled into Amanda's drive, put the car in park, and turned to study her. "I'd say that's fantastic, but I'm assuming this story doesn't end well."

Amanda shook her head miserably.

"Why don't you go wash your face while I make you a chocolate milkshake? We'll talk all night if you need to."

Amanda smiled at Leah. She was already feeling more rational. Leah was a soothing constant in her life. She wasn't sure what she'd do without her. "Thanks for rescuing me."

"You've rescued me plenty," Leah said, opening the door and climbing out into the balmy night air.

Cicadas cried repetitively to the summer sky. Crickets filled in the chorus with higher-pitched chirrups. The scent of freshly cut grass drifted over from a neighbor's yard, and a dog up the street barked a sharp warning. Nothing unusual about any of those things—Amanda must have experienced them hundreds of times—but she'd never taken note of how comforting the mundane could be. Amanda was glad Leah had brought her home. She wrapped the familiar around her like a protective cocoon.

"We're going to have to find a new hangout," Amanda said as the motion-sensing porch light switched on and she fit her key into the front door lock. "I'll never be able to show my face at Jack's again."

"No huge loss," Leah said glumly. "Only losers go there anyway."

Amanda glanced over her shoulder. "Something wrong?"

"Remember that guy Colton from Friday night?"

"Yeah."

"He never called me after . . ." Leah lowered her gaze.

"Did you sleep with him?"

"Maybe." Leah shrugged. "Okay, yeah, I did. We had lunch on Saturday, and I didn't mean to get so intimate so soon. It just sort of happened."

Which is why he didn't call you, Amanda thought, but Leah didn't need to hear that when she was hurt.

Amanda reached out and stroked Leah's silky jet-black hair. "I'm sorry he didn't call you. He seemed nice. Maybe he just needs a couple days to figure out how awesome you are."

"Men! They're such assholes." Leah scowled at the ground.

"Not all of them," Amanda said, her thoughts on the wonderful time she'd had with Jacob that weekend *before* she'd pulverized his heart and his pride.

"Okay, correction," Leah said as she followed Amanda into the house. "All the men *I've* ever been with are assholes."

"You'll find someone great," Amanda said. "My theory is that if you strike out enough times, eventually you'll get lucky and hit one out of the park." And when you finally do, you probably shouldn't make him hate your fucking guts, she added silently.

Setting her purse on her console table, she gave Tinkerbell a scratch behind the ears as she passed her lounging on the back of the sofa. The calico stretched out her paws and produced a mighty yawn, but obviously didn't give two shits that the human who fed her and cleaned her litter box had returned home. Amanda had always been more of a dog person, but when Tinkerbell had shredded one of Tina's curtains and Tina had threatened to take the stray Julie had found hiding in their drainpipe to the pound, Amanda had agreed to adopt the tiny kitten. She didn't regret the decision—Julie adored the standoffish cat—but was it asking too much for a tail wag of greeting when she came home after a hard day? Tinkerbell leaped off the couch and padded toward her food bowl in the kitchen. Apparently unmitigated affection *was* too much to ask from the furball.

Amanda entered the only bathroom in her small cottage and washed her face with cool water. She made the mistake of looking at her reflection in the mirror above the sink. She looked like she'd been to Hell and back, but she felt like she hadn't actually made it back.

The blender whirred to life in the kitchen as Leah started making the promised chocolate shake. Moments later, Amanda was slurping the cold creamy concoction while she continued to tell Leah about her weekend. Soon they were both sighing over the sexy, sensitive, and virile hunk that was Jacob Silverton. He really was amazing. Their sighs turned to mutual outrage when Amanda's story ended with Tina's attack and her demands that they break up.

"That's blackmail!" Leah said.

"It's worse than blackmail," Amanda said.

"I've always hated your sister, but now . . ." Leah snarled. "What she did . . ." Her entire body was shaking. "This is just too much."

"There isn't anything I can do about this, is there?" Amanda focused on Leah, hoping the woman's super brain could devise a plan to make everything work out.

Leah rolled the tip of her straw between her fingertips and got that far-off look she'd typically sported when she was puzzling out the answer to a tough school assignment. After a long moment, she shook her head. "I'm sorry. I can't think of anything. In every scenario, Julie is the one who gets hurt."

Amanda sighed, her shoulders slumping in defeat. "Exactly."

Leah reached over and touched the back of Amanda's hand. "Unless Tina's just bluffing," Leah said. "Maybe she's just talking out of that perfect ass of hers."

Amanda shook her head. "She isn't bluffing. Tina never bluffs. You know she'd have no problem using Julie as a wedge between Jacob and me. If I hadn't ended it tonight, the situation would have gotten worse, not better. Tina won't back down until it suits her."

What really irked Amanda was how Tina always managed to make everyone take her side. Somehow Tina would twist Amanda's affair with Jacob into something tawdry and cheap. Everything would end up being Amanda's fault when all was said and done. Except Leah. Leah had always been in her corner and

Amanda trusted that she always would be.

"How can anyone be so selfish?" Leah fumed.

"She's always gotten everything handed to her, so she thinks whatever she wants is owed to her. Nothing will stop her from taking what she wants. Did I mention that when we were having that brawl in Jacob's driveway, she said that she still loved him?"

Leah's eyes widened. "Shut the front door! Do you think it's true?"

"Of course not. She just doesn't want me or anyone else to have him."

Leah used her straw to stab at the hunk of ice cream at the bottom of her glass. "One of these days this is all going to bite her in the ass."

"God, I hope so. For now I'll bide my time to protect Julie and Jacob, but I'll be looking for an opening. And when I find one, she'll be sorry she ever crossed me."

The bitch better watch her back.

CHAPTER SEVENTEEN

SHADE HANDED his bag to the copilot, who stuffed it into the near-empty compartment beneath the plane. Shade had assumed he was late and that they were holding the plane for him, but apparently he wasn't the only one getting a late start.

"Please hurry, sir," the copilot said. "We're going to miss our departure time."

Shade climbed the awkward metal steps and ducked his head to enter the small craft. The only one inside was Owen, who offered him a smile and a friendly wave.

"Hey," Shade grumbled as he strode past Owen and took the seat in the far rear corner. He didn't want to chat with Owen. He didn't want to see or talk to anyone until he got his emotions completely in check.

He still wasn't exactly sure what had set Amanda off, but he was too pissed—too *hurt*—to want to set things straight with her. And he wasn't sure his pain or anger would diminish with time. He'd thought his lack of education—his stupidity—didn't matter to her. Well, apparently he'd been too dumb to recognize her disdain. Last night, he'd replayed every moment of the weekend as he'd stared at the darkened ceiling in Julie's bedroom. Sleeping on the couch had been out of the question—the first time he'd made love to Amanda had been on that couch—and her scent still clung to his own bed, so he'd found no rest there, only heartache. There was comfort in being surrounded by reminders of his daughter who never judged him even as her bitter mother tried to belittle him. But not comfort enough to let him find sleep.

He remembered every time Amanda had faced his struggle to read. Remembered well the look of pity on her face when he'd convinced Julie to give up her bedtime story so he could sing her to sleep. Remembered how she'd automatically read all the signs at the zoo when Julie had a question. That little speech she'd given him in the car about how she couldn't care deeply about an idiot had obviously been true. Maybe it had been the only truth she'd spoken to him all weekend. He kept hearing those words over and over in his head. "I could never care so deeply about an idiot." And the ones she'd said to him at the bar. "Do you really think someone like me would fall for an idiot like you?" Oh yeah? Well, fuck her. He'd gotten this far without having a firm grasp on written language. An illiterate moron could do a lot worse for himself.

Owen rose from the spot he'd chosen up the aisle and flopped himself into the seat across from Shade. "Have a good weekend?" Owen asked as he fastened his seat belt.

"Most of it," Shade admitted. Until last night, it had been one of the best weekends of his life. It had ended as one of his worst. "Where's Gabe?" Kellen and Adam had stayed behind in New Orleans, and he guessed that Owen had ditched Lindsey at his mom's house, but the plane was still emptier than it should have been.

Owen shrugged. "The pilot said he flew back last night. I have no idea why."

That was odd.

Shade didn't have time to fire off a text to Gabe asking him what was up before the scratchy voice of the pilot came over the intercom to remind them to turn off their devices during takeoff and that they were a few minutes behind schedule.

Owen grunted. "Well, I'm in the dog house, but—"

"I'm going to catch a nap," Shade interrupted. He wasn't in the mood to chat. And he was tired. There were no reminders of Amanda on the plane, so maybe he could actually sleep.

"Uh, okay," Owen said. "I wonder what Kelly's up to."

Owen apparently needed a friend at the moment, but Shade couldn't force himself to be that for him. Not now. He was sure Owen was feeling lost without the ever-present Kellen at his side, but Shade had his own shit to deal with. Or not deal with. Whatever.

Shade tried sorting through his thoughts while he feigned sleep and Owen played some loud shooter game on a handheld device. No matter which rabbit hole he went down trying to figure out how Amanda's feelings for him could do a one-eighty in less than an hour, he could only come to one conclusion: she'd finally figured out that he wasn't good enough for her.

His conclusion was as depressing as it was infuriating.

So much for catching some much-needed sleep.

By the time the plane landed in New Orleans, he was ready to get back to the life he understood. The life he lived for. Life on the road.

It wasn't hard to compartmentalize when his home life and his professional life were completely different. Here with his band he was Shade—badass egomaniac with the world at his feet. If not for Julie, he'd never leave this part of his life behind. This part of his life came easy. It made sense to him. If someone insulted him or *tried* to hurt him, he brushed it off. He was untouchable. Unreachable. He didn't give a fuck.

But he'd allowed himself to be vulnerable with Amanda. Let himself be Jacob—the sensitive, weak idiot he resented now more than ever. From now on, Shade would let that guy out for Julie and only Julie, but he'd never allow another woman see the Jacob part of him again. Jacob got his heart broken too easily. *Shade* didn't have time for heartache. Or for love.

"Adam has our room keys," Owen said when they exited the limo. Shade had almost forgotten Owen was even there.

"Okay, cool," Shade said. He tossed his bag over his shoulder and strode confidently into the hotel lobby.

Several women—and a couple of men—stopped what they were doing to gawk. He was used to people staring. He wore his confidence like a Kevlar vest. It had taken a few hits courtesy of one pretty schoolteacher from Austin, Texas, but he'd get over it. Hell, he was already over it. Over her. Fuck her. He didn't need her. He was much better off without her.

Liar, a little voice whispered to him.

He and Owen were directed to Adam's room by a gushing hotel clerk at the front desk. "I'm sorry," she said. "I can't stop talking. It's you, it's really you. I saw Adam Taylor and Force Banner go through the lobby a couple of times this weekend. But *Shade* Silverton?" She fanned her flushed face with both hands.

"And Tags," Owen said, shaking the dog tags around his neck at her.

She spared Owen a sideways glance before focusing on Shade again. "This is totally unprofessional of me, but could I get a picture with you?"

"Now?" Shade asked. "I'm in a hurry."

He couldn't help but chuckle when instead of going through the back and circling around the chest-high reception counter, the woman hiked up her uniform skirt and climbed over the top so as not to inconvenience him. Owen rescued her from falling flat on her face.

She thanked Owen briefly before plastering herself to Shade's side and holding her smartphone in front of them. Shade put on his fan-friendly face and waited for her to snap several pictures. But she eventually handed the device to Owen because she couldn't get a clear shot to come out.

"And one with you too," she said to Owen. Apparently his dejected-puppy look had finally gotten through to her.

After she was satisfied with her photos and had forced Shade to give her an inappropriately long hug, which involved more than one hand on his ass, she allowed him to escape. Owen trudged after him.

"Always an afterthought when I'm with you," Owen grumbled as they waited for the elevator.

"Can I help it that I'm cooler than you are?" Shade teased.

"Apparently you're also hotter than I am."

"Ah . . . well, hot gets you burned. And everyone actually *likes* lukewarm; lukewarm is comfortable." Shade hadn't meant it as an insult—Owen *was* easy to like—but the guy apparently took it the wrong way.

"Fuck you," he said before pushing his way past Shade to get on the elevator.

"So how was your weekend?" Shade asked Owen as he followed. Though still sleep deprived, he was feeling slightly more personable now that he was back in his element. And he really did care about Owen's problems. Somewhat.

"It sucked giant monkey balls," he said.

"I saw giant monkey balls this weekend," Shade said.

"Huh?"

He grinned at Owen's flabbergasted expression. "Took Julie to the zoo."

Owen smiled. He loved kids—especially Julie—and dogs, of course. "I bet she enjoyed that. Did you see Amanda?"

"Not really," he lied. He didn't want to talk about Amanda. Not now, not ever. Fuck her.

"That would explain why you're so cranky."

Adam answered their summons at his suite door with a dark expression and an even darker disposition. Shade hadn't seen this side of Adam in over a year. He couldn't help but wonder if he was using drugs again. Because that was what Adam did when his life turned to shit. He wrote deep, soulful metal music and got high out of his fucking mind.

"You okay?" Shade asked him.

"Never better," Adam said flatly. He handed Owen a keycard and another to Shade. "Gabe's woman took your spare key last night. So you might not want to barge in there without calling first."

"Why are they in my room?"

"Like I give a fuck." He closed the door in Shade's face.

"What was that all about?" Shade asked Owen. And why the fuck would Gabe and Melanie be in his room? Maybe it had something to do with Nikki inviting herself along for their romantic weekend. Perhaps they'd needed a little privacy from the mistress of cling.

"No clue. Maybe he had a weekend that sucked giant monkey balls too."

"Some monkeys have all the luck."

Owen snorted and then laughed. "It's good to be back."

"You never did say why your weekend sucked," Shade said as he fished his phone out of his pocket so he could call Gabe and alert him to his arrival. He tried not to let his heart sink when he found Amanda hadn't called to tell him she'd made a terrible mistake, but the stupid organ was apparently still hung up on the woman. Apparently his heart was just as dumb as his brain was.

"Not all of it," Owen said and slapped Shade on the back. "I'm gonna catch a nap. Didn't get much sleep last night."

And before Shade could ask why Owen had missed out on sleep, the guy had opened his suite door and disappeared inside.

Gabe sounded mostly asleep himself when he answered Shade's call. Shade could only think of one reason why Gabe would still be in bed with Melanie at noon.

"Can you vacate my room now?" Shade asked. "Adam said he gave my spare key to your girlfriend. Why are you guys in my room? Did you break another set of box springs?" At least someone was having a great morning.

"I'm not with her," Gabe said flatly. "She's in your room, and I'm in my room."

"Oh," Shade said, rubbing the side of his nose. "What's going on?"

"Shit. Lots of fucked-up shit."

That monkey with the giant pair must have the cleanest, most delighted pair of nuts ever conceived.

"Sounds like the morning I'm having." Or rather, the *life* he was having.

They agreed to approach the suite together—safety in numbers—and a moment later Gabe entered the corridor from his suite. He'd never looked worse. Both eyes were bloodshot and encircled by dark bruises. His crimson mohawk was flat and drooping. Hell, even the dragons tattooed on his scalp looked weary.

"What the hell happened to your face?" Shade asked, wincing at a pair of what had to be painful shiners.

"I bounced it off some guy's knuckles a couple dozen times," Gabe grumbled. "Good times."

Gabe pointed at Shade's forehead. "And what happened to you?"

Shade hadn't even noticed the dull pain of the bruise on his head until Gabe pointed it out. The ache in his chest had been a far greater distraction. "Ex-wife," Shade said vaguely.

Gabe sneered. He'd never been a fan of Tina. "Bitch."

"Ball-buster."

Gabe's sour expression brightened as he poked Shade's bruise and sent a sharp pain through his skull. "Head-buster."

Gabe grinned, and Shade couldn't help but smile back. Gabe was one of the few people who saw through Shade's façade and yet didn't give him grief about the softness hidden beneath his hardened outer shell. He wasn't exactly vulnerable around Gabe—not the way he had been with Amanda—but he was more genuine. He let his guard down. But Gabe had never betrayed him.

Shade wasn't sure which of them needed their back-pounding bro hug more as they crashed into each other and offered the manliest physical comfort possible. He actually felt a little better by the time Gabe opened the suite door with Shade's keycard.

Melanie and her very bendy friend Nikki were curled up together on the bed all sleep-tousled and feminine. Nikki's hand was cupped possessively over Melanie's breast, her beautiful face pressed into her bedmate's neck. Shade didn't know why lesbian lovers were such a turn-on to him, but he was definitely a fan.

"Well, what do we have here?" Shade asked with a crooked grin. This was a sandwich any man would want to be the filling in. Why exactly had Gabe defected to another room?

Melanie's eyes blinked open, and her intense dislike for him bubbled to the surface before she'd even taken a breath. "What are you doing in here?" she growled at him. "Get out!"

Shade was not in the mood for her sass. "This is my room. You get out!"

Nikki was more agreeable. She untangled herself from Melanie and stretched her arms over her head, showing off a strip of flat tanned belly at the hem of her tank top. "I guess I got to spend the night in Shade's bed after all," she said with a flirty smile.

And maybe Shade would have been better off with Nikki—or someone like her—in his bed. He'd have gotten his rocks off without the complications that came with emotional attachment. But even though Amanda had shredded his heart, he didn't regret a single moment he'd spent with her. He had loved her. *Still* loved her.

Maybe she'd change her mind about him. Would it be better to pressure her or give her time and space?

What was he thinking? She'd made it perfectly clear that she wasn't interested.

Oh hell, he didn't know. When it came to women, he'd never had this problem before. He was usually the one pushing them away, not the other way around. And he knew how fucking annoying it was for him when a woman he didn't want keep pestering him. It made him dislike her even more. How would he feel if he went after Amanda and her hated grew? Could he tolerate that?

Shade shook his head to clear it.

He didn't need Amanda in his life. He would not swallow his pride and go after her. Fuck her.

He turned his attention to the undercurrent of drama in the room. Nikki seemed her regular chipper self, but Melanie was definitely out of sorts. Gabe seemed shocked by Nikki's cheer. A bit puzzled himself, Shade couldn't help but stare at the dark bruises on Nikki's throat as she took Gabe's keycard, patted him on the butt, and left to return to Gabe's suite to get dressed.

"So what the hell happened?" Shade asked. "Owen said you two returned early from Austin, and there's obviously something going on with Nikki."

"I shouldn't have left her by herself," Melanie said, dragging a sheet from the bed to wrap around herself. She was wearing a nightgown, and it wasn't as if Shade had never seen a woman in her nightgown before, but the cover seemed to offer some comfort.

"She hooked up with the wrong guy," Gabe said. "An MMA fighter who wouldn't take no for an answer. I tried to kick his ass, but…" He shrugged and pointed to his blackened eyes.

"He did that to her neck?" Shade asked.

"Not just her neck," Gabe said.

"He fucking raped her!" Melanie shouted. "And no one was here to help her. She was all alone, lost in an unfamiliar city, broken and bruised."

"Mel, you can't blame yourself for what happened to Nikki," Gabe said, pulling her into his arms.

Shade half expected her to pull away, but she didn't. She melted into him and clung to his waist.

"Then who am I supposed to blame?"

"The fucking prick who hurt her."

"I wish she would press charges against him," Melanie said. "How could she let him walk?"

"I think she wants to forget it ever happened," Gabe said.

"Or she thinks she deserved it," Shade said. He'd spent enough time with Nikki to know how her mind worked. She had a victim mentality and until she figured out that she was in control of her destiny, life would continue to just happen to her.

"How can you say that? You're such an asshole," Melanie said. She shoved off Gabe's chest so she could flee Shade's odious presence.

"You really do bring out the worst in women," Gabe said, shaking his head at Shade before he followed Melanie out of the suite and shut the door with a loud bang.

Shade had to agree with him. He'd turned Tina into a bitter bitch and Amanda into a heartless shrew. They'd both been perfectly wonderful women until they'd tangled with him.

Still fully clothed, he collapsed on the crumpled bed and at long last found the sleep that had eluded him. He felt almost human when he woke several hours later. It was still light out—so he wasn't late for the show—and soon he realized that it was his rumbling stomach that had woken him. When had he last eaten? Sometime the day before. When he'd grilled burgers and brats for Julie and Amanda, he realized. Thinking of that happy time felt surreal. Had his world really been perfect just yesterday? He felt like he'd lost her a lifetime ago.

Shoving thoughts of Amanda aside—seriously, fuck her—he ordered room service and jumped into the shower while he waited for his food to arrive.

As water cascaded over his head and dripped from his jaw and the tip of his nose, he closed his eyes and tried to chase thoughts of Amanda from his head again. He didn't want to think about her or picture her floating topless in his pool. He sure as hell didn't want to continue to lust after her. He'd heard that absence made the heart grow fonder, but he was sure his dick would soon have other ideas. His need for her would diminish with time. Hopefully, real soon. How could he live with a huge achy hole in his chest where his heart had once beat strong and proud?

He was slipping into his leather pants when a knock sounded on the door. "Room service," a woman called from the corridor.

He tucked his dick against his thigh, careful not to catch his bare skin as he zipped his fly, and went to the door shirtless. The young woman's friendly smile was immediately replaced by slack-jawed gawking as her gaze roamed his exposed flesh. The dishes on the tray she carried rattled as she slumped against the door frame.

Her eyes lifted to meet his gaze, and he realized he wasn't wearing his sunglasses. He quickly turned to remedy that oversight and swore the woman gasped the second his backside came into view. Normally he'd have used her obvious attraction to him to his advantage—he was confident that getting the raven-haired beauty naked between the sheets wouldn't have been a challenge—but he honestly wasn't in the mood.

"Just set it on the desk," he said, sliding his shades into place and reaching for his wallet to offer the server a tip. It was apparent that she wanted more than a twenty when her hand touched the small of his back.

"If you'd like some company, it's time for my dinner break," she said.

Would he like some company? The image of Amanda laughing while sitting across the table from him entered his thoughts. That was the kind of company he wanted—the easy camaraderie and inside jokes, the warmth that glowed in his chest from being with her, and the knowledge that she liked him for himself and not because he was famous. But he'd been so wrong. So, so wrong. She *didn't* like him. She had never loved him. She thought he was stupid, and he must be if he thought what they'd had could have amounted to anything. He'd never share those simple moments with her again. So maybe losing himself between the thighs of some other woman—one who would never matter to him—would soothe the ache in his chest that was suddenly climbing his throat and making his eyes sting.

Shade turned, took the young woman by the upper arms, and gazed into her eyes. Her breath caught and her body immediately went soft and submissive.

He could practically hear her thoughts. *Oh God, this is going to happen. I'm going to fuck Shade Silverton. I can't wait to tell all my friends and my future grandchildren.* It was obvious she knew who he was and that was why she was offering herself as *company.*

He turned her toward the door and gave her a little shove so that she couldn't mistake his disinterest. "Show yourself out," he said, his voice taking on an authoritative edge. "And put out the Do Not Disturb sign. I'm not in the mood to be bothered by the help."

She practically sprinted to the door, and just before she slammed it, she shouted, "You're an asshole."

Her words had no effect on his feelings. She wasn't the first woman to call him that and he knew she wouldn't be the last. Shade knew he was an asshole. It made his life a whole lot easier.

As she hadn't followed his instructions, he went to the door and hung the Do Not Disturb sign. After closing the door, he flopped into the chair at the desk and uncovered his plate. Maybe his mood would lighten if he ate. Something needed to blow away the dark cloud brewing over his head. Sex was obviously out of the question.

While he shoveled rice into his mouth, his cellphone chimed when a new text message was delivered. His first thought was that it was from Amanda, so he scrambled after the device. The message and a whole string of others he'd missed either while sleeping or in the shower weren't from Amanda. They were from Tina. His heart sank with disappointment, and he blew out a long breath before having his phone read the messages to him.

"I know I should call you to have this conversation," the robotic tone of the app read aloud, "but I'm afraid I'll lose my nerve, so here goes.

"What I said last night about still being in love with you, it's true. I do still love you. I never stopped loving you. That was never the problem in our marriage. The problem was I couldn't trust you."

Shade rolled his eyes. She hadn't even tried to trust him.

"I've been thinking maybe we should start over . . ."

Shade dropped his fork. *What?*

". . . and try to be a family again, you and me and Julie. I think we can make it work. Julie needs a stable environment."

He did agree with that.

"And wouldn't it be nice to come home to a loving wife and a happy home and see your daughter as often as you'd like? I know that's what you want."

It was exactly what he wanted. Strange how Tina recognized his need so clearly. He just didn't want *her* to be that loving wife. Or the not so loving wife.

"Just think about it. Okay?"

He didn't have to think about it. He didn't want to be involved with Tina again. As much as it pained him, he was deeply in love with her heartbreaker of a sister. He lifted his phone and thumbed in a short reply: *No way in hell.* But he didn't send it. He deleted it before tossing his phone on the bed so he didn't have to look at it.

Why couldn't he have what he really wanted?

Why couldn't he have Amanda?

He glanced at his phone, wondering if it would do any good to call her. Maybe if he got his GED, she'd decide he wasn't a complete idiot and consider him an equal. Or maybe Tina was the best he could hope for. She said she still loved him—that was something, wasn't it? Amanda had never said the words. Obviously because she didn't feel the way he felt.

Shade pushed his nearly untouched food aside and stood to pull on a shirt. He couldn't stand to sit there alone trapped in his thoughts another moment. He needed to be surrounded by people he could depend on and who wouldn't make him feel lower than a slug's slime trail. He needed to be with the members of his band—his true friends. Or better yet, his fans.

After knocking on a few doors, he discovered that he was the only one staying at the hotel who hadn't yet left for the venue. Had they tried to rouse him or didn't they care that he was struggling?

No, that wasn't fair. They didn't know he was troubled. How could they if he didn't show his distress around them?

Shade found a ride and smiled as the limo drove past the venue. The show wouldn't start for hours, yet Sole Regret fans were already congregating outside the stadium and jockeying to be the first to enter so they could get prime general admission floor space close to the stage. Thousands—hell, *millions*—of people paid their hard-earned money to watch him perform. What did he care that some schoolteacher didn't want to have anything to do with him? Fuck her.

Shade tapped on the window that separated him from the driver. The glass slid down. "Stop right here and let me out," he said.

"Here?" The driver glanced anxiously at the black-wearing, tattooed, rough-looking crowd trying to peer through the tinted glass of the limo. "But—"

"Stop."

As soon as the car stopped, he opened the door before the press of bodies could trap him inside. It occurred to him that he'd busted Adam's balls for pulling a similar stunt a few days earlier. Crowds could quickly get out of control; Shade knew that. They also stroked his deflated ego; Shade needed that. He realized too late that he should have contacted his security team for assistance *before* he'd stepped out of the car. But he could command an entire stadium full of badass metal heads to jump and they fucking jumped, so how different could this situation be?

Once the crowd figured out that he planned to stay for a while and that he was genuinely interested in giving all of them some personal attention, they stopped trying to flatten him against the side of the car. Women wanted him, men wanted to be him, and not a single fan made him feel like he wasn't good enough. Their excitement and adulation lifted his spirits into the stratosphere— made him feel like a god. And he loved them for it. He'd been right, not that he was surprised. Shade was the persona he needed to cling to in order to feel good about himself. Jacob could go fuck himself.

Seeing as that loser got dumped every time he fell in love, masturbation *was* his best option.

Shade's phone vibrated in his pocket with the delivery of a text. His heart raced with anticipation. Amanda?

He scowled. Why was that his first thought every time he got a text? Fuck her.

He fished the device out of his pocket and viewed the message from Gabe. Something about Adam writing lyrics. Shade was too flustered to make out the details of the entire note. He couldn't concentrate on words with all the activity going on around him.

"I need to go get ready for the show," he said. He'd had his fill of fan worship and if Adam really was writing lyrics, he wanted to see it with his own eyes. "I hope you enjoy yourselves tonight."

After a few last handshakes and hugs, he slipped back into the limo and the crowd parted to let the car creep forward at a snail's pace.

"I thought they were going to kill you," the driver said, glancing anxiously at the fans visible through the windows.

"They love me," Shade said, with a smile. "Why would they kill me?"

"Not intentionally." The driver jumped when an eager fan slapped his palms against the hood of the car with a loud bang. People continued to walk beside the car all the way to the barrier fence that had been erected around the tour buses and equipment trucks. After verifying that it was Shade in the car, security let the limo through, but kept the crowd at bay.

"I love you, Shade!" a woman screamed from the crowd as he stepped from the car in the fan-free area behind the venue.

He waved to the people pushing against the barrier fence before trotting up the bus steps. He strode up the aisle and paused at the dining room table. Adam was sitting there with his sketchbook open and he was writing. Not drawing spiders. Not creating the fanciest "the" to ever grace a page. Lyrics were pouring from the tip of his pencil like he had no conscious control over the process. Shade's heart soared. They were going to be okay. With Adam's creativity on the loose, Sole Regret's success was guaranteed.

A long lean body blocked Shade's path, and he looked up into Gabe's grinning face.

"Is he writing?" Shade whispered, not wanting to disturb Adam.

Gabe nodded. "It's as if he can't stop. He also drew this wicked piece of artwork that we have to use for our next album cover. The dude has amazing talent."

Adam did have amazing talent. Shade could never do what he did. But he could try to keep Adam off drugs and scrape him off rock bottom every time he found himself there.

Shade pushed Gabe aside and slid into the empty booth across the table from Adam and waited for the guitarist to come up for air. Shade didn't want to be responsible for interrupting the man's flow of ideas, but he did want to witness what he'd feared he'd never experience again.

As soon as Shade settled into the seat, Adam glanced up and met his eyes.

"It's back?" Shade asked breathlessly and nodded, as if the motion would make it true.

"Yeah," Adam said, though the haunted look in his eyes didn't make him seem too happy about his breakthrough. "I guess it is."

"Any guitar music yet?" Shade asked. He couldn't wait any longer; he pulled the sketch pad toward himself. "Lats oGodbey" was his first impression of the title, but after a second of concentration, he decided that "Last Goodbye" made more sense. He'd ask Adam to read the lines to him later and blame the man's handwriting for his inability to make sense of the written words. The trick had worked before; he had confidence that it would work again. "I'm ready to harmonize."

"And I'm ready to bang out a new tempo," Gabe said as he leaned his hip against the back of the bench behind Adam and made drumming motions with both arms. His eyes were still blackened from his run-in with that MMA fighter, but he no longer looked like roadkill. He seemed almost as enthusiastic about Adam's sudden spawning of lyrics as Shade felt about it.

"And I'm ready to bang," Owen said from the back of the bus.

Nothing new there.

Shade flipped through Adam's notebook, excited to find several pages of scrawled words. His stomach turned when he came across a drawing of Melanie's friend Nikki, and rage pulsed through his skull. It wasn't the work that upset him. The details of the drawing were remarkable and if it had been of a woman he didn't know, he would have appreciated the meticulous care Adam had taken in his sketch. The subject matter, on the other hand . . . Shade couldn't tolerate that. Half of Nikki's beautiful face and flawless body was torn and decayed—her guts were spilling out, bits of muscle and lengths of bone showing through the gaps in her flesh. The sketchbook dropped from his suddenly numb fingers.

"What in the hell did you do to Nikki?" he yelled. Hadn't the woman been through enough? If she ever saw this drawing of herself, it would destroy her already delicate psyche.

"Isn't that awesome?" Gabe said. "That's the sketch I was talking about. It would make a fantastic album cover."

"It's sick." But maybe it would make a fantastic album cover. If the woman depicted weren't easily recognizable as someone they all knew, he'd have thought the drawing was badass. "How could you draw a living person all torn apart like that?"

"She *is* all torn apart like that." Adam pulled the sketch pad toward himself and began writing a new song on a blank page. "You're just too blind to see it."

Had something else happened to the poor woman? And why hadn't anyone told him? "What do you mean she's all torn up like that?" he yelled, not sure why he was so upset. He wasn't interested in Nikki, but he *had* slept with her. He didn't want anything bad to happen to her. Anything *else* bad to happen to her, he corrected.

Gabe grabbed Shade's shoulder. "He doesn't mean literally."

Thank God.

As the tension on the bus diminished, Adam's creative spark ignited into an inferno. Everything fed the fire within him. He was soon using every thread of conversation—even ridiculous ones—as inspiration for additional songs.

It felt so good to have the band all together, creating and joking around. Shade had forgotten what it was like to relax and enjoy the guys' company. He hadn't realized how tense things had become between them until that tension eased. He recognized that it hadn't been his insistence that had smoothed things over. It was Adam's palpable relief to be creating again.

Maybe Adam and the rest of the band had been as worried about their creative future as Shade had been. Maybe Shade didn't give the guys enough credit. He knew Adam didn't work best under pressure, but what did they expect? That Shade would take the back seat and wait this shit out? He was incapable of relinquishing control over the band's success. They all had to know that about him by now.

Shade wasn't sure what had unleashed Adam's creativity, but whatever it had been, he was grateful it had stirred Adam's soul. He couldn't help but wonder if Adam had returned to his heroin habit, but Adam's pupils weren't constricted, his skin wasn't flushed, and he hadn't sniffed his nose or scratched at his skin once. Shade had been around junkie-Adam enough to know what to look for. Adam wasn't high. At least not on heroin.

The entire band was in a good mood when Sally eventually came to get them for the show. Shade couldn't help but notice there were no longer any women on tour, which in his current state of mind proved that women were more trouble than they were worth. He was through with romantic relationships. Gabe's chick seemed more interested in keeping her friend in one piece than being with him; Melanie had abandoned Gabe to return home with Nikki a couple of hours ago. Shade wasn't sure what had happened to Adam's girlfriend. They'd been together the last he knew, but maybe her unexplained absence was why he was spewing dark hatred in the form of lyrics. And Owen wasn't messing with his iPad, buying useless tokens for the woman who'd supposedly stolen his heart. Kellen hadn't returned from his weekend with his pretty composer, and Owen seemed much more interested in where his friend was than what his maybe-girlfriend was up to. Was it wrong of Shade to feel connected to these guys because they were all romantically miserable at the moment?

"You know, if it were me," Owen said to Gabe as they headed down a long corridor toward the backstage area, "I'd get them both in bed and let my dick sort that shit out."

Shade chuckled. Owen's answer to everything. His dick.

"The problem with that," Gabe said, "is that Nikki would be more interested in Melanie's pussy than my dick."

Owen slapped him on the back. "That's not a problem in my book."

"Mine either," Shade said with a grin.

"So Melanie and Nikki are lovers?" Adam asked, his dark brow knitted with confusion.

Gabe shook his head. "Melanie isn't interested in Nikki that way, but Nikki is in love with her. Or she thinks she is. Maybe she's just confused."

"She didn't seem confused when she and I invited a waitress to our room last weekend for a little girl-on-girl action," Shade said. "Nikki went straight for the pussy, no hesitation. Had that chick coming in twenty seconds flat."

Gabe scowled at him. "Yeah, thanks. That does not make me feel any better."

Shade shrugged. "It made me feel pretty good."

"They live together now," Gabe said, wiping a hand over his lean jaw. He really seemed to be torn up about this. Didn't he realize this was the opportunity of a lifetime? "Nikki moved into Melanie's place this week."

"I'm sure Melanie will keep her legs closed even when your dick is a thousand miles away," Adam said.

"Nikki will wear her down eventually," Shade teased. "That wicked tongue of hers is very persistent."

Gabe shoved him in the shoulder. "Not funny."

"Still not seeing the problem," Owen said, shaking his head.

When they reached the backstage area, Adam and Owen settled their guitars in place. Adam immediately began fingering a new rift that made Shade's heart thud with excitement. The man's talent was astounding. He seemed to pull amazing music out of nowhere. Or maybe it was housed in his soul.

Kellen rushed backstage and reached for his guitar, but paused when he noticed the band gazing worshipfully at the lead guitarist.

"Nice," Owen said, mimicking Adam's string of notes on his bass guitar.

"Yeah, I like that," Kellen said as he listened to them play. "I assume your writer's block is gone." He grinned at his fellow guitarist.

"Yep."

"Well, keep it up." Kellen whacked Adam on the back. "Sounds great."

Kellen then greeted Owen, who began talking a mile a minute. Adam had quit playing his new riff to answer his phone, so Shade turned to Gabe.

"You're not really worried that Melanie is going to dump you for Nikki, are you?" Shade asked.

"Not much I can do about it if she does. So how did Tina take the news about you and Amanda?"

Shade hadn't told Gabe anything about the situation with Tina or Amanda, so how had he known to even ask? Now was not the time to discuss this. They had to be onstage in a few minutes and focusing on Tina *or* Amanda was sure to put him in a foul mood again.

"Not sure what you're talking about," Shade said with a shrug.

"So Tina just hit you in the head for fun? She still doesn't know?"

"She knows," Shade admitted, "but I broke it off with Amanda." He lied to save his ego further bruising. "I got what I wanted from her. Didn't seem smart to piss off Tina for a mediocre piece of ass."

Even referring to Amanda that way ate at him, but Gabe wouldn't harass him about it if he thought the breakup was Shade's idea.

"You don't mope like a teenage girl when you dump a mediocre piece of ass," Gabe observed before heading up the steps to find his place behind the drum kit.

Perceptive jerk, Shade thought darkly.

He turned to see if the rest of the band was ready to take the stage. Owen and Kellen were still chatting as if they hadn't seen each other in years, but Adam had disappeared.

CHAPTER EIGHTEEN

"WHERE'S ADAM?" Shade asked the other two guitarists.

Owen shrugged. "No idea."

Shade's gaze fell on a familiar guitar sitting on its stand next to the stage. "He left his guitar."

"Maybe he had to go to the bathroom," Kellen suggested. "Ever try to take a piss with a guitar strapped on?"

"Can't say that I have," Shade said, watching the wide double doors behind the stage for Adam's reappearance.

Several minutes ticked by with no sign of the lead guitarist. Shade grabbed the arm of a nearby roadie who was standing there with his arms crossed waiting for the performance to begin. "Will you run to the dressing room and tell Adam we're waiting for him? He's probably in the bathroom." He sent a second roadie to the bus, just in case he'd gone there instead.

A few minutes later, Gabe came down from the stage with drumsticks in hand. "What's the hold up?"

"Adam's missing," Shade said.

"Missing?"

"Yeah, he was just here." Shade turned to see if the incredible vanishing guitarist had returned in the few seconds he'd been distracted. Still no sign of him.

Shade didn't truly begin to worry until the two roadies returned without Adam in tow.

"He wasn't in the bathroom or the dressing room."

"Not on the bus either," the other roadie reported. "I found his earpiece on the ground behind the bus. At least I think it's his."

The guy dropped the earpiece into Shade's palm. It was probably Adam's, but he couldn't be sure. "Was his motorcycle still there?"

"I didn't see one."

"Fuck!" Shade yelled. "Did he say anything to any of you?" As Shade's glare landed on the members of his band, each shook his head in turn. "Fuck! What in the hell is he thinking?" The problem was Adam never thought things through. He was impulsive. Reactionary. An inconsiderate, self-absorbed jackass. Why had Shade let himself hope that Adam had changed?

"Maybe there's an emergency," Owen said.

"Even if there is, he could have taken a few seconds to tell someone. Fuck! I'm going after him."

"Do you know where he went?" Gabe asked.

Shade pulled his cellphone out of his pocket and pressed the icon for Adam's tracking app. He was already miles away heading west, but within seconds he moved out of range and the little orange dot that indicated his position blipped out of existence.

"Fuck!" Shade said again. "He's headed west."

"What's west?" Kellen asked.

"Texas. Madison. His fucking heroin dealer. How the hell should I know?"

"Calm down," Owen advised. "We'll figure something out."

Shade wasn't going to calm down. How could Adam leave just minutes before they were set to perform? What could possibly be that important? Nothing, as far as Shade was concerned. Granted, if something happened to Julie—God forbid—and he had to rush to her side, he would have walked out on a show, but he would have fucking told someone first.

"I'll try calling him," Kellen said rationally. "Maybe he'll answer."

While Kellen attempted to get Adam on the phone, Sally rushed toward Shade, almost colliding with him as her high heels skidded on the slippery concrete. She grabbed his arms to steady herself before looking up at him with wide eyes. "What's going on?" she demanded. "Why aren't you on stage?"

"Adam isn't here. We can't perform without our lead guitarist, can we?"

"I'm worried," Owen said, his eyes on Kellen as he shook his head to let them know Adam wasn't answering his phone. "He wouldn't just run off like that unless it was a life or death situation."

"*Yes*, he would," Shade said. "I was the one who dealt with him when he was at his worst. You all pretended everything was just fine while I was forced to get him lucid enough to perform. It was only a year ago. Don't tell me you've already forgotten."

"He's changed, Jacob," Gabe said, clutching the back of his neck with one hand as he stared at the floor.

"He has?" Shade shook his head in disagreement. "Sorry, but I don't see it."

Still beyond pissed, Shade stomped up the side steps and crossed the stage. The waiting crowd cheered when they recognized him. He took the mic out its stand and approached the audience, taking a moment to bask in the knowledge that they loved him almost as much as he needed them.

"Good evening, New Orleans. You look ready to rock!" When the fans cheered, his heart thudded with regret. He wouldn't get the chance to perform for this amazing crowd. He'd been so looking forward to it. "Unfortunately, our performance is not going to happen tonight," he said, his thoughts not matching his words. *Fucking Adam let us all down again.* A roar of disapproval circulated through the arena. "Our lead guitarist, Adam Taylor, was called away on an emergency." *And didn't bother to tell anyone. I will never forgive the asshole for forcing me to disappoint all these fans.* But as front man, he was expected to be the one who delivered such news, and he didn't shirk his responsibilities no matter how distasteful. Fucking Adam. "So we have to cancel the show."

A groan of disappointment reverberated through the stadium.

"I'm not sure if they'll issue refunds or reschedule the performance, but we'll square you away. I promise."

Grumbling, the crowd started to disperse.

"Hey! Hey, Shade!" The call came from some young guy among the group still hanging around the barrier fence directly in front of the stage. "I play lead guitar and know all your songs by heart. I could take Adam's place tonight."

It was as if Shade's guardian angel had fallen into the body of a skinny teenager in a black beanie hat.

Shade crouched down on the stage in front of him and stared into the kid's dark eyes. Long, jet-black bangs were smashed down to obscure those eyes, but the sincerity Shade read in his direct gaze gave him hope. "Are you sure?"

The kid nodded, oozing the kind of self-confidence of someone who was telling the truth or was *completely* delusional. "I'll prove it. Hand me a guitar."

"Wait!" Shade called to the retreating crowd. "We might have a solution. Can you give us a few minutes to see if the show can go on after all?"

Innumerable fans were probably already too pissed off to return, but the majority of them stopped their retreat to see what was in store for them.

Shade instructed security to let the young guitarist into the backstage area. His bandmates looked at him with narrowed eyes.

"Did you get a hold of Adam?" Shade asked Kellen, giving his longtime frenemy one last chance to not disappoint him.

Kellen frowned and shook his head.

"Okay," Shade said, nudging the kid forward. "This guy says he knows all our songs by heart and can take Adam's place onstage tonight."

None of his bandmates looked convinced, but they did look intrigued by the possible solution to their shitty situation.

"So I say we give him a chance to prove himself," Shade said. "What's your name?"

"Wes."

"Give Adam's guitar to Wes," Shade said to Adam's technician. "Let's see what he's got."

They put the kid through his paces. Riffs. Solos. Wes wasn't as skilled as Adam—no one was as skilled as Adam—but the talented kid would do in a bind.

"You don't get stage fright, do you?" Shade asked.

"I don't think so," Wes said uncertainly.

Well, it wasn't as if they had other options banging down their door.

"Are we all onboard with this idea?" Shade asked everyone who'd congregated to watch the spectacle. Bandmates, crew, and manager all nodded their approval.

"All right, kid, here's your chance to be a rock star for a night," Shade said. "Don't blow it."

Wes beamed at him and shook the devil horns he'd formed on one hand.

Shade returned to the stage and smiled down at the anxiously waiting and restless crowd.

"Well, he's no Adam Taylor, but he's going to do his best to pretend. Tonight we have Wes on lead guitar."

Wes jogged across the stage to stand at Shade's side and lifted both hands in the air triumphantly. Some of the audience members cheered, but most just stared up at them crossly.

Shade knew how to work a crowd. Undaunted, he'd have

them all excited about this idea in no time.

"How many of you have dreamed of being a rock star?" he called to the crowd. "Where are my aspiring vocalists?" He scowled at the pitiful response he received. "For a bunch of future rock singers, you aren't very loud," he complained. That evoked the response he wanted from them. "Okay, where are my rock stars who like to bang?" He placed a hand on his forehead as if shading his eyes so he could see all the wannabe drummers in the crowd. The audience exploded with cheers, and he noticed that some of the fans who had left earlier were filtering back in through the exit doors. "Force, get out here. Seems over half the audience wants to be like you."

Gabe jogged across the stage, waving at the crowd as he found a microphone. "I think they misunderstood your question," he said. "They don't want to waste their time on drums. They just want to bang."

Whistles of appreciation, whoops of delight, and loud catcalls filled the stadium.

"Anyone like to do it low and slow?" Shade asked. "Who out there always dreamed of being a famous bass player?"

Even though lots of people cheered, Shade had to tease Owen. "Anyone? No one wants to be Tags when they grow up?"

Owen entered the stage, which elicited more screams of excitement. He found a microphone. "Bassists never get any love."

"I love you, Tags!" several women yelled.

"So I guess the rest of you play air guitar in your underwear and dream of soloing in the spotlight," Shade said.

At least half the audience began playing air guitar. A few moments later, Kellen entered the stage and accompanied them on his real guitar. After several measures, Wes found the courage to join in. The crowd loved it.

"Now Wes here has the opportunity to do what most people only dream of doing—he gets to be a rock star for a night. So show him some love!" Shade shouted over the wailing guitars. Now that he had the crowd amped up and behind Wes, the kid had better not fuck this up.

Shade wrapped an arm around Wes's shoulders and showed him a paper taped to the floor. "This is the set list," he told him. "If there are any songs on there you don't know, just tell us; we'll work around it."

Wes's eyes scanned the list, and then he looked at Shade. "I know them all. Hey, is Adam okay?"

Shade wasn't sure why, but Wes's concern for Adam sent a spike of rage through him. "I'm sure he's fucking peachy," he said before dropping his arm and addressing the crowd. "It's time to get darker."

Usually Owen entered the stage first, extending the opening bass line of "Darker" by several measures to build up the song and the crowd's anticipation, but as the show was already off to an unusual start, the entire band started the song on Jacob's signal. Wes watched his fingers, working so hard at getting the notes right that he didn't seem to notice the crowd cheering him on. Kellen and Owen tried to coax him into enjoying himself, but their antics made him stumble over a riff, so they left him alone and worked extra hard to engage the crowd themselves.

When the song ended with one final reverberating wail of the lead guitar, Wes lifted his head and looked at Shade for approval.

"Not bad, Wes. Not bad at all. With a little more practice you could fill Adam Taylor's shoes." And Shade wasn't just saying that. He was more than ready to find someone to take the undependable lead guitarist's spot. And the longer he watched Wes—sounding almost like Adam in his first attempt—the more he thought a new guitarist would be the best solution for the band. Unfortunately, if they replaced Adam, they'd lose his songwriting skills. But if the only way he could compose was when his life was falling apart and he was dragging the rest of them down with him, Sole Regret was better off relying on those who wrote songs for a living. They could easily pay professionals to write their songs. So why not?

They played through their entire set list, and Shade could feel the uneasiness from the rest of the band—especially Owen. The guy was loyal to a fault. He probably felt guilty for sharing the stage with Wes instead of Adam. But Shade was experiencing something else entirely. Instead of trying to *fix* Adam—and what a monumental task that was—they could find someone who wasn't broken to replace him. Shade just had to get the other guys to see things his way. He refused to put up with Adam's bullshit any longer. He'd crossed the line one too many times.

When the concert was over, Shade took a sweat-drenched Wes aside and thanked him for his assistance. He made sure Sally took down his contact information. They could probably do better than a kid long on talent but short on experience, but they could definitely do a lot worse. Shade definitely wanted Wes to have a shot at being their new guitarist, but he also wanted to keep his options open, so he didn't reveal his thoughts to Wes. It *was* time to explain his plan to the band, however. They were rational men; they'd see it his way. He was sure of it.

He waited until all the guys were on the bus and they were headed east to their next destination before he broached the subject.

"Anyone hear from Adam yet?" he asked, checking his own phone to see if Adam had contacted him.

They all shook their heads, looking glum. He couldn't be the only one who saw Adam as more of a liability than an asset.

"I've had it with his bullshit," Shade said, his heart thundering with apprehension. "Adam's out of the band."

Gabe's eyes widened. Kellen's jaw dropped.

Owen blinked hard and sputtered, "What?"

"He's toxic," Shade said. "We need to get rid of him. Replace him with someone who takes our success seriously."

"Adam writes all of our music," Kellen said. "We can't just kick him out."

"We'll write the music ourselves and if necessary, hire songwriters," Shade said with a shrug.

"This is bullshit," Kellen said, crossing his arms over his bare chest. "Adam is one of us. He's always been one of us. We can't do this to him."

"We don't even know why he took off," Owen said. "I'm sure he had a good reason."

"More than two hours later and he still hasn't checked in to let us know what the fuck is going on!" Shade yelled. "He obviously doesn't give a shit about any of us or the fans or the music. All he cares about is himself. It's time to cut him loose. If he wants to destroy himself, fine, but I'm not letting him take the rest of us down with him."

"I want to hear what he has to say before I weigh in," Gabe said. "For all we know, he's dead in a ditch somewhere."

The blood drained from Owen's face. "Don't even say that."

"It would save me the trouble of telling him to fuck off," Shade growled.

"You're such an asshole," Owen said.

Shade stepped forward until his nose was an inch from Owen's. "I'd rather be an asshole than a spineless wuss."

"What's that supposed to mean?" Owen shoved him, and Shade was glad to see the guy actually had a little fight in him.

"You're a pushover, Owen. You always have been."

"Don't take your frustration with Adam out on Owen," Kellen said. "You're the one who never bends. You're the mighty oak, standing tall and rigid against any force that threatens your position." He slammed a fist against his chest.

"Someone has to be strong."

"Listen to what Kellen is trying to warn you about," Gabe said. "If you never bend, you will break, Jacob. Don't you see that?"

He didn't see it at all. Everyone just needed to fall in line with his plans and it would all work out for the best. Didn't *they* see that?

"We'll figure out what to do after we talk to Adam," Gabe said.

"Kellen could play lead," Shade said. Maybe they'd feel better about a change if they were replacing their rhythm guitarist instead of lead.

Owen scrunched his brow. "And Adam play rhythm? He'd never agree to that."

What part of *kick Adam the fuck out of the band* didn't these guys understand? "No. We'd get a new rhythm guitarist."

"I prefer rhythm guitar," Kellen said.

"Then we get a new lead guitarist," Shade said, exasperated. "I don't care either way, I just want Adam gone. And not temporarily. For good."

Owen shook his head. "What's wrong with you? I'm sure he'll explain everything when he gets back. He deserves a second chance."

"A *second* chance?" Shade asked, finding it difficult to draw air. Were these guys really so clueless to what had been going on with Adam for years?

Owen nodded. As did Kellen. Gabe had his gaze trained on the floor.

"He's already had a hundred second chances," Shade said. "Or more! He's gone too far this time. I'm not putting up with his shit anymore. So if you won't get rid of *him*, then I'm out of here."

"What?" Gabe's head snapped up, his disbelieving stare

forcing Shade to look away.

"There's the door," Owen said, pointing toward the front of the bus with his thumb.

Shade gaped at Owen. He supposed Owen was still pissed that he'd called him a spineless wuss, but Owen shouldn't push. Not right now. Shade wasn't fucking around. He was through with Adam, and if these guys wanted to side with a train-wreck of a recovering junkie, then Shade was through with the band entirely. He would *not* back down this time. Enough was enough.

"So Owen chooses Adam over me," Shade said. "What about you, Kellen? I'm sure you'll go along with whatever Owen says since you can't live without each other."

"Fuck you, Jacob," Kellen said.

Well, there was his answer to that question. He turned to Gabe. Of all of his bandmates, Gabe was the most sensible. He had to see reason. Either Adam had to go or Shade was going. Shade was beyond trying to fix this matter; he refused to compromise. He'd drawn a line on the stage and so far he was the only one willing to cross it. But he had crossed it and for him there was no turning back.

"Don't do this, Jacob. It isn't worth it," Gabe said.

Shade bit his lip and nodded. Gabe wasn't siding with him either; he'd lost his gamble. Not one of his bandmates was willing to back his decision. So be it. He could find another band to front. Perhaps Adam was the soul of Sole Regret, but Shade was its heart. They might survive without a soul, but without a heart? *Good luck with that, traitors.*

"I guess this is goodbye then," Shade said. "Good luck with Adam. He's only going to drag you down with him. I guess you'll just have to see it for yourself. I'm through being his buffer. None of you have any idea how bad he can get—you have absolutely no clue. But you'll figure it out soon enough, and I might have already moved on."

Shade had struggled alone for years to lift Adam out of the gutter he seemed to prefer, but he wasn't going to be there to help cover up Adam's dark reality from the rest of the band any longer. Or from the public. It wouldn't take long for them to realize Shade was right. He just had to wait this out and they'd be begging him to come back. And Sole Regret could have its future success without Adam. It was the only way they'd survive.

Shade grabbed the overnight bag he'd yet to unpack and headed to the front of the bus. He tapped Tex on the arm. "Stop the bus," he said.

Tex looked up at him eyes wide. "Here? Are you fucking nuts? We're miles from the next town," he said in his heavy Texas twang.

And the walk would do Shade some good. "I said stop the bus," he said more firmly.

Tex eased the bus over onto the highway's shoulder. It shuddered to a stop, idling loudly as a semi zipped past with a loud blare from its horn.

"What do you think you're doing?" Gabe asked.

"I'm leaving."

"Be reasonable, Jacob." Gabe laid a hand on Shade's shoulder, but Shade shrugged it off. "We can work through this. Stay. Let's talk about it."

"Open the door," Shade said to Tex.

The door creaked as it swung open, and Shade took the steps to the roadside before he could change his mind. He didn't want to leave, he had to leave. If he didn't, his bandmates wouldn't think he was serious. They'd think he'd get over Adam's massive fuck-up after he cooled down. But Shade was serious, and he wasn't going to get over it. He was through with Adam, and if the rest of them weren't, then it was time for him to move on.

"Great fucking plan, Jacob," Gabe called down to him as he flicked a hand toward the seemingly endless road to nowhere. "This doesn't solve a goddamned thing."

Shade ignored him and started walking. He didn't know if the closest town was ahead or behind, but as far as he was concerned, he could only move forward.

"Jacob!" Gabe called.

"Let him go if that's what he wants," Shade heard Kellen say. "God knows he's a stubborn son of a bitch."

"He might get hit by a car," Owen said. Even pissed off, he was still worried about Shade's safety. Shade shook his head and chuckled under his breath. Some things never changed.

When the bus pulled back onto the highway and drove past him slowly, Shade refused to look at it. A huge chunk of his life was on that bus along with most of his self-worth. Part of him wanted to bend, to admit he was wrong, to beg them to let him back on the bus, but if he did that, nothing would change. And things had to change.

"Fucking Adam," he grumbled when the taillights disappeared over a hill.

Jacob didn't find any answers along the deserted roadway. He did find a few blisters on his toes and a seedy motel with a vacancy. He was pretty sure the only occupants of the decrepit rooms had more than two legs and scurried close to the floor. The place was a shithole—a fitting place to reevaluate his life.

After entering his rented room, which smelled like a damp basement coated with stale cigarette smoke, he dropped his bag on the worn green quilt covering one of the beds and flopped back on the other bed to stare at a crack in the ceiling. A surge of emotions caught him so unaware that he gasped aloud.

What have I done?

He had nothing left that he cared about. Amanda hated him. His band hated him. He'd managed to destroy the career he loved. The fans would hate him for walking away, hate him for destroying Sole Regret. He knew they'd blame him since he'd taken the final step. In one shitty weekend, he'd lost everything.

I have nothing to live for.

Nothing to care about.

Nothing.

The image of his daughter's sweet, smiling face flitted through his thoughts. Jacob tugged his cellphone out of his back pocket to thumb through all the pictures he'd taken of Julie. The most recent shredded his heart. Riding the train at Austin Zoo, Julie had her head cocked slightly and was smiling her cutest, but he couldn't tear his gaze from Amanda. She looked delighted to be with them, fitting comfortably in their lives, making him think he could have everything he wanted just so she could rip it away less than a day later.

"Fuck her."

He edited the photo, cropping Amanda out of the image so that just he and Julie were visible. Apparently, it was as easy for him to erase her from his life as it was for her to delete him. Or not. Even though she was no longer visible in the photo, he knew she was there. He could practically feel the skin of her bare arm beneath his fingertips.

Swallowing the knot in his throat, Jacob flipped to the next image. It showed Julie with chocolate ice cream all over her face. He stared at the image for a long moment, his heart caught in a vice that tightened with each passing second. When he thought his heart would burst, he flicked to the next picture and started the process over again. At least he still had Julie's devotion. Well, he did until her mother managed to destroy her unconditional love for him. Jacob covered his eyes with one hand and rubbed the ache from them.

Fuck. How long would it be before his little girl hated him too?

He could never let it happen. If he did, he really would be left with nothing. He would do whatever it took to make Julie the center of his universe and keep her in that position. And he knew of only one way he could make that a reality. He had to keep her mother close and make her happy.

The delivery of a new text vibrated his phone, interrupting his emotional journey through four years of pictures. It was from Gabe. *When you remove your head from your ass, give me a call, we'll work this out.*

He didn't respond—let Gabe think about Shade's proposition for a few days or weeks or however long it took for him to come to Shade's side. Shade would not go crawling back and eat crow. His head wasn't in his ass, it was firmly in reality.

And the only part of his reality that didn't suck was his little girl.

Before Jacob could change his mind, he dialed Tina's number. He took a deep breath and held the phone to his ear.

When Tina answered, she said, "Julie's asleep. I told you not to call after ten. Are you capable of reading a clock, or is that beyond your mental facilities?"

Jacob closed his eyes, fighting the urge to tell her to fuck off. "Actually, I called to talk to you. I got your text messages."

"Oh," Tina whispered in an oddly breathless sigh.

"I've been thinking about what you said about making a real family for Julie."

"And?"

Jacob rubbed a hand over his face. Was he really considering this? "I agree. She deserves a stable home and to be surrounded by love."

"You agree?"

"Of course." He licked his lips, finding the courage—yes, courage—to take the next step. "Are you free for dinner tomorrow night? We need to talk about this in person."

"I'm free." Her voice was soft, full of hope.

Jacob covered the anxious knot in his belly with one hand.

"I'll pick you up at seven," he said.

"Okay."

He hung up before he could change his mind, and then he dropped his phone onto the bed beside him. He rubbed his eyes, wondering if he'd done the right thing. Wondering if he *ever* did the right thing. Sometimes a man had to make sacrifices to protect those he loved. And he had to protect not only Julie, but Amanda. Tina would make them both miserable if he didn't find a way to tame her wrath. His own misery was of little consequence.

Keep your friends close and your enemies closer—he'd heard the saying a thousand times. How close was he willing to let Tina get?

Could he make her believe that she was important to him? That he wanted not only Julie as a permanent fixture in his life, but her as well?

He could. He had to. If he wanted to hold on to all he held dear and reclaim what he'd lost, he would have to endure Tina's presence in his life. As he made reservations for two at Austin's most exclusive restaurant and set the next step of his plan into motion, he figured he wasn't as dumb as they all thought he was. His strategy was fucking brilliant.

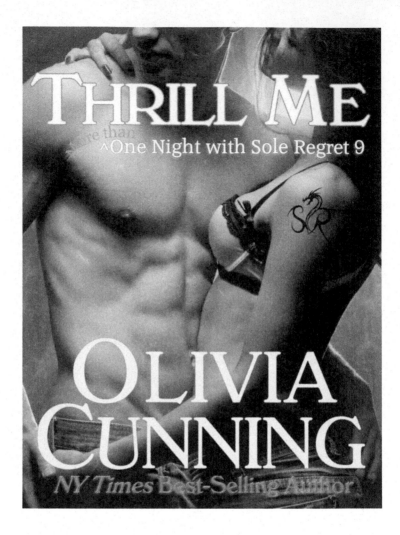

Thrill Me

More than ^One Night with Sole Regret 9

Olivia Cunning

NY Times Best-Selling Author

Thrill Me
One Night with Sole Regret #9

CHAPTER ONE

SOLE REGRET HADN'T even left the city limits of Houston, and their brand-spankablely-new pregnant problem was already making Owen's life hell. He flinched when Lindsey took his wrist in her hand. They probably should have left the chick behind the stadium instead of inviting her on the tour until the band—or more likely *he*—figured out what to do with her.

"I need to speak to you in private," she said.

She had backed Owen into a corner—both literally and figuratively. He looked down the aisle of the tour bus to his friends—his band brothers—for a bit of support, but it was as if he'd turned invisible. He didn't hate Lindsey, but he didn't want to talk to her either. Caitlyn had left because of the woman's odious timing, and while he felt bad for Lindsey—who was notably pregnant and apparently had no one in the world who cared—he had more important worries. Like how to convince Caitlyn they were meant to be together when he had a surprise pregnant groupie showing up on his bus step.

"It will only take a minute," Lindsey said, her blue eyes weary in her gaunt face.

He wondered if she was eating right. No matter how uncomfortable she made him, she was knocked-up and needed help. His conscience wouldn't let him disregard her without hearing what she had to say.

"I'm listening," he said.

Lindsey glanced at the other band members on the bus, guys trying so hard to ignore her that they'd fixated on her instead. He was pretty sure they were all holding their breath so she wouldn't notice they existed. Owen would like to play dead too, but she'd already zeroed in on him.

"Not here," she said under her breath. "I don't think you want them to listen in on this conversation."

He shrugged. "I don't think there's anything you can say that they shouldn't hear for themselves." Owen projected his voice toward the possum-playing rockers, but no one so much as blinked. Apparently they planned to throw him under the proverbial bus. And lucky for them, they had one handy.

Something about the intensity in Lindsey's gaze made him reconsider his claim to share her conversation with everyone. Without another word, he brushed past her to make his way to the open bedroom door. If she tried to make a move on him, he was sure he could handle himself. And if that wasn't why she wanted to speak to him in private . . . Well, maybe he was wrong about her.

He closed the door behind them and sat on the edge of the bed, crossing his leg over his knee so she couldn't sit too close to him. She released a shaky breath and didn't sit at all. Instead, she stood over him with a wide stance to maintain her balance. Concerned the bus might make a sudden move and send her tumbling, he patted the mattress beside him.

"Please sit. You look like you're about to fall over."

She considered him for a long moment, hooking her long blond hair behind one ear, and then she sat beside him, leaning forward and folding her arms over her belly.

"I'm not sure how to say this," she said.

"Just spit it out, Lindsey. Nothing you say can possibly be more upsetting than finding out I might be the father of your baby."

"You *are* the father," she insisted.

"Until you present some solid evidence, I'll hold off on installing a car seat in my Jeep."

She rubbed at her tired eyes and released a weary sigh.

"How well do you remember that night in the mountain pass?" she asked.

"Pretty well. I wasn't even drunk." Drunk on lust maybe, but not on alcohol.

"Then you'll recall the final time we were together that night. Everyone else had already passed out. That's when it happened. I'm sure of it."

He squinted as he tried to conjure up faded memories. He slept with a lot of woman and didn't recall each occurrence in vivid detail. "I know I wore a condom every time, even that last time. So unless you poked a hole in it—"

Her glare cut off his accusation. "Of course I didn't poke a hole in it. What kind of psycho do you think I am?"

He decided that was a question best left unanswered.

Her glare intensified. "*You* were the one who tried to put it on wrong side out."

He laughed. Oh yeah, that had been awkward. He'd been eager to fuck her one last time but had been forced to slow down when he'd tried unsuccessfully to unroll an inside-out condom over his dick. "I realized my mistake pretty quickly." And he'd felt like such an awkward idiot.

"You touched the outside of the condom to your . . ." She lifted her eyebrows and then glanced down at his crotch. "I know you had cum on your tip. I'd been rubbing it into your head with my thumb. Remember?"

He didn't remember clearly. He remembered being awoken in the middle of the night by her mouth sucking at his cock, and he remembered almost putting the condom on wrong side out before flipping it over and unrolling it. They'd gotten a good laugh out of how clumsy he was in his excitement. The woman had been hot and impatient—there was no denying that. But had he actually touched the outside of the rubber to his jizz-sticky skin? He wasn't sure. And he hadn't given the incident a single thought since it had happened all those months ago.

"Why would I do something that stupid?" he said, a heavy weight pressing down on him.

"You were excited," she said, "and it was your last condom. And I wanted you so bad, I wasn't thinking clearly either."

That was no excuse. Stupid mistakes like that got women pregnant. Owen suddenly felt light-headed.

This could not be happening.

"Are you sure I touched it to my . . ." He couldn't even bring himself to say cum. That stuff had potentially gotten him an unwanted heap of responsibility.

She nodded.

"And that's why you think the baby is mine?"

She nodded again. "The fault isn't entirely yours, Owen. I'm not blaming you. We both made mistakes. I could have told you I didn't want to do it with that contaminated condom, but I was on the pill. I didn't think it was a big deal."

"How did you get pregnant if you're on the pill?"

"My doctor said it was most likely the St. John's Wort I started taking a few months before. Did you know something like that can interfere with birth control pill effectiveness?"

How the hell would he know that? "So lots of women get pregnant that way."

She shook her head. "No, it's really rare. It's almost like a higher power wanted this to happen just to punish me."

"Punish you? For what?"

"For fooling around."

"We all fooled around."

And maybe they were all being punished. But not with a baby. A baby should be considered a joy, not a consequence. He was always so careful. Owen still wasn't a hundred percent convinced that Lindsey was pregnant with *his* baby, but if he'd done something as totally idiotic as fucking her with a contaminated condom, then more than likely she was.

This could not be happening.

"You can't tell the guys," Owen blurted.

"Why not?"

Because they'd think he was a total moron. If they thought he'd knocked her up because there'd been a hole in the condom, that was one thing. But if they knew he'd made the stupidest mistake of his life, he'd never live it down.

"I'll take responsibility for the baby for now," he said, "but don't tell them why."

"Owen . . ."

"Please." He reached for her hand and squeezed it for emphasis, and she made a pained sound of longing in the back of her throat. He chose to ignore what that reaction might mean. She was a beautiful young woman—he couldn't deny that obvious fact—but he'd just met someone he liked and they'd already forged a connection, one he hoped strengthened and lasted. Owen might be the kind of guy who fucked a lot of women, but he was not a cheater. Things would not progress with Lindsey, no matter how often she looked at him with longing. He knew how to keep it in his pants; he'd just rather let it out to play.

"I'll find you a place to stay," he said, "and get you the medical care you need." His mind scrambled for ways to sweeten the deal. "I'll even help you find a job, and if the baby is proven to be mine, I'll take full responsibility, but don't tell anyone the truth about why I'm helping you."

"People make mistakes, Owen. It's not the end of the world."

Oh, but it was. The end of his carefree days, in any case. He didn't even want Kelly to know that he'd fucked up so spectacularly, and Kelly knew everything about him. Owen planned to lie his ass off to his best friend for the first time in his life, and he didn't even feel a twinge of guilt about it.

"If you want my help, Lindsey, you have to promise not to tell anyone," Owen said, using his only bargaining chip. He knew he'd help her even if she held a press conference and told the world all about how stupid and irresponsible he'd been, but he was banking on her not knowing that. "Just let them think I'm a nice guy who wants to help you out. They'll probably think I'm a sucker."

In his book, being thought of as a nice-guy sucker was a lot better than being known as the idiot who attempted to apply a condom wrong side out and instead of discarding it, flipped it over and used it anyway.

"I think you should tell them why I think this baby is yours," Lindsey said. "So they don't keep wondering if it's theirs."

"Why does it matter as long as I'm helping you? You're getting what you want."

"I want more than financial support, Owen. I want my child to have a father."

"And that's why you waited until you were huge pregnant to come looking for one?"

Lindsey hung her head. "I was too ashamed. I'd been made to feel like getting pregnant was my fault alone because I was promiscuous *once*, but it takes two to make a baby, Owen."

And in the case of that fateful Christmas Eve, it took six—or had it been seven? The details were a little fuzzy.

"I wasn't the only one being promiscuous that night," she

continued. "Don't make me feel guilty with your double standards."

"I wasn't trying to make you feel guilty."

"And you shouldn't. I saw another example of your promiscuity just before we got on the bus." She crossed her arms over her chest.

"Leave Caitlyn out of this," Owen said, his stomach sinking even further. He liked Caitlyn. A lot. And Lindsey showing up out of the blue with a baby on board had more than likely ruined any chance he had to be with Caitlyn in any serious capacity.

"Is that her name, Caitlyn?" Lindsey sneered as she tried out the name for the first time.

Owen shook his head. "I said leave her out of it. She has nothing to do with this."

"How long have you been seeing her?"

One night. One amazing night that had felt like forever and mere seconds all at once.

"That's none of your business. And just so you don't think I'm going to start seeing you, I'm letting you know now that I plan to pursue Caitlyn. Even if that baby is mine . . ."

This could not be happening!

". . . I can still be a good father without getting entangled with you."

Lindsey shook her head. "I don't think that's possible."

"Why not? We can be friends, civil to each other. Make sound, unified decisions about any issues that arise with the child. Both be actively involved in the kid's life." He was saying the words calmly, but was pretty sure he was breaking out into hives. He was completely unprepared to be a father. He figured someday he'd settle down and have a family, but baby or no baby, he didn't want to settle for a woman he wasn't in love with.

"Do you really think you could do that?" she asked. At his nod, her shoulders sagged with relief. "I'm so glad this baby is yours and not someone like Adam's or that bus driver guy's. I can't even remember his name."

Owen was pretty sure she'd sucked the bus driver guy's dick while one of his bandmates fucked her doggy style, but she didn't remember his name? Owen was struggling with that double standard she'd called him on. "Tex."

She grimaced. "That's right."

"So do we have a deal? I'll help you get on your feet and you'll keep my condom mishap a secret from the guys."

"And if the baby is yours . . ."

"And if it isn't mine?"

Her long lashes lowered to cover her lovely but troubled blue eyes. "I guess we'll figure that part out after the baby is born," she said.

"How long do we have?"

"I'm due mid-September."

That was soon. Less than three months away.

"The tour will be winding down around then, so I'll be able to help with the baby." Ugh, why had he said it that way? It was almost as if he knew the baby was his when he truly didn't. Maybe he hadn't been the only idiot on the bus that cold December night. Maybe someone else had made a monumental mistake as well.

Lindsey touched his wrist, and an unwanted spark of attraction made his arm muscles tighten.

"Thank you, Tags. Owen," she corrected.

"For?"

"Being the man I thought you were. And for helping me out."

He smiled. He did love compliments. "Don't feel too special. I'd help out a stranger on the street."

"Exactly."

"You should get some rest," he said. "You look exhausted."

"And hungry?" she asked, sucking in her cheeks. "Do I look hungry?"

He had no idea what possessed him to stroke a lock of hair from her cheek and tuck it behind her ear. He didn't want her to get the wrong idea and have her think he actually cared about her. "You do look hungry," he said. "We should stop at a restaurant soon, but I'll go see if there's anything on the bus to eat besides beef jerky and peanuts. We might have some pretzels to tide you over."

Her body stiffened unexpectedly, and she laughed. "I think he heard you," she said, taking his hand and placing it on her distended abdomen. Something hard and round moved beneath her skin along his palm and then thumped against his hand. It was the strangest yet most awe-inspiring sensation he'd ever felt. There was a tiny person growing inside of her. A living being that might be half him.

"He's got quite a kick," Owen said, laughing when what he figured was a foot thumped against his palm again.

"I think he'd like some of those pretzels," Lindsey said.

Owen drew his hand from her belly, strangely reluctant to do so, and rose from the edge of the bed. "Make yourself comfortable," he said. "I'll scrounge up a snack for you. We'll stop for real food in about an hour."

"Thanks again, Owen," she said, scooting awkwardly up the mattress and rolling onto her side. She squirmed around for a full minute trying to get comfortable before stuffing a pillow between her knees. She was asleep almost instantly—her breathing even, her body relaxed. Owen covered her with a blanket and quietly shut the door on his way out. He didn't bother finding the probably stale pretzels he'd promised, but instead made his way to the front of the bus. "When are we stopping for dinner?"

Tex glanced at the cellphone he had stuck to the dashboard with directions to a suitable restaurant displayed through his map app. "Forty-seven minutes," Tex said. "Approximately."

"I'm hungry now."

"We called ahead, and they're already preparing to serve the busloads of crew headed their direction."

"Did you remember to include Lindsey in your head count?" he asked.

"The pregnant chick?"

"Lindsey." They might as well get used to saying her name and not referring to her as the object she'd been to them all the last time she'd been on the bus.

"No, I just gave them our usual numbers. But Kellen's not here, is he?"

No, Kelly wasn't on the bus. He'd gone off to Galveston to be depressed over Sara. A stupid thing to do, but Owen didn't understand life-altering grief. Luckily, he'd never personally experienced the loss of his soulmate or anyone close to him. Not even a grandparent. He hoped Kellen would get over Sara soon though. The guy needed to get laid so bad, just being around his celibate friend made Owen horny. He was duty bound to get laid enough for the both of them. "I guess she can have his dinner then."

Tex nodded. "So she's sure she got pregnant by one of us."

"She's sure."

"But she's almost certain it's yours, right? My wife won't want me bringing home some slut I knocked up by accident."

"I'm sure she wouldn't," Owen said, shaking his head in disgust.

"I mean, what happens on the bus, stays on the bus, right?"

That was their usual bargain, but this case was different. They couldn't force Lindsey to live as a prisoner on the bus with her baby. The father would eventually have to acknowledge the child's existence.

"Just pray it isn't yours," Owen said. Owen would rather the baby be his than have it be Tex's. The guy couldn't even stay faithful to his wife, so what kind of father would he make? A shitty one, Owen presumed.

"The Lord has been getting an earful of prayers from me tonight, that's for damn sure."

He'd probably be getting an earful of prayers from all of them tonight. "Yeah" was all Owen said before he turned and shuffled up the aisle between the sofa where Jacob was watching television and where Gabe was reading some obnoxiously thick book. Adam had hidden away in his bunk. Based on their body language and outright hiding, none of them wanted to talk. And Kelly wasn't around to listen to Owen's crushing problems. He headed for the cabinet and his old standby in times of crisis—food.

He was at the bottom of a bag of stale pretzels when the bus turned off the highway and into a 24-hour diner. He dusted the salt off his hands and moved to the back of the bus to get Lindsey. Everyone else fled, as if he were about to escort a man-eating shark out of the back bedroom.

"Are you ready to eat?" he asked from the doorway, thinking it wasn't wise to help her out of bed or even touch her. Not when he planned to keep as far from her as possible. He suspected that if he was too nice to her and allowed even friendship to bloom between them, she'd misread his intentions and think a romantic relationship stood a chance.

Lindsey sat up on the edge of the bed and stumbled as she attempted to get her feet beneath her. She chuckled at her clumsiness and dug her fingers into the headboard for the extra boost she needed to stand.

"I can't decide if I'm more tired or hungry," she murmured, rubbing her eyes with the back of her wrist.

"I can bring you some takeout," he offered, "if you'd rather stay here and rest."

"I'm up," she said and waddled past him, rubbing her belly with both hands. He followed her, stopping when she hesitated at the top of the steep bus steps.

"Can you manage?" he asked, doing his best to keep his distance when every instinct shouted at him to help her down the potentially dangerous steps.

"I think so," she said, gripping the shiny metal bar that served as a railing. "I'm just exhausted. My legs are a little wobbly."

Was she saying that so he'd take her arm and help her down the steps, or was she legitimately too tired to safely make it down on her own? He wasn't willing to risk her falling. A security guard had already shoved her and made her fall once that night; he refused to be responsible for another tumble.

"Take my arm," he insisted, shifting into the narrow stairwell beside her and assisting her as indifferently as possible as they took one step at a time.

"Thank you," she said quietly. "I wish I could get my shit together tonight."

"You've had an exhausting day." He wasn't sure why he was making excuses for her. He felt like such a doormat. None of the other guys were going out of their way to help this woman, so why should he?

Because the baby was most likely his.

This could not be happening.

"An exhausting three months," she said and squeezed his arm.

Maybe he'd ask her about those three months later, but now they had to navigate the crowd of opening bands and crew members already headed toward the entrance of the diner. By being the last off the bus, they'd missed their opportunity to be at the front of the line. Owen received a lot of confused stares from those waiting in front of them, but he kept his head down and his hands off Lindsey so everyone wouldn't wrongly assume that she was with him. Well, technically she was with him, but not because he wanted her to be. He glanced at her, finding her silky blond hair shielding her expression as she stared at the ground in front of them. He wasn't the only one feeling uncomfortable.

They were seated at a table for two—because all the larger

tables were already taken and his bandmates had betrayed him by allowing some other dudes to sit in his spot and the spot normally reserved for Kelly. Jackasses.

"Sorry you have to eat with me instead of your friends," Lindsey said as she settled into her chair.

"I'd rather eat with you anyway," he said, which at the moment was true. Jackasses.

"How nice of you to lie to save my feelings," Lindsey said with a smile of gratitude. She picked up the menu in front of her. Owen followed her lead.

A tired-looking waitress approached their table after a few minutes. "What would you like to drink?"

"Water is fine," Lindsey said.

"For me too," he said. Owen had already decided he was going to feast in abundance tonight, and he wouldn't be wasting those excess calories on beverages. He'd squeeze in an extra workout the next day to make up for his indulgence.

"I'm Katie and I'll be your server tonight," the waitress said as she filled their water glasses. "Are you ready to order?"

"I'm still trying to decide," Lindsey said. She nodded toward Owen. "I'll have it figured out by the time he's done ordering."

The diner was so crowded and noisy that Owen had to yell his order over the din. And seeing as he was stressed out and planning to feed that stress, his order was incredibly long and detailed.

"I'll just have some scrambled eggs and wheat toast," Lindsey said when it was her turn to order.

Owen felt like a complete pig for ordering the steak with the loaded baked potato and the shrimp platter with fries as well as a full-size chef salad and a bowl of chili. He'd even planned on getting dessert when the time came.

"I thought you were hungry," he said to Lindsey as the waitress walked away.

Her cheeks went pink. "I'm rather short on funds at the moment," she said.

"You don't have to worry about that. The band will pick up the tab for everyone." He indicated the giant crowd of people around him with the sweep of one hand.

"Yeah, but they work for you. I've already imposed and—"

"It's fine," he insisted. "I'll call the waitress back and you can order whatever you want."

She busied herself with loosening the paper napkin around her silverware and spreading the pathetic excuse for a table linen over her lap. "Scrambled eggs are fine," she said, obviously uncomfortable.

He didn't push the issue. He'd just insist he was too full to finish his own excessive meal and offer his leftovers to her. She wouldn't be able to refuse something that would otherwise go to waste, would she?

"So," he said after a long moment of painful silence, "what kind of work do you do?" If she was serious about finding a job, then he was serious about helping her with that if he could.

"Uh, before I got canned, you mean?"

He nodded and shifted his attention to his water glass, rubbing at the condensation collected on its exterior with one thumb.

"Banking," she said. "I was a teller and then I became a loan officer. I got fired for being pregnant, but my employee file will say I gave out too many bad loans. I'm somewhat of a sucker for the destitute."

He lifted his head and met her gaze.

"Sort of like you," she said with a smile.

He sipped his water, letting her insult or compliment—he couldn't tell which it was—slide. "Is that what you want to continue doing in the future? Banking, I mean. Not being a sucker for the destitute."

"I'm not sure anyone will hire me," she said. "I didn't leave my last job on good terms. I called my boss—my ex-boss—a few choice words when she fired me. She'll never give me a decent recommendation."

"You can try. Do you want to stay in Austin after the baby is born?"

"That's where my baby's father lives," she said. "Even if it turns out he isn't you."

Right.

This could not be happening.

"Maybe it'll be easier to get a job far away from your last place of employment," he said.

"Maybe."

She didn't seem too eager to get back to work. He watched

her for a moment, wondering if she was just looking for a handout. Surely she would have ordered herself a larger meal if she was a freeloader. Or maybe she'd done that so he wouldn't see what she was really after. He decided to give her the benefit of the doubt until she proved she was digging for gold. Kelly was a better judge of character than Owen had ever been; Owen wished his friend hadn't left for Galveston right after the performance since he could use a little advice in the Caitlyn department as well. Kelly seemed to like Caitlyn and like her with Owen. Kelly had never told any other woman Owen's closely guarded secrets, so she must have Kelly's stamp of approval, but how did Lindsey fit in? Or did she even have to? Yeah, if she was the mother of his child, he'd have to fit her in somewhere.

This could not be happening.

Lindsey's hand inched closer to his. "You seem distracted."

Now why would he be distracted? Owen tucked his hand beneath the table, relieved when the waitress appeared with an overflowing tray of food.

He dug into his steak first, trying not to feel too guilty about eating for two while the person at the table who was actually eating for two didn't even have enough food for one.

"Do you like shrimp?" he asked, picking a perfectly prepared breaded butterfly shrimp from his second plate.

She swallowed the last bite of her toast. "Who doesn't like shrimp?"

"I love them." He set one on the edge of her already empty plate. "Try one."

They each sampled a shrimp, and the tender-on-the-inside, crisp-on-the-outside morsels were amazing. So amazing he almost reconsidered his plan.

"Good, huh?" he said.

"Excellent."

He pushed the plate of shrimp, fries, and coleslaw toward her. "I can't eat all this and finish my steak," he said. "Eat those for me."

"I couldn't," she protested.

"They're just going to go to waste."

She stared at him for a moment, and he was pretty sure he was as transparent as a spotlessly clean window, but she didn't embarrass him by pointing out his generosity.

"Well, if it's just going to go to waste." She nibbled on a fry while a smile brightened her face.

He should probably be mean to her, he thought as he gulped down his glass of water, but it seemed she already had enough meanness in her life. What was wrong with showing her a bit of kindness and some compassion?

When her foot found his beneath the table and then her bare toe slid up his pants leg to stroke his calf, he immediately understood everything that was wrong with that plan.

CHAPTER TWO

CAITLYN GRABBED an unread copy of *Popular Science* and carried her cup of coffee to the round table in her breakfast nook. She normally didn't drink coffee late at night or have time to read the stack of magazines accumulating on her kitchen counter, but she knew she wouldn't be able to sleep. Not with a certain rock star dominating her thoughts.

Owen had seemed *so* nice, and that young, gorgeous groupie that had showed up after the concert—*Lindsey*—had been *so* pregnant. Caitlyn couldn't believe she'd allowed herself to call him within ten minutes of walking away from that scene. There was no way she was already that attached to the guy—they hardly knew each other. It had been an amazing one-night stand. Why couldn't she just leave it at that?

Because she still wanted him.

Caitlyn sipped the rich black coffee and flipped through articles that couldn't hold her attention. Instead, her mind was playing through the hot and dirty sex she'd experienced over the past twenty-four hours. She squirmed uncomfortably in her chair as she began to imagine all sorts of new scenarios she wanted to try with Owen. She had no doubt he could fulfill her every sexual fantasy. So maybe Owen wasn't the man she was supposed to spend the rest of her life with, but they could still enjoy each other's company. She'd just have to be careful that he didn't grab her heart the way she wanted him to grab her thighs before he filled her with that beguiling pierced cock of his.

She pushed her magazine aside and reached for her phone. Was he still awake? Should she call him again? How desperate would she look if she did something like that? She didn't want him to know how much she wanted him, so instead of calling him or texting him, she did something far more desperate. She searched his name via Google.

There wasn't too much information about him on the

Internet. She knew far more personal stuff about him than was included in a short paragraph on Wikipedia that was nearly identical to the bio on Sole Regret's official website. She found thousands of pictures of him, however, and he looked gorgeous in every single one. And in almost every shot he was posing with a different woman. Caitlyn might have convinced herself that all those women were just fans of his music, but they weren't touching him in a platonic way, and he wasn't trying to keep his distance.

"You are quite the man whore, Owen Mitchell," she said quietly to one of the few pictures of him without a woman clinging to his chest or arm or ass; he was glued to Kellen Jamison's side. She guessed she shouldn't be surprised by Owen's popularity. He was young and attractive and sensational in bed, not to mention famous in certain circles, but the man she'd spent last night and most of the day with had been sweet and charming and attentive. "I guess that's why they all fall for you." Including herself.

She sighed and switched off the screen of her phone. Could she pursue a man who wanted nothing from women but a good time and to get his rocks off?

"Yep," she said. She wasn't ready for a committed relationship anyway. Not after the way Charles had treated her. A man-whore rock star was exactly what she needed at this juncture in her life. Owen could fulfill her every fantasy without all the scary attachments that came with commitment and relationships. All that nonsense that Kellen had said the night before to make her feel like she could be special to his womanizing friend abandoned her instantly. Strangely, it was a relief. She could take Owen as a lover and use him the way he'd used so many women in the past. Assuming he still wanted her.

Her phone dinged with the delivery of a text message. She smiled when she saw it was from Owen.

Are you asleep? I'm lying here in my bunk thinking of you.

She giggled like a schoolgirl. He was sweeter than syrup. It was hard to believe he was the same guy who went through women the way most guys went through socks.

A second message dinged in.

And that makes me all hard and uncomfortable. Are you there?

Her breath caught as she read his words. Was this sexting? She knew about it, but Charles hadn't been interested at her lame attempts to gain his attention.

I'm here, she answered in a text of her own.

Can I jerk off?

He was asking her? Was this some sort of game he was playing?

Can I? she countered, suddenly feeling the urge to touch herself.

No. I want you horny the next time I see you.

Three days, she reminded him. He'd wanted to see her tomorrow, but she'd told him she was angry with him and was making him wait three days. What kind of idiot put the guy off for three days? He'd be completely over her by then. But she was sticking to her guns. They would not see each other until Sunday.

Tomorrow. Or I'm going to jerk one out right now.

She laughed. *Is that a threat?*

She waited anxiously for his response. And waited. And waited some more. Was he already tired of their little game?

Owen?

Shh. I'm trying to come.

Caitlyn wasn't sure why the thought of him touching himself had her beside herself with lust. A video appeared in their message thread. Before she pushed the little play arrow in the center, she could make out a very familiar thick cock wrapped in a tight fist. As she watched the short clip, the sight of him stroking his length was distracting, but his whispers to her had her wishing she could teleport through her phone and give him a hand—or a mouth— with that enormous hard-on.

"Caitlyn," he whispered so quietly, she could barely hear his words over the sounds of flesh stroking lubed-up flesh. "I can't stop thinking of you. Of the way you let me fuck your throat. How you looked up at me with your mouth stretched around me and my balls against your chin."

Shocked by what he was saying, by what he was *doing*, she slapped her phone face down on the table.

"Oh my God," she said aloud. What a dirty mouth he had on him. Did he actually think something like that would turn her on? Because she was currently on fire. She fanned her flushed face with one hand while using the other to turn her phone back over. She slid the video back to the beginning so she could watch and listen again.

"Caitlyn," he whispered to her again, his strong tanned fingers sliding up the length of his slippery-looking cock. "I can't stop thinking—"

Her phone rang, startling her so completely that the phone slid halfway across the table. She scrambled after it and scowled down at the name displayed on her caller ID. Why the fuck was Charles calling her after midnight? Why the fuck was he calling her at all? She didn't want to talk to her ex-husband, so she sent his call to voicemail and returned to Owen's string of messages to see if he'd sent anything else.

Do you want the money shot?

All over my tits, she typed back, feeling particularly brazen after being called out of the blue by her cheating ex-husband.

I can't reach them from here.

Then you'd better not come. Not until you see me.

Tomorrow?

Sunday. Don't come until then.

So cruel. My balls are going to ache so bad for you.

Good, she typed, not sure why making him wait made her feel more empowered than when she stood at the head of a board meeting. *Until Sunday then.*

Was she really going to be that woman, the one who teased a man to the extent of his patience? She was, she decided with a grin. Though she'd make sure the wait was worth his while. And hers.

If I can't come until then, neither can you, he texted her.

She didn't answer, deciding it was better to keep him guessing. And as aroused as watching his too short video made her, she didn't want to come without him. She wanted her desperate need to claw at her insides until she saw him again. That way she wouldn't be able to talk herself out of doing exactly what her body wanted when her head was telling her to run the other way.

~~~

Instead of returning to San Antonio to visit her friend Jenna on Thursday, Caitlyn decided to go to work. She figured it would keep her mind off Owen while he performed his concert in Beaumont that night and in New Orleans on Friday. At least she figured that until the gifts began to arrive. A little after nine, a huge bouquet of flowers was delivered. The card read: *Be kind and rewind. Owen*

What kind of message was that? She didn't get it, so she texted him. *Thanks for the flowers. They're gorgeous. But I'm too dense to figure out your message.*

She set aside her phone and went back to researching the current methods of converting water into hydrogen fuel, hoping to spark some new idea. She wasn't sure how much time had passed before her phone rang. It was Owen. Her palms went instantly damp, and she took a deep breath before answering.

"Hello?" Was that breathy, sexy sound really her voice?

"It means you should rewind and watch that video I sent you again." And could that deep, raspy voice of his be any sexier?

It took her a moment to realize he was talking about the card he'd sent with the flowers. She felt like an idiot for not figuring out his cryptic message on her own.

"Oh. But I'm at work." Even though she was supposed to be on vacation. Working was a habit she just couldn't seem to break.

"Afraid seeing me stroke my dick will make your panties all wet?"

She laughed. "Yes, actually."

"Don't worry, I've got you covered. Watch it again."

"Okay. But not because you told me to, but because I want to."

"You've been a bad girl, Caitlyn. I want you to think about what you did."

She scowled. Why did he think she was bad? "What did I do?"

"Do you have any idea how much my balls hurt after I had to get that hard-on under control without coming?"

Her breath caught, and she covered the throbbing pulse in her throat with her fingertips. "You obeyed my instructions?" Wow. This was a lot more fun than she'd anticipated. Long distance naughtiness played havoc on her nerve endings.

"I'm assuming you're going to make it up to me."

She grinned. "Not until Sunday." She hung up before he could respond. She found his video on her phone and watched it from the beginning.

The sound of her name being whispered by his deep gruff voice in the dark while the light from his camera illuminated his hand and cock made her thighs tremble. She decided she should be extra kind and rewind it twice more before she set her phone aside again. Her panties were indeed uncomfortably damp now, and despite what Owen had said, he didn't have her covered. She had to take a trip to the ladies room to do something about the hot, achy flesh between her legs. She considered sending him a video of the state she was in, but wasn't feeling quite that bold— not when she could hear a couple of her employees talking in the lab down the hallway. When she returned to her desk, she found a small shiny black box from some lingerie store across town. So that was what he'd meant by having her wet panties covered? He was sending her sexy lingerie at work—how inappropriate. And fun. She untied the red satin ribbon and lifted the lid. When she pulled out a pair of yellow panties with a chicken embroidered on the front, she burst into delighted laughter. Beneath the chicken, *Caitlyn's Sinday Panties* had been embroidered in black thread.

She reached for her phone again, trying to remember why she was supposed to be mad at him. Oh yeah, he'd knocked up some groupie six months ago. But his past didn't really matter to her. After knowing her less than two days, Owen understood her in a way that Charles had never figured out after twelve years of marriage.

She didn't bother texting this time, but called him directly. She was disappointed when he didn't answer but slightly appeased when she found he'd recorded a personal message for his voicemail greeting, so at least she could hear his voice.

"Sorry I missed your call. I'm either rocking on stage or rolling in the hay. Leave a message, and I'll call you after I catch my breath."

He'd better be rocking and not rolling, she thought as a loud beep told her she could begin recording her message. "It's Caitlyn. I got the um . . . *sexy* lingerie you sent me. Am I supposed to wear them when I see you on Sunday? They specifically say *Sin*day. Just making sure you know how to spell the days of the week. Lo— Bye." She hurriedly hung up the phone, glad she'd caught herself before she'd ended with her usual sign off of *love you*. She wasn't sure which of them would have been more disturbed by that slip.

Still smiling, she carefully tucked the thoughtful gift back into the box and secured the lid. She was staring wistfully into space when the chocolates arrived. She decided to wait until he called her back to thank him for those and tried to think of a gift she could get for him. He liked music—obviously—but she would undoubtedly screw up anything she attempted to get him in that arena. He liked pastrami sandwiches, dancing in diners, his friend Kellen, and sex clubs. Sex. He really liked sex. She definitely needed to get to know him better. While the flowers and chocolates were nice, she could tell he put some thought into the panties. She'd been embarrassed that for whatever stupid reason she'd worn a pair of sheep panties that first night he'd gotten into them. And when she'd had the opportunity to change into a new pair, she'd gone for the ones that had a cow on the front, since he'd gotten such a kick out of her sheep underwear. The chicken continued her barnyard theme, but it also reminded her that he'd made her do the Chicken Dance at a diner in the middle of the night. And she'd had a blast. So any gift she got him in return had to be just as personal to him as those custom embroidered chicken panties were to her.

Was it too soon in their relationship for him to have a matching pair of boxers?

Wait. Did she just think of this little tryst as a relationship? Wrong thinking, Caitlyn.

She was just going to have to thank him with sex. Lots of mind-blowing, load-blowing sex. But she was going to put some thought into how to get him off. And she'd start by doing a little research to educate herself. She wasn't a particularly spontaneous person. At her core, she'd always been a planner. Would he think it odd that she went online to look up sex acts and started a list?

Probably.

So she'd just keep her sexual fantasy list to herself. No one had to know about it but her.

She was watching a video showing a threesome between two women and a man when her phone rang. Her heart thudded as if she'd been doing something wrong. Hell, she was the boss and supposed to be on vacation; she could watch porn on her phone in her office if she felt like it. She scribbled threesome with another woman on her fantasy list before taking Owen's call.

"So you liked the panties?" he asked when she answered.

"Very sweet. Very thoughtful. The chocolates arrived as well. Thanks for thinking of me."

"It's what I've been doing all day."

She was having a hard time thinking at all. Her brain was still trying to wrap itself around eating another woman's pussy. She'd never thought about doing something like that until she wrote *threesome* on her list, but she wanted to try it now. Mostly to see if she was better at eating out a woman than her ex-husband had been. Charles couldn't find her clit with a map and a flashlight and her literally putting his fingers on it, so she'd had to figure out how to give herself orgasms. Owen had been incredibly skilled at oral stimulation—no problem locating her clit at all—but how would she fare? She knew how the female body worked better than any man could, so she'd probably be pretty good at pleasuring another woman. With her fingers. Her mouth. Her tongue.

". . . ready or not."

"I'm sorry," Caitlyn said, so distracted by her thoughts that she'd missed most of what he'd been saying. "Can you repeat that? I think we have a bad connection."

"I said, having Lindsey around is a pain in the ass. Everyone is worried that they're about to become a father, ready or not."

"So is she staying on tour with you guys until she gives birth?"

"No. I'm dropping her off at a hotel near my house in Austin after tomorrow night's show. I have the whole weekend off to get her settled."

Caitlyn touched the box on her desk to remind herself that he was thinking about her. He liked her even with Lindsey underfoot. Even if he seemed to be fixated on the girl, he'd still found time to send her gifts. "Why you? Why near your house? Why aren't any of the other guys taking responsibility for her?"

"Because."

Because? "Owen, is there something you aren't telling me?"

"I'm just being nice to her. What's the big deal?"

The big deal was that he had a very pregnant complication in his life. One that had showed up just after Caitlyn had decided she wanted to pursue Owen. Lindsey's pregnancy wouldn't stop Caitlyn from giving this thing—whatever their time together ended up being—with Owen a shot. She'd just have to keep her heart out of it. She was still getting over her ex-husband and couldn't let this guy get under her skin. If that baby was his—and the night before Lindsey had seemed entirely convinced it was—then he came with a whole slew of problems Caitlyn wasn't ready to deal with. She had been looking forward to a sweet and easy romance with a sweet and easy guy. And then bam, out of nowhere, a pregnant groupie shows up.

"It's fine," Caitlyn said. She could make this work; she just needed a different focus. Love was out, but lust? Lust she could do. "Are you still planning on seeing me this weekend?"

"Definitely. I just need to ditch Lindsey, and I'm yours."

"Are you taking me to another sex club?"

"Is that what you want to do?"

"Maybe," she said. "Will we be able to find a woman there willing to join us? In bed, I mean."

He coughed, and she smiled. He hadn't been expecting her to go there, she assumed. He probably thought she was being spontaneous and sexy, when in truth she was approaching her sexual awakening rather scientifically.

"Like a threesome?"

"Exactly like a threesome."

"Are you sure—" He coughed again. "Uh, I mean, yeah. I'm sure we could find a woman to hook up with us. What kind of chick are you into?"

"I'm not sure. I've never been with another woman before."

"But you want to be with one now?"

"Only if you're there to guide me."

"I'm so there," he said.

This was fun, she decided. She felt like she could tell him all her dirty fantasies and not only would he listen, but he'd help make them a reality.

"What about a threesome with another man?" she asked, jotting it down on her list. She'd watch some videos later to see if she was truly interested in something like that. "Can we try that too?"

"Yeah, um . . . Well, that might prove a little more difficult."

"Am I making you uncomfortable?" She wasn't sure why she found it so easy to request such things. Maybe it was because she was in her element here at the office. Or maybe it was because they were talking on the phone and she didn't have to look him in the eye when she asked. Or maybe it was because she'd written a list like she was shopping for groceries.

"No," Owen said. "I just didn't realize you were so kinky."

"I don't know if I'm kinky or not. I've never explored my kink except for the few things I tried with you. But you're kinky, right?"

He laughed softly. "I guess you could call me that."

"I want you to help me find my kink, Owen. Thrill me. Do

you think you can do that?"

"I'm sure I can."

"Great. I look forward to it." She rolled her eyes at how impersonal that sounded. Like they were discussing wine tasting or something.

"So should I come to your house when I return to Texas for the weekend, or do you want to meet me in Austin? Or . . . I'll go anywhere you want to go, Caitlyn. Take you anywhere you want to be."

She contemplated her options. If he met her at her house, she could be prepared to offer him a gift to repay him for his thoughtfulness. Something sexy and well planned. Something out of her usual comfort zone.

"Didn't you mention there was a sex club in Houston?" she asked.

"Several, actually. Houston's a big city with eclectic tastes."

She supposed that shouldn't surprise her, but as a local who didn't know of such things, she had to wonder what she'd been missing out on by getting married before she'd had a chance to explore her sexuality.

"Why don't you come to my house after you ditch Lindsey and we can discuss if we want to go to the club Sunday night."

"Sinday," he corrected, and she could picture the devilish gleam in his gorgeous blue eyes.

"Whatever we decide to do, we can spend the entire weekend at my place."

"Saturday too?"

It was breaking her plan to keep him hanging for three days, but if he was hanging, then she had to hang too. "Yes, Saturday too."

"Awesome. So you're going to tell me where you live?"

She chuckled. "Well, I was. Should I be worried? Are you a crazy stalker type or something?"

"Just a little crazy."

"Just the right amount of crazy," she said.

"But not dangerous."

"Just the right amount of dangerous," she said.

He groaned. "I'm going to have to get off the phone now."

"Sorry to keep you. I know you're busy."

"It isn't that. The sound of your voice and making plans with you . . . Knowing I get to see you a day earlier . . . Fuck, Caitlyn, you turn me on. I'm not sure I can handle another set of blue balls."

"You can," she said in her most authoritative voice. "And will."

He chuckled. "I love it when you talk bossy to me."

They hashed out their plans, and she gave him her address. It would probably be noon before he arrived on Saturday. It was about a three-hour drive from his house to Caitlyn's place, and she didn't want to be responsible for him falling asleep behind the wheel if he attempted the trip without resting. He had a big show in New Orleans Friday night, followed by a flight and then the ditching of a pregnant groupie in Austin. He had no business driving so far after a sure-to-be exhausting day.

"Can't wait to see you Saturday," he said.

"Sinday," she corrected, allowing her voice to drop to a husky timbre. She could be sexy when she put her mind to it.

"I thought we weren't waiting until Sunday."

"We're not. Every day with you is a Sinday."

He laughed, and she wished they were together now so she could see his amused smile.

"Well, then, I'm determined never to disappoint you. Until Sinday. Our first of many."

"I'll be waiting."

CHAPTER THREE

AFTER THEIR SHOW in New Orleans, Owen stood next to Kelly, trying to gain his attention. After several moments of shifting from one foot to the other and clearing his throat, Owen figured he was going to have to shove Kelly's singular fixation, Dawn, under the sofa to get him to look his way. The guy had been glued to her side since she showed up in Beaumont the night before. She'd even followed him to tonight's gig. Owen could understand Kelly's attraction to the stunning redhead; it was obvious why Kelly had broken his vow of celibacy with the beautiful, charming, and intelligent woman. But despite Dawn's abundant appeal, Owen was reminded of his friend's utter infatuation with his last great love, and Kelly's trend with obsessive romantic relationships was quite concerning.

Kelly had all but forgotten Owen was alive the entire time he'd been involved with Sara, and Owen was pretty sure Kelly had already forgotten he was alive now that Dawn was in the picture. He'd scarcely acknowledged Owen's existence all day, even though Owen really wanted to talk to him about how great Caitlyn was and about how worrisome Lindsey and the baby might become. Kelly didn't want to dwell on either topic. All he wanted to talk about—for the few moments Owen had caught him alone—was his new lover. *Isn't she amazing?* He'd said the same thing about Sara countless times. Owen and Kelly's friendship had scarcely survived that romance, and as Owen now touched Kelly's shoulder and was still ignored, he figured he had reason to worry that while Kelly had gained a new friend, Owen had lost one.

Dawn pulled her gaze from Kelly's lovesick face long enough to spare a glance for Owen. Only then did Kelly acknowledge that someone other than Dawn existed.

"Hey, what's up?" Kelly asked, his face lighting up with a smile.

Owen felt slightly better that Kelly at least looked happy to see him. "I talked to Sally, and she said we can charter a second flight tonight if you and Dawn want to head back to Austin with us for the weekend."

"We're staying in New Orleans tonight," Kelly said. He squeezed Dawn's hand. "And then we'll be off to Galveston in the morning."

Owen scrunched his brows together. "But you were just in Galveston." And because he'd made so many memories with Sara there, Galveston made Kelly moody. Why the hell would he want to keep going back there?

"I'll probably be spending a lot of time there since that's where Dawn lives," Kelly said.

Before Owen could remind him that *he* lived in Austin and maybe Kelly should consider splitting his attention between those who cared about him, Dawn leaned forward to catch Kelly's eye. He turned from Owen to stare at her again. Jeez, what was wrong with the guy?

"I just live there temporarily," she said. "I'll have to go back to LA soon. Now that the song is done, I have no reason to hide out there anymore."

"Maybe you should renew your lease and write a new song." Kelly lifted Dawn's hand to his lips to give her amazingly talented piano-playing fingers a reverent kiss.

"With you on my bench, I'll either be too distracted to write a single note or so inspired by your virility that I'll write scores and scores of measures."

As their heated gazes turned smoldering, the two lovebirds kissed. Ugh.

"I guess I'll see you in a few days," Owen said loudly.

Kelly waved him away before burying his hands in Dawn's fiery mane of hair and deepening their kiss.

Owen wondered if Kelly was ignoring him because he was still pissed at him for taking his precious cuff away. Maybe Kelly wasn't actually hypnotized by Dawn's magical, celibacy-breaking vagina. Maybe her presence just made it easier for him to give Owen the cold shoulder. Owen did feel bad about taking Kelly's security-blanket-of-a-wrist-cuff and tossing it into the luggage compartment under the bus—he knew how important that piece of jewelry was to the guy—but how could he convey his guilt and offer his apologies when Kelly was so busy trailing after Dawn?

Touching Dawn? Talking to Dawn? Teasing Dawn?

Of course, Owen couldn't blame his bad temper solely on Kelly and Dawn. His ill will was likely a result of him not having the privilege of spending time with Caitlyn while at the same time being stuck with Lindsey. That combination would make any horny guy cranky. Even mooning cows and the adrenaline rush of outrunning a charging bull that afternoon hadn't cheered him up. He knew Jacob had insisted on their outing to help him escape the ever-present Lindsey for a few hours, but Owen's bad mood was due more to Kelly being unavailable and Caitlyn making him promise not to blow a load than anything Lindsey had done. Stuffing his face with Cajun food had made him feel a little better and performing live with Kelly and the rest of the guys had made him feel almost like himself again. But as soon as the show had ended, Kelly had been back in Dawn's arms and pretending Owen didn't exist. The jerk. Was Kelly really *that* ticked off about that stupid fucking wrist cuff? Or worse, was he already wrapped so tightly around Dawn's little finger that he couldn't function without her?

Owen tried again to reach him. "If you really want your cuff back—"

Kelly pulled away from Dawn long enough to say, "Aren't you going to miss your flight?" before he leaned in for another kiss, a deeper kiss.

God, this fucking sucked. But he took Kelly's none-too-subtle cue and left.

Owen was forced—or perhaps expected—to sit next to Lindsey in the limo and on the plane and even on the shuttle to the parking lot to pick up his Jeep. He'd spent more time with her the last few days than anyone he actually wanted to hang out with. He couldn't wait to drop her off at a Holiday Inn and spend the night alone in his bed, even though he knew he wouldn't get much sleep with Caitlyn on his mind and, therefore, an unfulfilled boner in his boxers.

When the shuttle drew to a halt, Owen shook Lindsey awake. He wasn't sure if her hand was on his thigh intentionally or by chance, but he was so horny that even her accidental or on-purpose touch was making him hard. He'd made it through Thursday night and all of Friday without breaking his word to Caitlyn. Several women had tried to convince him to join them for some fun on a mattress, but he'd resisted. He hadn't come once in all that time, and he was so on edge, so keyed up, that everything seemed to give him wood. And he still had another twelve hours to go before he got to see Caitlyn. How would he make it?

"We're here," he whispered to Lindsey. "Wake up."

Lindsey shifted, her arm straightening, her hand slipping between his thighs. He groaned in semi-hard misery and grabbed her wrist, pulling her hand away from his lap.

"We're here?" She sat up straight and glanced around.

"Yep, let's go. I have to drop you off at the hotel before I get to go home."

Maybe he'd have a wet dream or something. Caitlyn couldn't count that as cheating at the little game they were playing. He'd never hoped for a wet dream before, but any relief from this torture was welcome.

Owen stood and helped Lindsey stand.

"I'm so tired," she said, a bit on the whiny side in her obvious exhaustion. "Do I really have to check into a hotel tonight? Can't I just crash on your couch?"

Hmm, potentially willing female staying at his place when he was so horny he couldn't walk fully upright? Yeah, not a good idea. He glanced at Jacob and Gabe for some backup, but Gabe's attention was on Melanie, and Jacob was pretending very hard that he was alone on the shuttle.

"I promise not to sneak into your bed and molest you while you're sleeping," she said.

He shook his head, wondering if she realized how easy he was at the moment, and started toward the front of the bus, ignoring the way she was rubbing both hands over her belly.

"I'm tired too," Owen said, sounding almost as out of sorts as he felt. Yeah, celibacy was so not his thing. Well, he could be celibate as long as he could masturbate, but Caitlyn said he couldn't do that either, and something about her telling him what to do made him gladly obey. She'd make it up to him. He had no doubt about that.

"Do you think I want to deal with this right now?" he snapped. "I'd much rather be with Caitlyn than trying to figure out what to do with you."

He heard Lindsey sniff and turned around to see why she was suddenly lagging behind, wishing he hadn't when he saw the tears welling up in her tired blue eyes. When she noticed him watching her, she turned her back and hugged herself. Guilt squeezed his insides. Yes, he was uncomfortably horny. Yes, he was exhausted. Yes, he was admittedly tired of being the only one looking out for Lindsey. But none of those things made it right to take out his frustration on her. She was struggling enough as it was. He closed his eyes and took a deep breath. Letting it out slowly, he put a hopefully comforting hand on her shoulder and squeezed.

"Fine. You can stay at my place tonight," he said. "But don't think it's going to be a permanent situation."

"Thank you," she said, giving him a weak one-armed hug. "I wouldn't have even asked to stay, but I'm so exhausted."

That made two of them. His tiredness was probably the reason why he had so few alarm bells going off over Lindsey staying in his home. He shifted her in front of him and followed her toward the exit.

"What time will Caitlyn be over tomorrow?" she asked. "I'll be sure to be gone before she gets there."

He grabbed his bag and Lindsey's from the shelves near the front of the shuttle, keeping an eye on her as she navigated the steps.

He stepped off the bus onto the overwarm asphalt of the parking lot where his Jeep—and the vehicles of his bandmates—was parked. He sighed in relief. Almost home. His sanctuary.

"Actually," he said, shifting Lindsey's bag onto his shoulder, "she's not coming to my house."

"Oh?" Lindsey asked. "Is she still mad at you? It isn't on my account, is it?"

Probably, but not for the reason she thought. "No. We just changed our plans. I'm heading to Houston in the morning to see her for the weekend instead of her coming to me."

Coming? He really needed to do some of that as soon as fucking possible.

"Oh . . . well . . ." Her smile wavered slightly as he gazed down at her beneath a humming streetlight. "That's fine. I hope you have fun together."

"I'm sure we'll have a lot of sex," he said with a grin, but then felt bad when Lindsey glanced away. "The black Jeep Wrangler is mine. Over there." He nodded toward his vehicle.

He'd have offered his arm for balance, but he was overloaded with luggage, so he headed off, hoping she'd be able to keep up. He unlocked the Jeep, tossed their bags into the back, and climbed into the driver's side. After a moment, Lindsey opened the passenger door and scrambled into her seat.

"You all right?" he asked.

"Fine," she said, but she didn't look at him as she closed her door and fastened her seat belt.

He started the Jeep and watched her for a moment as she intentionally avoided his gaze.

"What's wrong?"

"Nothing," she said.

"Look, Lindsey, I already told you I plan to keep seeing Caitlyn even if I did knock you up."

"I know that," she said quietly.

"Then why are you so upset about it?"

"It isn't that," she said. "You're ditching me in Austin, I get that. It's just . . ." She glanced at him and wasn't sporting the jealous look he'd been anticipating. Her eyes were wide with fear. "I don't know anyone in Austin."

"You'll be fine here," Owen said. "People are real friendly. And I live in a great neighborhood." Wait—why did that matter? She was only staying at his place for one night. Or until she could find her own place. Without any money. Shit, how did that work exactly?

"So what do I tell people?" she asked. "When they ask about us?"

"Us?" he said under his breath.

He floored the accelerator as he backed out of his parking spot so he didn't have to give her disturbing question an immediate answer.

She was still staring at him expectantly when he pulled out of the lot. "Uh, well, don't tell them anything," he said.

"I think they'll notice that I'm pregnant."

"So?"

She rubbed at her forehead. "Never mind. I'm too tired to think about this right now. Just take me home."

Home? She was already calling it home? Shit.

They had to drive only a few miles to *his* home. His body immediately relaxed when he pulled into *his* drive and parked *his* Jeep in *his* garage. *His.* Not hers.

"Nice place," she said. "What little I saw of it before you sped into the garage. Do you always drive like that?"

"Like what?" he asked.

"Like you're trying to outrun the devil."

"Yes," he said and climbed out.

He collected their bags again and was grateful that Lindsey opened the door for him and then closed it behind them. She followed him along the short sidewalk to the back porch, up the steps, and into the small mudroom off the kitchen. He always left the mudroom light on when he was out of town. The glow made him feel like someone was waiting for him.

"Do you want something to eat before you go to bed?"

"I just want to sleep, thanks," she said, glancing around the mudroom as if she'd just entered the Taj Mahal.

His house was on the small side, but he liked the homey touches of the Craftsman-style cottage. He'd bought the place as the worst house in his parents' neighborhood and spent most of his free time fixing it up. The house was almost complete now, and every square foot of the place had his stamp on it because he'd redone it all himself. From the refinished original floors and woodwork to the crown molding he'd pieced together over several years, this house was his. *His*, not hers. But she was his guest, and he would treat her as such.

"You can take the guest bedroom upstairs," he said, "but there's only one bathroom up there, so we'll have to share."

"Thanks for letting me stay," she said with a friendly smile. "I will warn you that I'll probably be up to pee at least ten times throughout the night." She seemed to have relaxed a bit now that she was inside his house. He was proud that his home had that kind of effect on everyone who entered. He just hoped she didn't get too attached to the place, because she was not staying for long. Was *not*.

He switched on a light as they entered the kitchen through the mudroom. "If you do get hungry, help yourself to anything not past its expiration date." He typically kept his kitchen well stocked and cooked regular meals, but when he was out on tour, sometimes his milk went bad or the bread molded.

"Thanks." She ran her finger along the light gray stone of the countertop as she took in the darker gray country-style cabinets and the farm sink that had been a total bitch to install. "You really are a sweetheart."

"And just the right amount of crazy and dangerous," he said, thinking of Caitlyn. She was never far from his thoughts. He wondered if she'd like his house as much as Lindsey seemed to. And also wondered what kind of house Caitlyn had. She was a well-off business owner. Would she have a modern loft in downtown Houston, a quaint townhouse near the city, or maybe something bigger out in the suburbs? He'd find out the next day. And the sooner he got to bed, the sooner the next day would arrive.

He shut off the kitchen light as they entered the cozy dining room that had a table so small it only comfortably sat four.

"It's so cute," she said. "I love it. Does your fireplace work?" she asked as she waddled into the living room.

"It does now. I had to replace the chimney flue. It used to blow all the smoke back into the house." He chuckled, recalling the first time he'd tried to light a relaxing fire and had ended up in the ER with smoke inhalation.

"This is exactly the kind of house I've always pictured myself living in."

Warning, warning! his brain blared at him.

"Raising a family in," she added, rubbing her large belly with one hand as she examined the framed photos on a shelf beside the mantel. Family photos, coincidentally. Family was important to him. It always had been. And he did want a family eventually. He just wanted one—in the distant future—with a woman he loved more than anything else in the world.

"It's too small for kids," he said, hoping to deter the direction of her homemaker thoughts. "Especially the upstairs."

"I think all kids should be raised in small houses," she said. "You'd have no choice but to spend time together."

"So your family is close?" he asked, wondering how she ended up with nothing and no one to look after her if she had a close family back in Idaho.

"Not really," she said, staring at him with a wide-eyed hopeful expression on her face. "But I want that for our baby, don't you?"

Owen started up the stairs, purposely avoiding her question. After a moment, he heard her footsteps on the meticulously refinished stairs behind him. He tossed his bag into the master bedroom, which was exactly twelve square feet larger than the guest room and scarcely fit his queen-size bed. He didn't need a big master bedroom. All he did was sleep in there, and he never brought a woman home with him.

Until tonight.

"The guest room," he announced as he crossed the small hallway and switched on the light. "Make yourself at home."

Sometimes his brother had stayed with Owen before he'd been deployed to Afghanistan. Chad had helped Owen with some of the construction for a few months before he'd left, and they'd often worked into the wee hours of the morning, so Owen had intentionally decorated the guest room in masculine shades of taupe, red, and navy blue because he'd honestly thought the only person who would ever use the room would be Chad or maybe Kelly if he was over and got too drunk to drive—something that had never happened.

"It's lovely," Lindsey said, stepping into the room. She glanced around before turning and hugging him fiercely. "I will pay you back somehow," she said. "Thank you for not making me feel like an unwanted whore."

He lifted his free arm to hug her in return, his stomach clenching because he might not have made her feel that way, but he had probably *thought* of her that way at least once, and that had been wrong of him.

"You're not unwanted or a whore," he said. "You're a friend, and friends help each other when they can."

She snuggled into him, and he became aware of her soft curves and the foreign—but pretty cool—feel of her large, firm belly against him. His body responded with instant, unwanted arousal, and he silently cursed Caitlyn for putting him in such a state. Lindsey was bound to get the wrong idea if he extended a major boner along with his hand in friendship.

"You're so wonderful," she murmured. "And you smell so good."

She smelled of vanilla and desperation.

Warning! Warning! his brain blared again. Owen backed away and handed her the striped tote bag that currently held all her possessions. Her car and the rest of her stuff had been abandoned along some highway in Oklahoma. He'd help her reclaim it in the morning. And maybe send her out shopping for some clothes.

"The bathroom is there." He nodded at the door at the end

of the hall. "I'm going to crash now. I'm exhausted." And he needed to put as much space between his aching balls and the woman who would probably give him the relief he needed if he so much as hinted that he wanted her. Normally he wasn't the kind of guy who turned down interested pussy, but he didn't want to mess things up with Caitlyn, and he didn't want Lindsey to think there could ever be anything more than friendship between them. And potentially parenting.

Shit.

"Good night," she said, watching him from her doorway as he entered his bedroom and closed the door.

Owen usually slept nude, but seeing as he had a guest, he climbed into bed in his underwear and a T-shirt. Even though he was utterly zonked, he found it impossible to sleep. He kept thinking of all the sexual requests Caitlyn had made over the past few days and wondering how he would ever find the stamina to fulfill all her fantasies. The woman had dozens of them, and she wasn't shy about sharing her desires with him. He loved that about her. His dick loved that about her. His sleep-deprived brain even loved her openness. But if he didn't get some sleep soon, he'd be totally useless the next day.

His cellphone, which was charging on the nightstand, dinged with the arrival of a text message. He wasn't getting any sleep anyway, so he reached for the phone. *Caitlyn.* Just seeing her name on the display had him rolling onto his belly to squash his hard-on into the mattress.

God, I want you, she'd messaged.

Not half as much as I want you, he responded.

Twice as much, she answered. And then, *If I give you permission to masturbate, will you do the same for me?*

It was a tempting proposition. If he jerked one out, he could probably sleep, but she'd been torturing him for days. He was glad she was as fucking horny as he was. She deserved the mutual misery.

No. You are not allowed to come until my dick is inside you.

He sent the message and was waiting for a reply when a thud outside his door made his heart race. He wasn't used to hearing strange noises in his house. Rushed footsteps hurried down the hall and the bathroom door closed. Just Lindsey, he decided.

Caitlyn's message arrived an instant later. *I'd respond with something sexy, but it will just make me hornier.*

He laughed softly and sent a reply.

Good night, Caitlyn.

Good night.

Fuck you tomorrow.

She sent him a rude emoticon—a one-finger salute—which drew another soft chuckle from him, and he dropped his phone on the nightstand before rolling onto his back and making a rather impressive tent in the covers.

He tried flattening it with his hand, but that led to touching it, which made him groan softly. The toilet flushed down the hall, water splashed in the sink, the bathroom door creaked slightly, and footsteps came back up the hall. They paused outside his door. He held his breath to be as quiet as possible. What would he do if Lindsey opened the door and found him with his hand trying to push his hard-as-stone dick into his thigh? What would she do? Would she be embarrassed? Try to touch him? Draw him into her sweet mouth and suck him, her hand sliding between his thighs to gently caress his balls?

No, he couldn't let himself think like that. He didn't want Lindsey, he wanted Caitlyn. But Caitlyn was so far away and Lindsey was standing right outside his door.

Finally she moved away, crossed the hall, and closed her bedroom door. Owen released a sigh of relief and rolled onto his belly, once again squashing his dick into the mattress. Rocking his hips slightly helped alleviate a bit of his suffering. Thinking about things other than women and all their delightful parts helped even more. Eventually he got his erection under control and drifted to sleep.

He was pulled awake before the sun was up by a strange and haunting noise. His eyes popped open, and he shifted them side to side, as if that could help him see in the dark. Nothing but silence met his ears, so he decided he'd been hearing things and rolled onto his side. He was almost asleep again when he heard the same sound. It was too human to be a wounded animal, but that was what it reminded him of. He listened to Lindsey groan as if she were in excruciating pain. Maybe she'd fallen, or maybe she'd gone into labor.

He untangled his legs from the covers and hopped out of bed, left his room and crossed the hall. He paused outside her door, listening.

"No," she shouted clearly enough for him to hear her through the closed door. "No, no. Please stop." She cried out in pain again.

Owen banged on her door. "Lindsey? Are you okay?"

He didn't hear any further sounds, so he pressed his ear to the door near the hinge, listening. He could hear her breathing— rapid and broken—but she wasn't moaning anymore. Wasn't shouting.

"Lindsey?"

"I'm okay," she called out. "Just a bad dream."

"Are you sure?"

He heard a thud on the other side of the door and reached for the knob. It turned in his hand, and the door swung inward.

"I didn't mean to wake you," she said.

It was too dark to see more than her outline. He wasn't sure what possessed him to lift a hand and touch her face. She was drenched in sweat, her hair sticking to her damp cheeks. Or maybe she'd been crying and the wetness on her face was tears.

"You sounded really scared," he said.

"Just a dream," she whispered.

"What about? Maybe it will help to talk about it."

"I—I don't remember. I never remember the dream. Just the feeling it gives me."

A terrible feeling, if the sounds she'd been making or the trembling in her body were any indication.

"You have it a lot?"

She nodded, and her head tipped forward, sending tendrils of hair slipping across her pale face. "I'm sure it's just the hormones. They make me a little crazy."

He stepped away. "Well, if you're okay, I'm going back to bed. I thought you had gone into labor or something."

When he turned, she grabbed the back of his T-shirt. "Just a minute," she said before pressing her face into the center of his back. "Stay just a minute. Until . . . until I feel safe again."

"Lindsey . . ." He tried to turn back around to comfort her properly.

"No. Don't look at me. Just . . . stay."

He stood there feeling foolish and uncertain of why she was clinging to the back of his shirt like a baby monkey. After a moment she pressed closer, straightening so that her face was between his shoulders and her breasts and belly were against his back. The hand that had been clutching his shirt now slid around his body, flattening against his belly

"Almost," she whispered.

Almost what? What was she doing back there? He noticed that her breathing was slowly returning to normal and the tremors of her body had gone still. She took one last deep breath and stepped away.

"Sorry about that," she said. "Sometimes . . ."

She took several steps backward until she'd crossed the threshold back into her room.

"Sometimes what?" he pressed, still not sure what she'd been doing as she held on to him. It hadn't felt like an attempt to seduce him. As horny as he was, it hadn't even excited him. It had tugged at other parts of him, though. Parts of him that usually made him do things like climb into a culvert to pull out a crying kitten or empty his wallet into the Salvation Army bucket.

"Sometimes a woman just needs something solid to hold on to."

She closed the door and left him standing in the hall puzzling over her words. He still hadn't figured them out when he crawled back into bed to lose a little more sleep.

~~~

The next morning Owen was woken by the smell of bacon. His stomach growled loud enough to make him laugh. He rolled out of bed and placed his hands on his hips, glaring down at his cock, as if that would make it behave. Hoping that a piss would cure him of his annoying problem, he cracked open his door and peered into the hallway for signs of Lindsey. He could hear her humming in the kitchen, her muted song accompanied by the sizzle of frying bacon and the occasional scrape or clang of a utensil against a pan.

He hurried down the hall, and it seemed to take a century for his stream to start. He was pretty sure he'd be permanently disfigured if he didn't see Caitlyn soon. He planned to get on the road to Houston as soon as he could drive. Of course, there was the problem of finding a place to put Lindsey before he left. He returned to his room to slip on a pair of jeans, convinced they'd conceal his overly excitable dick, and padded down the stairs in his bare feet. As he'd expected, Lindsey was cooking breakfast. What he hadn't expected was for her to look so tousled and beautiful while doing so.

It was his little head having such thoughts, he told himself as he leaned over the center kitchen island to watch. He refused to stare at the curve of her ass under her nightgown. Much.

"Good morning," he said quietly, and she jumped as if he'd shouted through a megaphone. "Something smells good."

"You said I could help myself," she said, stirring a huge skillet of scrambled eggs with a spatula.

"And I meant it on one condition."

Her eyes were wide as she turned to gape at him.

"That you'll share some with me."

"Oh!" She flushed prettily and turned back to the stove. "Of course. I was going to make toast, but—"

"Mold?"

She nodded. "The milk is still good, though. Do you drink coffee?"

"After not sleeping well?" he muttered, going to the coffee maker to start a pot and finding the coffee ready. He reached for his favorite mug. "I'll drink the whole pot."

"I'm sorry about waking you in the middle of the night," she said as she turned off the burner. "I don't know why, but ever since I got pregnant I've been having nightmares."

"Maybe it's the stress."

"Probably," she said. "That or my crazy hormonal swings. You can have all the coffee. I'm supposed to be watching my caffeine intake."

"I have some decaf around here somewhere," he said, opening a cabinet and shifting its contents around as he looked for the likely stale container of decaf—because, really, what was the point?

"I'll have orange juice," she said. "Unless it's fermented."

Her giggle made him laugh. Was it odd that he felt so at ease with her in his home? When she'd been around him on the tour bus or backstage, he'd been so tense he thought he'd snap. But here? Here he was at home. She was at home.

Shit.

He opened the fridge and pulled out the orange juice, sniffing it with trepidation but finding it consumable. He also discovered an English muffin and after determining that it was safe to eat, popped it into the toaster.

They filled their plates in the kitchen and carried their breakfast to the small table in the dining room. She smiled at him dreamily as she sat in the seat across from him. He concentrated on his food and not on the way the sunlight streaming through the window caught the golden highlights in her hair.

"Is there an employment agency nearby?" she asked.

He stopped eating with his fork halfway to his mouth. "I'm not sure it will be open on Saturday," he said.

"Oh. I can try calling and see."

Even if she found a job today, she wouldn't have an income for weeks. What was he going to do with her? Leave her here in his house making herself at home while he went to Houston to be with Caitlyn so he could fuck himself into oblivion? Maybe he could take Lindsey to a women's shelter or maybe—

"The garage apartment," he said aloud. His parents rented the apartment above the garage to college students, but he knew it was unoccupied until the fall. That would give them the time they needed to find Lindsey permanent accommodations.

Lindsey squinted at him. "What?"

"My mom will help you out while I'm on tour. She loves charity cases."

Before he could tell her about the apartment, Lindsey's blue eyes turned stormy. "You think I'm a charity case?"

"No," he said quickly. "You just need a little help to get back on your feet."

"I can't ask your mom for help," she said. "She'll think I'm a total slut."

"Why would she think that?"

She pointed both hands toward her pregnant belly. "Hello?"

"She doesn't need to know the story behind how you got in that condition." He poked another bite of eggs into his mouth.

"Do you plan on telling her it's yours?" Lindsey asked.

"No."

"Don't you think she'll wonder why you're helping me then?"

"Not really," he said with a shrug. He'd brought home all sorts of strays in his youth—wild animals, abandoned pets, Kellen Jamison. Lindsey seemed like a natural progression to him. His mom loved dealing with such things. She said his tendency to bring home strays proved that her son had a big heart and was a good person.

Or that he was a total sucker.

"What if she hates me?" Lindsey asked, shifting her eggs from one side of her plate to the other.

"She doesn't hate anyone. Trust me, okay?"

A crease formed between her pale eyebrows. "I kind of have to. I don't have many other options."

After they'd finished their breakfast and cleaned up, Owen checked his messages while Lindsey collected her things from upstairs.

Are you on your way? Caitlyn had messaged him almost an hour ago.

He smiled, glad she was as eager to see him as he was to see her. *Soon.*

He also had a message from Tony, who owned the series of underground sex clubs Owen frequented. *This weekend's passphrase is "Tangerines go well with mangos." Good for entry at any of my clubs until Monday.*

Owen wasn't sure if he'd take Caitlyn to another club or not, but if they did decide to go, he knew he could get them in.

"I'm ready," Lindsey said.

She looked so fresh and innocent with her recently scrubbed face and simple ponytail that he stuffed his phone into his pocket as if she'd find it offensive. He knew Lindsey was freaky in the sack from experience, but she looked positively angelic.

"Do you want to take the Jeep or walk?" he asked.

"Walk?"

"It's about a block. There's a sidewalk."

Lindsey blinked at him. "You, Owen Tags Mitchell the rock star, live a block away from your mother?"

"Hey, at least I don't live with her," he said. "Anymore."

She laughed and rocked forward on her toes as she leaned closer to him. "We can walk. I could use the exercise."

He insisted on carrying her bag as they headed out the back door and down the driveway. As they passed his neighbor's house, Mrs. Worth stopped watering her geraniums to stare.

"Did you get married, Owen?"

"Uh, no, Mrs. Worth," he said, feeling the heat of embarrassment rise up his throat and face. Perhaps they should have taken the Jeep after all.

"Does your mom know you're home?" Mrs. Worth called as they passed the end of her picket fence.

"Not yet. We're going to see her now."

"Maybe we should have called first," Lindsey said.

"And ruin the surprise? My mom loves surprises."

Lindsey didn't look convinced.

The houses got increasingly larger as they traveled up the block. They passed what was now the worst house on the block since Owen had fixed up his once-dilapidated home, and he noticed a For Sale sign in the yard. Perhaps a project for the winter, he thought. He could buy it, do the work, and resell it. Or . . .

He glanced down at Lindsey. "What do you think of that house?"

She paused at the end of the overgrown lawn and studied the Tudor-style cottage. The timbers and the once-white stucco between them could use fresh paint, and the brown shingles were curled in spots. They definitely needed to be replaced.

"It needs a lot of work," she said.

"I like working on houses. My house had squirrels living in it when I bought it."

"So you're thinking about buying this dump so you can live even closer to your mother?"

Owen laughed. "Maybe." Or maybe when Chad got back from Afghanistan he'd like a place of his own. Also near their mom. "My brother might like it."

"You have a brother?"

"Yep. Three years older. Chad is a soldier. The dog tags I wear are to honor him. He's been off at war, but he's coming home soon." Owen scowled at his words. Such a lame description for such a remarkable man.

"I'm glad to hear that."

"Oh," he said, remembering the last conversation he'd had with Chad. "You can't tell my mom he'll be home in a few weeks. He wants to surprise her. She loves surprises."

She grinned at him. "You said that already."

"It must be true then."

They crossed at the next corner, and Lindsey gawked at the large kid-friendly park across the street.

"It's a great neighborhood. Good schools too," Owen said. "The reason I met Kellen is because they were doing this experiment where they bused in a group of underprivileged kids and tracked their progress in our school district. I think they were trying to figure out if it was the low-income schools or the kids' home lives that made it so difficult for them to succeed and get ahead."

"Kellen is poor?" Lindsey asked, tearing her gaze from the perfectly tended park to look at him.

"He isn't now."

"And you never were."

"My parents are average middle-class citizens."

She shimmied her shoulders. "Who raised a rock star."

"And a war hero," Owen reminded her. That was far more important in his book.

At the end of the block, they stopped before a large gray house surrounded by a sturdy wooden fence. Dad said it was to keep kids out of his yard, but it was really there to keep the dogs in the yard.

Hawn, the family's golden retriever and who-knew-what mix, began to bounce excitedly at the gate, barking a friendly greeting at him.

"I probably should have asked if you like dogs before I brought you here," Owen said, reaching over the gate to give Hawn a vigorous rub on her furry neck.

"I love dogs," Lindsey said, holding out her hand for a sniff. It was soon covered in dog spit as Hawn immediately accepted Lindsey as a friend. Of course, Hawn accepted every decent person as a friend.

"Watch the little ones," Owen said as he opened the gate and ushered Lindsey inside.

As he and Lindsey shuffled carefully up the path, their three-legged Chihuahua, Maxie, and blind-in-one-eye Jack Russell, Toby, raced around and around their feet as Hawn leaped gleefully beside them. An unfamiliar gray kitten was sunning himself on the front porch next to the aging pair of ginger cats named Betsy and Ross.

"Looks like Mom picked up another stray," Owen said as he stretched out a cautious hand to give the newcomer a scratch behind the ear. The cat yawned and gave the now-sniffing-him Hawn an annoyed look before curling his crooked tail more securely around his body and returning to his nap.

"You have a lot of pets," Lindsey observed as she bent to give

Maxie and Toby the attention they craved. Maxie immediately peed in her excitement, but managed not to wet Lindsey's sneaker.

"Always have," Owen said. He was certain his mother would be over the moon to help Lindsey get back on her feet.

He rang the doorbell and waited for Mom to answer. The door was likely unlocked, but he'd once walked in on his parents engaged in a nooner on the foyer floor and would never again surprise them by letting himself into the house. He would also never look at his great-grandmother's Persian rug quite the same way.

"Owey," Mom said as she threw open the door and hugged him. "Mrs. Worth just called and said you were on your way."

"So much for surprises," Owen said under his breath. Mrs. Worth had babysat him when he'd been in elementary school, and apparently she'd never thought to stop.

"And this is . . ." Mom asked. Her dark blond bob shifted forward to cover one blue eye as she inclined her head in Lindsey's direction.

"This is Lindsey . . . uh . . . What's your last name?"

"It had better be Mitchell," Mom said, giving him a stern stare that made him feel about three inches high.

Lindsey flushed, and Owen was pretty sure he needed to throw up. "Uh, well, no . . . It's, uh . . ." Damn, he should have called first. Or come up with a feasible story before he delivered a pregnant groupie to his mother's doorstep. Especially since he had no clue what Lindsey's last name was.

"Donaldson," Lindsey supplied. "I should be going now."

She turned to escape—and abandon him to his mother's death stare—but Owen caught her arm before she could take a single step.

"I, uh, found her. Uh . . . at the arena in Houston." That was sort of true. Well, more like Lindsey had found him. "She doesn't have any place to go. She got fired, thrown out of her place. Her car broke down. She has no money, no family willing to help her, so I thought . . ." What had he thought? That his mom would just open her home and her heart to a perfect stranger? "Maybe you . . ." He tipped his head toward his mom, and she crossed her arms over her chest. "*I* could help her out. But I don't know where to start."

"First you start by claiming your baby," Mom said.

"Oh, it's not his," Lindsey said, pulling at the hem of her shirt with both hands. "Maybe."

"Hi, Owen!" someone called from the sidewalk outside the fence.

He waved at whoever it was and squeezed his mother's arm. "Can we talk about this inside?" There were plenty of good things about knowing all of your neighbors since birth and plenty of bad things too. "Please?"

"Of course," Mom said, meeting Lindsey's troubled gaze. "Please come inside, Lindsey."

Lindsey gave Owen a questioning look and when he nodded, she stepped over the threshold.

"Wow, Mrs. Mitchell, what a beautiful rug!" Lindsey said.

"It was my grandmother's," Mom said.

Owen cringed and made sure he stayed on the hardwood showing around its borders.

"You have a lovely home," Lindsey said. "And you raised a very thoughtful son."

"Why, thank you," Mom said with a sweet smile. Her frostiness was already melting, not that Owen was surprised. "Are you hungry? Thirsty?" She moved her mouth closer to Lindsey's ear and asked quietly, "Have to use the bathroom?"

Lindsey laughed. "Actually . . ."

"It's like they're standing directly on your bladder, isn't it?" Mom whispered. She pointed Lindsey toward the powder room.

As soon as Lindsey had shut the bathroom door behind her, his mom whirled on him. "Why didn't you tell me you were going to be a father?" she hissed.

"I—"

"If you're going to fool around, I thought you at least had the good sense to be safe."

Even though he was a grown-ass man, it still bothered him when he disappointed his mother. "Mom, it's not mine." He also agonized about lying to her. It probably was his baby.

"Then why did you bring her here?"

"I told you—she didn't have anywhere else to go."

"That's really the reason? The *only* reason?" She gave him *that* look, the one that made it psychologically impossible to lie to her.

"It might be mine," he admitted in a rush of breath. He immediately wanted to stab himself.

"Might?"

"She, uh . . . We, uh . . . The band, we . . ."

"Used your fame to take advantage of an innocent young woman."

Innocent? Yeah, Lindsey looked innocent, but she was far from virginal. Or even monogamous.

"It wasn't like that."

"Then what was it like?" Mom pressed. "Do you love her?"

"No."

"Do you even *like* her?"

"I don't hate her," he said.

Mom's eyebrows shot up, and she shook her head. "Wow, Owen, really?"

"It was a mistake to bring her here," he said, recognizing that Mom wasn't having any of his nonsense. "I'll figure out other arrangements for her."

Lindsey cracked the door open. He wondered how much she'd overheard. They'd been conversing in harsh whispers, but the powder room wasn't exactly soundproof.

Mom turned and smiled kindly at Lindsey. "Feel better?" she asked.

Lindsey had that terrified, hopeless expression on her face that had convinced Owen to bring her home with him in the first place.

Mom put an arm around Lindsey's slight shoulders and urged her toward the cozy living room off the foyer. Apparently he wasn't the only Mitchell on the planet affected by that look.

"Let's talk."

Lindsey was pressed into a patterned wingback chair, and Mom sat on the sofa across from her. Owen stood behind the sofa, behind his mom's back, just in case he had to lead the direction of Lindsey's answers with telepathic looks and/or had to run for his life if scary-mom made an appearance. No one was safe from scary-mom.

"When are you due, dear?" Mom asked.

Lindsey glanced up at Owen before settling her gaze on his mother's. "In about three months, I think."

"You think? Do you have a specific due date?"

She looked at Owen again. "September fifteenth."

"So we have a little time to get your life together before the baby arrives," Mom said. "Don't look so upset. Everything will be okay."

Oh sure, Mom comforted the stranger and made her own son feel like total shit.

"Is it a boy or a girl?"

The tiniest of smiles curved Lindsey's lips. "I think it's a boy."

"They couldn't tell for sure in the ultrasound?"

Lindsey ducked her head. "I haven't had one."

"Why not?"

Lindsey's ponytail shifted to cover her face, and she coiled her hair around one finger. "I haven't had . . . *time* to go to the doctor."

He was pretty sure she hadn't had the resources to go. Or maybe she'd been too ashamed. Owen circled the sofa and sat next to his mother, who reached over and squeezed his knee.

"I know a great ob/gyn," Mom said to Lindsey. "We'll get you an appointment this week. Have you been taking prenatal vitamins?"

"I bought some at the store." She looked up and met Mom's eyes. "Mrs. Mitchell, I appreciate what you're trying to do, but I can't afford to go to the doctor."

"So you're going to give birth in a public restroom?" Mom lifted both eyebrows at her. "Is that your plan?"

Lindsey cradled her belly in her arms. "I thought I could go to the ER and . . . not pay the bill. They can't turn you away, can they?"

"What? That's nonsense," Owen said. "I'll pay for everything."

Lindsey straightened and shook her head. "You can't."

"I have plenty of money, Lindsey. It's not a big deal."

"I can't. I can't just take a handout from you or, as Nessi suggested, from the welfare office or from anyone."

"If you won't take my money, then think of it as a loan," Owen said.

"Owen!" Mom chastised. "You aren't going to make her pay you back."

He didn't care if she did or not, but if he was reading Lindsey correctly, she might actually go to the doctor if she thought of his monetary assistance as a loan instead of a handout.

"I want to pay him back."

The relieved look on her face was payment enough for him. All the stress she'd been under couldn't be good for her or the baby.

"We'll get you some health insurance," Mom said. "And you can stay here with me and James until you find your own place."

There was the woman Owen knew his mother to be.

"I couldn't," Lindsey said.

"You will."

"Could she use the apartment?" Owen asked hopefully.

Mom glanced at Owen. "Yes. Perfect." Her attention shifted back to Lindsey. "We rent a room above our garage to college students during the school year, but it's vacant until late August. You are more than welcome to stay there."

"How much is the rent?" Lindsey asked.

Mom didn't bat an eyelash. "It's a small place. We get only a hundred dollars a month for it."

Liar, Owen thought. He knew for a fact that his parents usually got six times that amount for the nice one-bedroom apartment she'd referred to as a room above the garage. But he was glad for Mom's little fib, because Lindsey actually smiled.

"I can probably afford that even with a part-time job," she said.

"So you do have a job?" Mom asked.

"Not yet, but I'm sure I can find something around here." It was the first time Owen had seen her look hopeful.

"She's from Idaho, Mom," Owen said.

"Idaho! You're a long way from home."

"I need to make a new home," Lindsey said. "The old one isn't right for me or the baby."

"I'll see if I can find someone to go to Oklahoma to get your car," Owen said. "You'll need transportation to get you to work and doctor's appointments." And the store. She'd need to buy some things for herself and the baby.

Lindsey's smile faltered. "I'm sure it's been impounded by now. I left it on the side of a freeway."

"Don't worry about it. We'll get it here and running again. I'll just add all the expenses to your tab," Owen said with a wink.

She nodded and then reached out to take both his and Mom's hands. "Thanks for helping me," she said, "but not making me feel like a mooch. I've been feeling like such a mooch since I arrived in

Texas."

"Everyone can use a little help sometimes," Mom said, patting Lindsey's hand with her free one.

A *little* help? Owen thought, but he patted Lindsey's hand as well. The faster he had his mom onboard with Lindsey's care, the faster he could ditch her and head to Houston.

While Lindsey was in the bathroom—*again*—Owen gave his mom all the cash he had on him. It was only a few hundred bucks, but it should get her through the weekend. "She probably needs some clothes and stuff," he said, "and some necessities for the apartment." Luckily, the apartment was fully furnished, including kitchen wares and linens, but she'd still need a few things. "She has just that one little overnight bag of belongings until we get her car back."

"I'll take her shopping," Mom promised, not looking put out in the least.

"I hate to leave you with all the responsibility of taking care of her, but I have plans this weekend. I have to leave."

Mom crossed her arms over her chest and shook her head at him.

"Don't pretend like you can't wait to shop for baby clothes," he teased her, and she laughed.

"I'll take good care of her."

Of that, he had no doubt.

CHAPTER FOUR

CAITLYN NEARLY JUMPED out of her chair when her doorbell rang a little after noon. If her visitor was Owen, he was a tad early and must have driven like a maniac, but it could just be a delivery, so she cinched the belt of her big fluffy robe a bit tighter and went to the door. Her heart tripped over itself when she recognized the gorgeous face on her video monitor, even though he did appear slightly distorted and a touch grainy on the screen. She loosened her robe, stripped it from her shoulders, and tossed it on the bench in the foyer before opening the door.

His smile of greeting vanished as his jaw dropped.

She wasn't entirely naked. She wore the bright yellow Sinday chicken panties he'd so thoughtfully sent her.

"So much for small talk," he said with a wicked grin.

"How was your drive?" she asked as she stepped aside so he could enter.

"I do believe that qualifies as small talk."

Nerves fluttered through her belly as he stepped over the threshold and shut the solid wooden door behind him. He didn't take his eyes off hers once. Not even to stare at her bare breasts. She'd played this scenario through her head a dozen times that morning, but even though she'd let her thoughts take it in a different direction each time, she hadn't been prepared for the effect he's nearness would have on her. She was trembling. Her knees were shaky, and her heart and body both ached with longing. She hadn't experienced the feeling since the last time she'd fallen for the wrong man.

She didn't realize she was walking backwards and he was following until she bashed her hip into the foyer console. She whimpered, not in pain but because he was getting closer now and the deep longing within her intensified as the distance between them diminished.

"Are you trying to escape?" he asked, his voice low, hypnotic, and so sensual that she tingled from head to toe.

She shook her head. Her breath caught when he wrapped a hand around her throat and pinned her against the table with his lower body. His cock—thick and long and as hard as the marble at their feet—pressed into her lower belly.

She clung to the table behind her, afraid she might pass out if she filled her hands with his sculpted muscles. He shifted his hips away—stealing the reminder of his desire from her—and she moaned a protest. But then his free hand was on her hip and her panties were sliding down her thighs until they settled on the floor and he was fumbling between their bodies. He released his firm hold on her throat just long enough to lift her to sit on the edge of the console table and then he was inside her.

Only after he'd filled her completely did she touch him. She pulled at his shirt. The urgency to feel his bare chest against her achingly hard nipples made her tug at his clothes. He didn't help her—just stared into her eyes as he took her over and over with hard, deep, slow thrusts. And suddenly she didn't care that she couldn't press herself against his bare chest. The only things that mattered were the rhythmic connection between their bodies and the more intense one between their locked gazes.

Her favorite vase rattled on the console beside her each time he plunged into her. The wooden candlesticks she'd carefully chosen to match her décor tipped, rolled, and hit the floor with resounding thumps. But she didn't care. She wanted him. Wanted this. Wanted it to never end. Wanted to be lost in his gaze and in his rhythm forever.

Lifting her feet off the floor, she wrapped both legs around his hips to take him deeper. She gasped as the shift in position meant he rubbed her just right. Her eyelashes fluttered, and her mouth dropped open as the pleasure overwhelmed.

If it hadn't felt so fucking spectacular, she might have thought she ruined everything by coming. As she cried out lost in the throes of ecstasy, she couldn't help but break eye contact. Her nails raked down his back as she lost herself. Owen's entire body stiffened and he gasped brokenly. With a tormented moan, he buried his face in her throat, his fingers digging into her ass. After an intense moment of shallow, rapid strokes, he shuddered as he lost himself inside her.

He rubbed his open mouth against her throat as he struggled

to find enough air for his laboring lungs. She held him close, selfishly hoping he never took a steady breath, because she knew as soon as he did, he'd move away. She didn't think she'd ever be ready to release him.

After a long moment, he took a deep breath and lifted his head. His smile made her already thundering heart throb.

"Now that was wonderful greeting," he murmured, leaning in to kiss her.

"Hello," she said with a laugh and cupped his face between her palms so he'd stay close.

"And hello to you on this fine Sinday afternoon." He shifted away slightly, despite her unspoken wishes to remain glued to him, and glanced around the foyer. "Nice place you've got here. Enormous."

"I bought my husband out in the divorce settlement," she said. "I probably should have let it go and purchased something smaller, but it was my dream house, so I couldn't bear to part with it at the time."

"*Was* your dream house?"

"We were supposed to fill all five bedrooms with our children." She'd likely always feel sad and lonely in this huge house because it served to remind her that her dreams for a family had never been fulfilled.

"Maybe someday you'll have kids."

"Maybe." She didn't want to have this discussion with Owen. He must realize that she was only seeing him for the amazing sex. She had been thinking of starting something a bit more long term initially, but then that pregnant groupie had shown up, and it had been quite an awakening for Caitlyn. The guy was a seasoned player, and she'd just entered the field as a rookie. If Owen brought up something like having kids again, she'd have to set him straight. She'd been warned about how easily he got his feelings hurt, so she hoped he caught on without her having to tell him point blank that she had no plans to get serious about him. "Have you had lunch?" she asked.

His eyes lit up with interest. "Not yet. Did you cook?"

She laughed. *Her* cook? Yeah, no. "I don't cook much"—*or ever*—"but I am an expert at opening a takeout container."

He was pretty good at hiding his disappointment. "I could eat," he said. "Thanks."

He kissed her again and pulled out, putting far too much space between them. She stumbled as she got her feet beneath her. Sort of. She definitely wasn't accustomed to the kind of aerobics she'd just experienced. Her thighs were all shaky as she bent to retrieve her panties.

"So do you often open the door in the nude?" Owen asked.

She grinned. "Only if I'm hoping to get laid."

"Lucky me." He removed the condom she hadn't realized he'd applied and tied the open end into a knot.

"D-d-did you put that thing on in the car?" she sputtered.

He laughed as he tucked his cock into his pants and fastened his fly. "No, but I did open the package before I put it in my pocket. I hoped I'd need it upon arrival."

"So I guess opening the door in nothing but my panties was predictable?" They had been talking about how horny they both were for days, but they hadn't even made it out of the foyer.

"Appreciated," he murmured, kissing her bare shoulder. "You know, we could skip lunch and head directly to the bedroom."

"We're saving the bedroom for last." With her most mischievous smile, she turned and walked away, forcing herself not to look over her shoulder to see if he was following. She wasn't used to being a seductress, or even trying to be one, but she had a rich imagination and a long, detailed list of fantasies she wanted Owen to fulfill. She'd already set up each room of the house to accommodate a different sex act. She wondered, belatedly, if he'd find that odd.

She smiled to herself when his footsteps padded first against the marble and then the dark hardwood floor behind her as she made her way through the great room to the kitchen. She didn't look at the box on the coffee table as she passed, not wanting to draw his attention to it before the time was right.

"What do you mean, save the bedroom for last?"

"Considering it's the only room in this house where I ever had sex with my husband, I thought we'd save it for last. It's a big house, a clean house, and all the rooms could use a little dirtying."

"I do like the way you think."

She stopped at the counter and began to pull out the takeout containers from the bag she'd picked up from the deli on her way home from the sex shop she'd visited that morning. Not many locals went to sex shops at ten a.m., so she'd practically had the place to herself.

"I can't decide if I'd rather look at your tits or hold them," he said, leaning against the counter beside her. He was no longer focused on her eyes—not even close—and while she might despise and fight sexism at work on a daily basis, when she was in her own home, with this man? She wasn't fighting in the least. She liked that he looked at her as a desirable woman. Liked the way his tongue wet the corner of his mouth as if he were imagining her nipple between his lips.

"Can't you do both at the same time?" she asked. "I do have two of them."

He sucked in a sharp breath through his nose and lifted his gaze to meet hers. "I think that would result in sensory overload."

His befuddled grin made her laugh. "Maybe I should put on some clothes."

"I do feel overdressed," he said, but instead of encouraging her to cover up, he stripped down to his boxers.

She allowed her eyes to feast on his broad shoulders, firm chest, ripped stomach, and the devastating vee that drew her gaze from his narrow hips before unfortunately disappearing into his shorts.

"Still overdressed," she murmured, hoping he'd take a hint.

He slowly tugged his boxers lower, showing more vee and a hint of the root of his cock. Just a tease. Just enough to remind her how glad she was he'd come to visit.

"Enough?" he asked. She tore her gaze from his semi-peepshow to meet the challenge in his gorgeous blue eyes.

"For now," she said, inclining her head. "I wasn't sure what you liked—besides pastrami and rye bread—so I got a little of everything."

She opened the lids on her favorite potato salad and on a variety of pasta salads ranging from creamy to oily to vinegar-based. She pulled out three bean salad and coleslaw, mashed potatoes, and macaroni and cheese. Next came the cheese platter, the meat platter, the veggie platter, and the fruit tray, followed by assorted dips and crackers.

"Caitlyn?" he said, his eyes still on her breasts. "Would you be terribly offended if I changed my mind?"

Her heart gave an unpleasant lurch. Was he already tired of

looking at her? Jeez. At least it had taken her husband a few years before he'd started ignoring her.

"You don't want . . ." She couldn't bring herself to say it: *me?*

"I'm hungry for only one thing in this kitchen."

"Pastrami?" she guessed.

He chuckled. "No, beautiful. Earning my pastrami," he said. "With you."

She flushed with pleasure. She hadn't felt desired in so damned long, but he made her feel desirable, wanted, and beautiful. She did want to spend a little time with him that didn't involve him buried inside her. Granted, she hoped it was very little time, but still, some.

"I skipped breakfast," she said. "I'm starving."

"I had a big breakfast. Homemade."

Not from a restaurant, a deli counter, or a microwave? "You cook?"

He examined her spread of prepared foods and avoided her gaze. "Some."

She got the feeling he wasn't telling her the entire story and knew he was a bad liar, so she rephrased her question. "Did you cook yourself breakfast this morning?"

He reached across the counter and fixed himself a cracker with cheese and summer sausage before stuffing it into his mouth. "Uh, well," he said, still chewing, "Lindsey cooks, I guess."

"So Lindsey made you breakfast this morning."

"It didn't mean anything," he said. "She was just being nice because I gave her a place to sleep."

"At your house," Caitlyn said flatly. And when he nodded slightly, she added, "I thought you were taking her to a hotel."

"We got home really late." He met her eyes steadily. "Nothing happened."

She wanted to believe him, but the unwelcome vision of her husband fucking some nubile young college student on his desk invaded her thoughts. Lindsey appeared to be both nubile and college-age.

Caitlyn grabbed a paper plate and began filling it with food that no longer looked appetizing.

After a moment, Owen covered her wrist with his warm hand. "Look at me."

She glanced at him so swiftly, she didn't even register his

expression before turning her attention back to her plate.

"Look at me, Caitlyn."

She took a steadying breath and forced her eyes to meet his.

"Nothing happened. She slept across the hall in my guest room, and I tossed and turned all night aching with thoughts of you."

"She's very pretty." The image of the gorgeous pregnant blonde clinging to Owen when she floored him with her news was permanently etched in Caitlyn's mind. "And young."

"But I don't want her. I want you." He cupped her breast, his thumb brushing her nipple.

She closed her eyes and leaned into his touch. She wanted to believe him. She did. But some stupid part of her expected every man to betray her, every man to prefer a young, hot blonde with perfect firm tits and flawless skin. Every man to find her lacking.

"And I'd say it's only your body I want," he said, "but that would be a lie."

She moaned quietly as her body began to throb beneath the light, persistent stroke of his thumb.

"In addition to being beautiful, you're smart and funny and open-minded and beguilingly humble. Someone with your success should have a bigger ego."

She opened her eyes and found him watching her face. He smiled at her, and she smiled back. "I'll try not to be jealous of the gorgeous, young, pregnant blonde living under your roof."

"Oh, she's not staying with me anymore." He shook his head. "She's staying with my mom."

"Your mom? So you told her the baby is yours?" Why else would she take in a pregnant stranger?

He snorted on a laugh. "Uh, no. It's just my mother likes to take in strays—stray kids, stray animals, stray pregnant groupies."

"So you often drop off your pregnant groupies at your mother's house?"

He laughed again. An anxious laugh. "What? No, of course not. Lindsey is the first."

"But she's yours," Caitlyn pressed.

"Quit twisting my words," he said. "I could have let her stay at my place, but I didn't think you'd like that arrangement."

Fighting down the jealousy eating at her, she stared at him for a long moment. This was just a fling, she reminded herself. Sex and fun and nothing more. "Why would I care if she stays at your place?"

Yes, Caitlyn, why? Because she did care, even though she knew she shouldn't. She wasn't very good at this frivolous, meaningless relationship stuff. Maybe she'd eventually get the hang of it. But when he said all the right things and made her feel good about herself in addition to being an all-around great guy, keeping him at an emotional distance was difficult. And they hadn't even been together an hour.

"Can we not talk about Lindsey?" Owen asked. "I came here to spend time with you. To get to know you better. She's enough of an invasion into my life without me letting her dig her claws into me here as well."

"So you don't think it's your baby?" she asked.

"I don't know. I just want to be irresponsible and self-centered for a few more months. Is that too much to ask?"

She forced herself not to laugh. Maybe he had a reputation of being irresponsible and self-centered, but she never felt he was either of those things. He was kind, considerate, and thoughtful. And just the right amount of dirty and dangerous. But mostly he was nice.

"I don't want to talk about Lindsey either," she admitted, dipping a carrot stick into ranch dressing and biting into it with a satisfying crunch.

"Good," he said, his shoulders relaxing as the tension in his back eased.

"I'd rather talk to you about my list." She kept her eyes fixed on the countertop before her.

"What list?"

"A list of my fantasies."

"*Ride a unicorn in a crystal forest* fantasies or sexual fantasies?"

She met his gaze and grinned. "Well, I meant sexual fantasies, but do you have a unicorn?"

"I could probably find one."

She rolled her eyes at him. Even rock stars couldn't find a unicorn.

"Are you truly all-in on the threesome with another woman?" he asked.

"Yeah," she said, crinkling her brow. She felt that she was missing something important.

"Then I'll find us a unicorn. What's your type? I'm assuming no young blondes."

"Aren't all unicorns white?"

He lifted a brow at her. "Do you have something against women of color?"

"What?" She shook her head vigorously. She was of mixed heritage herself; how could he even ask her that? "Of course I don't. Are we even talking about the same thing?"

"A unicorn."

"Right."

"A woman who enjoys having sex with a committed heterosexual couple," he clarified.

She blinked at him. "They call that a *unicorn*?"

He chuckled. "Well, they are incredibly rare, but I've run across a few of them in my, um . . . *adventures*."

She massaged her forehead. "I feel so dense. I thought we were talking about an actual unicorn."

"Actual unicorns aren't real, but the kind I prefer are."

So he preferred two women at once, was that what he was saying? "A threesome with a woman is on my list, but it's not at the top."

She went to the refrigerator and pulled her fantasy list from its magnetic clip. She'd hung it between her grocery list and her to-do list.

"You made an actual list? And wrote it down?" He chuckled, but his laughter died when she glared at him.

"You can't make fun of me for this. I'd be mortified."

"I won't make fun."

She cozied up next to him at the kitchen island, her list pressed against her bare belly.

"I did some research."

"You did research?" He pressed his lips together, but managed not to laugh.

She nodded. "I did, and I ranked a handful of fantasies in accordance to my interest and then assigned each to a room in my house. If they required props, I went out and bought everything we'd need and set it up."

"I take it you're a planner?"

She flushed, trying not to be embarrassed. Focusing on every detail had seemed like a great idea at the time. Now she felt foolish.

"I, yeah, well, I can't help it. Is it better to just be spontaneous?"

He would know. He was the expert.

"Let's see the list," he said.

"You won't laugh at me?"

"I won't."

She wasn't sure if she believed him, but she begrudgingly handed over the list.

He read the first item and glanced at the wall clock. "Seems we're already off schedule," he said.

Her face flamed. "Those are just guidelines. And we added sex in the foyer. I hadn't planned for that one."

"You didn't appreciate my spontaneity?"

"Oh, trust me, I did. And this isn't set in stone. I'm flexible."

His grin was oh so naughty. "How flexible we talking here, Caitlyn?"

This double entendre didn't go over her head the way the unicorn one had.

"Well, if you'll skip down to number . . ." She glanced at the list and pointed to a line near the center of the page. ". . . seventeen, you'll recognize that I'm fairly flexible."

He grunted softly. "I see. What if I'm not that flexible?" He lifted his gaze, a worried scowl on his face.

"We can improvise."

"This is a lot of pressure to put on a guy," he said.

She hadn't even considered that when she'd been devising her list, but she recognized that he was right.

"Sorry," she said, pulling the paper from his fingers. "It was a stupid idea."

"It's a brilliant idea," he said, grabbing the page and crinkling it in his haste. He laid it on the countertop and smoothed it out. "How about we meet in the middle here?"

"Start with number twenty-five? I'm not sure we know each other well enough to do that just yet."

He read number twenty-five and actually blushed. "I think you might be right. That is pretty intimate." He tore his gaze from her list and met her eyes. "I meant, I have your list of fantasies, and I'd love to work at making them all a reality, but do we really need a schedule? Do we have to go through them one by one like a script, or can we be a little more spontaneous?"

"I know this might come as a huge shock to you, but I'm really not that spontaneous. The most spontaneous thing I've ever done in my life was have a one-night stand with you. Well, I'd thought it would be one night at the time," she quickly amended.

"And was it a truly terrible experience?" he asked.

"A bit unnerving," she admitted. "But no, not terrible." It could have gone terribly wrong, though. Thinking back, she wondered how she'd ever convinced herself to enter that sex club in the first place. "It was wonderful, actually. But I'm not sure I could do anything that spontaneous again."

He squeezed her hand. "I'm positive that you can. And I'd be more than happy to work near the edge of your comfort zone. Especially now that you've spelled it all out for me."

She licked her lips nervously. "Charles would have made fun of me for making a list. *Caitlyn, Caitlyn,*" she said in his typical condescending tone, *"you wouldn't know fun if it rode in on a hippopotamus playing the trombone."*

Owen laughed and pulled her into his arms for a hug. And maybe his hands did drift down to squeeze her ass, but she honestly didn't mind.

"You know how to have fun," he told her.

"But I don't. Not really. I haven't had any real fun in over a decade." Her night with Owen the one major exception.

"Did you ever consider that your lack of fun wasn't a personal problem but because you were with the wrong man?"

She shook her head. "Charles was always having fun without me."

"What kind of fun?"

"He'd play golf or read the classics or go to the theater or screw freshmen on his desk."

"And do you find any of those activities a complete and total blast?"

"I've never tried screwing a freshman, but I do like theater. Musicals, specifically, but Charles hates them. He's into character pieces. And political monologues."

Owen yawned exaggeratedly. "You aren't boring, Caitlyn," he said. "You were just married to a total, snobbish bore for so long, you haven't had a chance to figure out what you find fun." He leaned in to kiss the pulse point beneath her ear. "Or sexy."

"I find you to be both fun and sexy," she said, her fingers

burrowing into his soft hair to keep his mouth on her.

"So maybe now you've found the right man to bring you back to life."

She urged his head back by tugging on his hair. "You're not getting serious about us, are you?"

He searched her eyes for a long tense moment and then smiled as if he'd just told the biggest joke ever conceived. "Of course not. Whatever gave you that idea?"

Wishful thinking?

No, not that. She didn't want a serious relationship so soon after her divorce. Especially not with a younger man, a rock star, or a party animal. And Owen was all of those things. He was definitely what she needed to get out of her funk, but not life-partner material. Not that she was looking for that anytime soon. Because she wasn't.

"You said I'd found the right man."

"To bring you back to life." He produced a scoffing snort and stared off over her shoulder. "Not to marry you."

"Right," she said, thinking he was a bit too affected to be entirely sincere about his detachment. In her head she could still hear Kellen's warning about Owen falling too hard and fast and how easily he got his feelings hurt, as well as her promise not to destroy him. "I just want to be clear: I'm not looking for more than a little fun and a lot of amazing sex."

"Well, then," he said. "You've come to the right player."

CHAPTER FIVE

WHAT THE HELL was wrong with him? Why did he get attached to women so quickly? Owen could manwhore the hell out of a one-night stand, but if he so much as had a decent conversation with a woman, his heart and mind were already making room for her to become the center of his universe. It scared the hell out of any woman who had a shred of self-identity, and he couldn't blame them for putting up barriers. But, damn, it was hard to keep his head on straight when it was already spinning. He was just going to have to think of Caitlyn—and her fantasy list—as a series of one-night stands. They could have fun and fuck, and he could walk away in two days with fond memories of getting his rocks off with a beautiful woman without any emotional connection to her.

Sure he could. He hugged her against him and looked over her shoulder at the list that lay on the counter. He'd been serious about fulfilling all her fantasies and showing her a few she didn't realize she had, but he wasn't a robot. He couldn't see himself licking whipped cream off her at 1:30 p.m., fucking her bent over a stool at 1:45, adding a vibrator to her ass at 1:50, and spanking her until they both reached orgasm. Okay, he was a liar; he could totally see himself doing all those things. It was the schedule that was destroying his mojo. Maybe he wanted to spank her before he stuck a vibrator up her ass. Or maybe he wanted the vibrator in her pussy and his dick pounding her ass. Had she ever considered those possibilities? He knew he'd rather lick chocolate off her body than whipped cream—chocolate required more thorough tongue action.

But he didn't want to disappoint her, so he backed her into the counter and reached for the can of whipped cream sitting beside a small tube of lube, a slender vibrator, and a wooden paddle. She had lined them all up in a neat row next to a tub of wet wipes and a box of the brand of condoms he always used. He was surprised she hadn't labeled everything and added a place card labeled "Kitchen Fantasy #1" followed by step-by-step instructions.

He wouldn't tease her for knowing—or thinking she knew—exactly what she wanted, but he would mix things up a bit. She was an intelligent woman. She'd soon see that spontaneity was the most exciting part of making love.

Pinning her butt against the cabinets by pressing his pelvis firmly against hers, he leaned back and sprayed a dot of whipped cream into the hollow of her throat. He collected the cream with a gentle swipe of his tongue, and she moaned. Surprised by her excessive reaction, he tried to meet her eyes, but she had them closed.

"Are you up for a little experimentation?" he asked.

Maybe having him follow a script was a total turn-on for her. Maybe it was thinking she was completely in control that had her nipples so hot and hard they seared his chest. Maybe bossing him around made her ache for him the way her sexy voice and thick mane of black hair made him ache for her.

Her eyes cracked open, and she met his gaze with an inquisitive brow raised. "What kind of experimentation?"

She was a scientist, so maybe that word meant something more to her than it did to him.

"Do you have any chocolate syrup? I want to show you something."

She looked relieved that he hadn't suggested something more wicked. "I'll get it."

She squeezed out from between him and the counter and circled the island. His gaze moving from ankle to ass, he admired her smooth, curvy legs. His otherwise unrestricted view of her nudity was blocked by a narrow swatch of yellow fabric.

"Take off your panties," he demanded quietly. "I want to see your ass while you obey me."

She turned abruptly, her hair shifting across her bare back and shoulders, and her soft brown eyes sparking with challenge. When she caught him smirking at her, a bit of the fire went out of her. Or at least that was what he thought until she said, "Make me."

That was not the reaction he'd expected out of Little Miss Make a Schedule for My Fantasy List. "What?"

"You heard me," she said, straightening her shoulders, which lifted her breasts into high, perfect globes that demanded he put his mouth on them immediately. "If you want me to take them off, you'll have to make me."

He rubbed the back of his neck as he considered her challenge. "I'm not the kind of guy who makes a woman do something she doesn't want to do."

One corner of her mouth lifted, as if she thought she'd won. "I guess they stay on, then."

"I'm the kind of guy who makes a woman want something she shouldn't so much that she willingly obeys."

"Is that so?"

She opened the refrigerator and pulled out the bottle of chocolate syrup he'd requested. He didn't bother pointing out that she was doing what he'd told her to do.

"You haven't figured that out about me yet?" he asked, watching the gentle bounce of her breasts as she returned to him with the chocolate syrup in hand.

"We haven't known each other for long," she reminded him.

"I keep forgetting."

He popped the top of the syrup and drizzled a thin line along her collarbone. He licked it with the same gentle caress he'd used when he'd collected the whipped cream from the same spot. Traces of sticky chocolate remained on her skin, so he licked more rigorously and then suckled and licked a little more.

"See the difference?" he murmured.

"N equals one," she said.

He lifted his gaze to meet hers and found her watching him with interest. "Huh?"

"Your experiment has only one piece of data," she said. "You're going to need far more trials to prove your hypothesis."

"What's my hypothesis?"

"You tell me."

Brainy chicks . . . always a challenge. And definitely worth the effort. "Licking chocolate syrup off your lover's body brings more delight to them than licking off whipped cream."

She nodded curtly. "Proceed with your experiment, Mr. Mitchell," she said.

He grinned and shook his head at her serious tone. "Someone needs to get laid."

"You can proceed with that as well," she said.

He sprayed a dab of whipped cream on her nipple and licked

it off with one gentle sweep of his tongue. She shuddered and leaned back against the counter for support. He squirted a small sample of chocolate on the same nipple before licking and sucking it clean again.

Switching to the other nipple, he started with chocolate and then once he had her skin clean and her body trembling, he finished with a dab of whipped cream.

"So?" he whispered. "What's the verdict?"

"Am I allowed to like them both?" she asked.

"Do you like them both?"

She nodded.

"Absolutely not," he teased, cupping her face and rubbing his thumb across her lips. "You're only allowed to enjoy what I want you to enjoy."

"And what would that be?"

"Everything I do to you." He kissed her gently. "If something feels a little strange or uncomfortable, I ask that you give it a chance, but if you don't like something, just tell me."

She nodded. "I ask that you do the same."

She took the bottle of syrup from him and squeezed a drip onto the center of his belly. She squatted in front of him and licked it off, slowly at first and then with more enthusiasm. Excitement stirred low in his gut and his cock began to rise. She'd failed to mention that this would be a reciprocal experiment. Not that he was complaining. His breath caught when she hooked her fingers in his shorts and tugged them off over his ass. She took the whipped cream from his hand—which was good, because he was liable to drop it in his distraction—and sprayed it on the head of his cock. The gentle slip of her tongue against his rapidly engorging flesh made his knees weak.

"Whipped cream wins that trial," he said, "but I think you're supposed to test both in the same location to make the experiment valid."

"I didn't realize you were so well versed in scientific experimentation," she said, drizzling chocolate just inside his hip and along the ridge of the vee he hoped would point her tongue in the right direction. By the time she finished licking and sucking that bit of chocolate off, his fingers were tangled in her hair and his head was tipped back in complete abandon. Apparently she'd decided to take command of the experiment, but she wasn't being very scientific about it as she again sprayed whipped cream on the tip of his cock and drove him insane with overly gentle, teasing licks.

His breath came out in an excited sputter. Caitlyn rose to her feet and handed him the bottle of chocolate syrup and the spray can of whipped cream.

"Your turn," she said.

As much as he wanted to make a banana split out of her pussy, she still had her panties on, and he refused to take them off for her or force her to take them off. He was on a self-directed mission to get her to take them off without him having to tell her again. He pulled a stool toward them with one foot and turned her to face it. Setting their food experiment aside, he slid the paddle off the counter, watching her closely for her reaction. Her eyes darted to her fantasy list and then the paddle in his hand.

"Bend over, Caitlyn."

She made a sound in the back of her throat, a sort of anxious moan, and he thought she would refuse his request. That was okay, because he wouldn't force her to do anything. Not even the things she'd written on her list. But she bent over the stool and grabbed the sturdy legs with both hands. She was all sorts of tense when she gushed, "I'm ready."

He moved to stand behind her and pressed the head of his cock into the heated flesh exposed to him. Unfortunately, his progress was stalled by the pair of panties he'd so thoughtfully—*stupidly!*—purchased for her. He rubbed a hand along the bare skin of her flank and then the covered part of her ass to remind her that she was still partially clothed. He took a step back and flicked his wrist to tap her ass with the paddle.

Her body tensed, and she cried out in surprise. But not pain. He hadn't swatted her hard enough to cause pain.

"Again," she said breathlessly.

He gave her one firm swat and then set the paddle on the countertop. He moved in close again, making sure she could feel how turned-on he was, and reached for their experimental props again. He dripped some chocolate onto her spine between her shoulder blades and then added a mound of whipped cream on top.

"This," he said as he licked at the sweetness, "is what I'd be doing to your pussy." He licked a little more rigorously. "And your asshole." Her breath caught, and he sucked at the chocolate on her back. "If you knew how to obey."

"I bent over the stool," she protested.

He rubbed his cock up and down her seam the best he could with those damned panties holding him back.

"Take them off me," she said, widening her stance. Opening herself to him. Driving him insane with his need to be inside her. "I won't stop you."

"I told you to take them off," he reminded her, and with every shred of willpower he possessed, he took a step back.

She groaned in protest, but changed her tune when he reached for the paddle and smacked her ass twice, the sound muffled by fabric. He figured that would gain her cooperation, but she stood there, ass in the air, rocking her hips slightly as if trying to hypnotize him with thoughts of her flesh completely exposed to his fevered gaze.

He shook his head to clear his thoughts. It would be so easy to reach over and peel her panties down her thighs, but this was a test of wills he planned to ace. Setting the paddle aside, he traced the entire length of Caitlyn's spine with a single line of chocolate syrup. She shuddered when he added dots of whipped cream on either side of the chocolate. This time as he bent over her to sample the chocolate along her back, he rocked into her, pressing her wet panties into her opening with his distractingly hard cock. She surprised him by jerking her panties down her thighs. He surprised them both when he sank into her warmth unprotected.

"Oh God," she groaned, surprising him further by pressing backward, driving him deeper.

He gritted his teeth together as pleasure completely encompassed him, trying to rob him of every fragment of logic he possessed. Yet the image of a very pregnant Lindsey brought him partially back to his senses.

"Cai-Cait-ly-lyn," he said, gasping on every syllable. "I don't have a condom on."

"Is that why your piercing feels so fantastic?"

She rocked into him, encouraging him to thrust. His fingers dug into her hips as he gave in to what she wanted, what they both wanted—warm, slick softness holding him, grasping and tugging at him.

He needed to be deeper. Deeper. His balls slapped against

her, and she groaned, meeting him stroke for stroke as he pounded into her.

One terrifying thought of finding himself the father of not one but two illegitimate babies gave him the strength to pull out. He reached for the box of condoms, fingers fumbling with the packaging. He was ready to fulfill her being-spanked-while-getting-fucked agenda item, but he needed the proper protection first.

"I don't want you to wear a condom," she said.

He dropped the box, sending colorful strips of condoms scattering across the kitchen floor.

"What?"

"I guess I should be worried about disease or something, but I'm not. Are you? If you are—"

"Pregnancy," he said. "That's what I'm worried about."

"There's no chance of that, Owen. We're covered." She laughed and turned to look at him. "Actually, I hope you don't cover it ever again. That felt so good."

"No condoms?"

She nodded slightly. "No condoms."

"Are you on the pill?"

"IUD."

"Are you taking St. John's Warts?"

"Nooooo," she said, looking concerned for his sanity.

Did he trust her? He did with his body, but with his future? What if she tried to trap him the same way Lindsey was trying to trap him? He knew that was what Lyndsey was trying to do, and still he was too much of a pushover to tell her to fuck off.

"I'm sorry," Caitlyn said, reaching for his hand and squeezing it. "I'm being selfish. If you want to wear a condom, of course you should wear one."

But he didn't want to wear one.

"Bend over that stool, Caitlyn," he said, reaching not for the paddle but for the whipped cream. She didn't argue with him at all as she turned and grabbed the legs of the stool again. Now he could see everything she had to offer between her thighs, and he was more than ready to experiment.

CHAPTER SIX

CAITLYN SUCKED in a breath as something cool landed on one ass cheek and then the other, and she nearly hurdled the stool when the same sensation awakened the oft-neglected hole between them. Owen's soft, warm tongue collected the near-weightless cream from each cheek—a delightful enough sensation—but it was the anticipation of him sampling the whipped topping at the center that had her belly quivering. One barely perceptible swipe of his tongue against her back door had her knees wobbly and her lungs laboring for air.

"You like that?" he asked.

"I couldn't tell," she said, hiding a teasing grin as she kept her focus on the floor. "Better try it again."

With a metallic clatter, he set the whipped cream aside which hopefully meant he was reaching for the chocolate syrup. She remembered what they'd learned from their experiment—chocolate took more pressure and effort to lick from the skin. So with breathless anticipation, she spread her feet another few inches and squeezed her eyes shut. The syrup felt foreign against her flesh, and she clutched the legs of the stool to steady herself as he began to lick her in a place she'd only imagined having licked. She never thought she'd be with a man dirty and kinky enough to actually do it. The sensation of his tongue teasing the periphery of her hole in firm, wet, and slippery strokes had her craving something more.

"Owen," she said desperately, "fuck my ass."

He stopped delighting her ass with his tongue to say, "No can do. That's not on your list."

She knew that list had been a mistake.

He stood straight, and a moment later the slender vibrator she'd purchased for this particular fantasy buzzed to life. She whimpered at the thought of him ramming it into her needy ass, but he didn't give her what she wanted—or what she *thought* she wanted, what she'd planned to want—and instead rubbed the vibrating tip against her clit. Her body jerked at the intense pleasure, which was apparently a distraction technique to keep her occupied while he squirted lube onto her ass with his free hand. Her orgasm was almost within reach when he dragged the vibrator up her slit, teasing lips and pussy and asshole as he twisted the vibrator to get plenty of her fluids as well as lube to coat the length of the vibrator's shaft.

She was on the verge of begging when he finally slipped the vibrator's pointed tip into her ass. Her mouth dropped open and her eyes squeezed shut as Owen revolved the end of the vibrator to stretch her wider, slowly working that maddening vibration deep inside her.

"Yes," she said, ending in a deep moan.

"More?"

"More."

She expected the more he'd mentioned to be more amazing vibrator action in her ass, but he pressed his cock into her pussy, filling both holes at once.

He groaned as he found a rhythm between his thrusting cock and the vibrator he worked in and out of her ass. She wasn't sure if he was working the vibrator at that angle for her benefit or his own, but dear lord, that piercing at his tip was even more mind-blowing when it rubbed against the toy sharing space inside her.

After a moment of driving her insane with sensation, he asked, "More?"

There couldn't possibly be anything beyond what she was experiencing, but the word burst from her anyway. "More!"

He released his stabilizing grip on her hip, and she heard the paddle scrape off the nearby countertop. The sound in no way prepared her for the thrill of its sharp sting as it smacked against the fleshiest part of her ass cheek. She'd never expected reality to supersede her dirty fantasies, but the convergence of so many powerful sensations—friction and heat; stinging pain and blinding pleasure; slick, deep thrusts and churning vibration; smooth, thick, hard flesh filling her, and the even harder tiny ball driving her further to distraction—she couldn't handle all at once, and yet she shouted, "More, more!"

"I don't have a spare hand, angel," Owen said. "You know where your clit is."

She did? Yes, she did. She released her hold on the stool and shoved her hand between her legs, working her fingers against her clit until she exploded. When she came, her head spun dizzily as she screamed at the intensity of shattering into a billion pieces. Unable to stand further stimulation to her clit, she shifted her hand back a couple inches to feel his cock thrusting in and out of her.

"Oh God," he groaned as he spanked her with the paddle—she gasped and clenched her core around him—and then he gave himself over to the excitement between them.

The paddle clattered to the floor when he grasped her hip to push himself balls deep inside her, and he shuddered and groaned through his release. She sagged against the stool, glad it was there to keep her standing, but suddenly wished for a comfortable bed. She winced when he pulled the vibrator out of her ass and again when he withdrew his spent cock. She adored that cock piercing of his, but it was harsh on her tender flesh, especially without the buffer of a condom.

"We're going to have to take it a little easier on you," he said, "or your first fantasy might have to be the only one I fulfill this weekend."

"It felt amazing," she said. "All of it."

She stood upright and forced herself not to show any discomfort. She was definitely going to be feeling that encounter for days to come, and she relished knowing why she was sore. Owen had fucked her liked she'd never been fucked before, and she felt utterly satisfied. Sex usually left her wanting, and she could never figure out why.

He began to clean himself with the Handi Wipes she'd placed on the counter for that very purpose.

"I think I'm going to enjoy this fantasy list of yours."

She grinned at him and decided as his cum dripped down the inside of her thigh that those wipes weren't going to cut it. She was going to need go upstairs to wash up.

"Especially knowing it's going to take ages to get through all the scenarios." He smiled at her and then glanced at the list resting on the counter.

Ages? Well, as long as they kept their interactions light and all about the sex, she was fine with extending their time together indefinitely.

"I'll probably come up with new ideas as we go," she said. "Are you sure you want to start this journey with me?"

"I don't want to just start it, babe," he said. "I plan to finish it."

CHAPTER SEVEN

OWEN CHECKED his phone while Caitlyn was upstairs. He had three text messages from his mom asking questions about Lindsey, whose pet name was apparently *doll*. Could he add her to his health insurance if they weren't married? He had no idea. Was it okay to buy her some maternity clothes? Of course that was okay. And then Owen got to the one that made his heart almost stop. *Lindsey insisted we buy all the baby stuff second-hand. Isn't she a doll? I hope the baby's a girl. I always wanted a little girl to spoil. Or twins. Twins would be so cute.* And she ended her terrifying message with a bunch of baby-themed emojis. Forcing a knot of panic back down his throat, Owen typed appropriate responses to her first two queries and left the last one unanswered. Mom did realize that the baby might not be his, didn't she? He hoped she didn't get too attached.

Of course she would get too attached. This was his mother he'd gotten involved. The woman got attached to the little toads that lived under the back steps. What had he been thinking when he'd left a destitute pregnant groupie with the woman who'd given birth to him?

He covered his eyes with one hand, hoping to erase his mother's message from his memory.

"Fuck."

"If you insist," Caitlyn said, sliding up against his back and rubbing her hands over his bare belly. "I thought you might want to eat first."

Her naked breasts pressed into his back, and there was no way he could ignore that invitation.

Owen set his phone face down on the counter and covered her questing hands with his. "I'm not sure we'll have time to cover much on your list if we take breaks for unnecessary activities like washing and eating and sleeping."

She chuckled and kissed his shoulder. "I'm glad you're so willing to accommodate my fantasies, but we can take our time.

I'm not in any rush."

But he had little to offer her besides great sex. The woman was so far out of his league, they were playing different sports. He wasn't the kind of guy who ended up with the intelligent, sophisticated, driven, successful, and obviously rich hottie. Nope, he was the guy who ended up with the desperate, pregnant groupie. Everyone knew that. Even him.

He turned in Caitlyn's arms and wrapped her in a tight embrace, lowering his head to claim her lips in a searing kiss. She tasted of minty freshness and smelled of clean soap with a hint of jasmine. "You're too clean." He nibbled her jaw. "I have an overwhelming need to dirty you up again."

"Charles wouldn't touch me unless I'd just recently washed. I thought . . ."

He lifted his head to look at her, meeting her dark brown eyes. "You thought what?"

"That cum dripping down my leg would gross you out."

He chuckled. "Sex is messy, gorgeous." He stroked several long black strands of hair from her face. "The messier the better."

She looked over his shoulder and nibbled on her lip. "So I probably shouldn't have douched."

It was her body—who was he to tell her how best to care for it? "If it makes you more comfortable."

She shook her head. "Charles—"

He covered her full lips with one finger. "I'm not Charles. I like my cum on you. In you. Dripping down your thigh. I'm all about sloppy seconds." He grinned. "Or thirds."

She pulled out of his grasp and went to her list on the counter. She uncapped a black marker and added two items to her agenda. He peered over her shoulder and read: *sloppy seconds* followed by *sloppy thirds*.

He chuckled. "I'm not sure those are fantasies."

"They are to me," she said. "Especially if you enjoy them."

"I'm going to enjoy everything on that list." And he would make certain that she enjoyed them as well.

Her stomach rumbled, and he captured her hand, leading her to the elegant, round glass table in the kitchen nook. He didn't allow himself to smile when she spread a cloth napkin over the seat of the plum-colored velveteen chair before she sat her naked butt on it. Sex wasn't the only need he could fulfill for her. He could feed her belly as well.

"Has a naked man ever hand fed you in your kitchen?" Owen went to the spread she'd set out before they'd been so wonderfully distracted and filled a plate with a variety of finger foods.

"No. Especially not one who looks like you."

She laughed, her pretty eyes following his every move. She seemed to pay the most attention to his ass, so he spent plenty of time with his back to her, ensuring she got an eyeful. After spending his teen years as the icky fat kid no girl would offer a second glance, he rather enjoyed being a beautiful woman's eye candy.

He returned to the table and set the plate on the table between her seat and the empty one next to her. When he reached for a cloth napkin to spread over the chair's plump cushion, Caitlyn reached not for her food but for his ass.

"You're absolutely perfect," she murmured under her breath. "What are you doing here with me?"

There were dozens of reasons, not all hinging on physical attraction, but he said, "Serving your every whim."

She moved her hand so he could sit. "And what do you get out of this?" she asked.

"To be with you."

She licked her lips and glanced away. "This frivolous affair is exactly what I want," she said, "what I need right now. But I don't want to just use you. It doesn't seem right."

He'd prefer if she was just a user. If they were going to keep their interactions light, frivolous, and fun, she couldn't be wonderful. If she treated him with consideration and showed him affection, he could easily give her his heart. He was well aware of his habit of falling fast and hard for nice women. And strong women. Intelligent women. *Most* women. If she wanted to fool around without attachment, then she had to be a bitch. He needed her to treat him like shit, or he wouldn't be able to keep his heart out of the equation. And he knew where that would lead—another ex for her, another broken heart for him.

"You aren't using me," he said. "I'm using you."

"For sex?"

He grinned and reached for a chunk of pineapple. "What else?"

"Just making sure," she said. "I don't think I'm ready to love you. Not so soon after Charles."

"I understand," he said, poking the pineapple into her mouth, mostly to keep her from talking about her ex-husband.

"It's okay that I like you, though, isn't it?" she asked around the pineapple.

His heart twisted, and he helped himself to a grape. Sweet juice burst onto his tongue when he bit into the small fruit. "It's probably best to keep your feelings to yourself," he said cautiously. "Unless you want this to turn into something more serious."

He did. He couldn't deny his need for a strong and lasting connection with her, but he knew from experience—too much experience—that one-sided love affairs were hell on the heart. How many women had he scared off by moving too fast? A dozen? And he'd gotten his heart broken every time.

"I don't want this to be serious," she said. "At least not yet."

"Understood."

But by offering him the hope of *yet*, she was opening a door. Just a little. And his foolish heart was already trying to squeeze itself through the crack. He squashed down the tenderness he longed to express—with adoring gazes and gentle caresses that had nothing to do with sex—and offered her a bite of cheese. He held her gaze as she accepted the cube of Swiss and chewed slowly. She surprised him by reaching for a piece of cheese and feeding it to him.

"We should open a bottle of wine," she said as he followed the cheese with a grape. She reciprocated by offering him a savory slice of pepperoni.

"If that's your desire." He pulled his gaze from hers to locate a bottle of wine, but she palmed his cheek, returning his attention to her eyes.

"Later, maybe," she murmured before leaning in to kiss him.

If he'd been struggling to keep his feelings in check before, they grew completely out of control as she caressed his lips with hers. He definitely felt more than desire in her kiss, and though his head was shouting at him to take control, to shift their focus to pure, burning passion and away from emotion, his heart wouldn't let him. Bittersweet relief swamped him when her hand slid down his chest and stomach before circling his cock. Lust slammed into his lower belly when he deepened the maddeningly sweet kiss, and his dick stirred with excitement.

"I guess this is one benefit of being with a younger man," she said, stroking him to readiness before scooting her chair closer and opening her legs wide. "You don't have a recovery time of two weeks."

She was thinking of *him* again. Not fondly, but Charles was definitely on her mind. Owen had to do something about that. Could he fuck the thoughts of that bastard out of her? Maybe temporarily at least.

He took a grape between his thumb and forefinger and lowered it between her legs. He traced the boundary of her clit with the firm, smooth globe before centering it over the sensitive flesh and rubbing her there until she gasped. He then popped the grape into her open mouth.

Her eyes blinked wide with shock, and she lifted a hand toward her mouth. He caught her wrist before she could pull out the grape.

"Eat it," he said, keeping his voice deep and demanding.

"But you had that on my . . ."

"I know exactly where I had it. Chew."

She obeyed, never taking her eyes off his.

"Swallow."

She swallowed with a gulp.

"You have taste a woman's cum on your list," he said.

"I do?" She looked adorable when she was uncertain of herself.

He grinned. "If you're in a threesome with another woman, it's bound to happen."

"Oh. I thought you'd be doing all the licking."

"I could," he said, reaching for another grape, "but you wouldn't get the full extent of the encounter if I did all the licking."

He traced her pussy lips with the new grape, making her shiver.

"I want the full experience, Owen. Promise you'll whisper instructions to me. I've never done anything like that before, but I don't want our partner to realize it."

Owen's dick throbbed with arousal at the thought of Caitlyn getting freaky with another woman while he gave instructions. The gentle tug of her hand on him only added to his excitement.

"I'll help you."

She sagged back against her chair. "Thank you."

No, thank you, he thought as he dipped the tips of his fingers and the grape into her rapidly awakening pussy. Her breath caught, and her gaze shifted to the area between her splayed legs. He swirled his fingers in the margin of her opening and then lifted them, shiny with her fluids, and brought them to her lips. "Lick," he said.

She hesitated for the briefest moment before the pink tip of her tongue stroked his fingertips.

"How do you taste?"

She licked his fingers with more attention. "I can't taste much," she said.

He relinquished the grape to her. "Can you taste yourself there?"

She sucked on that grape for a long moment, until his balls started to ache with their need for release, and he asked brokenly, "Caitlyn?"

"I still can't really taste it." One corner of her mouth quirked upward. "Maybe if you made me come."

Now there was an idea he could get behind. He reached for another grape, but she caught his wrist. "On your cock," she said, her chest flushing with desire. "And I'll suck it off there."

The woman was a fucking genius.

He pulled her chair closer, angling his hips so they'd fit together easily. She moaned when he pressed his cock into her opening and spread her legs wider. He smiled to himself when he tried to meet her eyes and found her staring at the place where their bodies were joined. He rocked slightly, so that he was barely entering her before withdrawing completely.

"Do you like to watch?" he asked, loving the little gasps of protest she released every time he pulled out.

"I think I'd be embarrassed."

It took him a moment to gather his thoughts enough to figure out what she meant. Even the small amount of contact between his bare skin and hers felt amazing. "I meant watch me inside you, not watch another couple."

"Mmm," she murmured. "I definitely like that."

She tipped forward to rest her forehead against his shoulder and moved her hand to trace the length of his shaft with one finger. That teasing touch made him tremble, until the urge to thrust deep became undeniable. His chair crashed behind him as he stood and rammed himself into her.

"Slow," she whispered, her head unmoving against his shoulder. He presumed she was still watching his body claiming hers. "Deep but slow."

It was damned hard to keep his emotions in check when he took it slow, but he did his best to give her what she wanted. Slow, deep strokes did give him plenty of time to relish the pleasure of each motion rather than focusing on the urgency to attain orgasm.

"I think that might be enough," she said.

"Huh?" Fuck, she wasn't going to make him stop, was she?

"Looks really slick and shiny. I should be able to taste my cum now."

He'd been so caught up in the pleasure, he'd already forgotten why he'd entered her in the first place—so she could suck her fluid off his dick.

"You didn't come yet, did you?" he asked.

"I came less than an hour ago, so I probably won't be able to come again for a while."

"That's okay, take your time." But not too long, he thought, or I'll be the one coming.

He explored her body with both palms, grateful for her chair's support so he could use his hands for something other than lifting her to his height. Completely lost in her, he began to churn his hips each time their bodies came together, wanting to feel more of her inside and out.

"I'm close," she said, moving her hand between her legs to rub at her clit. He caught her hand and brought her wrist to his lips, kissing the rapid pulse thrumming there just beneath the skin.

"Don't rush your orgasm," he said. "Give it time to build."

She groaned and lifted her head from his shoulder to meet his eyes. If it was hard to keep his emotions out of sex when he took it slow, it was doubly difficult to do so when she was looking at him all glassy eyed and trusting.

"I've never had a vaginal orgasm," she said.

"Is that on your list?" he asked.

"I didn't add it to my list, because I don't think it's possible for me."

"I love a challenge," he murmured, kissing her neck.

"Maybe with the piercing—Oh!"

"Maybe with less thinking."

He was completely drenched in sweat and far less frustrated with her body's inability to find release than she was. She was trying too hard, and that was most of her problem. He'd tackle giving her a vaginal orgasm when she wasn't aware of his intentions.

He didn't warn her that he'd changed his plans, just shifted his belly away from hers so he could rub her clit. She exploded within seconds, her breasts pressing into his chest and her heels digging into his ass as her back arched and she cried out with release. The tightening of her pussy around him almost pulled him over the brink with her, but he clenched every muscle in his body to hold back. She hadn't even caught her breath when she pushed him away.

He groaned in agony when his cock popped free of her warmth. She slipped from the chair and knelt at his feet, licking and sucking her cum off his dick and balls until he fisted her hair in his hands. She opened wide for him as he thrust into her mouth. He marveled at her diminished gag reflex for a short moment, and then the pleasure of fucking her throat while she sucked was the only thing he could concentrate on. After a few strokes he pulled out to give her time to draw several labored breaths before thrusting into her mouth again.

Minutes later, she pulled back to make a new request. "Come inside me. Mix our cum together so I can taste that too."

The thought sent him tumbling with her to the hard, cold floor. She reached between them to help him find her when he couldn't locate the presence of mind to untangle his fingers from her hair. Within several fast strokes, he exploded, forcing his hips to continue to pump while he came. He closed his eyes as sparks of light flashed in his vision. She squirmed to get him to roll onto his back and then slowly lifted her hips until his cock fell free. She seemed oblivious to the pull of his hands in her hair as she shifted down his body and sucked his still twitching cock into her mouth.

He cried out—in a mix of agony and bliss—as she sampled their comingled cum with licks and kisses and dizzying suction. When his cock had been cleaned to her satisfaction, she turned her attention to his balls.

"Cai-Caitlyn," he panted. Her name was the only word he knew.

"No two licks taste the same," she said from somewhere between his legs. When her tongue brushed his asshole, his eyes popped open and he sat up involuntarily.

"Okay, I think you've had enough," he said.

"I'll never get enough of you."

She licked her finger, and if he hadn't just had one of the most explosive orgasms of his life, the sight would have made him come.

"I feel so dirty right now."

He was feeling pretty dirty himself, so he kissed her—excited by knowing all the places her tongue had just been. He had a naughty reputation for a reason.

When their mouths separated, she cupped his cheek in one hand and stared into his eyes. His heart started thudding on cue.

"I love getting dirty with you, Owen."

"I love making you dirty, Cait."

"Where are you taking me tonight?" she asked, her eyes flashing with excitement.

"You don't want to stay here for sloppy seconds and thirds?" he asked. Because that sounded like a perfect plan to him, and she was definitely sloppy at the moment.

"The other day you mentioned Houston has several sex clubs."

That sounded like a pretty good plan too.

"More than a few," he said. "What are you in the mood for?"

"What are my options?"

"There's a BDSM club for people who want to experiment with alternate forms of pleasure and pain."

She shook her head. "Not really my thing."

Good. Because it wasn't really his thing either. "If you have any fetishes—"

"Pierced cocks," she said, reaching for his and rubbing her finger over the little balls that spanned the rim of his head.

"You're a bit under-pierced for the piercing fetish crowd, but I know a guy who could pierce your clit—"

"Ow!"

"It's actually the hood of skin that gets pierced, but you can buy jewelry that rubs against you all the time."

Her thoughtful look made him chuckle.

"Are you considering it?" he asked.

"Maybe," she said, a delightful blush staining her face and throat. "Are there other clubs?

"If you're into cosplay, there's a sci-fi club that includes interesting uses of light sabers."

"I really just want to try out the threesome thing."

"Okay," he said. "I'll take you to the Red Door. You'll have to wear a mask and nothing but red underwear."

"That doesn't sound too over the top. Are you sure we can find a partner there?"

He'd been to the Red Door several times and had never had a problem finding a partner or two. And with a beauty like Caitlyn at his side, they were sure to be approached. "I have no doubt."

CHAPTER EIGHT

CAITLYN CLUNG to Owen's arm, wondering if she had the courage to pull this off. When they'd entered the back of the warehouse and walked a narrow hallway to a red door, she'd been nervous yet excited. But now that Owen had given the password and they were inside, she was wishing they'd just stayed home.

The man at the entrance wore a pair of red leather shorts and a black mask that reminded her of Halle Berry's Catwoman, except it lacked the cute ears.

"Men, women, or both?" he asked Owen.

"Just women," Owen said. The guy handed Owen a white mask similar in shape to his own.

"And you?" he asked Caitlyn.

She was trembling, but somehow managed to say, "Both."

He started to hand her a red mask, but Owen grabbed it and handed it back. "By both, she means me and just women."

The guy's mouth twisted with an annoyed smile. "That's entirely different."

How was she supposed to know that? The doorman handed her a white mask.

"You brought appropriate attire, I hope."

"I've been here before," Owen said. "We know our part."

"She didn't know about the masks," the man pointed out.

"So if I say both, that means I'm looking to hook up with both women and men strangers?"

"You're not looking for men." Owen led her into a changing room before the doorman could hand her a mask of a different color.

"Take off all your clothes and jewelry except your underwear."

He'd helped her choose a lacy red thong and bra to wear under her street clothes, so she'd been expecting this. What she hadn't been expecting was to be a jumble of nerves as he tucked their clothes, her bracelet, and his dog tags into a locker and locked it with a combination he punched into the keypad. He took her hand and led her to a second door in the room. This one was also red, and she could hear muffled sounds on the other side.

"Are you ready?"

"Since we're both wearing white masks and we're together, people will realize we're looking for another woman, right?"

Owen nodded. "Yeah, it makes this easier. Men probably won't hit on us."

"Probably?"

"Some like the challenge of convincing others to want something they don't think they want."

"I do want to try two men," Caitlyn said. "But I'm not quite ready for that yet."

"I'm not ready for that at all," Owen said. He opened the door.

She wasn't sure what he'd meant by that—was he saying he didn't want her to be with two men or that he wasn't prepared to be a part of her threesome experience—but she didn't have time to come to a conclusion before her eyeballs were bombarded by images of near naked people.

She'd thought what she wanted and needed was a bunch of impersonal yet mind-blowing sex and that any partner would do, but now that she was confronted with it from every angle, it wasn't as sexy as she imagined.

"I've never brought a woman with me to one of these clubs," Owen said as he tugged her forward.

"Yet I'm sure you never leave empty-handed."

"True," he said. "I'm not sure if anyone will approach us as a couple."

His concern was unfounded. They hadn't even had time to order drinks before a young woman in a white mask sat in the empty seat beside Caitlyn.

"You're gorgeous," she shouted over the loud, throbbing club music. "What are you doing here with this guy?"

Caitlyn had never had a woman hit on her before, so it took her a moment to respond. "Uh, he's my boyfriend."

Was he her boyfriend? Maybe she shouldn't have introduced Owen that way. She glanced at him to see if her claim had bothered him, but he was looking at the drink menu as if he hadn't noticed the blonde who'd invited herself to their table.

"Not fulfilling your needs? I've got the cure for that." She leaned over and licked Caitlyn's breast above the lacy edge of her bra.

Um, wow. Forward much? Caitlyn supposed there wasn't any reason to play coy or pretend that any of them were there for something other than sex.

"He's fulfilling all of my fantasies," Caitlyn said, rubbing a hand over the inside of Owen's bare thigh. "That's why he brought me here."

"So is this a lesbian fantasy while he watches thing or a threesome thing? Because I don't do dick. I don't want dick anywhere near me."

Caitlyn laughed, hoping the woman wasn't offended. She didn't think she was funny per se, but rather refreshing in her ballsy outlandishness. "I hadn't thought that far ahead," Caitlyn said, which wasn't entirely true.

"She wants to be the center of our attention," Owen said. "She wants dick in her pussy. Your tongue and fingers and fist in her pussy."

Fist? They'd never discussed a fist. They hadn't discussed tongue and fingers, for that matter.

"Does she speak for herself?" the woman asked, never taking her eyes off Caitlyn.

"I'd like to try licking." She glanced at Owen and then back at the blonde. "I want to eat your pussy too," she said, "but I don't want my man to touch you or be touched by you."

The blonde chuckled and slid a hand up Caitlyn's leg. "I like a woman who knows what she wants. I just wish we could leave the dick out of this entirely."

"Then you should find some other woman to hit on," Owen said. "One who doesn't crave my cock."

The blonde laughed and slapped him in the chest. "My, aren't you full of yourself?"

Actually, he wasn't usually the type who boasted about his appeal—though he had tons to spare—but Caitlyn noticed this woman had him on edge and not in a good way.

"He's right," Caitlyn said. "I do crave his cock. I think I want him to be pounding me while I eat you out."

"As long as he's not pounding you while *I* eat you out."

Caitlyn's pussy tightened at the thought. "That does sound exciting." Caitlyn turned to Owen and wrapped her arm around his lower back, pressing her breast into his hard-muscled arm. "Is that possible, to be licked and fucked at the same time?"

"Yeah. But probably not if your partner is afraid of cock."

"I'm not afraid of cock," the blonde said. "It's just gross. All hard and veiny." Her lip curled. "Ew."

"Mmm," Caitlyn purred. "I like them all hard and veiny."

The blonde shuddered and stood. "If you change your mind, I'll be over there, far, far from the penis you brought with you." She planted a soft kiss on Caitlyn's lips. Caitlyn was too stunned to kiss her back. And even more stunned to discover she hadn't been even slightly repulsed by another woman's mouth against hers.

Her eyes still on the blonde as she walked away, Caitlyn leaned toward Owen and asked, "Are the people who frequent these places always so forward?" At her first and only other experience in a sex club, Owen had been the only one to approach her, and he hadn't been quite that brusque when making it clear their interactions would be sexual in nature.

When he didn't answer her question, she turned to find a woman draped over the back of his chair, one hand on his devastatingly distracting abs and another inching down the front of his red silk boxers.

Caitlyn grabbed the woman's wrists and yanked her hands off Owen's body, all sorts of overwhelming and confusing feelings swarming through her. "What are you doing?"

"Inviting myself to his party," the woman said. The red of her hooded mask brought out the blue of her eyes and told Caitlyn that this one was looking for both a man and a woman. That might have had interesting possibilities if it hadn't meant that she'd expect Owen to touch her, to *fuck* her. It probably wasn't fair of Caitlyn to expect him to be okay with her having sex with another woman while she was decidedly *not okay* with him having sex with one, but the unfairness didn't change her opinion on the matter.

"I don't like her touching you," Caitlyn said to Owen. She released the woman's wrists with a shove.

"Would you prefer her to touch you?" Owen asked.

Caitlyn couldn't meet the woman's eyes as she made her intentions clear. "No."

The woman shrugged and wandered off to find more

reasonable prospects.

"She would have let us do anything to her," Owen said.

"She would have wanted you inside her."

"And you have a problem with that?"

"Of course I have a problem with that."

His grin completely disarmed her. Why was he smiling? He should be perturbed that Caitlyn's fantasies were so unyielding to *his* preferences, yet he seemed happy that she'd erected barriers not around herself, but around him.

"I like a woman who knows what she wants," he said.

Oh, was that why he was smiling? Well, that was okay. Just as long as he wasn't feeling smug because Caitlyn was out of her head at the mere thought of him fucking some other woman at a sex club. Maybe it was because he looked so hot and mysterious in that white mask. She couldn't blame women for putting their hands on him.

Owen ordered drinks—whiskey for himself and a crisp white wine for her—and they people-watched for a while. With the normal boundaries of society left at the door, the women became rather predatory, she noticed. She watched one curvy lady take a man to the back, only to return ten minutes later and collect two more. Were they having an orgy back there? Caitlyn wondered if she'd be able to disconnect from her personal morals enough to get gang fucked. Probably not, she decided when several additional men tagged along behind the trio heading to the back of the establishment. The thought of six men taking turns banging her worried Caitlyn far more than it turned her on. Things could so rapidly get out of control in a mob situation. But wasn't that what had happened between the members of Sole Regret and that Lindsey woman? As sexy as she found all the members of the band, Caitlyn didn't think she'd enjoy them taking turns fucking her.

"I think I see exactly what we're looking for," Owen said after a moment. "Stay here; I'll bring her to you."

He kissed her before rising from the table and crossing the room. She couldn't take her eyes off him even when a pair of giggling women streaked completely naked through her line of vision with a bouncer following them, shouting, "No nudity on the floor."

Owen slid into a booth with a woman sitting alone and wearing a pink hooded mask. She was very thin and very pale and actually jumped when Owen spoke to her. She reminded Caitlyn of herself—not in appearance, but in the way she'd reacted when Owen had first approached her in that sex club in San Antonio. Caitlyn wished she were a lip reader when Owen continued to speak to the stranger and the woman turned her head to gaze at Caitlyn. Caitlyn smiled, hoping she didn't look as freaked out as she suddenly felt, and the woman smiled in return before turning back to Owen and nodding.

He slid from the booth and took her hand, leading her across the floor. He stopped as the giggling streakers tried to use him as a human shield against the bouncer holding bra and panty sets in each outstretched hand. They circled him and then raced down the corridor that led to the partitioned rooms.

Owen placed a hand on the pink-hooded woman's back and escorted her to the table. "C," he said, nodding in Caitlyn's direction. They weren't supposed to use names, but an initial would make interactions less confusing. "This is M."

"Hello," Caitlyn said, feeling all sorts of awkward. She supposed the more often a person frequented one of these clubs, the more at ease they became. She wasn't sure she'd come often enough to find that level of comfort.

"Hi. O says you're curious too."

Caitlyn looked to Owen for an explanation.

"Pink," he said, pointing at the woman's mask, "means she's curious but not sure how far she'll go. That's why these horndogs haven't approached her. She might say no."

Caitlyn wished she'd known about the pink mask. She'd have asked for one herself even if it meant she didn't have strangers feeling her up and kissing her without provocation.

"But I might say yes," M said. "Can I sit down?"

"Of course." Caitlyn scooted her chair slightly away from the free chair. She wasn't sure if she was giving M or herself more personal space.

Owen sat on Caitlyn's opposite side and took her hand before reaching for his drink.

Caitlyn examined M more closely. She appeared to be in her early twenties. Her long brown hair—obscured and flattened by the hood on her head—hung in a long mass to the middle of her back. She'd been close to Owen in height—nearing six foot—and had a slender athletic build, with small breasts and narrow hips.

"Would you like a drink, M?" Owen asked as the two women gawked at each other awkwardly.

"Something strong," M said, a hint of humor in her tone.

"Have you been to one of these places before?" Caitlyn asked.

"This is my third time," she said.

"Second time for me," Caitlyn said.

"I haven't done much more than watch," M said.

Caitlyn couldn't claim the same. She sipped her wine, intrigued by the woman in the pink hood. "Why's that?"

"I'm curious, but, uh"—she glanced across the room—"afraid to explore my fantasies. I've been trying to work up the courage to ask for a red hood."

"So you're attracted to both men and women?" Caitlyn asked.

"I'm attracted to men, curious about women."

"Me too!" Caitlyn said and then laughed at how totally unprovocative that sounded. Like they were choosing paint colors or something.

"Does your guy just want to watch?" M asked.

"I want him to make love to me while we are, erm, *curious* with each other."

She glanced at Owen and found him smiling into his glass, completely content to allow Caitlyn to hash out plans with M.

"So I'll get to watch you two together and participate with just you?" M asked.

"You can say no, M, but those are my terms."

"Yes," M said.

Caitlyn's pussy gave an unexpected throb, and she turned to Owen. "Are you okay with this?"

He took her hand and slid it over the rock-hard cock in his boxers. "What do you think?"

"You feel okay with it, but you have to say it."

"Yes, I'm more than okay with it," Owen said. "I'll go see if they have a room ready."

"He's cute," M said as they watched him walk toward a reception counter near the hall that led to the back rooms.

"And sweet," Caitlyn said, knowing she was grinning like an imbecile but unable to help it. "And sexy."

"I sure wouldn't bring him to a place like this if he were mine." M took a swallow of her drink and choked. "I didn't realize vodka came in ten thousand proof."

"Why wouldn't you bring him here? I trust him."

"Maybe," she said, "but do you trust me?"

Caitlyn studied the pretty young woman who was watching Owen like a hawk who'd spotted a tasty young rabbit.

"I don't know you."

"Exactly."

Caitlyn slipped from her chair and hurried after Owen. "Let's just go," she said when she caught up to him.

"There's less than a twenty-minute wait," he said. "They're cleaning a room now."

"I've changed my mind. I don't want to do this. Not with a stranger."

"I was a stranger when we hooked up the first time."

"But you're not a stranger anymore."

"Did M say something that set off alarm bells?"

Caitlyn tugged on his arm. "Please, can we just go?"

"I know her, okay? She's cool. I promise."

Caitlyn quit pulling on his arm to glower at him. "You *know* her?"

"Not outside the club; she's a regular. She likes to pretend she's innocent. It's how she gets her kicks."

She narrowed her eyes at him. "So you were playing me for a fool."

Owen shook his head. "Of course not. I was just trying to get you what you want."

"I want to leave," she said.

"You don't want to fulfill your threesome fantasy?"

"I do," she said, tracing the line between his gorgeous pecs as she tried to sort through her thoughts and feelings.

"So you want to leave because you don't like M? You're not attracted to her?"

"It's not that. I don't like the way she was looking at you."

Owen smiled. "I can handle myself. She's not a threat to either of us. It's just casual sex."

Which was what Caitlyn wanted—she thought. So why was she so jumpy and looking for any excuse to call this off?

"If you really want to leave—"

"I'm not sure."

"I didn't mean to scare you," M said from behind Caitlyn.

Caitlyn spun around and felt incredibly exposed as M looked

at her the same way she'd looked at Owen a few moments ago.

"Let's start over," M said, leaning in close to Caitlyn's ear. "I want to be your fantasy, but just for tonight. I can pretend I don't know what I'm doing if that turns you on, or I can show you what it's like to be pleasured by a woman who knows her way around a pussy."

"M," Owen said, "you aren't helping."

But she was, actually. Because if M was onboard with fulfilling Caitlyn's fantasies and nothing more, then Caitlyn was sure she could give this a try, but if M was interested in Owen or even pursuing Caitlyn beyond one encounter, she wouldn't be able to go through with it. Caitlyn decided this was more her hang-up than M's or Owen's. She was the one who couldn't fuck a guy in a sex club without taking him home. M and Owen had managed to avoid personal connections with past sexual partners—why did she worry this would be different?

"The room is ready," the attendant said. "Did you still want it, or should I page the next guests?"

"We want it," Owen said. And taking Caitlyn's hand, he led her down the corridor with M following close behind.

CHAPTER NINE

AS SOON AS THE DOOR SHUT, Caitlyn found herself in Owen's arms. He kissed her deeply, stealing her reservations and igniting her body. The fingers that unhooked her bra weren't his; his hands were holding her waist. The hands that slipped her bra straps from her shoulders and pulled the garment free weren't his either. Caitlyn kissed him more desperately and reminded herself that this had been her idea, not his or M's. She'd wanted this. Or she thought she had.

She shuddered as M's hands covered her breasts and teased her nipples into hard points.

"You're gorgeous, love," M said, "but you never told me if you wanted me to play the saint or the sinner."

Caitlyn pulled away from Owen's kiss and stared up into his eyes. "I'm going to play the sinner," she said and turned to face M.

M gasped when Caitlyn wrapped an arm around the back of her neck and pulled their mouths together for a deep kiss. Caitlyn allowed herself to get lost in the moment. No more thinking. No more worrying about the outcome. She focused on the present and how exciting it felt to be kissing a woman—who had a thrilling tongue technique as she returned Caitlyn's kisses—while Owen rubbed his hardened cock against her ass.

Caitlyn made short work of M's bra as she slowly backed her toward the small sterile-looking bed. There was no romance at all in this place, Caitlyn thought as the back of M's legs bumped the mattress and she lowered to the bed, pulling Caitlyn with her. Caitlyn caught herself with her hands, breaking the kiss. She held M's gaze for a moment—a stranger behind a mask—and wondered if she was actually going to do this. Before Owen, she'd never fucked anyone besides Charles. And now here she was, standing at the end of a bed between M's legs, mouth watering with anticipation over exploring the taste of another woman. Caitlyn lowered her head to suck one of M's pink nipples—smaller than her own and exotic somehow—while she eased M's panties down her thighs. Once the tiny garment was tossed aside, M opened her thighs without a shred of inhibition or shyness. Her pretty folds were flushed with excitement and shiny with wetness.

Owen shifted away from Caitlyn's backside to remove her panties and apparently his shorts since their next contact was the bare head of his cock seeking entrance into Caitlyn's unquestionably excited body. She crawled onto the end of the bed and spread her knees so that Owen's hips were perfectly aligned for fucking her. M scooted up the bed until her pussy was even with Caitlyn's face, and Caitlyn didn't need any additional encouragement to lower her head and lick M's center.

M's taste was a bit sweeter than what Caitlyn remembered of her own flavor. She swirled her tongue into M's opening, her heart thundering in her chest. At M's soft moan of encouragement, she pressed her tongue deeper. M's scent grew musky with excitement and completely intoxicated Caitlyn. When M's hand tangled in Caitlyn's hair and tugged her up toward her clit, Caitlyn smiled softly and followed her lead. As soon as Caitlyn's tongue brushed the swollen clit, M's thighs quivered and she cried out.

Caitlyn's breath caught when Owen slid into her, shattering her concentration. She panted through several toe-curling thrusts before latching on to M's clit, Owen's steady strokes inciting her boldness. M's moans of pleasure fueled Caitlyn's desire to please her, to bring her to orgasm with licks and kisses and gentle suction.

"She's so sweet," M's whispered.

Sweet? Though this was new to her, Caitlyn had been going for *skilled*.

Finding her courage, Caitlyn slid two fingers into M's silky pussy, curling her fingertips upward and hunting for the spot inside her that would make her hips buckle. When she found it, she rubbed until M's pussy tightened, and then she held her hand still while she sucked and licked at M's clit. M's thighs began to tremble and she drew her knees up, toes curling into the sheets, back arching off the mattress. Caitlyn gentled her sucking kisses and used her fingers to rub at M's front inner wall again.

"Fuck, woman!" M cried. "Are you trying to give me a vag O or a clit O?"

Both, Caitlyn thought with a smirk, waiting until M was almost coming before switching her attention back to her clit, and then when she almost reached her peak, returning to finger-fucking her.

"I'm adding that to my skill set," Owen said. He was so busy paying attention to what Caitlyn was doing to M that he was scarcely moving, but Caitlyn didn't mind. She'd be getting her fill of both of them soon enough.

As M's excitement peaked, she squeezed her breasts and rocked against Caitlyn's fingers. "Yeah," she said, "yeah, make me come. Oh!"

She shook violently as she let go. Caitlyn rotated her hand, stretching M's pussy wide as her inner muscles tightened around her fingers. Caitlyn smiled before latching onto M's clit with a tight suction to draw her even higher. M's second orgasm had her thrashing against the bed.

M collapsed with a satisfied moan, her sweat-dampened body going limp. Caitlyn licked at her center, finding M's freely flowing fluids had a more metallic taste now.

"Don't be selfish, M," Owen said. "C wants to know a woman's mouth on her as well."

"Ah," M said, "she's good. Give me a moment to catch my breath."

Caitlyn lifted her head, concentrating now on the slow deep thrusts of Owen's cock. She closed her eyes and rocked back to meet him, the friction and fullness building her pleasure. She groaned when he pulled out, and she opened her eyes. M had turned so her head was at the foot of the mattress and her feet were resting against the bars of the headboard.

"Come, love," she said. "Put your pussy in my mouth."

Caitlyn looked to Owen, who smiled at her in encouragement. She was surprised by how easy it was to have sex with him and another woman. There was no animosity in him, nor any judgment. He was excited and encouraging. She'd found the perfect man to help her explore her previously repressed sexuality. He even helped her find a good position on M's face. The woman ate pussy with total abandon and after sending Caitlyn flying in less than a minute, she tore her mouth away and said, "You could reciprocate, love."

Caitlyn looked down at M's shaven mound, wondering if she'd be able to reach for a proper sixty-nine. M was half a foot taller than she was, but as she bent forward and licked at the cleft that housed M's clit, Caitlyn decided she could please her without touching her vagina at all. The shift in position moved M's mouth to Caitlyn's clit as well. Caitlyn was really getting into her task and enjoying M's tight suction and rapid tongue flicks, when the mattress sagged between Caitlyn's legs.

"I hope you're okay with balls in your face," Owen said.

M murmured what sounded like agreement, and Caitlyn gasped as the head of his cock pressed into her. He had to take her shallow—their positions wouldn't allow for the deep penetration she craved—but it felt so good to be sucked and fucked at the same time, Caitlyn completely lost herself to soaring bliss. She tried to remember to give M a taste of the pleasure she was enjoying, but mostly she just panted against the pussy in her face.

Owen grabbed her hips and pulled her off M's tight suction, which sent Caitlyn spiraling out of control. He pounded into her hard and deep as she cried out in ecstasy before he let go inside her. Owen's mouth tickled her shoulder as he rubbed his lips against her flushed skin.

"Now I need a man," M said, sitting up on the edge of the bed and rubbing her pussy with one hand, her fingers plunging deep into her body.

Breathless, Caitlyn said, "You can't have mine. Sorry."

Owen kissed her shoulder and neck as if he appreciated her words. She figured most men would want to bang both women involved in a threesome, but he really did seem to be satisfied with just her. The man was absolutely amazing, the perfect sex partner. She had to do something to thank him for his open-mindedness and understanding.

M hopped off the bed and reached for her panties, sliding them up her long legs. Caitlyn suddenly had a hard time looking at her. She still wasn't accustomed to sex for the sake of sex. Shouldn't they exchange gifts or at least thanks? She tried to look at Owen, but he was glued to her back, his softening cock still buried inside her, one arm securely around her waist, his free hand gently massaging her breasts. It was as if he didn't even realize M was still in the room.

"Thanks for the Os," M said. "You two are the hottest couple I've ever been with." She kissed Caitlyn on the mouth and Owen on the cheek. "I'm going to go find a big thick stiffy to ride. I've got a deep, deep itch that needs scratching."

And just like that, she was gone.

"Um," Caitlyn said. "Is that really all there is to this?"

"Usually," Owen murmured. "That's exactly what I'm used to at these places. You're the odd one here."

"Odd?"

She tried to struggle out of his grasp, but he held her tight. "Why do you think I wanted to make you mine?"

What?

"You're the perfect mix of nice girl I want to take home to my mother and sex club vixen who's up for anything in the bedroom."

Meet his mother? Surely he was joking.

"Owen, I don't want this to get serious, remember?"

"Of course I remember." He released her and went to the small sink in the corner to wash his cock. "So are we going to fulfill your *other* threesome fantasy tonight, or would you rather go someplace fun?"

"More fun than a sex club?"

"You don't really like these places, do you?"

She shrugged. "They provide opportunities I'd struggle to find elsewhere." Where else could she discover she enjoyed eating pussy without it feeling incredibly awkward?

He laughed. "I love the way you talk," he said. "So refined even when you're talking about hooking up with strangers."

She tried another approach. "I ate pussy tonight."

"And you liked it."

She grinned. She couldn't deny the truth; the experience had far surpassed her expectations. "I loved it." And she'd probably want to try it again someday, as long as it didn't come with the strings of an actual relationship. "I especially liked when you participated."

"What can I say?" His devilish grin was completely disarming. "I'm a team player."

CHAPTER TEN

"SO WHAT do you want to do now?" Owen asked as they left the anonymous-sex room. "Are there other fantasies you want to try tonight?"

Caitlyn squeezed his hand and smiled. "I'd like to savor that one before moving on to the next. You've been beyond wonderful to me."

Owen snorted. Because watching two hot chicks get it on while you fucked one of them was such a heavy load to bear.

"I'd rather know what you'd like to do now," she said. "You should have your needs met as well."

"My needs have been more than met," he said. Well, his sexual needs had. But unlike Caitlyn, he'd like to enjoy more than sex during their time together. Maybe she'd be open to going out in public with him without having to disguise themselves with masks and refer to each other by initials—like an actual date or something.

"Do you want to go back to my place?" she asked. "We can cozy up on the sofa and relax."

In other words, not be seen together in public.

"I was thinking we could go out to dinner."

The farther they walked down the corridor, the louder the club music got, so she had to shout. "I'd rather stay in for pizza."

It seemed she really didn't want to go out with him, but he wasn't ready to give up yet. "Are there any good shows playing at the theater?" he asked, remembering that she'd said she liked musicals and her ex-husband never took her. Owen's goal was to be the opposite of that dolt.

"Probably," she said, "but we'll never get tickets."

"If I can get tickets, will you go?"

"I'd love to, but you'll never get tickets."

"Have a little faith." He grinned and dropped off their key with the attendant before leading Caitlyn toward the dressing room exit.

He located their shared locker and punched in the code to unlock it. He'd used Chad's birthday, so had no trouble remembering the four-digit combination. He slipped into his pants and pulled out his phone while Caitlyn dressed. He knew exactly who to call for tickets.

~~~

Owen was still chuckling when he escorted Caitlyn out of the theater a few hours later. He'd never realized he liked musicals, but in his attempt to find some common ground with Caitlyn, he'd actually enjoyed *The Book of Mormon.* Maybe because it had been written by the same hilarious dudes who wrote the TV show *South Park* or maybe because his date—who refused to call their time together dating—was so charming. At first he'd expected her to be offended by the script's over the top hijinks and crude language, but she'd laughed along with the rest of the audience. And Owen had laughed so hard he'd had to dab tears from his eyes.

"Did you enjoy yourself?" Caitlyn asked as they walked hand in hand to her car.

"Surprisingly, yes." He leaned in to claim her lips, and she allowed his kiss. Even though she said she didn't want to start a serious relationship, she'd agreed to their second real date. It gave him hope that that they could forge a relationship that was more than just one amazing sexual encounter after another. "Kelly would have loved it. I'll have to take him to see it."

Caitlyn stumbled over a step. "Kellen," she said. "What's he up to this weekend?"

"Oh." A cold, heavy lump settled in the pit of Owen's stomach. "He met a woman when he went to Galveston. I guess they hit it off; he's spending the weekend with her." And completely ignoring Owen. Owen understood that Kelly was upset about losing his cuff, but Owen couldn't stand Kelly to be cross with him, and though he should be happy about Kelly being so lost in a chick that he didn't have three seconds for his best friend, he wasn't. Owen figured after the newness of Dawn and of having sex again wore off, Kelly might find a few moments to spare for the guy who stood by him through every disaster thrown his direction. Kelly had been the same way when he'd been with Sara too, so caught up in her that he seemed to forget that Owen existed.

"A woman?" Caitlyn smiled and unlocked her doors with her key fob. "That's great news."

"Yeah," Owen said, so why did he feel so miserable when he thought about Kelly with Dawn? Kelly deserved someone to love. He deserved happiness. Owen decided he was just missing him. They'd been inseparable for years. Had it not been for Caitlyn and Dawn, the two guys would have undoubtedly spent the weekend together like they usually did. He'd probably be scoping out some unknown rock band in a bar in Austin right now if his and Kelly's lives hadn't suddenly detoured into female territory. Not that he minded. He was having a great time with Caitlyn. He'd just have been even more content if Kelly were serving as their third wheel.

Owen opened the passenger door and climbed in, only remembering he should have opened Caitlyn's door for her after she slid into the driver's seat next to him.

"You don't sound happy." Caitlyn started the Camaro, her attention shifting from the backup cam's screen to the rearview mirror as she waited for traffic to clear behind the car.

"I am happy for him. God knows the dude needed to get laid."

"He had *sex* with her?"

Owen laughed. "I know, right? About damned time he got over Sara." And Owen meant that. He just wasn't sure that going from completely celibate and single for five years to being adhered to Dawn was best for Kelly. The dumbass was probably in over his head, and Owen couldn't even talk to him about it because the woman had been standing right beside him every time Owen tried to approach him.

Caitlyn shrugged, and when she finally found her opening to back out of the parking spot, she gunned the engine. "I guess I was wrong."

"About what?"

"I thought he was waiting for you to come around."

The muscle car seemed to shrink and evacuate itself of air. Owen grabbed the handle above the window to steady himself. "Waiting for me?" he squeaked. He cleared his throat before chuckling uncomfortably. "Whatever gave you that idea?"

"Something about the way he looks at you and touches you. Not to mention that you called his name when I was ass-fucking you with a dildo. I thought maybe there was something more than friendship between you."

Owen shook his head, because for some lame reason, the word no got stuck in his throat and never materialized.

"I shouldn't have said anything," Caitlyn said. "I probably imagined an attraction between you when I was fantasizing about the two of you kissing."

If Owen had been driving, he would have slammed on the brakes. "You fantasize about us kissing?"

"I saw him stroke your cock just days ago, Owen. My little fantasy about you sucking face is tame by comparison."

At her words, Owen's thoughts immediately shifted to the memory of being tied to a pommel and unable to move while Kelly's hand rubbed him. Kelly had been showing Caitlyn how to touch Owen to give him the most pleasure. At least that was what Kelly had used as his excuse. And then after he'd boned Dawn, he'd decided he needed to awkwardly apologize for touching Owen, which had made Owen incredibly uncomfortable. His apology had made something substantial out of what Owen had thought they both considered nothing. Owen had put it out of his mind because he still didn't understand why Kelly had said he was sorry.

"Do you really think he might want me?" Owen asked, confused as to why talking about Kelly's possible attraction gave him a boner on par with the one he'd gotten while watching Caitlyn and M sixty-nine. Lord, what the fuck was wrong with him? Watching hot chicks eating each other out was definitely boner-worthy. Talking about his best friend platonically stroking his cock in demonstration shouldn't be.

"I do," Caitlyn said, "but I don't think he's prepared to admit it. Not even to himself. The question I have is: do you want him?"

Owen scoffed. "Uh, no. Of course not." But the stiffy in his pants declared him a fucking liar.

Caitlyn drove through the city of Houston like she was trying to deliver a bomb before it exploded. Owen shoved all thoughts of Kelly aside to focus on not shrieking like a little girl every time Caitlyn got a bit too close to another driver's bumper. His imaginary passenger-side brake was getting quite a workout.

"So what do you like to eat?" she asked. "I'm starved."

"Pa—"

"If you say pastrami on rye, I'm going to vomit."

Owen chuckled. He had been going to say that. "Pasta?"

"Awesome. I know a great place that serves dinner late."

He gripped the handle above the window tighter as she did a U-turn at the next intersection and gunned the engine again. He'd have never taken her for the kind of woman who drove a muscle car—he'd have placed her in something a bit more practical, like a Volvo—but he had to admit that she looked hot behind the wheel of her brand new yellow Camaro. She'd called it her divorcee ego-recovery car when she'd insisted on driving to the sex club.

The small Italian restaurant they went to was not one he'd expect her to frequent. After seeing her house—he could have fit four or five of his little cottage inside her giant McMansion—he assumed she dined at five-star restaurants and had been ashamed that he'd taken her to some greasy-spoon diner on their first date. This little hole in the wall didn't even have a lit sign out front, and they'd had to park on the street. The tables were crammed into the small space so close that their hippy hostess had to walk sideways to seat them.

"I haven't been here in years," Caitlyn said, scouring her menu.

Ah, so she didn't frequent this place.

"Charles says it's too claustrophobic."

Owen could see the man's point as he accidentally elbowed a perfect stranger at the next table. "Sorry," he said, rubbing the woman's arm to undo any damage.

"It's okay," she said with a friendly smile.

Owen liked the place already.

"You have to try the portabella tortellini," Caitlyn said. "Do you like mushrooms?"

"They're okay. I prefer pastrami."

Caitlyn laughed and smacked at him with her menu. "Is prosciutto a good enough substitute?"

"I suppose." He actually loved prosciutto and was surprised she understood his tastes enough to suggest it.

They ordered and after finishing their tangy Caesar salads, they munched on chewy slices of warm bread with creamy butter while they waited for their entrees. Owen was already in food heaven.

"So what else do you like to do that ol' Charlie hates?" Owen asked, happy to be a part of Caitlyn finding herself again.

She laughed and buttered the last piece of bread, tearing it in half and offering him a section. "First and foremost, he loathes being called Charlie."

Then that was exactly what Owen would call him from now on.

"Let's see. Backgammon. He hates to lose, and I always win."

"Unless you're playing Gabe," Owen reminded her. She and the band's drummer had engaged in several serious battles, and Caitlyn had managed to claim only one victory against the master.

"Oh jeez, I'd forgotten Gabe had skunked me." She bit into her bread. "Charles also hates science museums."

Owen didn't think any museum would be much fun, but he'd thought the same about musical theater until Caitlyn had shown him otherwise.

"He could spend all day in the library, though. We both enjoy reading. Different tastes in books, but we often sat quietly and read for hours."

"Are you sure you weren't married to Gabe?" Owen said, seeing many parallels between his friend and her ex.

"I think I would have remembered that. Especially the crimson-red Mohawk and scalp tattoos."

He laughed, and she reached over to squeeze his hand. "And what do you like to do in your spare time?" she asked.

Was she trying to get to know him more personally? Score! "Besides music?"

"Do you attend a lot of concerts when you aren't performing?"

"Kelly and I like to scope out unknown talent in Austin. There's an amazing music scene there, so that's always fun. We spend a lot of time at the gym so I can still eat the foods I love. Especially carbs." He licked his finger to pick up a stray crumb off the empty bread plate and put it on his tongue. He hoped their pasta arrived soon. "And he makes me go kayaking." Which wasn't his favorite activity—he'd much rather take an exciting ride in Gabe's speedboat followed by some relaxing fishing on the lake— but if Kelly was happy paddling around with his legs jammed inside a claustrophobic boat, then Owen was happy to follow him around.

"And you make Kellen go to sex clubs."

When she put it that way, it sounded pretty douche-y. "Yeah."

Their food arrived, and Owen was in taste-bud bliss as he devoured his prosciutto, peas, and cream sauce over perfectly al dente fettuccini. Caitlyn offered him a bite of her portabella tortellini, and it was equally delicious. As they ate, he made her laugh with stories about touring with his band. He couldn't get enough of the delightful sound and was glad he could bring her joy. After finishing their entrees, they fed each other bites of the most incredible tiramisu he'd ever tasted. He was going to have to hit the gym extra hard for the next few days, but, damn, was the meal worth it.

"Do you think you have one more fantasy in you tonight?" she asked as she insisted on paying the check.

"You should have asked before I gorged myself on carbs." He produced a large yawn for effect.

"I've always wanted to make love beneath the stars," she said. "I set up a spot in my backyard if you're game. If not—"

He caught her hand and brought her knuckles to his lips. He stared deeply into her eyes and used his most seductive voice as he said, "My pants are already around my knees."

CHAPTER ELEVEN

CAITLYN TOOK Owen's hand and led him out to the backyard. The gentle lap of the bay water against the bulkhead hidden by the inky darkness provided a rhythmic backdrop to the chorus of squalling cicadas and chirping crickets. She'd had a great time with Owen that night, first at the sex club, then at the theater, and finally at dinner, and though making love under the stars really was on her list of fantasies, she wanted this encounter to be more about him than it was about her.

She pushed aside the mosquito netting that kept biting critters from entering the glass gazebo while allowing a cool onshore breeze to blow through. She didn't light the torches, but there was enough moonlight to make out the creamy white sheet draped over the pillows she'd pulled from the dark wicker sofa, loveseat, and various lounge chairs. They wouldn't exactly be roughing it, but they'd be able to see the stars through the glass ceiling and almost feel one with nature without having to deal with the bugs.

"Someone has been planning again," Owen commented as he stepped onto the low deck inside the gazebo.

"Expect the best, plan for the better," she said, kicking off her shoes and pulling her blouse over her head.

"I'm not sure that's how the saying goes," he said, reaching for the hem of his shirt. She caught his hands.

"Allow me," she murmured, bending forward so she could kiss his belly and chest as she removed his shirt.

He helped her pull off the rest of her clothes, and then she grabbed a pillow for her knees before she knelt at his feet. She planned to be there for a while. He stared down at her as she unfastened his pants and slowly slid them over the tight curve of his perfect ass. "Now your pants are at your knees," she murmured before licking his cock until it danced to life.

"You're so beautiful." His hand lightly stroked her hair from her face.

"Do you know any constellations?" she asked.

"Does it matter?"

"Look up at the stars, Owen." She kissed the head of his now fully erect cock. "Let me take you to them."

He tilted his head back, and she licked and sucked at his tip, loving the way the metal balls in his piercing felt against her lips and tongue.

"Don't close your eyes." She sucked him into her mouth and, after taking a deep breath through her nose, drew him into her throat.

He shuddered and released a breathy moan. She caressed his smooth ass with both palms as she slowly pulled back and then took him deep again.

"So beautiful," he whispered to the sky, and she wasn't sure if he was speaking of her or the sea of sparkling stars above.

His breath quickened, and he tangled his fingers in her hair, meeting her movement with gentle thrusts of his hips. With a tormented groan, he pulled out and urged her to her feet. She blinked at him, wondering if he wasn't enjoying something as ordinary as oral pleasure after spending an evening in a sex club. Fingers tangled in her hair, he moved his hands forward to cup her face.

"I want this to last," he said and leaned in to claim her lips.

Make what last? His erection? This perfect night? Their potential forever? She wasn't sure what he expected from their time together—hell, she wasn't sure what *she* expected anymore—but she didn't resist when he lifted her and carried her to the nest of cushions. Instead, she cupped his face as he held her and kissed him back with an unguarded heart as he gently laid her down.

His touch, his kisses, his tender nibbles were unhurried as he explored her body. When she remembered to open her eyes, she stared up at the stars, but mostly she let her eyes drift shut and just felt him. *Owen*. She felt him everywhere, not only against her skin. And when he claimed her at last, she felt him even deeper. Not just where their bodies were joined but inside her heart, her soul, the parts of her she kept carefully hidden. She felt him. *Owen*.

She'd never bargained for this. She wasn't ready to feel for another man. It was much too soon; she was still trying to sort herself out. No matter how wonderful he was, she didn't want to get tangled up in a relationship just yet.

"Caitlyn," he whispered, his infectious rhythm rocking them together in perfect harmony.

She opened her eyes and though his face was obscured by shadows, she could feel the intensity of his emotions as he held her gaze. In the moonlight, could he read the feelings expressed on her face?

"I want to say it," he whispered, his lips seeking hers for a tender kiss. "I want to say it."

Her heart slammed into her ribs. If he meant what she thought he meant, she didn't want to hear it. It was too soon for him to love her. "Not yet," she said. "Wait for me to catch up with you."

He lowered his body against hers and buried his face in her neck, never once losing the sensual rhythm his body played into hers. "I won't say it," he murmured, "but you can't stop me from feeling it."

She wrapped her arms around him and hugged him tight. He couldn't stop her from feeling it either. In fact, her unwanted feelings of affection for him were all his fault. He absolutely should not be her every dream come true. How was she supposed to resist him and his damned tender heart?

When his focus shifted from connecting with her to seeking release, she clung to his shoulders and let him take her body to the dizzying heights of the stars above. After they drifted back down to their soft bed of pillows and she was wrapped securely in his arms, she realized that for the first time in her life, an orgasm hadn't been the best part of sex. Nor had the pleasure or the raw remembrance of his body locked in hers. The best part had been connecting with this man—this virtual stranger—on a level far deeper than the physical. She couldn't remember ever feeling that with Charles. They'd had sex, and it had connected them on a physical level. They'd often connected on a mental level and had stimulating conversations. But their emotional connection had never been deep. Not like this. She'd always assumed that she was the type of woman who could only form strong emotional attachments with her future children—it was why she'd so wanted a baby and had never gotten over Charles's refusal to meet that need. Caitlyn wasn't sure if she should be glad to have found this uncommon connection with Owen or be terrified out of her mind.

Too soon, she reminded herself as she snuggled closer against his sleeping body, seeking not only warmth but comfort and that scary as hell connection he'd shared with her. Too soon, she reminded herself one last time before she drifted to sleep.

CHAPTER TWELVE

OWEN RUBBED a hand over Caitlyn's chilled arm and watched the sun rise over the choppy horizon of the bay. Gradually pink and orange gave way to a pale blue sky. Perhaps he should wake her to witness the splendor surrounding them, but Owen needed a moment to collect his thoughts. Last night something had changed between them. He'd seen it in her moonlight-kissed face when he'd made love to her. Owen tried not to let himself get too excited about potential prospects. His heart had been broken so many times in the past, he knew better than to rush this—whatever this was becoming. In the past he'd put himself out there over and over again. Sometimes his efforts would be rewarded with the love he craved, but it never lasted. He got too intense too fast, and the sensible women he always fell for frightened easily. So even though his heart was already all-in, he was going to follow Caitlyn's advice and wait until she caught up with him before he told her how he felt. But could she ever really catch up with him? He wasn't sure it was possible.

Caitlyn took a deep breath when the sun rose high enough to bathe her face in golden brilliance. She shivered and snuggled closer to his warmth. He reached for the edge of the sheet and pulled it around her bare back.

"Am I really sleeping naked in my backyard?" she murmured groggily.

"Yep."

"And is there really a gorgeous tattooed and pierced hunk plastered to my side?"

He smiled at her compliment. "Yep."

"And is that a spider crawling up my leg?"

Owen sat up and flicked the offensive arachnid from her ankle.

"Poisonous?" she asked, calmly.

"Nope. Wolf spider."

She shivered. "I'm chilly," she said, her gorgeous brown eyes still glassy with sleep.

He tucked the sheet more closely around her and pulled her into his lap, rubbing her with both hands to warm her.

"I have a better idea for getting warm," she said.

"Go inside?"

She touched his face, her gaze filled with warmth and affection. "Kiss me."

Her taste was sharper in the morning, he noted, but that didn't stop him from deepening his kiss.

"Better?" he asked when they drew apart. Personally, he was overheated.

She nodded. "You know what I wish?"

His heart thudded, knowing that the woman wished for incredible things that brought indescribable pleasure to his eager body. "What's that?"

"That I didn't have to pee so badly. This is a wonderful way to wake up. I'd like to enjoy it."

He chuckled and kissed her nose before tipping her onto her feet. "Nature calls."

Struck by her beauty—the tangle of her dark hair, the sheet that covered parts of her curves but not others, and the swollen quality of her recently kissed lips—he sat there and watched her leave the glass gazebo and tiptoe up the sloped yard toward the house.

"Are you coming?" she called to him.

He scooped up a wad of discarded clothing and pressed it against his already rising dick before he followed her. The grass was cool and damp beneath his bare feet, and the onshore breeze chilled his naked ass, but he was still on fire.

"Join me in the shower?" she asked when he followed her into the house.

He tugged a small leaf from her tangled locks. "Is that on your fantasy list?"

She grinned. "If it wasn't, it is now."

She had him exhausted, yet clean and satisfied, before breakfast. He was as horny as the next guy, but his stamina did have a few bounds. So when she reached for her fantasy list over a bowl of cereal—to undoubtedly determine what the rest of their day would bring—Owen took it from her and shoved it into his pocket.

"Let's go to a museum," he said.

She gave him an odd look. "Why?"

"You said you like them." *And ol' Charlie doesn't.* "And as much as I enjoy every minute with your naked body, I wouldn't mind spending time with the clothed version of you."

"So the nudist museum is out," she said.

He laughed. "Didn't know there was such a thing, but maybe next time."

"Next time."

The future promised in her eyes made his heart skip a beat. He pulled his attention back to his bowl of wheat flakes—her idea of cooking breakfast. "So do you like art museums?"

"I do," she said, "but my favorites are science museums."

He managed not to make a face of displeasure. "Science, huh?"

She reached for his hand and gave it a squeeze. "Art it is," she said.

Maybe he wasn't as good at hiding his disinterest in science as he thought. "We can do science."

"We can do both," she said with a smile. She scooped another bite of cornflakes into her mouth.

"That might be a bit more of the clothed version of you than I can tolerate at once."

She laughed, covering her mouth as she choked on her cereal. He stood to whack her on the back, but she held up a hand to let him know she wasn't dying.

When she regained her composure, she said, "You're so bad, you're good."

"You shouldn't encourage me."

"Why not? I'm in this for the fun and excitement, and the more I encourage you, the more fun and exciting you become."

He couldn't deny that truth, but hoped she'd eventually add a little depth to the superficial relationship she thought she wanted.

When they later climbed into her Camaro for their day of adventure, he asked, "Where are we going?"

"Someplace cool," she said. "You might want to look over that list in your pocket while I drive." She lifted her eyebrows suggestively. "Maybe we can multitask."

"Maybe."

The seat belt dug into his shoulder as she shot backward down the drive. She shifted into drive, punched the accelerator, and took off with a squeal of tires that pressed him solidly into the leather seat. While she drove like they'd just robbed a bank in her bay area suburb and planned to escape into the urban center of Houston, Owen slipped the list out of his pocket and refreshed his memory. There were a few they could make work on their adventure today—sex in an elevator being his favorite—but one item caught his attention.

"You've never had sex in a car?" Considering how much she loved to drive like a getaway driver—they had that in common, actually—her back-seat virginity surprised him.

"Not yet." She grinned and zoomed along in the fast lane of the interstate until they spotted a state trooper, which effectively removed the lead from her foot.

Okay, he'd be looking for the opportunity to make that particular fantasy a reality. He peered over his shoulder and decided the proper descriptor for the small back seat was *cozy*. Not much room back there for a vigorous romp. Maybe they could take his Jeep out for a spin later.

"Are there any local beaches that allow vehicle traffic?"

"Uh, Crystal Beach on Bolivar Peninsula. Closer to my house there's Seaside, but that's on the Bay, not the Gulf, and I think you need a permit. I don't go to the beach often."

But sex on the beach was on her list.

"What about Galveston?" Mentioning Galveston made Owen think of Kelly. Maybe if he visited the island with Caitlyn that evening he'd have the opportunity to see his friend. Maybe they could double date. Now *that* would be fun. Especially if Dawn couldn't go with them.

"Not that I know of. You might be able to park on the west end, but there are sea turtle nesting areas, so you can't just drive wherever you want. I thought you wanted to do the museum thing today."

"I do. I was just planning what to do tonight. Gotta fulfill your fantasies somehow." He winked at her.

"I am so glad I wrote that list." Seeming to have forgotten about the cop they'd seen earlier, she floored the accelerator to pass several semi-trucks. "I thought showing it to you might be embarrassing, but it actually makes things easier. You know what

I want, so I don't have to fret about telling you."

"And I can try to be a little spontaneous, which I hope is more exciting for us than you setting up sex stations in your house."

She laughed and coasted to a slower speed again. "Ah God, I'm such a dork."

"Charming," he corrected. She was a bit of a dork, but he found it to be one of her most charming qualities. "You know what you want, and you go after it."

"That's not the dorky part. The dorky part is making a nested list for each one of those fantasies and taking it to a sex shop. I even made place cards for each station, but hid them in a drawer." She laughed so hard, the car crossed the dotted white line. He reached for the wheel, heart hammering like mad in his chest, but she quickly corrected into her lane. "If you can't tell, I have no idea what I'm doing when it comes to you."

He chuckled. "So you thought you'd give micromanagement a try?"

"Not my best idea!" She blinked tears of mirth out of her eyes and purposely crossed several lanes to merge onto another interstate. Owen had no idea where they were headed. If his memory served correctly, they should have headed due west, not north, to get to Houston's museum district.

"Where are we going?" he asked.

"It's a surprise."

"I thought we were going to a museum."

"We are. It's the coolest museum I know of."

Cool and museum didn't belong in the same sentence, but he was having fun just talking with her while she maneuvered her "divorce therapy" to dodge traffic. And not once that morning had he felt the need to act like a buffoon to make her laugh. They just clicked—and not only in the bedroom. He hoped she recognized how rare that was, and if not, he would be sure to point it out to her.

They pulled up to a metal fortress of a building surrounded by a chain-link fence. The entire structure was chrome, with exhaust pipes and car grills fashioned into works of art near the roof line. Large cones of metal worked into menacing spikes adorned the roof and surrounded the door frames. If not for the letters cut out of sheet metal that spelled out Art Car Museum in an arch, Owen would never have reckoned the place for a museum.

"Welcome to the Garage Mahal," Caitlyn said. She pecked him on the cheek—likely because his mouth was unattractively agape as he stared at the building—and opened her door.

He was still trying to take in the structure—a work of metal art in itself—when Caitlyn opened his door. "Are you coming?"

"Nice call, babe. This place is badass." He pulled out his cellphone to snap a picture. He then pulled Caitlyn against his side and extended his arm to get them in frame for a selfie. He caught little of the building, her blinking, and only half of his face, but it was the memory that was important, not the composition of the picture.

"Wow," Caitlyn said, examining the shot he'd taken. "You suck at selfies."

"I'd like to see you do better."

Her selfie attempt was marginally better if he'd wanted a shot up his nostrils. He didn't.

"Oh God, that's even worse," she said, laughing at her sidelong expression as she'd been trying to find the right button to push.

He laughed and hugged her tightly. "You can't say we don't have anything but sex in common," he said. "We both suck at selfies."

The museum was free but accepted donations, so Owen offered up a few twenties. The building was smaller than he'd expected. Four art cars were on display, each decorated in very different styles. One reminded him of a futuristic metallic demon. Another had an outlandish alligator theme, complete with stuffed alligators on the hood. A third had been painted by an insanely skilled artist in a brightly colored motif. There were other modern works of art on display as well, and it turned out he and Caitlyn had a similar taste in art. Or at least she claimed to like the same pieces that inspired him. Maybe she was just looking for more common ground. They took a few more selfies—all of which sucked and made them laugh—before returning to Caitlyn's car.

"Now we'll go to a real museum," she said, "but first—do you like beer?"

"Who doesn't like beer?"

"A lot of people, but I'll take that as a yes." She drove a bit off the beaten path to a small silver house. "Beer-can house," she said, unnecessarily pointing it out as they creeped past. The house

OLIVIA CUNNING

was silver because every inch, even the roof, was covered with beer-can tops. A curtain of dangling silver tops hung from the eaves like gaudy icicle lights.

"The band could decorate the tour bus this way," Caitlyn said. "It wouldn't take long to collect enough cans."

Less than a block past the glittering attraction, Caitlyn pulled to a stop on the side of the road and put the car in park. When he reached for the door handle, she caught his arm. "We don't need to see the inside," she said.

"Then why did you stop?"

"I had a powerful urge to do this."

Her cool fingers slid up the back of his neck to delve into the hair at his nape, and she tugged him close for a kiss.

Lust heated his blood as he pulled her against him the best he could with a console between them. It had been a few hours since he'd taken her in the shower, and that stamina he'd been concerned about earlier became a nonissue. He wanted her desperately. He found himself tugging her toward the back seat, ready to fulfill her sex-in-a-car fantasy right there on the side of the road.

"We'd better stop," she said against his mouth, though her tongue brushed his, prompting his hands to tug at her clothes. He reached for her breast, palming the soft, full globe, and she moaned.

"Owen," she murmured. "Not here."

"Then where?" He didn't think he could wait the hour it would take them to return to her house. "Is there a hotel nearby?"

"My office isn't far."

He had seen that fantasy on her list, but hadn't expected they'd tackle that one today.

"Do you want to fuck me on my desk, Owen?"

He pressed her hand against his stiff cock. "He's answering for me at the moment."

She rubbed him just enough to make his breath catch. "I think he's saying yes."

He always said yes.

Owen's hand moved between Caitlyn's legs. Desire slammed into his gut as the heat coming off of her pussy registered. "Drive," he growled.

The short trip to the deserted office building was a blur. She

312

didn't stop him when he rubbed her mound through her shorts or her tit through her shirt as she drove. She merely moaned encouragement when he kissed her neck and pinched one hard nipple. By the time they stumbled out of the car and she used her key to open the front door of the building, he was about to bust the zipper out of his pants.

"Is there anyone here?" He followed her into an attractively decorated reception area, lit only by natural light pouring in through a bank of high windows.

"It's a Sunday," she reminded him, "so no."

"I think you mean it's Sinday." He pushed her up against the back of the door and unfastened her shorts. "I'm going to assume this is your office, because I can't wait another second."

Her shorts dropped to her ankles, and she kicked them aside. He fumbled with her panties while she freed his cock, and then he found her center, sinking deep into her hot, slick flesh. She kissed him desperately, hands pressing into his face, his shoulders, stretching to hold his ass as he fucked her so hard her body shifted up and down the back of the door.

"Is that your desk?" he asked, lifting her by the ass and turning her to settle on a meticulously kept desk.

She reclined back and swept her arms over the surface, sending a stapler, pen cup, and several outboxes tumbling to the floor.

"Belongs to my partner's receptionist," she said breathlessly. "I overheard her in the breakroom talking about me. She said my husband cheated on me because I was a dried-up prude."

He snorted. "No clue where she got that idea."

She sent a framed picture of the receptionist's man tumbling to the floor, shattering the glass on impact.

"Make me come on her desk," Caitlyn said, grabbing the front of his shirt and pulling him against her. Her ankles dug into his thighs as he pounded her to her peak. Her cries of release echoed through the cavernous room. He wasn't finished with her yet, though. They still hadn't fucked on her desk, and that was why they'd gone there in the first place.

"Where's your office?" he asked when her body went slack and she lay sprawled across the surface of the receptionist's desk trying to catch her breath.

"Third floor."

He probably could have carried her down the hall, but not up two flights of stairs.

"The elevator is down that way." She tilted her head toward a corridor.

"Elevator?" He grinned and scooped her off the desk. She wrapped her arms around his neck and her legs around his waist as he carried her toward the stainless steel doors obscured by shadows in the dark hallway. "Why didn't you say there was an elevator here?"

"Sorry. Didn't know elevators were your thing."

"Everything is my thing," he assured her.

She kissed him desperately, her fingers toying with his hair as he slapped at the button to open the elevator door. She pulled away long enough to say, "I know I just came, but I can't stand you not being inside me. Hurry." She crushed her mouth to his again.

The elevator dinged and the door slid open. His muscles were starting to fatigue, so he set her on her feet. Their gazes locked and then were torn apart momentarily as she removed his shirt and tossed it onto the floor. She removed her own shirt next and then her bra to stand naked before him. Her tits were too gorgeous not to catch his attention. He sank to his knees at her feet, cupping the perfect, soft globes in his hands and drawing one nipple into his mouth.

"Fuck, you're hot, Caitlyn," he murmured as he moved his mouth to her other breast.

She laughed and buried her fingers in his hair, holding him to her. "No one has ever accused me of that."

"They don't see you the way I see you."

"Naked in an elevator?" she said. "Probably not."

She slapped a button, and the elevator car began to rise. At the same time, she sank down, directing his straining cock into the warmth between her thighs. He groaned, pulling her against him as she rose and sank over him, loving the feel of her breasts caressing his chest almost as much as the sweet friction of her pussy around him. Her head dropped back, long silky hair tickling the arm he held securely around her back. Cries of passion punctuated her every motion, her vocalizations growing louder and faster as she took what she wanted from him and gave him so much in return. He kissed her neck, using his tongue to collect the salty moisture that rose to the surface of her skin. When the elevator dinged and the doors slid open, she reached over and slapped a button and they began their descent. The unsettling feeling of his body dropping while he thrust up into her made him dizzy. Or maybe it was being with her that had him out of his head.

"We're not getting off this elevator until you come," he murmured against her throat.

"Almost there," she said between broken gasps. "I do love your pierced cock."

Based on the way she was grinding against him as if trying to keep it inside her forever, he'd figured as much.

She shuddered, her pussy tightening around him as she cried out. Owen squeezed his eyes shut and recited the alphabet backward in his head—an attempt to calm himself so he didn't follow her over the edge. He still had to fuck her on her desk.

The elevator dinged again, and the doors slid open. He held her against him, trying to still the trembling of her body and the spasms tugging at his cock.

"Don't move for a second," he pleaded, sucking air into his lungs and forcing the pressure building inside his pelvis not to burst.

The elevator door slid shut, but the car didn't move as he sat there collecting his wits—what was left of them.

"Slowly now," he said as he took her by the hips and lifted her from his lap. When his cock fell free of her soft haven, he sucked an agonized breath through his teeth.

"Oh, sweetheart," Caitlyn said, reaching for his overly engorged and very pissed-off cock.

"Don't touch it." He grabbed her hand.

"Let me help. I'll suck—"

"Ah God, don't put that image in my head. I'll never last. Where's your desk?"

"You held back for me?"

He had no idea why her eyes were suddenly brimming with tears. Of course he'd held back for her. He couldn't remember ever needing to come as badly as he did at that moment.

Caitlyn climbed to her feet and opened the elevator door. She reached for his hand and tugged him to standing, then raced naked down the hall to an open door at its very end. Seeing her desk—all covered in journals and stacks of papers and manila folders—unlocked something primal in him. There was no tenderness or concern in the way he bent her over the desk, his hand pressing the side of her head against the solid surface, and rammed his aching cock into her. She didn't seem to mind his harsh treatment. In fact, she shifted into his rigorous thrusts, meeting him stroke for stroke.

"Fuck me, Owen," she said. "Harder. Fuck me."

He slapped her flank, and her pussy tightened around him. He liked it so much he smacked the same spot again.

"Oh God," she said, her hand sliding between her legs to touch the place where their bodies were coming together. That tiny bit of added stimulation sent him flying.

He cried out as pleasure ripped through his center and blessed release consumed him. She rocked into him, drawing his orgasm out until he had to grab her hips to still her body. When the waves of ecstasy finally subsided, he leaned over her back and kissed her spine.

When their breathing had returned to almost normal, she said, "I'm going to have to change offices."

He lifted his head, his heart suddenly panging with hurt. "I didn't live up to your expectations?"

"Baby, you exceeded them so much that I'll never get any work done. I'll be too busy dwelling on the things you did to my body here. And in the elevator. And downstairs."

He grinned, feeling better. Not as good as he would have felt if she'd dwelled on the things he did to her emotions—to her heart and to her soul—but he had faith that he'd bring her to that point eventually.

"So instead of working, you'll be fantasizing?" he asked, pulling out of her body, his breath catching as he watched their combined cum dribble from her reddened pussy and down her thigh. He knelt at her feet and licked at the salty, slightly bitter mess they'd made together.

She gasped. "Jesus, Owen, you're so dirty."

He stopped just shy of her pussy lips. "Sorry."

"Why are you sorry? I fucking love it. I won't just sit here fantasizing about you when I'm behind this desk; I'll have my hand in my panties touching myself."

He groaned in appreciation of that visual and gently licked her drenched hole.

She sucked a pained breath through her teeth, and he

immediately knew what that meant. "Sore?"

"Very," she admitted.

He kissed her tender flesh, hoping to heal her agony. "I should have taken the piercing out."

"No, it was wonderful. Perfect. I wouldn't change a second of it. And you're wonderful. Perfect. I wouldn't change anything about you."

This woman was very good for his ego.

She sighed. "But being this sore means you'll have to spend more time with the clothed version of me."

He traced her opening with the tip of his tongue. "I happen to like the clothed version of you."

"Even if she's walking like a cowboy who rode a thousand miles on a spiked saddle?"

He chuckled, loving her wit. "Especially if she's walking like that."

He leaned away, and she lifted herself from the desk before dropping to her knees so they were face to face. "Would it be dirty of me to kiss you after you've been licking my cum-filled pussy?"

"Very dirty."

She melded her mouth to his in a tongue-teasing, lips-caressing, teeth-nibbling kiss. She pulled away after a moment, her dark eyes searching his.

"Would it be dirty of me to lick the cum off your cock?"

"Dirty and dangerous," he said.

"I'm not worried about germs."

He chuckled. "Dangerous because you might get a rise out of me, and then I'll either have to fuck that sore pussy again or take your ass."

"Or I could suck you off," she said, lowering her head until her warm breath teased the head of his cock.

When her tongue danced over his sensitive flesh and lust slammed into his gut once again, he figured they never would make it to the next museum.

CHAPTER THIRTEEN

BY THE TIME CAITLYN HAD GIVEN Owen the best blow job of his life—his words—and found all of her discarded clothes—half in the elevator and half next to Joyce's desk—and given him a brief tour of her research lab, it was well past lunch and nearing dinner time. If they were going to bring another two of her sexual fantasies to life, they'd have to start making their way home to pick up Owen's Jeep and then head to the Gulf Coast. She was going to have to ask him to take the jewelry out of his piercing for their next encounter, which was a bummer, but she needed the break. Not from him, just from his jewelry.

"Do you want to go out to dinner or have a picnic in the back of the Jeep?" she asked as she relocked the office's front door and hoped no one ever had a reason to review today's incriminating security tapes.

"Which is more likely to make you smile?" he asked.

"Whichever involves more of you." She took his hand as they walked to her eye-catching car in the otherwise deserted parking lot. She knew she shouldn't encourage this lovey-dovey crap, but her heart and her brain were at total odds. And as scary as it was, her heart was currently in control. She was pretty sure her oversexed body was unfairly swaying said heart in the man's direction.

"I will be present either way," he said.

But they'd have to keep their hands to themselves if they dined in public. Still, maybe that was for the best. The more time she spent with her hands on Owen's body, the less her brain functioned in a logical and coherent fashion.

"Picnic on the beach," popped out of her mouth before she could get her thoughts in any semblance of order.

"My mind-control techniques are working," he said, releasing an evil-sounding laugh.

So he'd rather picnic alone with her on the beach? Her belly began to quiver with butterflies at the thought of being with him from sunrise over the Bay to sunset over the Gulf. They'd have spent the *entire* day together, and she was in no way looking forward to him returning to his band's tour the next day. She normally liked her interactions with other people to come in small doses; she'd always been a bit of a loner. But where Owen was involved, she feared she'd never get enough.

"You're staying the night, aren't you?" she asked, her hand involuntarily tightening on his.

"I hope to. Will you come see me later this week after a show? Before a show? During a show? I'm not sure I can wait until our next tour break to see you again."

"Of course," she gushed, wishing the foot she had in her mouth was bigger so stupid happy shit would stop falling from her lips. But she did want to see him as soon as possible. And that was a bad sign. Very bad. Was she falling for him? Truly? That fast? It wasn't possible, was it? Even in her impressionable and naive youth, her handsome, intelligent, and worldly English professor hadn't won her heart this quickly. Perhaps she should have encouraged Owen to leave rather than stay the night. A little space would let her clear her head before she did something as ridiculous as fall in love with her rebound guy. Her younger man—sexually explorative, ego boosting, and awesome—was not long-term-commitment material. At least that was what she'd thought when she'd hooked up with him. Now she was starting to think beyond their weekend together. Even beyond that silly sexual fantasy list she'd made. She was thinking of him as her boyfriend. Crap.

"You're starting to give off men-suck vibes," he said, drawing her up against the side of the car.

"Are you sure?" She hooked an arm around his neck and kissed him. Her heart thundered in her chest. She knew her throbbing heart had little to do with the burning sexual chemistry between them and everything to do with the junior-high-level crush she had going on for the guy. Her scientific mind could explain her giddiness away by knowing the release of endorphins in her brain was tricking her into thinking she'd found her soulmate, but, lord, how she wanted these overwhelming feelings to be more than a chemical maelstrom brewing in her system.

"Maybe I was mistaken," he said, the movement of his mouth tickling her lips.

"If I'm giving off vibes, they're not directed at you. You don't suck," she assured him.

"I can if you'd like."

She felt his grin against her lips.

"I'm feeling things for you I'm not ready to feel yet." And his close proximity must be affecting her judgement, because she wasn't ready to admit even that much to him.

The grin against her lips widened.

"Maybe we need to spend some time apart," she said, hating the words as soon as they escaped her, even as she knew that time apart was the sensible reaction to moving way too fast. And they were definitely moving way too fast. Even her Camaro—with its accelerator mashed to the floor—wouldn't be able to keep pace with the progression of their relationship.

"Okay," he said. "Starting tomorrow I promise to give you some space. At least until you come see me on Tuesday."

"Wow, twenty-four hours without you? I'm not sure I can handle that."

"You can always come to the show in New Orleans. Can you survive twelve hours apart? If not, you can follow me back to Austin and stow away on the plane. I'll hide you in my pants. No one will think anything is up."

"Except the *enormous* cock you suddenly have hidden in your pants."

"Nothing new there."

She laughed and turned the gentle touch of their inseparable lips into another deep kiss. When she finally pulled away, she was breathless. "We'd better go if we want to watch the sunset on the beach."

"Do you want to go to Galveston? Kelly has a beach house—"

"We won't be alone if Kelly's there."

"Right," he said, almost managing to hide his disappointment from her. But she already knew how to make it up to him. He reached for the door handle, but she pressed a hand along the door seal to keep him from escaping.

"Call me selfish, Owen, but I want you all to myself this weekend. Maybe if you weren't so gorgeous and sweet and charming, I'd be willing to share you with Kellen. But you are, so I'm not."

He looked at her over his shoulder, his face flushed with pleasure, and shrugged. "I see your point. Kelly's probably too busy screwing Dawn to hang out with us anyway. He has a lot of years of sexual frustration to work out of his system."

"So Dawn and I will both be walking funny for a few days."

He laughed and opened the passenger door. "How about you let me drive?"

No one had driven her car besides her, so she hesitated before asking, "You don't drive like a granny, do you?"

"I guess you'll have to wait and see."

She held his gaze for a moment and decided there was no way this man drove like an overcautious senior citizen.

Her knees a bit wobbly all of a sudden, she sank into the passenger seat and took a deep breath when he closed her door. He was grinning ear to ear when he climbed behind the wheel, and after a few seat and mirror adjustments, he started the engine with the push start. The car roared to life, the big engine rumbling when he revved it.

"Nice," he said before shifting into reverse and peeling out of the parking spot. He did several donuts in reverse, narrowly missing a curb, before screeching to a halt and shifting into first. Caitlyn clung to the console and her armrest to hold herself steady and blinked at him before bursting into laughter.

"Ah, the allure of an empty parking lot," Owen said, doing several more donuts, this time in the forward direction, before finally turning into traffic.

He was a bit more cautious on the road than she was and spent most of the drive cussing out idiots while at the same time courteously letting other speed demons into his lane without cutting them off.

"So why do you drive a Jeep when you obviously love a fast car as much as I do?" Caitlyn asked.

"I tend to ignore curbs," Owen said.

The smile dropped from Caitlyn's face. "Now you tell me."

"I promise I won't damage your car. I only take curbs in the Jeep because I can."

Traffic wasn't bad for a Sunday afternoon—and good compared to the typical weekday bumper-to-bumper crush—so they made it to her home in record time.

She was laughing at what was probably whiplash from being

slammed against the seat when Owen screeched to a halt in her driveway, but her wide smile—and the day's fun—evaporated when she recognized the familiar Mercedes parked there.

"What the fuck is he doing here?" Caitlyn narrowed her eyes. "He's supposed to be in Rome banging his coed all summer."

"You have a visitor?" Owen asked, looking far more morose than he had for a single second that entire day.

"That's my ex-husband's car." She hoped it had materialized in her driveway without its owner attached.

"We could, uh, just leave," Owen suggested, suddenly looking way younger than her. Embarrassingly younger. Not quite college-freshman embarrassing, but definitely younger.

"He better not be in my house," she said as she opened her door, climbed out of the car, and slammed it with the fury she always felt whenever Charles invaded her life.

It turned out he was in the house. She'd had the locks changed, but she still kept her spare key in the place they'd always kept it, so he hadn't had any difficulty finding it.

"Breaking and entering!" she shouted at him when she found him lounging in the den reading some dusty work of literary fiction.

The bastard had the audacity to look even more gorgeous than usual with his newly acquired tan and stress-free expression as he lifted his head from his book.

"Ah, Caity dear," he said. "I was hoping you'd turn up soon. I tried to call . . ."

He lifted his hands and shrugged. A lock of dark hair curved over his high forehead. The traces of gray flecking his otherwise perfectly maintained short hairstyle made him look more attractive, not less so. And those deep, inquisitive eyes of his still managed to make her feel exposed. Not her body—he'd never ruled her body the way Owen did. But her soul and her mind, those were the parts of her that he'd always understood best.

"Aren't you supposed to be in Rome?"

The small smile that twisted the corner of his mouth wasn't even slightly happy. "Rome was magnificent, as usual. Remember when we went to the Colosseum and discussed what it must have been like there at the height of the Roman Empire?"

Of course she remembered. Fondly even. And she didn't want to entertain fond memories of her marriage to Charles. She wanted to remember it as all bad so she could continue to despise his very existence. She crossed her arms over her chest and glared at him.

"You need to get out of my house, Charles. You have no business being here."

He rose from the wing chair and set his book in his seat. He took a step toward her, looking all tall and stern and in control of himself. But not in control of her. Not anymore. Caitlyn forced herself not to take a step back.

"I made a mistake, Caity. She's nothing like you were at the beginning."

"You do not get to come here now and try to make amends, Charles. You tried to destroy me in the divorce. Tried to take my company, tried to force me from my home." He'd definitely stripped her of her pride, but she wouldn't give him the satisfaction of admitting that to his face.

"Those things were *ours*," Charles said. "Not just yours. Ours."

"Just because we were married when I built the business from the ground up and used some of the earnings to build my dream house—"

"Our dream house," he interjected.

"*My* dream house, does not mean any of it was *ours*," she spat at him. All her hard work had been responsible for their financial and business success. Her hard work, not his.

"That's the definition of marriage, Caity. What's mine is yours, what's yours is mine."

But he didn't have anything. And it still pissed her off that she had had to buy him out of both the business and the house—millions upon millions of *her* hard-earned money—when they'd divorced. She was still making fucking alimony payments because most of her money wasn't liquid but was tied up in her successful business. She'd done that—all of that—with no help from him, and no one would ever convince her otherwise.

"Don't you mean what's mine is yours and you have nothing to offer me? Never had anything to offer me?"

"I didn't come here to fight, Caity."

"Stop calling me Caity!" It was much too intimate. She could still hear the way he whispered her name when they'd made love. Caity was what he'd called her when they came together.

"Um, Caitlyn?" Owen spoke from behind her.

Fuck! How long had he been standing there? Maybe not long. Charles hadn't even registered his existence. But then Charles had a way of making a person feel less than human and inferior without even trying.

"I think I should bail," Owen said. "Give me a call when you get this sorted out."

"No, don't leave. I don't want you to leave, I want him to leave." Caitlyn threw out a hand in Charles's direction.

"He's cute," Charles said with a dismissive chuckle. "I wondered why there were vibrators, dildos, and condoms all over the house. I guess you're more like me than you want to admit. Sex with the young and inexperienced is always more fun."

Owen's brows scrunched together. "Did he just call me inexperienced?"

Caitlyn laughed, some of the tension draining from her body. She'd almost forgotten that a man could make her feel something other than angry. A man didn't have to subject her to constant condescension. A man—this man—could make her feel happy and good about herself. Good about being with him.

"So where did you pick him up?" Charles asked.

"A sex club," Owen said. "I'd like to thank you for pissing her off so much that she was giving off men-suck vibes. Her attitude scared off all the other men in the room long enough for me to approach her."

There was something embarrassing about Owen sharing details with Charles. Embarrassing, yet karmic. She wanted that affronted look on Charles's face to be captured, enlarged, printed, and framed so she could remember it eternally.

"Well, when you've had your fill screwing this *boy*," Charles said, "and are looking for something more substantial, I'd like to talk."

Caitlyn scowled. "What makes you think what I have with Owen isn't substantial?"

Charles lifted his brows, and she again hated that he was Pierce Bronson handsome. She wished he was as ugly as he made her feel—like a snot-and-wart-covered troll.

"Maybe by the way you're walking. Sex isn't everything, Caity. You need to have more in common to make a relationship work for longer than a few weeks."

Charles brushed past her, bombarding her with his familiar scent. She still liked the way he smelled. The way he looked. The sound of his voice. But she couldn't stomach the way he spoke to her like she was still that naïve freshman who cared more about his opinions of her than her self-respect.

"Says a man who never fucked his wife in an elevator or on her desk," Owen called after him.

"Owen," Caitlyn said, shaking her head. The dig was unnecessary and gave some substantiation to what Charles had said. Sex wasn't everything, yet it was all she was prepared to share with Owen at the moment. Charles's intrusion had somehow diminished her already superficial relationship with her sweet rock star. And when she heard the front door close as Charles saw himself out, it was exactly the figurative cold shower she needed to finally get her head on straight.

"Maybe you should go," she said to Owen, crossing her arms over her chest and staring at the wall. She no longer felt like going to the beach and picnicking as they watched the sun set. The only reason they were going there was to have sex again, to check off another fantasy from her list. And she was no longer in the mood for fantasies.

"Do you want him back?" Owen asked, turning toward the doorway through which Charles had just walked.

"Of course not," she said, "but maybe now you can see why I'm not ready to get serious with another man. Not even someone as good and kind as you. It's too soon. I need to find more of me before I have anything to offer you but my body."

"I can help you find yourself," he said. "You've come out of your shell so much already since we've been together."

She smiled sadly. "That's just the part of me that complements you, Owen. It's not all of me. Not much of me, really. Just like when I was with Charles. I showed him the parts of me that complemented him. So when I began to find myself— especially my ambitious side—we no longer worked. I don't want to end up in the same place with you."

Owen's jaw was hard, his eyes a bit glassy. She could tell he was struggling with emotion, but she couldn't give him much wiggle room.

"I thought this relationship was just about sex," he said, the crack in his voice shredding her heart.

"It can be," she said. "If that's what you really want, then stay. I can handle that sort of relationship with you and discard you when I get bored. But if you want something more—and today has shown me that I do want more—you have to give me some time to sort myself out. And you have to go."

He stared at her for a long moment. Part of her wanted him to stay and ruin any future they could have together by them fucking until they tired of each other, but the bigger part of her needed him to make the decision that being with her was worth more than the blistering hot sex they shared. They could have both the serious, fulfilled relationship and the amazing sex life if he was patient. Just a little patient. She didn't expect him to wait around forever, just until the ink was dry on her divorce papers and she figured out what her next step was going to be. She'd really thought she'd be single for a while—a long while—not fall for her rebound guy.

"I had a wonderful time with you this weekend," Owen said, tugging her into a gentle embrace.

He kissed her temple, and she blinked back tears. She was the one forcing him to give her time to find herself, so she didn't have the right to cry. At least not in front of him.

"I hope you don't keep me waiting for long. I don't think I can stand it," he said. "Goodbye for now."

He kissed her just long enough to make her heart ache and then turned. She clung to the hem of her shirt so she didn't reach for him as she watched him stride away. He'd chosen her—not her body—but *her*. So why did she feel so fucking miserable about it?

CHAPTER FOURTEEN

DURING THE DRIVE BACK to Austin, Owen had had a long time to second guess his decision to leave Caitlyn even temporarily. It was obvious that her *old* ex-husband—dude had to be pushing fifty—wanted her back. Owen trusted that Caitlyn just wanted a little time to sort through her feelings, but he didn't trust that ol' Charlie would stay away for long. Owen just had to make sure the ex- stayed away longer than he did.

Owen had just tossed his overnight bag into the mudroom when his doorbell rang. A small part of him wondered if Caitlyn had already decided she'd made a mistake and had followed him home, but he probably would have noticed her bright yellow Camaro in his rearview mirror, so he went to the door to investigate, not in the mood to listen to a salesman's spiel or have his soul saved by Jesus or even endure a friendly visit from a neighbor. Peeking out the postcard-size window in his front door, he groaned aloud. Normally he'd have been happy to see his mom—and tell her about his latest heartache—but she had Lindsey with her. Since he'd last seen her yesterday morning, he'd almost forgotten Lindsey existed. Her presence on his doorstep was like a bucket of ice water thrown over his head.

He opened the door.

"I saw you drive by," Mom said. "I thought you were going to be out of town until tomorrow."

"Change of plans," he said.

"Can we come in?"

He wanted to say no, especially when he noticed Lindsey was staring at him all doe-eyed as she clutched a plastic container to her chest, but he couldn't tell his mother to get lost, so he stepped aside and ushered them in.

"We have a little problem," Mom said.

And they were hoping he could fix it, so he said, "How can I help?" Why did he have to be such a nice guy? Or maybe he was a doormat.

"Lindsey had an asthma attack in her new place, so I called Ben and he came out and tested for mold."

There was one reason to continue to be nice like his mom, Owen mused; nice sometimes earned benefits. Busy contractors like Ben didn't usually drop everything on a weekend to test for mold.

"It's everywhere. Apparently the apartment shower has been leaking behind the walls for months, and we're going to have to rip it all out and redo it."

"I'll grab my tools," Owen said.

"You don't need to do that," Mom said. "We've already hired Ben to do it."

Which meant the job would be done right, but they'd have to wait months.

"I can at least rip out the old stuff. Get the mold out of there so she doesn't have another attack."

"She can't stay there without a functioning bathroom, Owen. She's pregnant." Mom squeezed Lindsey's arm. "And pregnant women definitely need a functioning bathroom."

He refused to look at Lindsey, knowing that if he did, he'd give in to her plight. "I can give you some more money. I'm sure you can help her find a place nearby. There's an apartment building over on—"

"Owen," Mom interrupted, reaching out to pat his hand. Now *she* was giving him the doe eyes. "There's already a place nearby that she can stay for free."

Owen's stomach dropped. He knew what she was going to ask of him.

"It's preferable that you two are married before you live together, but she can keep an eye on your house while you're gone, and I'll be just a block away if she needs anything."

"Joan," Lindsey said, "this isn't a good idea."

"Of course it's a good idea," Mom said.

"I'm not marrying her, Mom," Owen said. Might as well get that all out in the open. "I know you're old-fashioned and think the parents of a child have to be married—"

"Old-fashioned?" Mom interrupted. "It's not old-fashioned to want what's best for my grandchild. So even if you aren't married to the mother of your child, I don't understand why she can't live here. It's not like you'll be home much before the baby is born anyway."

"Mom," Owen said, trying to reason with her without breaking his promise to Lindsey. He wouldn't tell her that there were other potential fathers. And he did want to help the woman. But he absolutely did not want her to live in his home. His home was his sanctuary, and if Lindsey moved in, he'd be the one with no place to go. "She's not moving in here."

"Just until they get the bathroom remodeled," she bargained. "Ben promised it would only be a few weeks."

"I don't want to be a burden," Lindsey said.

"You're not a burden, doll," Mom said, patting her shoulder before turning a harsh glare on Owen. "And I can't believe you insist on making her feel like one."

"Me?"

"Yes, you. You get a sweet innocent girl in trouble . . ."

Owen couldn't hold back his scoff. Lindsey might be a lot of things, but innocent wasn't one of them.

". . . and then make her feel like a villain."

"I'm not the villain either, Mom."

"I know that, sweetheart. Just think about it, okay? I'm sure she doesn't want to stay at my house in your old room with posters of half-naked starlets staring down at her."

For some reason, the thought of Lindsey staying in his childhood bedroom was even worse than her sharing a roof with him.

Lindsey handed him the plastic container she'd been holding. "Your mom taught me how to bake your favorite cookies."

And thus it began, the war against Owen's bachelorhood. He should have known better than to bring Lindsey to his mother. He'd thought he'd have less to worry about if his mother was around to look after her, but his mom didn't just take in strays, she made them a part of her family. And with a baby in the equation, of course his mother would get attached to the young woman and share her oatmeal cookie recipe with her.

"Thanks," Owen said, accepting her thoughtful gift. He opened the lid, selected a cookie, and stuffed it into his mouth. He was going to need the entire batch to get him through this night.

"So she can stay here until the bathroom is remodeled, right?"

Owen swallowed the sweet, chewy delight in his mouth.

"She'll be lonely here by herself. I leave tomorrow. She doesn't know anyone in Austin but me."

"And me," Mom said.

"I won't be lonely," Lindsey said. "I'll be too busy to be lonely. I'm going out looking for a job tomorrow, and then I'll be working."

That didn't change the fact that he didn't want her to live with him. Even if the baby was his, he'd have a room for the child in his house so he could be a part of the baby's life, but he didn't want to get involved with Lindsey. Even if it would make things easier on all of them.

"Lindsey—"

Lindsey grabbed his arm, her pretty blue eyes searching his. "Owen, I promise as soon as I have the funds, I'll move out. Even if the bathroom remodel isn't finished. I'll find my own place."

"I thought you loved the apartment," Mom said.

"I do," Lindsey said, giving Mom a quick hug. "The little office would make a perfect nursery."

She might as well have punched Owen directly in the gut.

"There's that lovely park on the corner," Lindsey continued. "And the rent is so reasonable."

Owen knew apartments in the area were not reasonable at all. Unless she found a really good job—and he hoped she did—she'd be raising his kid in a low-income area. If it was his kid, and even if it wasn't, he was sure any father would want what was best for his baby and the baby's mother. Living here was what was best for everyone. Except for Owen.

He selected another cookie and said, "You can stay at my place until the bathroom is remodeled."

"Oh, thank you," Lindsey said, hugging him tight. "I'm keeping track of everything you do for me, Owen. I will pay you back."

"Unnecessary," Owen said, stuffing the cookie into his mouth.

"Charity is given without expectation of reciprocation." Mom repeated a saying she'd taught Owen when he young.

"This isn't charity," Lindsey said. "It's just a loan."

Owen swallowed the cookie. "Lindsey, you don't have to—"

"A loan," she interrupted him, ferocity in her eyes.

"If it will make you feel better."

"It will."

Mom was all smiles as she went out on the porch and picked up Lindsey's overnight bag. Owen rolled his eyes. His mother had known he'd cave long before she'd arrived.

"I'll see you Tuesday morning and take you to meet Dr. Kurt. She delivered Owen. Did you know that?"

Lindsey smiled. "Thanks, Joan."

"She can borrow your Jeep to job search tomorrow, right?" Mom asked Owen. "If not, I can cancel my appointments and drive her around."

His mother was a master manipulator, yet he knew she really would cancel her appointments and not complain about being Lindsey's taxi.

"She can borrow it, but she'll have to take me to the airstrip in the morning unless I can get one of the guys to give me a lift."

"Of course I'll take you," Lindsey said. She blinked at him, her eyes wide with incredulity. "Are you really going to let me borrow your car?"

"Just until we can get yours here from Oklahoma." He still wasn't sure how they'd accomplish that feat. If he'd had more time off, he'd have taken a road trip.

"You are the sweetest guy," Lindsey said. He tensed when she hugged him.

"I'll leave you two alone," Mom said, looking far too pleased for Owen's comfort.

Within seconds Mom had vanished and he really was alone with Lindsey. He sighed and picked up his bag and hers and carried them upstairs. He heard her light footsteps on the stairs behind him, but he wasn't in the mood to talk to her. Kelly was the one he wanted to talk to. The guy always gave the best advice, and Owen could use a truckload of the stuff at the moment. But Kelly was undoubtedly busy with Dawn. He hadn't even answered his phone when Owen had called him on the drive back to Austin.

"I hope you don't mind me asking . . ."

Lindsey shifted from foot to foot when he dropped off her bag in the guest room. He was pretty sure he was going to mind her questions very much.

"What do your parents really charge to rent that place? It's way too nice to charge what they do. They could easily get three times that amount, I'm sure."

"They don't get anything for it most summers," he said, "because they're fair enough to give students a nine-month lease instead of charging them for a full year. So they're actually making extra money off you."

She rolled her eyes. "What a bunch of crooks."

"New shirt?" Owen asked, nodding at her soft blue tunic. It made her enlarged belly very noticeable.

"And pants. I kept all the receipts so I can pay you back."

That again. "Look, Lindsey, you don't have to pay me back for anything. It's a gift."

"I don't feel comfortable accepting gifts from people I hardly know."

"Would you feel comfortable if we were married and having a baby together?"

She released a soft gasp, and Owen mentally kicked himself for putting that image in her head.

"Go ahead and keep your receipts if it makes you feel better," he said.

She nodded, still looking at him like he was her personal savior.

"Whoever fathered the kid will pay me back."

"I'll pay you back," she insisted.

Damn, the woman was stubborn, but then maybe he was making her feel incapable of paying her own debts.

"Don't forget to ask that doctor to do one of those early DNA tests." There. Now she wouldn't think he was such a nice guy.

"You expect me to ask for a paternity test in front of your mother?"

"She won't be there through the entire appointment." As soon as he said it, he knew he was wrong. His mom would totally be there for the entire appointment. She'd probably take notes and write dates on her calendar in whatever color she chose to represent Lindsey's schedule—Owen's was orange, Chad's was red, Dad's was blue, and Mom's was purple. She'd even kept track of Kelly's high school schedule in green. Owen supposed Lindsey's schedule would be written in pink.

With a heavy sigh—he'd done this to himself by trying to pawn off his responsibility for Lindsey on his mom—he dropped his bag in his room and checked his phone. Nothing from Caitlyn.

Nothing from Kelly.

"Have you eaten?" Lindsey asked. "I can make you something."

"You already made me cookies."

"Why are you home early?" she asked in a rush, as if she'd lose the courage to ask if she spoke at a normal pace.

He glanced up from his phone and found it too dark to read her expression in the dim pink-tinged light filtering in through the windows. That light reminded him that he was supposed to be picnicking on the beach with Caitlyn right now. He was supposed to be making love to her in his Jeep while they watched the sun set over the Gulf.

"Something came up," he said vaguely. "I'm really tired. I think I'll go to bed early."

"It's not even nine o'clock," she said.

"Make yourself at home." He closed his bedroom door.

"What time do we need to be at the airstrip in the morning?" she called through the door.

"Not until noon." Which meant he'd have to spend even more time in her company. He felt like a prisoner in his own house.

"Okay. Good night."

He waited until he heard her move away from the door before he flopped back on his bed and rubbed his face with both hands. He checked his phone again, in case he'd somehow missed a message or call, and after staring at the darkening ceiling for several long minutes, he chanced texting Kelly. Maybe he wasn't having the time of his life with Dawn. Maybe he was as miserable as Owen felt at the moment.

Caitlyn says she needs time to find herself and wanted me to leave. What exactly does that mean?

He was surprised when Kelly responded almost immediately.

It means she's too nice to dump you outright.

So it's over? If that was the case, he should have just stayed for the sex. At least that was something. This waiting for her to figure shit out was nothing.

Sounds like it. Sorry.

Fuck. How's Dawn?

Amazing. I gotta go.

Owen knew he should be happy for Kelly, but Owen was miserable and alone. He'd very much like some company in that feeling, though he doubted anyone was half as miserable as he was. Well, with the exception of Lindsey. Her life was even shittier than his. Lying across his bed, staring at the ceiling wasn't making him feel even slightly better, but he knew something that would take his mind off his troubles for a couple of hours.

He pulled himself to his feet and opened his bedroom door. He could see Lindsey in her room, unpacking her overnight bag and tucking her belongings into the dresser he kept empty for visitors.

"You want to go out?" he asked.

She sucked in a startled breath and spun in his direction.

"To a movie," he added.

"Like on a date?"

There he went giving her the wrong idea again. "Friend outing."

"I can't affor—"

"Yes, a date. And where I'm from, the guy pays and the gal doesn't make him feel like an ass about it." Anything to get her off her running-a-tab mantra.

Her pretty blue eyes brightened with her smile. "I'd love to go to the movies with you. Just let me pee first."

They were halfway to the movie theater when he asked, "When a woman asks you to wait for her while she finds herself, does that mean she's dumped you?"

"Did Caitlyn dump you?"

"I don't know. That's why I'm asking you."

"She's an idiot. Doesn't she realize how great you are? You're perfect, and she doesn't deserve you."

"I think she does realize how great I am." He smirked and tried to find a good parking spot so Lindsey didn't have too far to waddle. "Her ex-husband showed up, and they got into a huge fight."

"That's not good. If they're still passionate enough about each other to fight, they still mean something to each other."

Owen hadn't thought about it that way. "She said she doesn't want to get back together with him."

"But she doesn't want you either."

"I'm not sure." He pulled into a parking spot and shut off the engine. "Should I call her?"

"You'll seem desperate."

He nodded at her wisdom. "So I'll just obsessively check my cell all night."

Lindsey laughed. "The modern version of waiting by the phone."

"Yep. Except now you can go out to a movie while you wait."

They chose a slapstick comedy, which was good. They both needed a laugh. In the concession line, Lindsey had insisted she didn't want popcorn, but her hand kept dipping into Owen's giant tub of buttery kernels the entire movie. At least she'd let him buy her a Sprite without mentioning she owed him. Sharing a straw would have been far more intimate than he was willing to go.

As they were leaving after the show, an older woman smiled at them and said, "Such a lovely young couple. When is your baby due?"

Lindsey glanced sidelong at Owen, her mouth opening and closing as she struggled to answer.

Owen smiled at the curious woman, placed a hand on Lindsey's distended belly, and said, "Mid-September."

The woman giggled. "I know what someone was doing around Christmas time last year."

Uh, probably not exactly what they'd been doing, but an exchange of genetic material had been involved.

"Congratulations," the woman said. "Any baby of yours will be a blue-eyed little cutie pie."

"Thanks," Owen said.

The woman patted Lindsey's belly without permission before she wandered off through the theater lobby.

"Thanks for handling that," Lindsey said to Owen. "I never know what to say."

"When you're with me, we'll just let everyone assume the baby is mine. It will make situations like those a lot less awkward."

Lindsey turned toward the exit. He was pretty sure she muttered something like, "That woman is a fucking idiot," as she waddled off. Maybe Lindsey was referring to the nosy stranger, but he figured she was actually referring to Caitlyn. Which reminded him to turn on his phone.

She still hadn't contacted him.

Just how many hours did it take a woman to find herself, anyway?

CHAPTER FIFTEEN

CAITLYN PACED back and forth as she spoke to Jenna on the phone. Thank God she had someone to talk to about what she'd done. She'd been flipping out by herself for a couple hours by the time she thought to call her best friend. In Caitlyn's jumbled head, Owen was already out with some other woman, and she'd been forgotten. "I should call him, right? Reassure him that we're not over."

"When did you suggest he leave?"

Caitlyn checked the digital clock on her oven. "A few hours ago."

"He's going to think you're indecisive if you call him this soon."

"I *am* indecisive," Caitlyn said. "I thought I wanted time to find myself, and yet within ten minutes of him walking out the door, I'd already decided that I'm an idiot. I can figure myself out some other time. Not now. Now is not the time to find myself. Tomorrow would have made more sense."

"This is like Charles all over again," Jenna said in her voice of reason. Caitlyn hadn't listened to it in college, so what made Jenna think she'd listen to it now?

"He's nothing like Charles," Caitlyn said. "Owen is kind and considerate. He's always lifting people up instead of bringing them down. He's cool and funny and ridiculously attractive."

"And great in bed."

"Yeah, whatever," she said, though his sexual expertise was an undeniable fact. "That's not what I miss about him. I miss his smile and his laugh. The way he says my name."

"Oh my God, Caitlyn." Jenna's voice burst through Caitlyn's daydreams of Owen. "You're in love with him." It was an accusation, one that made Caitlyn's breath catch. "How could you let this happen? You just got divorced."

"I know. That's what I've been telling myself all weekend. I shouldn't let myself have feelings for him yet; it's too soon. I *know* it's too soon." And yet she definitely felt something for Owen. A lot of something. And it wasn't just lust.

"At least you have a bit of sense. It was smart of you to put on the brakes when you did."

"I don't feel smart, I feel lonely." She traced the edge of the kitchen counter with one fingertip, staring down at the swirled marble surface but not really seeing it. "What if he forgets about me?"

"He won't; how could he? You're fabulous. And if he cares about you, he'll wait a little while. You don't need to see him again right away."

"Even if I don't see him, I should call him, right? Let him know I'm still interested." Like she had when Lindsey had shown up and Caitlyn had run from him. She hadn't lasted fifteen minutes before she'd called to make amends. Did that make her a pathetic loser? "I just need an hour or two to figure myself out, decide what I want to do with my life."

Jenna laughed. "An hour or two? I've been trying to figure myself out for thirty-two years, and it still hasn't happened. I have no idea what I want to do with my life."

"I'm afraid if I don't call him, he'll think I dumped him. I don't want him to think I dumped him. I didn't mean to dump him."

"Is he really going to go off and date some other woman right away? He won't do that if you mean anything to him. He's probably as torn up about this as you are."

Or more so. And she knew enough about him to realize he healed his ego with women and his heart with food. She didn't know which she'd damaged more—his pride or his sentimentality.

"He definitely has his choice of women," Caitlyn said. "And he loves going to sex clubs." The collection of her kitchen-fantasy implements still resting on the kitchen island caught her attention. Had it really been only yesterday that he'd taken her over that stool and spanked her while he fucked her?

"Caitlyn? You still there?"

"Yeah."

"Promise you'll listen to my advice."

"I'm listening."

"You have to wait at least forty-eight hours before you call him."

Caitlyn cringed. "What? No, I can't wait that long." Why had she sent him away in the first place? She could have waited and sorted herself out while he was on tour. Granted, the man was an expert at mixing her emotions and lust into a frenzied slurry, but she wouldn't have spontaneously combusted in the twelve hours they had remaining together that weekend. "How about two more hours."

"Two days, Caitlyn, not two hours. Why did you send him away if you're only going to beg him to come back?"

"I don't know—that's why I called you. You're supposed to help me figure this mess out."

Jenna sighed. "I'm trying, but you aren't listening. Take a deep breath."

Caitlyn gulped air and leaned against the kitchen sink, gazing out the window. She stared at the glass roof of the gazebo, her thoughts instantly replaying making love with Owen beneath the stars. That was when she'd started to care about him. She'd been brimming with emotions the entire time and had woken the next morning still feeling tenderness for him. Wasn't the morning after supposed to be awkward? Wasn't she supposed to have come to her senses after a good night's sleep rather than losing them altogether?

"Repeat after me," Jenna said. "I, Caitlyn Marie Mattock."

"Hanson," Caitlyn corrected. She'd decided to go back to her maiden name in the divorce.

"Even better. Say it."

"I, Caitlyn Marie Hanson."

"Do solemnly swear."

Caitlyn repeated the words.

"Not to call Owen for forty-eight hours."

"Not to call Owen for . . ." Caitlyn hesitated.

"Caitlyn?"

"Twenty-four hours," she said. "That's more than long enough."

Jenna released another sigh, but apparently decided not to press the issue. "Okay, now set an alarm on your phone and under no circumstances are you to call him until it goes off."

Caitlyn figured that for the next day she'd be staring at her phone alarm like it was the countdown on a doomsday device.

"Okay."

"Stop thinking about him," Jenna said, and Caitlyn snorted. "And use this time to think about what you want. You don't have to give up everything to be with him."

"I wasn't planning on giving up everything."

"But you were considering it."

Her friend knew her too well. Caitlyn couldn't deny she'd been wondering if it was time to retire and sell her house and follow a rock band around the country. And that might make her happy for a little while, yet she needed more in her life than a man to love. But she did want a man to be a part of her life, and that was something she hadn't anticipated wanting ever again after her marriage had fallen apart.

She chatted with Jenna for a few more minutes, fighting the urge to wax poetic about the time she'd spent with Owen—she really was pathetic when she was newly in love. As soon as they said their goodbyes, she followed Jenna's advice and set the alarm on her phone. She was glad she had to work the next day. That might keep her mind off Owen for a few hours. But then, there were plenty of memories of him in her office, the elevator, and her car. There would be no escaping him.

The most terrifying part of that realization was that she didn't want to escape.

CHAPTER SIXTEEN

WHEN OWEN'S EYES OPENED the next morning, the first thing he did was reach for his phone. The last time he'd checked it—for the thousandth time—it had been four a.m. It was now six, and Caitlyn still hadn't called. Still hadn't texted. It really was over between them. With two hours of sleep under his belt, he tossed on his workout clothes, yanked on his cross-trainers, and rushed to the bathroom. He had a few hours before he had to leave to meet the chartered plane that would take him back to New Orleans. He planned to spend them all at the gym working out his frustration. He also needed to work off all that popcorn and those oatmeal cookies he'd eaten the night before. The bathroom door was closed, and he didn't think to knock when he barged right in.

Lindsey gasped, one bare foot still in the tub, the other on the floor as she reached for a towel.

"Sorry!" Owen slammed the door.

He'd never seen a pregnant woman naked before. Seeing Lindsey's body—so lush and full of life—stirred a mix of strange feelings in him. It wasn't lust—not in the general sense—but longing and wonder and admiration.

"Weird," he said aloud as he turned from the door. "I'm going to the gym," he yelled over his shoulder and waited for her muffled *okay* before he raced down the steps and used the half bathroom downstairs. He grabbed his keys with the gym membership fob and jogged—more like sprinted—the four blocks to the gym.

Working out did relieve his stress, but it gave him a lot of time to think. No matter how hard he tried to concentrate on his form and no matter how many repetitions he counted, he couldn't stop thinking about Caitlyn. He would call her when he got home, he decided, wiping the sweat from his face with a towel. He should probably respect her wish for space, but what about *his* wishes? He didn't want space, he wanted her.

He'd fallen into the same trap before. He'd move too fast, then the woman would ask to slow down and for him to give her space. He'd stubbornly refuse to do either, and she'd wind up pushing him away for good. Maybe Owen was insane for thinking that repeating the same action would get him different results this time, but he had to believe that someone out there was willing to take a chance on someone like him, a guy who could easily center his entire universe around one special person. And he convinced himself while doing hundreds of angry sit-ups that his one special person was Caitlyn.

His jog home was a bit slow—he'd expended too much energy at the gym—but he felt better. He let himself into his house through the mudroom and found Lindsey in the kitchen nook, scouring a newspaper with a pen between her teeth. Should he apologize for barging in on her when she'd been getting out of the shower or just pretend it had never happened?

Her eyes lifted from the newspaper, and the pen tumbled from her mouth as her jaw dropped and she gawked at him.

"Sorry, I must reek," he said, suddenly self-conscious about his soaked clothes and his sweat-drenched hair that was probably sticking out in all directions. He lifted the hem of his shirt to dab sweat off his face, hoping to make himself marginally presentable.

"You look . . ." She swallowed. "Really hot."

He wasn't sure if she meant hot as in attractive or in the sense that he was overheated and dripping sweat, so he said, "I'm going to jump in the shower. We need to leave in a couple of hours."

She pulled her gaze from him and moved it to the thick Sunday newspaper in front of her. "I found a couple of jobs in here that I'm qualified for."

"That's great," he said.

"You want breakfast? I can make eggs or something." She refused to look at him for some reason.

"That would be awesome. Thanks."

He hurried upstairs and took a cool shower. He was in a fantastic mood by the time he was dried off and dressed. He hoped Caitlyn was awake. It was Monday, and her vacation was supposedly over, so she probably had to work. He dialed her cell number.

"I'm not supposed to talk to you for another eight hours," she said. He could hear background noise—road noise, maybe. A car honked. He decided she was in the car, most likely braving Houston morning traffic.

"Why eight hours?"

"I promised Jenna I wouldn't call you for twenty-four hours. That was at around six last night. It's now a little after ten. Eight hours."

He chuckled. "You're good at math."

"I actually have a countdown timer on my phone."

He laughed again, surprised it was so easy to talk to her. He'd imagined this conversation being a lot more difficult. Of course, they hadn't said anything important yet. "I want to see you," he said. "Soon."

"Don't you have to go to New Orleans for a show tonight?"

"Yeah," he said. "You can meet me there."

"I'd have to skip work to pull that off."

"So? You're the boss. You can take off whenever you want."

"Actually . . ." Her voice faded before she yelled, "Get the fuck out of the fast lane, Grandpa! You're making me later than I already am."

Owen heard the loud blare of a horn and the roar of the Camaro's engine as she maneuvered around Grandpa.

"Actually," she repeated, now speaking to Owen again, "I can't take time off *because* I'm the boss. People depend on me."

"Oh," he said flatly.

"So I'm thinking of taking on another partner—an engineer who can do some of the tasks I do. That way I can take more time off work. Eventually. That can't happen overnight."

He was probably jumping to conclusions by thinking she was considering that step so she could spend more time with him, but he couldn't help it. She wouldn't have mentioned it if it wasn't related to him in some way, would she?

"Owen, your eggs are getting cold," Lindsey called from the bottom of the stairs.

"Be down in a minute."

"Where you are?" Caitlyn asked.

"I'm at home."

"And there's a woman in your house concerned about your cold eggs?"

"It's just Lindsey," he said.

"She's staying at your house?"

Owen ruffled his hair with his towel one last time before tossing it into the hamper. "I don't want to talk about Lindsey. I want to talk about us."

"I thought she was at your mom's."

"She was, but circumstances changed and—"

"Are you fucking kidding me?"

"What? No, she needed a place—"

"Don't call me again, Owen."

The phone went dead in his ear and going against her final demand, he immediately dialed her number again.

"I said don't fucking call me!" Caitlyn answered and then hung up on him before he could get in a single word.

"Owen!" Lindsey called up at him. "Are you coming?"

He growled at his phone and shoved it into his pocket before thundering down the steps. He glared at Lindsey—the reason for all of his problems—and she skittered back. "Sorry to rush you," she said.

"Caitlyn heard you."

"You were talking to Caitlyn? I thought she dumped you."

"Apparently she hadn't, but thanks to you, she has now."

He strode into the kitchen with Lindsey tagging along behind him. He stopped at the edge of the table, already feeling guilty for snapping at her.

"I didn't mean to cause you problems," she said.

He knew that, and he couldn't be mad at her. She'd made him a breakfast of scrambled eggs, sliced tomatoes, toast, and orange juice. Her identical plate sat beside his untouched, growing cold while she waited for him to join her.

"It's not your fault," he said before he sat down. "I'll get things with Caitlyn sorted out." After he got some food in his belly, he'd text Caitlyn and explain everything to her. She'd demanded that he didn't call her—she hadn't said anything about sending text messages.

About halfway through breakfast, his phone dinged with a message. He knew it was rude to check his phone while he was sharing a pleasant meal with Lindsey, but he couldn't help himself. The message was from Caitlyn.

Don't text me either, Owen. I mean it. I'll talk to you when I'm ready to talk to you. Not before.

His shoulders dropped, and he sighed as he stuffed the phone back into his pocket. He was really in the doghouse here, and he hadn't done anything wrong. Unless taking your baby mama to a late night movie and seeing her naked was wrong. He didn't think they counted since nothing had happened between him and Lindsey. Seeing her nude hadn't even given him a stiffy. But how could he assure Caitlyn of the platonic state of his relationship with his new roomie if she wouldn't take his calls or read his texts?

"Maybe I should send her flowers again," Owen said.

"She's stupid," Lindsey said, nibbling on her toast. "You deserve better. She should be nicer to you."

Her *I would be nicer to you* was left unspoken, but Owen could read it in the way she leaned closer to him, as if he needed her to offer comfort.

"She's great, you know," Owen said. "If she wasn't, I wouldn't give two shits that she dumped me." And he still wasn't clear on that little detail. Was there potential for them to reconcile? He had to believe there was, or he'd end up doing something really idiotic—like waiting naked for her in her office with a rose clamped between his teeth.

Desperately wanting to change the topic of conversation—he didn't need or want relationship advice from Lindsey—he asked, "So what did you find in the paper?"

"There's a bank teller job I could do. It doesn't pay well, but has benefits."

"Were you a bank teller before?" She might have told him months before, but if she had, he'd forgotten.

"I started as one, then I trained to be an investment broker. I'd finally found my stride and was making good money for the bank when my boss found out about—" She folded her arms around her middle and hunched forward. "Well, you know. And she fired me."

"She fired you for fucking a rock band?" He'd heard of some pretty stupid reasons to fire someone, but that had to take the grand prize.

"She fired me because she's always hated me. She used my reputation—it being bad for business—as her excuse to get rid of me. I'm from a small town with two banks. She's the president of one, and guess who's the president of the other?"

"Her?"

"Might as well be. It's her good ol' boy daddy, who should

have retired about twenty years ago. The man is eighty years old."

"Hey, I plan to still be rocking the stage on my bass when I'm eighty."

"That would be awesome—Sole Regret, the geriatric years." She giggled. "I'd definitely pay to see that."

Owen smiled. He liked making her laugh. She'd been so anxious and defensive since she'd shown up with her baby on board, he'd honestly wanted to dump her off on his mother and never interact with her again. She'd been super fun and adventurous when they'd shared that wild night of sex on the tour bus on Christmas Eve—no holds barred and anything goes. Still, he supposed any woman in her current position would be anxious and defensive. But she didn't have to feel that way around him.

She glanced at the time and squeezed out from behind the table, collecting her plate and putting it in the sink. She turned on the water to clean the skillet, but Owen jumped up from the table and nudged her aside. "You cooked; I'll get the dishes."

"But—"

"I insist. Plus my mom would skin me if she knew I made you cook and do the dishes."

"You didn't make me," Lindsey said, her thick lashes shielding her wide blue eyes. "I wanted to."

She wanted to what, play Susie Homemaker? With him? And in the house she'd told him was perfect for raising kids? He shuddered.

"Uh, why don't you see if you can figure out how to get your car back?" he suggested. "Call Oklahoma State Patrol. They should be able to tell you how to proceed."

She nodded slightly and then sat down with her cellphone to look up the appropriate phone numbers online. She was talking with someone when he went upstairs to pack a bag and collect dirty clothes to throw in a load of laundry.

When he came back down, Lindsey followed him into the mudroom to watch him load the washing machine.

"Did you know they dispose of vehicles if they aren't claimed within thirty days and if they do, you still have to pay all the impound and storage fees in cash?"

"That's to encourage you to get your piece of junk out of their hair as quickly as possible."

She scowled at him. "It's not a piece of junk. I ran out of gas."

"And then hitched a ride with a trucker."

"Don't remind me of how stupid I was. I was running on pure adrenaline at that point. I had to get to Houston before you guys took off for your next tour stop."

She just couldn't wait to find them and ruin some lives. Owen mentally slapped himself; it wasn't fair to blame her for how things had turned out. He was ashamed of himself for even thinking she was trying to ruin anyone.

"I need to get to the airstrip." He'd arrive extra early, but maybe someone else in the band was as desperate to leave home as he was. He was drowning in estrogen here.

"I'm ready when you are."

"I hope you can drive a stick." He hadn't even wondered if she could handle the Jeep's standard transmission.

"If I have to," she said.

She ground only two gears before she dropped him off in the parking lot where the band members usually parked their cars to catch a chartered flight. He was the first one there, but didn't mind waiting. Adam had stayed in New Orleans, and Kelly would be driving from Galveston, so it was no surprise when neither of them showed up, but as the small plane arrived and they allowed him to board, he was surprised that Gabe and Jacob hadn't turned up yet.

As their scheduled departure time got closer and closer, he began to worry. He squeezed through the narrow aisle and stuck his head into the cockpit. "Where is everyone?" he asked the copilot, who was scowling at a clipboard.

"Well, the tall guy—what's his name?"

Gabe and Jacob were both well over six feet, but Gabe was of thinner build and so seemed much taller than broad-shouldered Jacob. "Gabe?"

"Mohawk guy."

"Yeah, that's Gabe."

"He and his girlfriend went back to New Orleans last night. Some emergency."

Owen's heart dropped. "What kind of emergency?"

"They didn't share details. I think it had something to do with a friend of the woman's. I don't know for sure, but she was extremely upset."

"Did Jacob leave with them?"

"Nope. We're still waiting for him."

"So it's just me and Jacob on this trip?"

"Assuming he shows up."

Of course Jacob would show up. He was the most responsible, driven member of the band. Hell, he'd missed the birth of his own daughter to keep Adam from dying of an overdose. Jacob was the guy they could all depend on. He always did what was right.

"I'll just sit and wait then," Owen said. He took a moment to call Gabe to see if he could help with the emergency the copilot had mentioned. When Gabe didn't answer, he left a voicemail and also sent him a text to assure him that he could ask Owen for help—no matter what the emergency—if he needed anything.

Jacob eventually entered the plane, and Owen beamed at him, glad he finally had a friend to talk to. Since Jacob brushed past without so much as a howdy and plopped into a seat at the back, Owen unfastened his seat belt and moved to the seat across from him.

"Have a good weekend?" Owen asked.

"Most of it," Jacob said, not so much as glancing Owen's way. He was obviously in a bad mood. "Where's Gabe?"

Owen shrugged. "The pilot said he flew back last night. I have no idea why."

When Jacob didn't comment, Owen tried broaching the subject of his situation with Caitlyn. Maybe Jacob had a suggestion on how to proceed. He was always smooth with the ladies. "Well, I'm in the doghouse, but—"

"I'm going to catch a nap," Jacob interrupted.

Owen ignored the sting of Jacob's rejection. Still, he needed an actual bro to talk to, yet now that the plane was taxiing, he couldn't even call or text Kelly. Owen realized too late that he should have contacted Kelly while he'd been waiting for Jacob to board.

"Uh, okay," Owen said. "I wonder what Kelly's up to."

While Jacob pretended to sleep, which was pretty hurtful, Owen occupied himself with a shooter game on his phone. He couldn't remember ever wanting to be back on the road so much in his life. He usually treasured his time at home, but he needed the normal give and take of the band and the routine of playing. Maybe he'd get to talk to his brother this evening; Chad's calls from Afghanistan always cheered him up. And he'd get to see Kelly soon. That also cheered Owen up. They rarely spent a day apart, and Owen legit missed the guy.

In New Orleans, after a bit of a mix-up at the hotel's front desk—Adam apparently had their keycards—he and Jacob went upstairs. Jacob seemed a bit more amenable to conversation in the elevator, but Owen no longer felt like sharing his problems with the jerk, so he decided to wait in his room until the concert.

Once there, he checked his messages—one from his mom asking if he knew anyone who could get Lindsey's car in Oklahoma and one from Lindsey saying she hadn't completely destroyed his transmission but that she'd feel more comfortable driving her own vehicle. No messages from Kelly or Caitlyn. Since he was forbidden to contact Caitlyn, he called Kelly. When Kelly answered, Owen could hear road noise in the background.

"Glad you called. I was getting really bored," Kelly said.

"How far out are you?" Owen didn't mind talking on the phone, but he much preferred face to face conversations.

"I got a late start this morning," he said. "If traffic cooperates, I should get there about an hour before we go onstage."

"Oh." That sucked.

"How are you holding up?" Kelly asked. "I know what you're like after a chick dumps you."

"She didn't dump me. At least I don't think she did. I'm not sure. She's none too happy about Lindsey living with me."

"Lindsey is living with you? I thought Mom was going to take her in." Kelly had called Owen's mother Mom since he'd been in junior high.

"She tried. My parents were going to rent the apartment to her."

"That's a nice place."

"Was a nice place." Owen caught Kelly up on the mold situation and ended by telling him that Caitlyn had overheard Lindsey calling him down to breakfast.

"Well, you know how you could have avoided the entire situation."

"How?"

"Told her up front that Lindsey was living with you and not tried to hide it."

"I wasn't trying to hide it. Lindsey wasn't staying at my place when I'd last spoken with Caitlyn. Circumstances changed."

"So you really want to make this thing with Caitlyn work?"

"I do."

Kelly sighed. "Whatever makes you happy. I'm stopping for gas now. I'll see you when I get into New Orleans."

"Okay," Owen said. He didn't realize he hadn't asked Kelly about his weekend with Dawn until they hung up. They'd have plenty of time to catch up later.

Owen was drifting in and out of sleep across the hotel bed when his phone rang. He was absolutely stunned to see the caller was Caitlyn. He glanced at the clock radio—exactly six p.m. Wasn't that when she'd said she was allowed to call?

"Hello?" he answered. "Caitlyn?"

"Okay, I have a list of all the things I want to say to you," she said, her words rushed, as if she'd lose her nerve if she didn't blurt everything out at once. "Please hold your questions and comments until the end."

He laughed at her making a list—it was definitely something she'd do—and at her treating a phone call like a press conference.

"Number One," she said.

And of course she'd number the list.

"I don't like that the pregnant girl is staying with you, but I understand that you feel obligated and want to help her out, so I won't throw a big fit about it. If she's staying with you, there can be no touching. I mean it. I will throw a fit about that."

"No touching Lindsey," he said, smiling at her bossy tone. "Got it."

"Number Two. I regret sending you away when I did. We could have enjoyed the rest of our weekend without me suddenly having to find myself. Charles reminded me how I get when I fall in love. I completely forget who I am and focus on complementing the man I'm with."

"You're in love," he said, his smile broadening. "Got it."

"Don't put words in my mouth, Owen."

"You're the one who said it."

She chuckled. "Fine. Number Three. I checked your concert schedule and see that you'll be in Atlanta on Thursday. If I take a flight right after work, I think I can catch the tail end of the concert and spend the night with you. Take Friday off and hang out with you all weekend."

"You can't wait to see me again," he said. "Got it."

"I'm trying to be serious here."

"How's that working for you?"

"It was going well in my head, but I can't seem to stick to my agenda when you're involved."

"I don't do agendas," he said, "but I can compromise, and I do want to see you again as soon as possible because I have feelings to confess and I don't want to do it in a line-itemed list over the phone."

"You got a problem with how I confess my feelings?"

He could hear the teasing laugh in her voice. He wished he could also see it on her face.

"No problem," he said. "I just do things a bit differently."

"That's good. So do I. I just have to keep reminding myself that it's okay to be me."

"It's better than okay. You're amazing."

"I should have just driven to New Orleans instead of pacing my office all day. I'd have almost been there by now."

"Are you finished with your list? I have a few things to say as well."

"No. It has twenty-four points."

"Twenty-four?"

"Well, some of them are pretty specific and not that important."

"So summarize for me."

"I want to be your girlfriend."

"Done," he said.

"I want to meet your family."

"This is getting serious," he said.

"We need to spend less time with our clothes off. I can't so much as sneeze without feeling you were inside me."

He grinned. "How about we compromise on that one? One solid fuck with the stud in my piercing per day. No more."

"Amending list item Seven," she said.

He could actually hear the sound of her pen scraping against the page as he assumed she added a note to her list.

"Unlimited fucking without the stud in."

"Yes," she said. "That's good. Unlimited fucking. Okay, Number Eight."

"Caitlyn?"

"Yeah?"

"Why don't you fax your list to me and we can discuss it at our next meeting."

"I'm being silly, aren't I?"

"You're being wonderful you. I just want to make sure you add my items to your list before I have to go. They'll be calling me to the bus for sound check and dinner soon."

"Oh, sorry for keeping you."

"Owen's list Number One: no making me wonder for twenty-four hours if I'm going to see you again. Dump me for real or keep our line of communication open."

"Good one," she said. Again he could hear her scribbling.

"Owen's Number Two: no more lists."

"I need lists," she insisted.

"Okay, but you don't have to share them with me. We can operate on different levels and still work together."

"That's the part that freaks me out. We're so different."

"That's the part that makes this exciting."

"It is exciting."

He kept her on the line until Jordan came for him.

The guys hung out on the bus before they had to head backstage and prepare for the show. Except for Kelly. Kelly hadn't made it back yet. Adam, who was apparently inspired by his woman leaving him, was having a great songwriting day. Owen couldn't remember the last time the lyrics and music had flowed so easily for him. The entire band was riding Adam's creative high. Owen was in a better mood now that he and Caitlyn had talked and she'd made her list of plans, so he joked around with his bandmates like old times. The camaraderie between them actually felt normal for a change.

About an hour before the show, Owen began to feel that something was wrong. The band was getting along better than it ever had and was currently goofing off backstage with some VIP guests, so that bit of anxiety was missing and couldn't explain the dread he was feeling. Kelly still hadn't arrived, and Owen started to think maybe something terrible had happened to him. They'd been friends so long that he sometimes thought they shared a psychic link. He called Kelly to put his mind at ease, and Kelly answered on the first ring.

"I'm stuck in traffic. Some accident has the entire highway closed. I hope I can get to the show in time."

"You're okay, though?" Owen asked.

"Of course. Other than being highly annoyed. Sorry to worry you."

"Like I'd ever worry about you." But he had been worried, because even though he was talking to Kelly, something still felt wrong. "I'll let the guys know you might be late."

"I refuse to be late, even if I have to hydroplane this rental car through the bayou."

Owen laughed at the mental image and told Kelly he'd see him soon. He called Caitlyn next. She was fine and not even slightly annoyed that he'd called. He phoned his mom and asked how her day with Lindsey had gone—maybe something was wrong with the baby. But all was well on the home front too.

"Did Chad call you tonight?" Mom asked.

Chad! That was why he was feeling off. His brother called every couple of nights. It wasn't unusual for him to miss calling; he was a busy soldier, after all. But that had to be why Owen felt off. "Maybe he called Josie." Chad was less likely to miss calling his long-time girlfriend than his parents and younger brother.

"Nope. That's why I asked if he called you. Josie asked if I'd heard from him."

"I'm sure he's fine," Owen said, clutching the dog tags around his neck and sending a silent prayer to his brother's protector. He almost let it slip to Mom that they'd be seeing Chad soon, but remembered in time that Chad had sworn him to secrecy. Chad wanted to surprise everyone by returning from his tour of duty unannounced.

"I'm sure he is too," Mom said. "Don't worry about Lindsey and the baby. I'll take good care of them while you're away."

Owen bit his lip to hold back a laugh. Did his mother imagine he was sitting around ringing his hands over Lindsey? She'd be sorely disappointed by her son in that regard. Lindsey was out of sight, out of mind.

Owen texted several people on his contact list—including his grandmother—to assure himself that everyone was okay. Yet he still couldn't shake the feeling that all was not right in the world. While Owen was saying goodbye to his "perfectly fine" cousin Pete, Kelly rushed behind the stage, joining the rest of the band just minutes before they were to go on.

"You made it," Owen said, slapping him on the arm.

"Remind me never to *drive* from Galveston to New Orleans again."

Owen glanced around. He'd suspected it when he'd talked to Kelly in the car, but the lack of a woman in tow confirmed his suspicions. "Dawn didn't come back with you?"

Kelly shook his head. "We're trying to sort out where we go next."

Owen scratched his jaw. "Yeah, Caitlyn and I hit that point as well. Fortunately, we talked it out and are moving forward."

Kelly offered him a weak smile. "That's great."

Owen frowned. He felt Kelly was feigning enthusiasm, but he threw off his concern to ask, "You ever get the feeling that something is wrong? Or that something bad is about to happen?"

"Sometimes," Kelly said.

"I've been feeling like that for about an hour. I called a bunch of people, and everyone assures me they're okay, but this feeling of dread won't go away."

"Where's Adam?" Jacob unexpectedly interjected himself into Owen and Kelly's conversation.

Owen glanced around, not seeing any sign of their lead guitarist, and shrugged. "No idea."

Jacob turned his attention to the black guitar—Adam's favorite—sitting in a stand next to the stage. "He left his guitar."

"Maybe he had to go to the bathroom," Kelly suggested, his grin wide. "Ever try to take a piss with a guitar strapped on?"

"Can't say that I have," Jacob said, his gaze trained on the double doors that led to the dressing room.

Maybe that was what was giving Owen unshakable anxiety. Maybe something had happened to Adam during the minutes Owen had been contacting almost every person he knew. As far as he knew, Adam hadn't been using heroin again, but he had been working on his songwriting today, and in the past he'd abused drugs to get the edge he needed to write. Owen was grateful when Jacob sent a couple of roadies to search for the missing guitarist, praying they wouldn't find him in some bathroom stall suffering another heroin overdose.

They waited in terse silence for signs of the guitarist. Gabe eventually came down from the stage where he'd been waiting behind his drum kit to start the show. "What's the holdup?"

"Adam's missing," Jacob said.

"Missing?"

"Yeah, he was just here."

And it was as if he'd vanished.

"Should we go look for him?" Owen asked Kelly.

"Let the road crew handle it. We wouldn't want them to have to round us all up again when they find him."

Except when the crew returned about ten minutes later, Adam wasn't with them.

"He wasn't in the bathroom or the dressing room," one roadie said.

"Not on the bus either," another told them. "I found his earpiece on the ground behind the bus. At least I think it's his."

The guy dropped the earpiece into Jacob's outstretched hand. "Was his motorcycle still there?" Jacob asked.

"I didn't see one."

"Fuck!" Jacob yelled. "Did he say anything to any of you?"

When Jacob's glare landed on Owen, Owen shook his head and glanced at Kelly, who shook his head as well.

"Fuck!" Jacob shouted again. "What in the hell is he thinking?"

The feeling of dread intensified in Owen, so strong that he rubbed at his chest. And Owen figured he knew what had caused it. "Maybe there's an emergency." It seemed the only logical reason why their lead guitarist would leave right before the show without telling anyone where he was going.

"Even if there is, he could have taken a few seconds to tell someone," Jacob said.

That was true. Unless he was unconscious.

"Fuck!" Jacob yelled his favorite word again. "I'm going after him."

"Do you know where he went?" Gabe asked.

Jacob checked his phone, and Owen realized he was tracking him with that creepy app he had installed to keep tabs on their recovering-addict guitarist.

"Fuck!" he yelled when apparently the app confirmed his fears. "He's headed west."

"What's west?" Kelly asked.

"Texas. Madison. His fucking heroin dealer. How the hell should I know?"

"Calm down," Owen said. Throwing a tantrum wouldn't get

them anywhere. "We'll figure something out."

"I'll try calling him," Kelly said in a calm voice. Owen was glad one of them was calm. Even Gabe was pacing now. "Maybe he'll answer."

"What's going on?" Sally said, announcing her arrival backstage. "Why aren't you on stage?"

"Adam isn't here," Jacob said. "We can't perform without our lead guitarist, can we?"

"I'm worried," Owen said, his eyes on Kelly as he shook his head to let them know Adam wasn't answering his phone. "He wouldn't just run off like that unless it was a life or death situation." Adam was in trouble. Not the regular trouble that followed the guy like a plague, but trouble that caused him to run off without saying a word. Huge trouble.

"Yes, he would."

Of course Jacob would contradict Owen's assessment of the situation. Jacob was incapable of seeing the world through anyone's eyes but his own.

"I was the one who dealt with him when he was at his worst. You all pretended everything was just fine while I was forced to get him lucid enough to perform. It was only a year ago. Don't tell me you've already forgotten."

Of course they hadn't forgotten. And while Jacob had taken a very exasperating hands-on approach to Adam's struggles with addiction, the rest of them had tried to keep the bomb of a relationship between the two of them from exploding and taking them all out.

"He's changed, Jacob." Gabe clutched the back of his neck with one hand as he stared at the floor.

"He has?" Jacob shook his head, his angry voice finally going soft. "Sorry, but I don't see it."

Without another word, Jacob climbed up on stage and took his microphone out of its stand. What the fuck was he doing?

"Good evening, New Orleans," he called out to the audience. "You look ready to rock!" They cheered in anticipation. "Unfortunately, our performance is not going to happen tonight. Our lead guitarist, Adam Taylor, was called away on an emergency. So we have to cancel the show."

At least he hadn't thrown Adam under the bus and claimed he was a thoughtless, irresponsible asshole who hadn't bothered to tell anyone where he was going. Owen truly believed that Adam *had* been called away on an emergency. An emergency so terrible that he'd forgotten his other responsibilities.

A roar of discontent reverberated through the stadium. The crowd didn't seem too forgiving of Adam's troubles.

"I'm not sure if they'll issue refunds or reschedule the performance," Jacob said, "but we'll square you away. I promise."

"This is a fucking nightmare," Gabe said.

"Understatement of the century. The fans are pissed," Owen said. And he couldn't blame them. If he was in their shoes, he'd be pissed too.

Within a minute Jacob was back to calling out to the crowd and asking them to stay. What the fuck was he thinking? They couldn't go onstage without a lead guitarist.

A moment later Jacob ushered a skinny teenage boy in a black beanie into the backstage area. Now what was he up to?

"Did you get ahold of Adam?" he asked Kelly.

Kelly frowned and shook his head.

"Okay." Jacob nudged the wide-eyed kid forward. "This guy says he knows all our songs by heart and can take Adam's place onstage tonight."

For real? Owen highly doubted that, but he was willing to give this solution a shot. None of them wanted to disappoint the fans. The fans made the whole rock star gig possible.

"So I say we give him a chance to prove himself," Jacob said. "What's your name?"

"Wes."

"Give Adam's guitar to Wes," Jacob said to Adam's technician. "Let's see what he's got."

Surprisingly, the kid was an excellent guitarist. Not as good as the professional he'd be temporarily replacing, but he had definite talent.

They gave Wes his shot in the spotlight, and he didn't let them down. Jacob even managed to get the audience behind the young man's one night as a rock star. Owen felt guilty for allowing someone to fill Adam's shoes. Maybe they should have just canceled the show, but fan satisfaction was more important than his feelings of loyalty. He just hoped Adam would be back for their next show. They couldn't continue without him for long.

They played through their entire set list and when the concert was over, Owen couldn't get to the tour bus fast enough. He wanted to put tonight and New Orleans behind him. He still had a niggling feeling that something was terribly wrong. He kept expecting the state patrol to call and tell them that Adam had been involved in a deadly accident.

"I actually think Jacob was okay with that little scenario," Kelly commented as he flopped down next to Owen on the tour bus sofa.

"More than okay with it," Gabe said. "I think he preferred it. He had Sally get that kid's information."

"He's a nice kid and all," Owen said, "but . . ."

". . . he's no Adam Taylor," he, Kelly, and Gabe finished in unison.

Jacob was near the back of the bus, ignoring them, or maybe just putting off the conversation they had to have. Turning their backs on Adam was not an option, yet Owen was pretty sure Jacob had already done so. He would probably never forgive Adam this time. Disappointing his bandmates was one thing; letting the fans down was an unforgivable offense. And Owen was pretty sure Jacob had never truly forgiven Adam for all the shit he'd put them through in the past. Tonight was one more brick of a burden stacked on an already laboring relationship.

"Anyone hear from Adam yet?" Jacob asked nonchalantly.

None of them had.

"I've had it with his bullshit," Jacob said. "Adam's out of the band."

The entire world flipped upside down. Owen blinked to reset his reeling mind and managed to say, "What?"

"He's toxic," Jacob continued. "We need to get rid of him. Replace him with someone who takes our success seriously."

"Adam writes all of our music," Kelly said. "We can't just kick him out."

And not only that, he was a freaking amazing guitarist. They worked in perfect harmony on stage and in the recording studio, even if their personal relationships were a bit rocky—on par with the mountain range kind of rocky—but they cared about each other.

"We'll write the music ourselves and if necessary, hire songwriters," Jacob said with a shrug.

Songwriters? *Songwriters!* They couldn't hire fucking

songwriters. No songwriter could ever match the feel of their music, the sound of it, or the purpose behind it. Had Jacob lost his fucking mind?

"This is bullshit," Kelly said, giving voice to Owen's jumbled thoughts. "Adam is one of us. He's always been one of us. We can't do this to him."

"We don't even know why he took off," Owen added. "I'm sure he had a good reason."

"More than two hours later, and he still hasn't checked in to let us know what the fuck is going on!" Jacob yelled. "He obviously doesn't give a shit about any of us or the fans or the music. All he cares about is himself. It's time to cut him loose. If he wants to destroy himself, fine, but I'm not letting him take the rest of us down with him."

"I want to hear what he has to say before I weigh in," Gabe said. "For all we know, he's dead in a ditch somewhere."

Owen went light-headed. "Don't even say that." It was very possible that Adam *was* dead in a ditch somewhere. In fact, he was almost sure of it. They hadn't heard from him for hours.

Then again, maybe he was too afraid to call them, knowing that Jacob would likely overreact.

"It would save me the trouble of telling him to fuck off," Jacob said in a growl of a voice.

Owen couldn't believe he would say that about a friend. A brother. Not a brother by blood, maybe, but they'd been through so much together, they had important bonds. "You're such an asshole."

Jacob got in Owen's face, so close that their noses were almost touching. "I'd rather be an asshole than a spineless wuss."

"What's that supposed to mean?" Owen shoved him away. What a fucking prick. Just because Owen didn't march around like some self-important blowhard didn't mean he was spineless or a wuss.

"You're a pushover, Owen. You always have been."

"Don't take your frustration with Adam out on Owen," Kelly said, placing a calming hand on Owen's thigh. "You're the one who never bends. You're the mighty oak, standing tall and rigid against any force that threatens your position." He slammed his other fist against his own chest.

"Someone has to be strong."

"Listen to what Kellen is trying to warn you about," Gabe said. "If you never bend, you will break, Jacob. Don't you see that? We'll figure out what to do after we talk to Adam."

They listened to Jacob's solution that Kelly play lead or that they replace Adam outright with a new guitarist. Neither option was a solution as far as Owen was concerned.

"I just want Adam gone," Jacob spat. "And not temporarily. For good."

Owen shook his head. How could he even think that was the best solution, much less suggest it? "What's wrong with you? I'm sure he'll explain everything when he gets back. He deserves a second chance."

"A second chance?"

Owen nodded, and Kelly's hand tightened on Owen's leg. At least he and Kelly were on the same page. He still wasn't sure about Gabe, who'd withdrawn completely into himself.

"He's already had a hundred second chances," Jacob said. "Or more! He's gone too far this time. I'm not putting up with his shit anymore. So if you won't get rid of him, then I'm out of here."

"What?" Gabe's head snapped up as he stared at Jacob, looking stunned.

Best idea Jacob had had all evening as far as Owen was concerned. He was currently beyond his limit with the inconsiderate jerk. "There's the door." He jabbed his thumb in the direction of the exit.

Jacob's jaw dropped, and Owen was glad to see something had derailed him. He was on a collision course with the band's demise. This decision of his affected everyone, not just him. Not just Adam. Not even just the band members, but the crew, the fans, and even their record label.

"So Owen chooses Adam over me," Jacob said. "What about you, Kellen? I'm sure you'll go along with whatever Owen says since you can't live without each other."

"Fuck you, Jacob," Kelly said.

Indeed, Owen thought, glad Kelly had his priorities straight.

"Don't do this, Jacob. It isn't worth it," Gabe said.

Jacob's shoulders sagged as his last possible ally chose the other side. He bit his lip and nodded. "I guess this is goodbye then. Good luck with Adam. He's only going to drag you down with him. I guess you'll just have to see it for yourself. I'm through being his buffer. None of you have any idea how bad he can get—you have absolutely no clue. But you'll figure it out soon enough, and I might have already moved on."

Jacob grabbed his overnight bag and headed to the front of the bus, where he instructed Tex to pull over.

After some argument, Tex eased the bus onto the shoulder of the road.

"What do you think you're doing?" Gabe asked.

Owen exchanged a concerned glance with Kelly. If the band was really breaking up, that was one thing. But tossing Jacob out on the side of the road in the middle of nowhere was unquestionably wrong.

"I'm leaving," Jacob said.

"Be reasonable, Jacob." Gabe tried to soothe him with a hand on the shoulder, but Jacob shrugged it off. "We can work through this. Stay. Let's talk about it."

"Open the door," Jacob said to Tex.

Before Owen could even rise to his feet, Jacob was off the bus. Gone. Jacob was gone.

"Great fucking plan, Jacob," Gabe yelled out the door. "This doesn't solve a goddamned thing. Jacob!"

"Let him go if that's what he wants," Kelly said. "God knows he's a stubborn son of a bitch."

"He might get hit by a car," Owen said, but Jacob didn't return. Instead, Tex pulled back onto the road, and Owen watched in disbelief as the dark figure walking up the deserted shoulder disappeared from view.

"What the fuck just happened?" Gabe asked, turning from the exit to stare at them. "What the *fuck* just happened?"

"Jacob just screwed us all, that's what happened," Kelly said.

"Did Sole Regret just break up?" Owen asked, grabbing Kelly's arm to steady himself. "Did he actually leave? He's coming back, though, right? After we find Adam and Jacob clears his head, he'll be back."

"I'm not so sure," Kelly said. "I think we're through."

This could not be happening.

CHAPTER SEVENTEEN

CAITLYN BLINKED awake, her mind scrambling to identify the sound blaring from the nightstand by her bed. She rolled over and slapped around for her phone, noting that according to her clock radio, it was after midnight. Her phone rang again and slipped out of her fumbling hand, landing on the floor with a thud. Groaning, she rolled out of bed and lay flat on her belly, reaching under her bed to find the damned thing. This had better be important.

"Hello?"

"I'm sorry," Owen said. "I know it's late. Were you sleeping?"

Caitlyn rolled onto her back and rubbed at her eyes. "Yeah. But I'm awake now. Please don't tell me you woke me up just because you were thinking of me." Which would have been a nice gesture and something totally Owen, but she was tired and had to be up early for a staff meeting.

"My band broke up."

Caitlyn sat up and bumped her head on the corner of the nightstand. *Ow!* Wincing, she rubbed the smarting spot and flipped over to her knees. "What? What do you mean your band broke up?" Last she'd talked to him, Sole Regret was preparing to go on stage in New Orleans and he'd called just to make sure she was safe. Another very Owen thing to do.

"I mean Sole Regret broke up. Our guitarist took off right before the show, and we had some kid take Adam's place onstage, and then Jacob decided he'd had enough irresponsible behavior and he left."

"Did something happen to Adam?"

"I'm not sure. We still haven't heard from him. But I'm used to Adam doing stupid shit. This isn't like Jacob. He *left* us."

"Maybe once he cools down—"

"You sound like Kelly," Owen said. "I told you I had a bad feeling tonight. I should have expected something like this to happen."

"Where are you?" she asked. "You sound like you need a hug." And she had the sudden urge to be the one who gave him what he needed.

"We're on our way to Jackson. Sally is trying to get this shit sorted out and figure out if we're going to play tomorrow or if we should just cancel the show before all the fans show up and we have to turn them away."

"Sally?"

"Our tour manager."

"Do you want me to meet you in Jackson?"

He was silent for a long moment. "You'd do that?"

"Of course. I'd have to rearrange my schedule a little, but I'll be there for you if you need me."

He was quiet for another moment before he said, "I'm okay. Kelly and the guys are here with me. I just wanted to hear your voice."

"Are you sure?" She wouldn't have offered if she wasn't sincere about seeing him.

"If this show doesn't happen, we'll fly home to Austin tomorrow. Maybe you could . . . Never mind."

"I'll be there," she said. "Just be sure to give me a little warning so I can sort out my schedule and travel plans before I come running to you."

He chuckled. "You're so obsessed with my happiness, almost like you love me or something."

His tone was teasing, but she knew he wanted to hear her say the words. However, she'd wait until they saw each other in person to make that kind of confession. Eventually. Her head was still telling her to slow down, even if her heart was racing in the fast lane.

"If you don't want me to come to Austin—"

"I do. I just hope it doesn't come to that. We won't leave for Austin unless there's no way to fix things before the concert."

"Then I hope to see you in Jackson."

"I'll let you go back to bed," he said. "Sorry I woke you."

"I'm glad you called." She felt that he needed her support, and she was happy to offer it.

When they hung up, she crawled back into bed, but couldn't sleep. Her heart ached for him. His entire career had been turned upside down by the thoughtless actions of two people he considered friends. She could only imagine how devastating that would be. Caitlyn decided she'd be making a nuisance of herself and going to Owen no matter where he happened to be the next day. If he decided to take a trip to the moon, she'd find a way to join him.

Since sleep wasn't happening, Caitlyn got up and fired off an email to her staff, canceling their morning meeting and vaguely citing an emergency as her excuse, and then she packed a small suitcase. She couldn't predict where she'd be going the next day— Mississippi or Texas or the moon—but wherever Owen was, that was where she wanted to be.

~~~

Caitlyn didn't know what she'd expected Owen's house to look like, but as soon as she pulled into his drive, she realized the meticulously maintained blue cottage was perfect for him. She wasn't sure if he'd made it home yet—his flight from Jackson had landed a while ago, but she wasn't familiar with Austin's layout or how far the airport was from his house. He had texted her when he'd landed safely, but she hadn't heard from him since. His Jeep wasn't in the drive, but it might be in the small garage off to the side of the house. She'd try knocking and if he wasn't home, she'd wait for him in her car. Or maybe in that inviting porch swing that was swaying gently in the warm spring breeze.

She rang the front doorbell, and after a moment, a woman's voice called, "Who is it?"

Her heart froze in her chest.

Lindsey? Caitlyn had forgotten the woman was her boyfriend's temporary roommate. She shook off a spike of jealousy and said, "It's Caitlyn. Has Owen made it home yet?"

The door swung open, and Lindsey stood framed by the small foyer behind her. She placed a hand on her pregnant belly and smiled—it didn't quite reach her eyes.

"Oh, he'll be home soon. He's such a sweetheart, he ran to the store to get me some chocolate ice cream. You know what these pregnant cravings are like."

Caitlyn didn't, actually, and she wasn't sure if Lindsey's comment was meant to be a barb or just small talk. Lindsey wouldn't know how much Caitlyn had longed to have a baby. Even Owen didn't know that.

"That must be rough," Caitlyn said, hoping she sounded nicer than she felt. "At least you aren't craving pickles dipped in peanut butter."

"Actually," Lindsey said with a giggle, "that doesn't sound half bad." She stepped aside. "Come in. I'm sure Owen would be upset if he knew I'd kept you waiting on his doorstep."

Lindsey showed Caitlyn around the small yet homey interior of Owen's house as if she lived there—probably because she did. Caitlyn had left her suitcase in her trunk, but was now wishing she'd brought it inside so she could not-so-nonchalantly stow it in Owen's room. On his bed. The one he would share with Caitlyn and not with Lindsey that night.

Caitlyn mentally rolled her eyes at herself. What was she, thirteen? She took a breath and blew it out slowly, trying to assure herself that this beautiful, young, and pregnant roommate of Owen's wasn't a threat.

"Caitlyn?" She hadn't realized Owen was home until she heard him call her name.

"Upstairs!" she called back. He thundered up the stairs, and Lindsey was shuffled to the side as he pulled Caitlyn into his arms and kissed her as if it had been months rather than days since they'd last touched.

"I showed her around a little," Lindsey said.

Owen tugged his mouth from Caitlyn's, rolled his eyes, and then turned. "Thanks for entertaining my guest. Your ice cream is in the freezer."

He pushed Lindsey out into the hallway and closed the door in her face.

"Any word from Adam?" Caitlyn asked.

"He's in Dallas. His girlfriend fell off a horse."

Caitlyn cringed. "Sounds painful. Is Jacob ready to forgive him?"

"No one can find Jacob, so I guess not."

She touched his face, delighting in his beard stubble which was rough against her fingertips. The beard growth made him look a bit older. A bit rougher. She could easily get used to his less polished look. "I'm sorry you're dealing with this."

He kissed her again and tightened his hold, one hand sliding up her back to cradle her head and press her face closer to his neck. She inhaled his slightly musky scent and sighed in contentment. This was where she belonged. In his arms.

"Should I admit to you how excited I was to see a yellow Camaro parked in my driveway?"

"Probably not," she teased.

"Should I tell you how much I need to see you naked in my bed right now?"

"How about you show me instead?"

He undressed her slowly, filling his strong hands with her curves, his warm mouth with her flesh. He was trying out the technique Caitlyn had used on M at the sex club when an unfamiliar voice echoed through the house.

"Owey?" the woman called. "Come down and help us pick out tile."

Owen stopped moving, his fingers sliding out of Caitlyn's overexcited pussy, his suction going slack on her throbbing clit.

"Just how many ladies live with you?" she asked, lifting her head to look down at him and finding his face flushed with something other than excitement.

"That's my mom," he whispered.

"Does she know you're seeing me?" Caitlyn asked.

"Yeah, but just so you know, she's pulling for Lindsey."

Caitlyn bit her lip. Everything she knew about Owen pointed to him being a mama's boy. She wondered how much influence his mother's wishes held over his decisions. "And who are you pulling for?"

"You have nothing to worry about," he said as he slid from the bed. "Get dressed. I'll introduce you."

Caitlyn could still feel the thickness of his fingers stretching her pussy and the tug of his mouth on her clit. In addition, the rawness of his beard stubble had scratched into the skin of her thighs, turning her on, so she didn't much feel like meeting his mother at that exact moment. But when he collected her clothes and dropped them on the mattress beside her, she supposed she had little choice.

"Owey? Are you up there?" His mother's voice carried up the stairwell.

"Coming, Ma!" he yelled before turning to Caitlyn. "Hurry, baby. She's liable to come up here looking for me if we don't go down quickly."

Caitlyn struggled into her clothes, noting that Owen didn't help her even though he was still fully dressed. He basically stared at the door as if the thought of her naked with his mother in the house was completely mortifying. When Caitlyn was mostly presentable—assuming his mom didn't recognize her incriminating tousled hair for what it meant—Owen took her hand and opened the bedroom door.

"This shouldn't be my decision," Lindsey said, her voice drifting up from somewhere below them. "I'm just a renter."

"Oh, please," the other woman—his mother—said. "You're family, Lindsey. You can help me pick out tile for your bathroom."

"Hey, Mom," Owen said to the woman sitting on the sofa beside Lindsey.

She looked so much like her gorgeous son that Caitlyn's breath caught. When his mom rose to offer him a kiss, he quickly turned his head so that her peck landed on his cheek rather than on his lips. If the woman had any idea where her son's mouth had just been, she would definitely thank him for brushing her off.

"This is my girlfriend, Caitlyn."

Caitlyn's palms grew damp and her mouth dry. *Wow, Owen, way not to beat around the bush.*

"Oh!" His mother's eyes opened wide as they focused on Caitlyn.

"Hello," Caitlyn said with an awkward little wave.

"This is my mom, Joan." Owen nodded at his mom.

"Nice to meet you," Joan said with a welcoming smile—which instantly reminded Caitlyn of Owen's—and Caitlyn was surprised that she felt no animosity from the woman, especially if she was pulling for Lindsey.

"I think the gray," Lindsey said a bit loudly. "What do you think, Owen?"

"Um . . ." Owen turned to a large cardboard sheet with squares of tile affixed to it. He shrugged. "Sure."

"Or maybe the beige," Lindsey said, drawing her fingers over a sample. "This is pretty close to the tile you laid in your powder room."

Owen laid tile? Caitlyn thought he played bass.

"So how did you and Owen meet?" Joan asked Caitlyn.

Caitlyn's face burned with embarrassment. It was one thing to blatantly tell her ex-husband how they'd met, quite another to tell Owen's mother.

"At a club," Owen said. Not a lie, just an understatement of the truth. Caitlyn could handle that.

"Oh, oh," Lindsey said, covering her belly with one hand. "The baby is kicking."

Joan and Owen plopped down on either side of her, their hands searching Lindsey's belly for signs of baby movement. Caitlyn tried not to feel stabby toward the pregnant woman, but it was quite obvious to her that Lindsey was doing everything she could to wedge herself squarely into Owen's life. Rather Lindsey was pregnant or not, Caitlyn would not be putting up with her obvious ploys. Caitlyn couldn't have a frank discussion with Lindsey while Joan was present, though. If Caitlyn went off on Lindsey now, she'd likely earn Joan as an enemy, and she didn't want to start her relationship with Owen with that hanging over them.

"Do you want to feel him kick too?" Lindsey asked Caitlyn, throwing her so off guard that Caitlyn merely blinked at her.

"It's really cool," Owen said, his fingers and his mother's overlapping as they found the right spot.

Joan laughed. "He's got quite a kick! He's either going to punt footballs or be a swimmer."

"Football," Owen said. "I definitely vote for football."

Lindsey's adoring gaze as she stared at Owen had Caitlyn's hands balling into fists. Did he not see what kind of situation he'd gotten himself into here? Or maybe he wanted Lindsey. He definitely wanted the baby.

The amazed smile on Owen's face faded, and he sank back into the sofa, removing his hand from Lindsey's belly. "He stopped."

"You always calm him down," Lindsey said.

Owen lifted an eyebrow at her. "I do?"

Lindsey's laugh rang false as she patted Owen on the leg. "You know that."

Owen shook his head and then rose from the sofa to wrap an arm around Caitlyn's lower back. "Are you hungry? We should probably think about dinner. Do you want to go out or—"

"I have chicken thawed," Lindsey said. "I was going to fry it for dinner. There will be plenty."

"Is that okay?" Owen asked.

Eating a dinner that Lindsey cooked in Owen's kitchen? Yeah, *no*, that wasn't even slightly okay, but Joan was staring directly at her, so she plastered a smile on her face and choked out a yes.

"You can help me cook," Lindsey said, rocking forward to get her feet under her.

"Oh," Caitlyn said. "I don't cook."

Lindsey cocked her head. "You don't?"

"She's too busy changing the world to cook," Owen said. He kissed Caitlyn's temple.

Caitlyn appreciated that he stood up for her, but his defense didn't change the curious way Joan was suddenly looking at her.

"I can give you a hand," Joan said, standing.

"That's not necessary," Lindsey said. "Are you staying for dinner?"

"No, I need to head home and get supper started for James."

"That's my dad," Owen whispered next to Caitlyn's ear. "I'll take you over to meet him later."

It occurred to Caitlyn that Lindsey and Joan had a lot more in common with each other than she had in common with either of them. And didn't they say men always married women like their mothers? Panic clawed up Caitlyn's throat. If she was going to have any sort of meaningful relationship with Owen, Lindsey had to go.

Joan pointed to her tile samples and asked Lindsey, "Beige, then?"

"Gray," she said. "No, wait—beige. Or cream. Maybe cream."

"I'll leave this with you and you can decide," Joan said. "I need to know by tomorrow so we can get the tile ordered, okay?"

"I'll figure it out by then," Lindsey promised. She hugged Joan before waddling off toward the kitchen.

"It was a pleasure to meet you, Caitlyn," Joan said, taking her hand and clasping it. Her pretty blue eyes were both kind and welcoming, but Caitlyn still felt she was at a disadvantage when compared to Lindsey. "We need to get together while you're in town and get to know each other better."

"I'd like that," Caitlyn said.

"Lindsey and I are doing lunch after her appointment tomorrow; maybe you could join us?"

She wouldn't like that, but she said, "Okay."

"Mom, don't subject her to even more Lindsey," Owen said in a harsh whisper. "You should hang out with Caitlyn without her."

"Owen, you're not asking me to exclude Lindsey, are you?"

"That's exactly what I'm asking."

Caitlyn squeezed his hand, grateful that he understood how being around Lindsey made her feel.

Joan smiled at her son and reached over to cup his cheek. "Walk me out?"

Owen apparently figured that meant his mother needed a private word with him. He picked up the television remote and handed it to Caitlyn.

"Find something to watch, a ball game or something. I'll be back in a minute."

"Okay," Caitlyn said, watching him walk with his mother to the foyer. She wasn't the type to eavesdrop, but after she turned on the television, she silently followed them. She couldn't help herself. She needed to know if she'd be battling one woman or two for Owen's affection.

"You really like her, don't you?" Joan asked quietly.

"Madly in love with her," Owen said, and Caitlyn's heart skipped a beat.

"If you aren't careful, Lindsey is going to scare her off."

Not happening.

"You were the one who insisted she stay with me until the bathroom is finished," Owen said.

"I didn't realize you were so serious about Caitlyn. I was trying to help. I'm sure Ben will rush the bathroom repairs if I ask nicely."

"That would be awesome."

"That doesn't help you now, though. I'll call Lindsey after dinner and beg her to keep me company tonight. We'll have a girls' night in. That will give you and Caitlyn some alone time."

Owen blew out an audible breath. "You're the best, Mom."

Caitlyn slunk back into the living room, a wide smile on her face, and settled on the sofa. She had absolutely nothing to worry about. Owen's heart belonged to her. At least until that baby was born.

CHAPTER EIGHTEEN

OWEN CLOSED his front door and leaned against its solid back. He took a deep breath and let it out slowly. Mom seemed to like Caitlyn, and maybe now that the two had met, Mom would stop pressuring him about Lindsey. His career was still in shambles and his bandmates were acting like a bunch of idiots, but Caitlyn had Mom's approval, so he had one less worry.

He found Caitlyn in the living room, smiling to herself. He plopped down next to her on the sofa and kissed her cheek. "What are you grinning about?"

"I *love* your mom." Her eyes flipped upward with emphasis.

And now Owen was smiling as well. "She's great, isn't she?"

"She reminds me of my mom. I want you to meet her, and Daddy too."

Now *that* sounded serious. Owen's smile broadened. "I'd like that."

He leaned in to claim her mouth with his, but his phone chose that inopportune moment to ring, so he was only able to give her a swift peck instead of diving in for the deep, satisfying kiss he craved.

"Sorry," he said, scooping his phone out of his pocket and checking caller ID. *Adam.* Owen's heart hammered in his chest. He'd been waiting for this call all afternoon. "I need to take this."

Caitlyn smiled in understanding as he answered.

"Did you talk to Jacob?" Owen asked without greeting.

"I tried," Adam said. "He hung up on me."

After he'd taken off on his rented motorcycle, Adam hadn't contacted anyone for almost twenty-four hours. Owen had been on the phone with the Texas State Patrol to report him as a missing person when Adam had finally called Gabe and informed him that he was in Dallas because Madison had taken a nasty fall off her horse. Adam had agreed to try to sort things out with Jacob for the sake of the band, but if Jacob wouldn't even talk to him, how could they make amends and fix this fucking disaster?

Caitlyn linked her fingers through his and leaned against his shoulder to offer support. He was so glad she'd decided to make the trip from Houston to stay with him for a few days. She couldn't possibly know how great it felt to have her in his corner.

"Did you try going to his house to see him in person?" Owen asked Adam. Maybe Jacob would listen to him if they met face to face. Or maybe they'd come to blows.

"I'm still at the hospital."

In Dallas with Madison. "Of course," Owen said. "I wasn't thinking. I'll go."

"Don't bother. Gabe went to find him, but Jacob wasn't home." Adam released a long breath. "And there's a For Sale By Owner sign on his lawn."

"You're kidding."

"Nope." Adam snorted. "Maybe I should buy the place."

"That would really piss him off. How's Madison?"

"Sleeping. I might get to take her home tomorrow. Or maybe the next day."

"Jacob would have done the same thing if Amanda had been hurt." And Owen would have dropped everything for Caitlyn. He wouldn't have remained out of touch for an entire day, but he'd have gone to her, just as she had come to him. Of course, Owen had a huge network of support and knew someone would be there in a crisis if he ever needed help. Other than Madison, Adam didn't have anyone like that in his life. Jacob had once been that person, but that relationship had been strained one time too many. So Madison was Adam's only champion. Of course he'd panic if he thought he might lose her. Owen silently vowed to forge a stronger bond with Adam. The guy obviously needed more support, and Owen had failed him.

"He might," Adam said, his voice subdued.

"I could come to Dallas and hang out with you if you want." Owen offered his olive branch. Caitlyn squeezed his hand in encouragement, her support clear. He kissed her forehead to let her know he appreciated her.

"Nah."

Owen's phone beeped. "I've got another call. Will you hold on for a second?"

Before Adam could respond, Owen released Caitlyn's hand

so he could switch calls.

"Did you see that he's going to be on TV tonight?" Kelly asked

"Who?"

"Jacob. He's going to be on the local news to explain what's going on with the tour."

"So we're supposed to be on the news tonight? Nice of him to warn us." And nice of him to explain to *them* what was going on with the tour, because Owen was sure he wasn't the only member of the band Jacob had left out of the loop.

"Nope. Just him."

"What the fuck is going on with him?" Owen rubbed his forehead with his free hand. He was getting a headache. Jacob was giving him a headache. Maybe even a stroke.

"I think he's lost his shit entirely," Kelly said. "Have you heard from Adam or Gabe?"

"Actually, I have Adam on hold. Jacob hung up on him. I guess Gabe went to Jacob's house to hunt him down, but the ass wasn't there. Did Jacob mention anything to you about putting his house up for sale?"

"I'm telling you, he's lost his mind, Owen. I'm on my way to your place, so I'll see you in a few."

"Okay." Owen hung up and reconnected with Adam. "You still there?"

"No," Adam said, drawing a chuckle from Owen.

"That was Kelly. He said Jacob will be on the local news tonight."

"In Austin? I'm in Dallas, and I don't want to leave Madison, but—"

"Just him," Owen said. "A news segment *all* about him."

"What the fuck is his problem?"

Owen would say that Adam was much of Jacob's problem, that Jacob had finally taken all he could take from their lead guitarist, but there had to be more to the situation than that. Something with Amanda. Or with his daughter, Julie. "Maybe we'll figure it out if we watch the news. See what he has to say."

"So he'll talk to the media, but not to us?"

"I guess so."

Owen's doorbell rang, and Lindsey called from the kitchen. "I'll get it. It's probably your mom."

Or Kelly.

He would never ever get used to having Lindsey living in his house as if she belonged there. He'd come home to a spotless kitchen and she was an excellent cook. Owen didn't hate that she was living there. It just felt odd.

"I can get the door," Caitlyn said. "She's cooking."

And the fried chicken smelled fantastic.

But before Caitlyn could rise from the couch, Lindsey's hurried footsteps crossed the foyer next to the living room.

"I'll find out as much as I can and call you back," Owen said to Adam.

"I'm sorry I set Jacob off again," Adam said. "I should have told someone where I was going. I just panicked. All I could think about was getting to Madi as fast as I could."

"It's over and done with, Adam. We can't change any of it now." And Owen wasn't convinced Adam's disappearance right before a show was the reason Jacob had gone off the deep end. Part of the problem, sure, but not the only reason. Jacob had been acting strange on the plane from Austin too. "We have to move forward from here."

"Force!" Lindsey said at the front door. "We weren't expecting you."

We?

"Uh," Gabe said. "Hi, Lindsey. I didn't know you'd be here."

Because Owen hadn't exactly told his band that she was living with him. He hadn't told them Caitlyn was visiting either. They were sure to have him committed to an asylum when they found out he had two women staying with him.

"I'm staying with Owen until my apartment is ready."

"Gabe is here," Owen told Adam. "I'll keep you posted."

"Thanks, man," Adam said.

Owen pulled himself off the couch, shoved his phone into his pocket, and after offering Caitlyn a smile, hurried to the front door. Gabe looked a little queasy, as if he crossed the threshold, he'd be forever haunted by evil spirits.

It was funny that something as unthreatening as an unborn baby could strike fear into the hearts of rock stars, but Owen understood where Gabe was coming from.

"Come in. Make yourself at home," Owen said. "Did you ever reach Jacob?"

Gabe stepped into the house and followed Owen toward the living room. He stopped short in the doorway when he saw Caitlyn sitting on the sofa.

"Are you staying for dinner?" Lindsey asked him.

Gabe blinked at Owen, pretending Lindsey hadn't addressed him.

"Yeah, he's staying. Kelly is on his way too."

Lindsey lifted her brows. "And Caitlyn. So that makes five of us?"

"Sorry to keep adding to the guest list."

"It's no problem. You know I love to serve Sole Regret."

Owen managed not to laugh at her claim. She'd served them more than once.

Lindsey glanced longingly at Gabe, who still wouldn't look at her, and then hurried back into the kitchen.

"What is she doing?" Gabe asked, watching her retreating back until she was no longer visible.

"Trying too hard." Owen sighed. "She wants love and marriage and babies and to make a home."

"And you want?"

Owen smiled. "Caitlyn."

"And Lindsey still wants to live here? Even though you're not interested in her?"

"Yep."

Gabe shook his head, tugged off his baseball cap, and stuffed it into his back pocket. "If you don't know how stupid you are, there's no sense in me trying to explain everything that's wrong with this situation."

"It's just temporary." And Caitlyn seemed okay with it. Maybe. They hadn't had an opportunity to talk much with Lindsey turning up every few minutes.

"If you say so."

Gabe followed Owen into the living room and dropped into the chair next to the sofa. Owen returned to his spot next to Caitlyn.

"How are you holding up?" Caitlyn asked Gabe.

He smiled at her "Me? I'll be fine," Gabe said. "But I fear Jacob has completely lost his mind."

"That's the same thing Kelly said," Owen said.

"He's under a lot of stress," Caitlyn said. "You all are. Maybe he'll pull himself together."

"I don't think so," Gabe said. "There's a For Sale sign on his lawn. It says fully furnished."

"Fully furnished?" Owen asked. That sounded drastic.

"Yeah, like he's up and left his life, not just the band. His entire life."

"He wouldn't leave Julie," Owen said. Jacob could be a hardass and self-centered and a complete control freak, but his entire world revolved around that little girl. Jacob would never, ever do anything to jeopardize Julie.

"If he hasn't left town, then where the hell is he?" Gabe asked.

"Did you try talking to Amanda? Surely, she knows—"

"She refused to talk about him." Gabe massaged the back of his neck, refusing to meet Owen's gaze. "She started sobbing the moment I mentioned his name. I think they broke up."

"What? Why would he break up with her?" Owen had thought things were going well between Jacob and Amanda.

"I think *she* broke up with him."

"Poor guy," Caitlyn whispered, and Owen was glad she was there, but she didn't really understand the depth of Jacob's betrayal. Owen hadn't taken a decent breath for two days.

"I can't say that I blame her for dumping his ass," Owen said. "He's acting all weird. He got off the fucking bus in the middle of nowhere. Who does that?"

Gabe released a sigh and rubbed a hand over his face. "I'm worried about him. I know I should be pissed, but I'm worried."

Owen had started that way, but now he was just angry. They'd located Adam, and if Jacob would just pull his head out of his ass, Owen was sure they could straighten things out. But Jacob had his head jammed up there more securely than an industrial-size butt plug.

"Jacob can take care of himself," Owen said. "If he's scheduled a news segment, he obviously didn't get run over on the side of the road. He's avoiding us."

"We did sort of turn our backs on him. Not take his side or back him up."

"Because he was acting crazy," Owen reminded him.

"I think everything's been piling up on him for months and he snapped. You don't think he'd try to end it all, do you?"

Leaving his band, dumping his girlfriend, selling his house— Owen had heard that a person who was suicidal tended to distance himself from everything important in his life.

"Great," Owen said. "Now I'm worried about him too. Thanks, dude."

"Maybe the news segment will shed some light on all this," Caitlyn said. "But if you really think he might be suicidal, you have to get him help, Owen."

Owen nodded. "You're right." He and Gabe exchanged a long look. God, he hoped Jacob wasn't that far gone.

The front door opened as Kelly let himself inside. "Is Gabe here too? Isn't that his truck taking up half the street?"

"Hey," Gabe said.

Kelly barely acknowledged anyone's presence and flopped down on the sofa next to Owen.

"Turn the channel," Kelly said, flicking a hand toward the television. "It should be starting."

"Already?" Owen asked. "I thought you said tonight."

"At five," Kellen said.

Surprised it was already that late, Owen switched through the local channels until he found Jacob's familiar face. He exchanged a look of surprise with Kelly when the camera focused on Jacob and his despised ex-wife. He looked good and even sane, except for the fact that he was holding Tina's fucking hand.

Owen rubbed his eyes. He must be seeing things. "What the . . .?"

"That settles it," Gabe said while Owen cranked up the volume to catch what Jacob was saying. "He's completely lost his shit. We're having him committed."

". . . time I got my priorities straight and focused on what's really important," Jacob spoke to the camera in a calm, almost rehearsed cadence. "Not fame, not success, not money, but family. So the rest of Sole Regret's summer tour is canceled. I'll personally repay the fans for any nonrefundable tickets."

"What?" Tina said, the satisfied smile slipping from her model-perfect face.

"What?" Gabe repeated to the television, his voice raised in anger.

"Are you back together with your ex-wife?" a reporter asked. "If I recall correctly, your divorce was rather messy."

"And final!" Gabe shouted at the TV.

"We're going to live together as a family," Jacob said. "I won't be able to afford two homes once all the lawsuits start being filed, so I've moved back in with my wife and daughter."

"He can barely get the word *wife* out," Caitlyn noted.

"Lawsuits?" Tina asked, her head whipping around so she could gawk at Jacob.

"I'm breaking all sorts of contracts to be with you," Jacob said, feeding her a lovey-dovey look that made Owen want to vomit. "But none of that's important. My career is over. I'll be utterly broke, but none of that matters. All that matters is that you get what you want, Tina. You want me, right?"

Tina blinked at him and then looked down at the hands she had folded in her lap. "Of course I do."

"Does he really not care that he's going to lose everything?" Gabe yelled. "He doesn't even like her!"

"All we need is love," Jacob said. "Isn't that right, sweetheart?" He lifted Tina's hand to his lips and kissed it.

"That's right," she said weakly.

Something didn't feel right, Owen thought. Why would Jacob ever take Tina back? He hated the woman. He loved his daughter—and Tina had custody of Julie—but Jacob couldn't stand his ex-wife. The dumbass was in love with her sister, Amanda, *not* with Tina. And yet they certainly looked like a happy couple on television.

"We're missing something," Owen said. "Something monumental."

Kelly snorted. "Don't you see what he's doing?"

"Being the biggest fucking idiot who ever lived?" Gabe bellowed.

"He's calling her bluff."

"What bluff?" Owen asked.

"I don't know," Kelly said, "but look at her face. She started off smug—like she had him by the balls, like she was in charge and held all the aces. And now she looks like she's ready to fold."

"You don't honestly think he's willing to give up everything just to get back at her?" Gabe said. "And he's not the only one he's screwing here. What about us? We have a stake in this too. Did he ever consider how this would affect anyone but himself?"

"It has to have something to do with Julie," Owen said. He

absolutely would not believe that Jacob could be so callous toward his friends—his band brothers—for any other reason. And even then Owen couldn't wrap his head around the drastic measures Jacob was willing to take to get whatever it was he was after without consulting any of those affected by his rash decision. If any of them had pulled such a stunt, he'd have been pissed. But maybe he expected them to be pissed and didn't care.

"I'm going to kill him," Gabe said. "If Adam doesn't get to him before I do, I'm going to reach into his gut and yank out his balls from the inside."

"Give him a little time to sort himself out," Kelly said.

"He's getting back together with Tina." Owen pointed to the television where Jacob was now telling the interviewer he might never go back to singing.

"I might paint houses," Jacob was saying. "Or sell tires. I do want to finish my education—get my GED and set the right example for my daughter."

"I don't think he is," Kelly said, scrutinizing what was playing out on the screen with his head tilted slightly.

"You're going to let him get away with this bullshit?" Gabe said. "He walked out on us, Kellen. And without him fronting the band, Sole Regret will never be the same."

"Maybe he'll change his mind," Owen said.

"And maybe we'll tell him to fuck off," Gabe said.

"He's obviously struggling. Look at him," Kelly said. He stood and jabbed at the TV. "Look at his posture."

Owen couldn't see what Kelly was apparently seeing. Jacob seemed to know exactly what he was saying as he clearly stated his only future plans were to spend time with his family. A family which inexplicably included the ex-wife he despised.

"He was acting off before Adam left, you morons," Kelly said. "I'm telling you, something is going on with him that he didn't share with us."

"Obviously," Gabe said. "But that's no excuse to stab your friends in the back. He just up and left."

"Adam also fucking left," Kelly said, his voice raised for the first time.

Gabe slammed his fist into the sofa's arm. Beside Owen, Caitlyn jumped, but she didn't say anything. She probably didn't know what to say.

"And the three of us are left here holding our dicks," Gabe said.

"Jacob has only fucked us over this once; Adam has left us high and dry dozens of times," Owen said. They all knew it. They treaded lightly on the subject because Adam was an addict, because Adam was unstable.

They were used to Adam living by his own agenda; they decidedly were not used to Jacob putting himself before the rest of them. They were used to Jacob fixing Adam, Jacob keeping them together, Jacob being dependable. The dude on TV looked like Jacob and he sounded like Jacob, but he sure as fuck didn't *act* like Jacob.

"I think we have to support him until he figures out what he wants," Kelly said.

"I'm not supporting his insanity." Gabe stood and pulled his baseball cap on. "We put all our faith in him and he left us. Without a word, he left."

And they'd never had faith in Adam. It didn't hurt when he disappointed them all time and again. They expected his self-centered behavior. They didn't expect the same from Jacob.

"You need to think this through before you go off, Gabe," Kelly said. "You could make things worse."

"Stop being so goddamned even-tempered, Cuff! This doesn't piss you off? Not even a little?"

Kelly shook his head. "It makes me sad."

Gabe turned his attention to Owen. "And I suppose you're in agreement with your friend here. You two practically share a brain."

Owen glanced at Kelly. He found his friend's calm admirable, but Owen wasn't calm or sad. He wasn't angry either. He was in denial. This could not be happening. They'd worked so hard to get where they were, and Owen could not wrap his head around the idea that any of this was real. He had to be dreaming or something. Jacob would not trade his career for Tina, he just wouldn't. But he might give it up for Amanda. Maybe. And he would definitely give it up for his daughter.

"Maybe Julie is sick," he said, not sure where the idea had come from, but at least it made logical sense to him. Jacob suddenly being in love with Tina and giving up the music he valued in order to be with a woman he hated made no sense at all.

Gabe blinked at him in confusion. "Why would you think that?"

"He's been adamant about spending time with Julie lately. Scheduled the entire tour around his visitation days. So maybe something is terribly wrong with her." The mere thought was heartbreaking.

"It could be that," Kelly said. "But I don't think he'd hide that from us." He looked up at Gabe. "Will you sit down? We need to figure this mess out."

"We need to get Shade back," Owen said. Kelly smiled at him and nodded.

"Maybe I don't want him back," Gabe said, but he sat and they brainstormed—rather ineffectually—until Lindsey entered the room. Her nose was red and her cheeks tear streaked.

"Are you okay?" Owen said, rising from the sofa and grasping her shoulder. "Are you in pain? Is it the baby?"

She shook her head. "Is Sole Regret really breaking up?"

"We hope not," Owen said. When she wrapped her arms around him, he tried his best to comfort her casually. He glanced at Caitlyn, knowing she wouldn't like him that close to Lindsey. *If she's staying with you, there can be no touching,* she'd included on her list of conditions. But now Caitlyn just shrugged, as if to say, *someone needs to hug the poor woman—might as well be you.*

"It's all my fault," Lindsey said. "I show up pregnant and you all start arguing and then Adam leaves and now Shade is gone and . . . and . . ."

"This has nothing to do with you," Gabe said. "Adam has been unreliable and self-absorbed since the day I met him."

"But he left to be reliable for Madison," Kelly said. "*Selfless* for Madison."

Kelly and his uncanny ability to see things from every perspective—Owen wished he thought that way.

"How very nice for Madison," Gabe said, his temper still not entirely cool. "How utterly devastating for the rest of us. Did Adam even admit he was in the wrong when you talked to him? Because when I talked to him all he wanted to know was what Jacob had done."

"He admitted he should have told us where he was going," Owen said. "He seemed sorry."

"But he didn't say it."

Owen shook his head.

"Adam's always been unapologetic," Kelly said. "It doesn't mean he doesn't feel remorse. He just doesn't express it."

Owen pulled Lindsey away from his chest to look down into her eyes. "We're going to do whatever we can to keep Sole Regret together. No more crying over this."

She wiped at her face with the back of her hand and nodded. "I came to tell you dinner is ready and overheard you talking about the band."

"I can't stay," Gabe said, but his expression as he looked at Lindsey said *I don't want to stay*. "I'm going to see if I can find out some real information. Maybe I can corner Jacob outside the news studio if I hurry."

Owen exchanged a fist bump with Gabe. "Keep us posted."

"Once things settle down, I want a backgammon rematch," Caitlyn called after him.

Gabe paused in the doorway and grinned at her. "Eager to lose again?"

"Oh, I'll be winning this time."

"We'll see about that," Gabe said, and with a wave he hurried out of the house. Owen hoped he'd be able to catch up with Jacob. Gabe might actually be able to talk some sense into the dude.

"Are you staying?" Owen asked Kelly.

"Free home-cooked meal?" He inhaled deeply through his nose. "Fried chicken, if I'm not mistaken. Do you need to ask?"

Owen laughed, a bit of tension draining from his body. He hadn't seen much of this version of Kelly since the guy had gotten laid. Maybe this time he hadn't lost a friend when Kelly had gained a romantic interest. He pounded Kelly on the back and then helped Caitlyn to her feet. He still had plenty of good in his life. He just needed to focus on the positives and hope the negatives righted themselves.

At dinner he and Kelly talked about most of their usual topics of conversation: baseball and music, family and plans, the weather and news. Caitlyn weighed in as though she'd always sat at his side. They purposefully skated around more serious topics—like band breakups and Jacob's apparent meltdown. Even Lindsey seemed in her element as the elephant in the room—her pregnancy—was tactfully ignored.

"Have you gotten any job interviews yet?" Owen asked her

as they cleared the table.

She sighed. "Not yet, but I've had a few good leads—most telling me to come back in six months. The problem is that no one is going to offer me a job when I'm going to need to be on maternity leave very soon."

"I don't have a problem with you waiting to find work until after the baby is born," Owen said. He wasn't sure why Kelly was suddenly grimacing at him and shaking his head.

"I have a problem with it," Lindsey said. "I'm not a mooch."

"I might have some contacts in Austin that could help you out," Caitlyn offered. "I'll look into it when I return to the office."

"That's nice of you," Lindsey said with a smile.

Owen was starting to think this might work. Caitlyn hadn't tried to stab Lindsey at the dinner table, and everyone seemed to be getting along well. If he could just get his band back together.

"Have you thought about temp work for now?" Kelly asked, his grimace replaced with an encouraging smile. "Maybe an agency has an assignment that will last a couple of months. And then you can find something permanent later."

"That's a great idea, Cuff," Lindsey said, placing the dishes she carried into the sink and giving him a hug.

To Owen's surprise, Kelly actually hugged her back. Owen supposed Kelly was the only member of the band who knew for a certainty that the baby wasn't his, so he could relax in her company. And she really wasn't a bad person; she was just in a bad situation. A situation he had probably gotten her into by idiotically using a contaminated condom. She'd kept her word as far as he knew and hadn't told anyone how stupid he was. And he hadn't told anyone either. Not even Caitlyn. Maybe he should confide in her. As he watched her fill the sink with soapy water, he decided he'd wait to rock that particular boat when the waters of his life were a tad less choppy.

"Have you been to the doctor?" Kelly asked Lindsey.

"Joan took me to meet her ob/gyn yesterday. We scheduled a thorough appointment for Friday. I'm going to have an ultrasound and everything."

"And a paternity test?" Kelly asked.

Lindsey glanced at Owen and then flushed when her gaze landed on Caitlyn. "If I have to."

"If it's not Owen's baby, do you still plan on staying here?"

Caitlyn asked.

"I suppose I'll have to leave."

When Lindsey's eyes met Owen's, he could see the fear behind her gaze. Was she afraid that there'd be no one there for her and the baby when the time came to give birth? With all the shit that Jacob and Adam were currently going through, Owen doubted that either of them would take proper care of her. And Tex was fucking married. Owen was sure his wife would *love* to have a pregnant groupie move in with them. Gabe would probably do right by her, but his girlfriend might have issue with him taking on another woman on the side. Caitlyn had already come to terms with the situation. She didn't like the arrangement, but she trusted Owen and she had reason to. He would never break her trust.

"She can stay here," Owen said with a shrug. "Even if it's not my kid."

Caitlyn dropped a pan in the sink with a loud bang.

Kelly rubbed a hand over his eyes. "I'd accuse you of being an idiot . . ."

Oh I'm definitely an idiot.

". . . but your family took me in and made me feel welcome, so I can't insist you offer Lindsey any less." He turned to Lindsey. "I can help you out too."

"But it's definitely not yours, Cuff," Lindsey said, rubbing a hand over her belly.

He smiled, and Owen had to wonder if he saw as much of Sara in the pretty blonde as Owen did. The resemblance between Lindsey and Kelly's lost love was almost eerie.

"I don't have to be responsible to want to help you, do I?"

Silverware clattered loudly as Caitlyn slammed the utensils into the dishwasher. He'd never heard anyone load the machine so noisily.

Lindsey gave Kelly another hug. "Thank you so much, Cuff. You're almost as nice as Owen is."

"Almost," Kelly said, winking at Owen over her head.

"Excuse me," Caitlyn said, giving Owen a pointed look he didn't understand. "I need to use the bathroom." She stared at him for a long moment before adding, "Upstairs."

Owen took that to mean she had to go number two and didn't want to smell up the main floor, but wasn't sure why she was announcing her bathroom situation to everyone. She gave him another hard stare before blotting her hands dry on a towel and leaving the room with a frustrated growl.

"You're supposed to go after her," Kelly said.

Owen made a face of disgust. "No thanks. What she does in that bathroom is her business."

"Trust me. You need to go after her."

Owen shrugged, but before he could hang out with Caitlyn in the upstairs bathroom, his phone rang. He was smiling in relief as he answered. "Hey, Mom, we just fin—"

Her broken sob cut him off. "Owey?"

"What's wrong?"

"I can't say it," she said. "Not on the phone."

"I'll be right there," he said, his heart hammering so hard, he could scarcely breathe.

He raced from the house, not bothering to close the front door. He jumped his front steps and sprinted the block to his mother's house, vaguely aware of Kelly racing after him and calling, "Owen, what is it?"

He opened his parents' front gate—none of the dogs were in the yard to greet him—and hurried to the front door. From the porch, he could hear his mother sobbing inside. Knocking loudly, he yelled for her before trying the handle and finding the door unlocked. He followed the sounds of her crying to the living room and found her in a heap on the floor, fiercely hugging one of her rescue dogs while the others either watched or licked the tears off her face.

"Mom!" He knelt in front of her and took her hands. "What is it? Are you hurt?"

The pain in her eyes when she lifted her head wasn't the physical sort. It was of the soul-crushing variety.

"Ch-Chad."

Owen shook his head. Whatever she was about to tell him about his brother, he wasn't prepared to believe a word of it.

"His helicopter went down."

Owen shook his head harder. No. He was coming home soon. That was what she'd meant to tell him. Chad was coming home.

"Monday. It happened Monday, and they didn't bother to tell us until now!"

"Is he—" Owen couldn't actually say the word *dead*, because

Chad's death was too unreal to consider.

"Alive," she gasped. "In a hospital in Germany."

Owen released a sigh of relief. Alive. They could handle anything but dead. He couldn't handle dead.

"They're not sure he's going to make it."

"That bad?" he heard himself say over the growing buzz in his ears.

She nodded. "His CO said he was the only survivor. The only survivor."

He pulled her into his arms, her little three-legged dog squirming in protest between them. "He's going to make it."

"They said not to get our hopes up," she gasped out between sobs.

Too bad. Owen's hopes were sky high.

"He's going to make it," Owen repeated, squeezing tighter.

Footsteps stopped behind him, and he looked up to see Kelly standing there with Lindsey behind him. Kelly's concerned face blurred beyond the sudden flood of tears in his eyes.

"Is it Chad?" Kelly asked.

Owen couldn't answer him. He turned his face into his mother's neck, his mind racing, his heart aching, his soul completely empty. "He's going to make it."

That was all that mattered to Owen. The shit with his band and with Lindsey—none of it mattered. Getting Chad home alive was all that he cared about.

"Can we go to Germany and see him?" Owen asked.

"Once he's stable they'll transfer him to a hospital stateside. I should have prayed harder," Mom said.

Owen had a ritual where he prayed for Chad's safe return, so that couldn't be why his helicopter had crashed. Owen always prayed hard. Every night he prayed for Chad.

Oh shit. Owen's heart turned to ice in his chest. "Did you say it happened Monday?"

"That's why he never called. He was supposed to call."

And that had been the evening Owen had experienced an unshakable feeling of dread. He'd thought it was because Adam had gone missing and Jacob had destroyed the band, but he knew now that was when Chad had been injured, when he'd been fighting to live. And Owen been so caught up in his own much smaller tragedies that he *hadn't* prayed for him that night. He hadn't prayed.

"My brave, brave boy," Mom whimpered. "This wasn't supposed to happen."

The back door banged shut, and Dad called into the house, "Joan? Where are you?"

"James!" She didn't get another word out as sobs racked her body. Apparently she'd been holding herself together the best she could for Owen's benefit.

Dad ran in, face drawn, hands clenched, his gaze searching the room. "Did the officer leave?"

"What officer?" Owen asked.

"The death squad officer!"

Owen didn't know if there was such a thing as a death squad officer, but Dad's meaning was clear. When a soldier was killed in action, a high-ranking uniformed officer delivered the news in person.

"He's not dead," Owen said. And he would not allow himself to even consider the possibility.

Dad's sturdy shoulders sagged, and he covered his face with one hand before bending to scoop Mom against him with the other. "Why didn't you tell me that on the phone? I thought—I thought we'd lost him."

"W-wounded," Mom said, her tears flowing nonstop. "Terribly."

Owen couldn't listen to her tell his father the mortal danger Chad still faced. His heart wouldn't survive a repeat of those words. He turned and rushed for the door, needing a moment or ten alone so he could collect his thoughts.

This could not be happening.

Lindsey caught his arm as he brushed past. "Is there anything I can do?"

"Fix my brother," he snapped. "Can you do that?"

She ducked her head and whispered, "I'm so sorry," as he pulled free and fled to the front porch, where he stopped short before he careened into Kelly's back. Kelly was staring out across the front yard, a hand on either hip.

He turned. Had the tears swimming in Kelly's eyes not chosen that moment to course down his cheeks, Owen might not have shattered. He covered his mouth with one hand to choke back a sob and found himself crushed in a tight embrace. Kelly's hand cupped the back of Owen's head as he held him close. Afraid he'd crumple to the porch, Owen wrapped his arms around Kelly and held on to the solid strength he hadn't realized he needed from his friend.

Agony choked him until it burst from him in a sob.

"He'll be all right," Kelly whispered. "You have to believe he'll be all right."

Owen did believe that. He believed it so much that he mentally promised God everything he could think of to make the wish a reality.

When at last Owen was able to shove his grief into the darkest pit of his soul, he lifted his head and got lost in Kelly's turbulent gaze. Kelly didn't drop his arms, didn't release Owen from his embrace, instead he leaned close—closer still—until his face blurred. Kelly's lips brushed Owen's, so feather-light that Owen convinced himself he was imagining his kiss.

What?

Kelly groaned, his lips parting as he deepened his claim on Owen's mouth.

For a moment, the darkness clouding Owen's heart dissipated. Every worry vanished. The world outside Kellen's kiss didn't exist. Hunger, passion, and a forbidden pleasure centered on Owen's mouth and spread down his throat and into his chest, forming a shield of trust around his heart. The deep-rooted connection that had always existed between them manifested into physical form. The beauty of it stole Owen's every thought for one glorious moment.

But then Kelly pulled away, and the magic shattered.

Kelly searched Owen's eyes and said, "I'm sorry."

Owen might have understood Kellen's apology if he hadn't just been kissed into emotional oblivion, but this was no joke. He could see a change in the way Kelly looked at him, with feelings just realized. Painful, inappropriate feelings.

Owen was shaking.

How did Kelly expect him to react? What did he expect him to say? Maybe he wasn't supposed to do or say anything.

"Owen," Kelly said, curving his fingers into Owen's face and leaning closer. "I'm so sorry."

"For what?" Owen asked, confusion hammering at his reeling mind. "For Chad? For doing . . . doing *that* to me?"

"I'm not sorry I kissed you. I'm also not sorry I enjoyed it or that you enjoyed it."

What? He hadn't enjoyed it. He'd just . . . He'd needed to feel a deep emotional bond with someone and Caitlyn was back at his place taking a dump.

Owen shook his head at the lie he was trying to pass over on himself. What he really wished was that Kelly was still kissing him, had never stopped kissing him. While their lips had been pressed together, Owen had felt none of the fear or confusion or anxiety that he felt now. He'd only felt right.

This could not be happening.

Kelly pressed his forehead against Owen's and closed his eyes. Peace stole over Owen for an instant, and then more confusing thoughts bombarded him. What had caused this sudden change between them? The band breaking up? Chad's horrible situation? Owen's reaction to it? Something that had happened during Kelly's weekend with Dawn? What? Why was Kelly acting like this was totally normal? There was nothing normal about this. Nothing!

"I don't understand," Owen mumbled.

"I am beyond sorry about Chad."

Of course he was. Chad was an older brother to both of them—Owen's by blood, Kelly's by circumstance.

"But I'm mostly sorry that I've been blind for so long."

What?

"I want you, Owen."

Owen stiffened and backed away. Kelly *wanted* him. Want, not love. What did that mean? He shook his head. What the *hell* did Kelly mean?

"Owen?"

Owen waved him off, unable to meet his eyes. "This cannot be happening."

He stumbled backwards down the steps and ran so hard that he was unable to slow his momentum before he slammed into the gate. He fumbled with the latch and threw the gate open before sprinting toward home. He needed to run from it all. From his brother's injury, from the responsibility of Lindsey and the baby, from the end of his career and aspirations, even from Kelly—the one person he'd counted on his entire adult life.

He ran to the only sane thing, the only good thing in his

world. He ran to Caitlyn.

ABOUT THE AUTHOR

Combining her love for romantic fiction and rock 'n roll, Olivia Cunning writes erotic romance centered around rock musicians. Raised on hard rock music from the cradle, she attended her first Styx concert at age six and fell instantly in love with live music. She's been known to travel over a thousand miles just to see a favorite band in concert. As a teen, she discovered her second love, romantic fiction—first, voraciously reading steamy romance novels and then penning her own. Growing up as the daughter of a career soldier, she's lived all over the United States and overseas. She currently lives in Illinois. To learn more about Olivia and her books, please visit www.oliviacunning.com.